THE SMUGGLER'S WIFE

Kent, 1815. When the beautiful but naive Grace Lennicker falls for Isaiah Feasey, son of a rival smuggling family and owner of a local tavern, her sisters try to intervene. Grace is unwittingly drawn back into the world of smuggling that her sisters fought hard to leave behind, and as violence erupts, she finds herself unable to stand by, knowing the rival gangs will kill anyone who stands in their way.

THE SMUGGLER'S WIFE

Kent, 1815. When the beautiful but naive Grace Lannicker falls for Isaiah Feasey, son of a rival smuggling family and owner of a local tavern, her sisters try to intervene. Grace is unwittingly drawn back into the world of smuggling that her sisters fought hard to leave behind, and as violence erupts, she finds herself unable to stand by, knowing the rival gangs will kill anyone who stands in their way.

EVIE GRACE

THE SMUGGLER'S WIFE

Complete and Unabridged

MAGNA
Leicester

First published in Great Britain in 2020 by
Arrow Books
London

First Ulverscroft Edition
published 2021
by arrangement with
Arrow Books
Penguin Random House UK
London

*A catalogue record for this book is available
from the British Library.*

ISBN 978–0–7505–4868–7

Published by
Ulverscroft Limited
Anstey, Leicestershire

Set by Words & Graphics Ltd.
Anstey, Leicestershire
Printed and bound in Great Britain by
TJ Books Ltd., Padstow, Cornwall

This book is printed on acid-free paper

To Mum, with love

Acknowledgements

I should like to thank Laura and everyone at MBA Literary Agents, and Jennie and the team at Penguin Random House UK for their unwavering enthusiasm and support for 'The Smuggler's Daughters' series.

1

A Breath of Fresh Air

Deal, June 1815

It was all very well Louisa warning her off. Grace's eldest sister had her best interests at heart, but she didn't know that she had a fancy for Isaiah so strong that she couldn't eat or sleep.

Not only was he a Deal boatman who could be relied upon to go out in the fiercest of storms, risking his life to save others whose vessels foundered on the Sands, he was landlord of the Rattling Cat pub and a notorious smuggler. He was a loner — Grace often saw him walking along the beach with his grey longdog at his heels — yet he was leader of a gang, capable of inspiring respect and loyalty. The contradictions intrigued her, and it helped enormously that he was also dark and handsome and *at least* as tall as her, she thought, smiling to herself.

'Where do you think you're going?' Louisa stepped across the hall and stood between Grace and the front door as she tied the laces on her boots.

'Back to the market before it closes — I forgot to buy the bread.' It wasn't a lie exactly — she had accidentally on purpose forgotten to pick up

1

a loaf with the rest of the shopping.

'Haven't I told you before to take a list with you?'

On many an occasion, Grace wanted to say, but she managed to bite her tongue just in time.

'I don't feel so good, having been staring at the accounts all morning. Maybe a breath of fresh air will perk me up. Why don't I come with you?'

'You look well enough to me,' Grace said, standing up. Tall, slender and blue eyed, they were peas from the same pod, except that Louisa was five years older than Grace and an inch shorter, and her hair was a dark brown while Grace's was the colour of ebony.

'Where is your sympathy for your hardworking sister? Let me put my ledger away and fetch my bonnet. It's a lovely day. We can walk along the beach afterwards.'

'Are you sure you wouldn't prefer to go and have a lie-down?' Grace suggested, but Louisa had made up her mind.

Her plot foiled to see Isaiah again, Grace reached for the willow basket on the shelf, at which a pair of green eyes peered over the top.

'Oh Kitty,' she said.

'What's that creature doing, lazing around in there when she's supposed to be earning her keep?' Louisa grumbled lightly.

'She's done her work for today — tell me when you last saw or heard a meaker?'

'Not for a while,' Louisa admitted.

'Mrs Witherall next door says she's overrun with them while we have none, proof of Kitty's prowess.'

2

'I'll suggest she gives her board and lodgings then — on a permanent basis.'

Grace's exclamation of protest sent the fluffy black cat leaping out of the basket on to the floor.

'You wouldn't? I couldn't bear it!' Grace noticed the alteration in Louisa's expression. 'You are shamming me?'

'I am indeed. Although I was very annoyed when Isaiah pressed you into having her, she's turned out to be rather endearing.' Smiling, Louisa looked down to where Kitty was winding herself around her legs, then glanced back up. 'Hark. Do you hear that?'

Straining her ears, Grace listened for the faint medley of sound coming from the distance. Gradually it grew louder, and she began to distinguish the individual parts: the voice of the town crier; the steady beat of a drum; cheering and laughter; a piper's merry hornpipe; a troupe of fiddlers scraping their strings. The church bells pealed, and the ships' bells clanged relentlessly from the roadstead.

'What is it? Has the world come to an end?' She pushed the front door open. Kitty dashed outside and shot back in again.

'Miss, miss, 'ave you 'eard the news?' One of a gaggle of shore boys who were half running, half walking along the alley stopped outside Compass Cottage. Fourteen-year-old Cromwell's face was as brown as a nut, his eyes alight with excitement.

'I can't say that I have,' Grace said, as Louisa leaned on her shoulder to listen to what he had to say.

'The Dooke of Wellin'ton and 'is men 'ave

3

beaten Ol' Boney at Wa'erloo.'

'Is that the truth of it?' Grace touched her throat. She was seventeen — almost eighteen — and she couldn't recall a time when England hadn't been at war with France, when they hadn't lived in fear of Napoleon and his great army crossing the Channel and invading their shores. 'It isn't going to turn out the same as last time?' In February of the previous year she had been bitterly disappointed to find out that the announcement of Napoleon's death had been a hoax created to allow several so-called gentlemen to defraud the London Stock Market.

'Everybody's sayin' it's true and I think it 'as to be cos lightnin' don't strike twice. Major Percy of the 14th Light Dragoons carried the dispatches to Lord Liverpool and Prinny.' He was referring to the Prince Regent. 'Apparently, 'e was still wearin' 'is bloodstained clothes when 'e rode day and night from the battlefield to Ostend where 'e boarded the Peruvian. It weren't plain sailin' even then because there weren't no wind, so they 'ad to lower a gig and row the rest of the way.'

'What is the proof, though?' Grace wanted to be sure.

'They 'ad two French Eagles in the boat with them, the standards what they captured in the fight.' Without waiting to see if he had managed to convince her, he punched the air and ran on.

'What do you think?' Grace said, turning to Louisa who was looking past her, watching the elderly couple struggle out of the cottage next door.

'I don't know. Mrs Witherall, have you heard

4

that the war against the Frenchies is over?'

'We 'aven't 'eard nothin' about it afore now.' Louisa's mother-in-law nodded towards her husband. 'Mr Witherall's been sufferin' from another nasty bout of gout and gravel which 'as kept us indoors.'

'Hush.' Mr Witherall frowned. His hair was silver, his eyes creased at the corners, and his complexion weathered by the elements. 'Spare dear Louisa and Grace the gory details.'

Grace smiled to herself — everyone who lived on the spit knew about Mr Witherall's state of health. Seeing that Louisa would be distracted for a while, she took advantage and slipped away towards the beach. When she reached the street that ran along the top of the shore, she was swept into a milling throng of men, women and children, marvelling at the news they had wished for since Bonaparte had escaped from exile on Elba over one hundred days before.

'Let me 'elp you along, miss.' A bow-legged sailor, wearing a blue shirt and wide trousers with stripes, who was swaggering along with his mate, offered her his arm.

'I can manage very well, thank you,' she replied hastily. 'Excuse my friend for bein' so bold,' the sailor's mate said, doffing his tarpot hat.

'The excitement 'as gone to me 'ead.'

'The rum, yer mean. I think you've 'ad a drop too much.'

Amused, Grace squeezed through the crowds until she found her way blocked by a group of elbow-crookers who were standing outside the Rattling Cat, clashing their tankards together and

5

spilling foaming ale as they toasted Wellington's victory. She recognised Lawless and Awful Doins, a pair of middle-aged smugglers who'd troubled her family in the past.

'Greetin's, Miss Lennicker,' Awful Doins said, grinning inanely and exposing a single grey tooth — one that he'd acquired as a relic from another gentleman upon his death and had wired into the middle of his upper jaw.

'Let me pass,' she said sharply.

'I dunno about that.' Lawless, who was dressed top to toe in black, leaned in close, repulsing her with his foul breath. 'I think we should 'ave a chat about 'ow we can 'elp each other, you bein' party to certain information . . .'

'If you think you can bribe me, you're wrong.' She glared at him. 'Step aside.'

'Oi, leave the young lady alone!' Her heart missed a beat as the landlord of the tavern and object of her affection emerged from the open doorway. 'Do as I tell you, you pair o' lobcocks.' The men backed off as Isaiah walked across to her, his rough-coated longdog at his heels. 'Pardon my language, Grace.' He stopped a few feet from her and grinned, revealing a fine set of teeth that were all his own. In his middle twenties, he was handsome in a rugged kind of way, his curly hair the colour of jet and his eyes deep brown. 'Aren't you goin' to thank me for rescuin' you?'

'I can stand up for myself.'

'I 'ave no doubt of that — you're very much like your sister.' He was referring to Louisa, not Winnie or her half-sister, Nancy, she thought, her brow tightening as she looked him up and down.

6

'What's wrong?'

'You look like a gentleman, not a tatterdemalion,' she said, recalling his usual state of undress, wearing torn clothing and no shoes.

'Only look like one? What a low opinion you 'ave of me.' He smoothed the lapels of his patterned waistcoat and tweaked his shirt's high-standing collar, leaving a smudge on the white linen.

'I didn't intend to cause offence. I'm sure you have some . . . gentlemanly qualities.'

'If you're goin' to dig yourself into an 'ole, make sure you dig it deep.' He chuckled. 'Just because I was born low don't mean I can't rise like cream to the top of the milk in society. I've 'ad a run of good luck recently, if you know what I mean, and I'm makin' the most of it. I'm 'avin' some buildin' work done— ' He nodded towards the tavern. 'The war's over for good — they won't let Old Boney come back a third time. Life's goin' to be better for all of us, you'll see.'

'How can you be certain?' she asked, unconvinced. 'When Bonaparte went into exile last year, the people who depended on the commerce of war began to struggle to make ends meet. It'll be worse now. With the soldiers gone and the barracks empty, who will buy the boot-makers' wares? Who will place orders at the boatyards? When the naval yard closes because there are no ships to provision, who will buy the market gardeners' fruit and veg?'

'Oh Grace, you're soundin' old beyond your years. You shouldn't listen to the doom-mongers and naysayers. Our neighbours are for the most part seafarin', that's true, but new trades

7

will rise from the ashes, ones we 'aven't thought of yet. People will come to Deal for business and seabathin', and I'm makin' sure I 'ave a piece of it. I'm 'avin' the kitchen extended and several more lettin' rooms added.' He changed the subject, apparently emboldened by the mood of the crowd. 'You're lookin' well.'

'Thank you.' It was merely an observation, not a compliment, she told herself as her cheeks grew hot.

'Come and join me. Bring your sisters and their menfolk. Let past arguments and strife be forgot,' he said earnestly.

'It's kind of you, but my sisters won't allow it. They don't approve of me talking to you.'

'I understand — there's bad blood between our families, and for good reason, but this is an inauspicious occasion — '

'I think you mean 'auspicious',' she cut in.

'Whatever it is, clever boots, it's a good time for makin' a fresh start. Bein' neighbours, livin' cheek by jowl, we should try bein' civil for a change.'

'Do I not speak civilly to you?' she said archly.

'Always,' he smiled. 'Although I do recall an occasion when you told me off — it was in no uncertain terms.'

It was strange how she could remember every word that had ever passed between them.

'You made a cruel joke, saying you would pelt Winnie when she was in — ' She stopped abruptly, not wishing to be reminded of how her middle sister had ended up in the stocks after one of the Riding officers of the Revenue had arrested her for being in possession of a half-anker — a small

8

barrel — containing cognac. 'You upset Louisa when you gave me the kitten,' she said instead. 'Knowin' 'ow much you like animals, I thought it would make you 'appy.'

'It pleased me very much.' 'How is the dear little puss?'

'Kitty's an excellent mouser as you said she would be, and she's very affectionate.'

'I'm delighted to 'ear it.'

'I'd better run,' she said, taking her leave. 'Louisa will be wondering where I am.' She wished she hadn't said that — it made her sound childish and dull when she wanted to appear as intriguing as he was dark and dangerous. 'I'm not under her thumb though. I offered to fetch a loaf of bread,' she added hastily by way of explanation.

'The last time I looked, the market was in that direction.' He pointed and quirked one eyebrow.

'I thought I'd go the long way — for the scenery.'

'Again? I saw you with your basket earlier. Anyone would think you were 'opin' to run into someone.'

'Not really. I mean, not at all,' she stammered. 'I forgot to buy the bread the first time and Jason gets crabby when there's nothing to eat when he comes home.'

'Ah yes. Marlin's a ten-shillin' man now.' Isaiah used Jason's nickname, a shortened version of marlinspike. 'Who'd 'ave thought it, eh? I can't believe 'e turned 'is coat like that.'

Grace wasn't sure why her brother-in-law and Louisa had given up smuggling spirits and lace when they had made such a success of it. As a

9

Deal boatman like Isaiah, the occupation that Jason used to follow was hovelling, which involved ferrying pilots and supplies such as anchors and cables back and forth to the ships in the Downs, the sheltered stretch of water between the coast and the Goodwin Sands. He'd also gone out to save lives and property when a vessel was in trouble. For that purpose, he'd used his giant lugger, the *Whimbrel*, a boat built for speed and perfect for smuggling contraband.

However, the *Whimbrel* had been re-rigged as a cutter in the service of the King's Navy — given a large spread of sail and extended bowsprit — and renamed. Now Jason was a Revenue man, commander of HMS *Legacy*, prey turned predator.

'They say 'e made enough from the guinea boat to retire,' Isaiah commented.

'I don't think that was the reason.' It was true that her brother-in-law had made a small fortune from running gold across the Channel to fund Wellington's army — and possibly Bonaparte's too — in the past. The guinea runs were funded by wealthy investors and organised by an agent, a Mr Cork who had since suffered the ignominy of being convicted and imprisoned with his co-conspirators for the fraud that brought the false dawn of peace the previous spring. Grace's family were comfortably off and she didn't believe that Jason's decision had anything to do with money.

'Don't tell me 'e 'ad a sudden crisis of conscience.'

Grace noticed the spark of humour in Isaiah's eyes and the way he ran his hand through his dishevelled curls. His sideburns were long and his chin was shadowed with stubble, and she was staring.

10

She glanced away, looking along the street where a band of musicians was marching towards them, escorted by a group of small children banging saucepans with spoons and blowing on whistles.

''E makes out that he's some kind of 'ero, but we all know 'e used to sail close to the wind. We were always runnin' up against each other, even when we were workin' on the same side: one gang against the other; your lot against the Rattlers.' A smile played on his lips.

'I really should go,' she said, even more reluctantly than before.

'You'll be back for the dancin' later? We'll be celebratin' on the beach till dawn.'

'Wild horses couldn't keep me away — I love to dance. Now, I've wasted more than enough time talking to you — I have to run. I must find Louisa before she finds me.'

Laughing and hitching up her skirts, Grace turned and hurried towards the junction of Beach Street and Cockle Swamp Alley. She hoped she hadn't offended him with her last remark. She hoped too that she hadn't attracted the attention of the gossips — they'd soon have her down as Isaiah's bit of muslin and then Louisa would find out, and she'd never hear the end of it.

She stopped at the corner where Old Mr Witherall and Smoker Edwards were talking.

'The Dooke 'as the 'eart of a lion,' she heard Old Mr Witherall say as he leaned on his stick, looking out to sea. 'I never thought there'd be anybody who'd come close to matchin' Admiral Nelson for 'is tactics on the battlefield, but I reckon Wellin'ton's surpassed 'im.'

11

'I look up to 'em for their bravery and leadership,' Smoker Edwards said, drawing on his pipe, 'but it was a close contest. Old Boney's army fell foul of the rain, 'is cannons sinkin' into the flooded ground. I keep sorrowin' for the men we've lost, 'undreds an' thousands of 'em, their bodies lyin' broken in the mud. Many families, 'igh born and low, won't be seein' their 'usbands, fathers, brothers and sons again.'

'It's a terr'ble price that we've 'ad to pay, but I don't think it's wrong to mark the occasion. Life goes on. And as we know all too well, it can be brutally short, so while we're 'ere, we should make the most of it. Oh Grace, your sister's lookin' for you. I'm not sure I'd want to be in your shoes when she finds you. Ah, there she is.'

'Where have you been? I'm guessing that you're harbouring a guilty conscience,' Louisa said, walking up to her.

Grace didn't know what to say. How had her sister found out that she'd been speaking to Isaiah?

'News travels fast,' Grace said tentatively as they stood at the top of the steeply shelving beach, looking down at the waves lapping the shingle forty feet below, turning the stones shining red and gold. Further along the beach, she could see the *Curlew*, her family's fishing boat, perched at the top of the rollers beside the hut that Pa had built from reclaimed timbers.

Frowning, Louisa lifted the corner of the cloth and peered into Grace's basket. 'Wasn't there any bread left?'

'They'd sold out, I'm afraid.' For a moment, Grace thought she was about to receive a scolding, but Louisa went on, 'Never mind. We'll have pies from Molly's for supper tonight.'

With a sigh of relief and salt-laden air, Grace gazed at the sea and the treacherous beauty of the ever-changing sandbanks that glistened in the late afternoon sun. Between the giant ship gobbler of the Goodwin Sands and the East Kent coast, the roadstead that provided shelter from dangerous winds and tides was filled with men-o'-war, fishing boats and merchantmen.

'I can't see the *Legacy*,' she said, looking for the armed cutter with her hull painted black and the white gigs and galleys hoisted on her deck.

'She'll be on her way — they'll have heard the news by now.' Louisa smiled. 'Let's go home. You can put my hair up for me and I'll do yours in return.'

Having arrived back at the cottage, they went up to Grace's room where Louisa sat down on the edge of the bed. Grace prayed that she wouldn't notice the dust that she'd swept underneath it in her hurry to finish her chores that morning.

'I don't know what to wear: the primrose gown or the puce one, or the pale blue satin? What do you think?' Grace smoothed the front of her everyday dress — the printed brown cotton hid a multitude of stains.

'What about the grey silk with the silver headdress?' Louisa joined in with her pretence. 'Or the white tulle with the golden threads running through it?'

'Oh, that won't do. The ladies of the ton have seen it before. I can't possibly wear it twice.' Smiling, Grace gazed at her reflection in the mirror

13

that stood on the dressing table. Isaiah had been right when he said she looked well, she thought, too well to be considered à la mode when the current fashion was for complexions lightened with wafers and soap, and virtually no eyebrows to speak of. Blue eyed with a pink hue to her cheeks, tall and elegant, she could pass for a princess, if only she didn't have to wear her sister's hand-me-downs.

Within the hour, they were dressed in their Sunday best. Grace's alterations to Louisa's old lilac muslin gown, replacing the frayed hem with a strip of contrasting material and adjusting the side seams of the bodice, had improved the fit, and the bonnet she had trimmed with matching ribbons complemented it perfectly, but would it be enough to impress Isaiah?

'Grace, you are in a world of your own. I've asked you thrice why you aren't wearing your shawl and gloves?'

'It's summertime, not midwinter.' Their dearly departed mother had insisted on high standards — refined speech and modest behaviour — and sometimes Grace found it hard to live up to them. 'What's wrong? I look perfectly respectable like this.'

'I don't like the idea of you attracting the wrong kind of attention, that's all. You know how men stare so.'

'That's rather hypocritical. You used to take advantage of their weakness, encouraging me to flirt with the Riding officers when they challenged us, and chat up the sailors when we were out on the *Curlew*, selling contraband and fresh produce.

14

Do you recall the lecherous purser?'

'He would always make exceptionally free with his money when you were present.' With a grin, Louisa went on, 'But those days are behind us. You have your reputation to think of. And to that end, I'll be keeping a close eye on you, young lady. Remember what happened to Winnie when she ended up alone in the sandhills.'

'It isn't the same.' Grace had been running goods inland with her sisters when Louisa had sprained her ankle in the dark, leaving her unable to walk unaided, or ride one of the ponies they'd had with them. Grace had helped Louisa home while Winnie went on to the rendezvous. On the way, a stranger had confronted and assaulted her. Grace had never been sure exactly what he'd done to her, only that he hadn't touched Winnie 'in that way' as her sisters had so delicately put it. 'I love how much you care for me, but I do have my own mind.'

Louisa pulled a face. 'That's what I'm afraid of.'

'Do you think we'll see Winnie soon?' Their middle sister had married and moved to West-cliffe, a hamlet four miles from Deal and Dover and not far from St Margaret's Bay.

'We should call on her. We don't see enough of her and the children . . .' Louisa's voice trailed off and Grace wondered if the mention of Winnie's littluns had reminded her of her failure to produce a child. Grace knew that it preyed on her mind. It wasn't for lack of trying, but she had observed — although she'd rather not have done — that the creaking of the bedsprings from

15

the marital bedroom had become less frequent than before. She wondered too if Louisa's rather scratchy mood meant she was with child again.

'Are you ready?' Grace asked, changing the subject.

'I am. I'm waiting for you.' Louisa tilted her head to one side in mock impatience.

With reluctance, Grace collected her gloves and shawl.

'That's better. Now we can go.'

As they left the cottage, Grace put her arm through Louisa's and half walked, half ran towards the shore.

'Slow down,' Louisa grumbled lightly. 'What's the rush?'

'I don't want to miss anything,' Grace exclaimed, the sound of music and laughter making her footsteps quicken. She particularly didn't want to miss out on the chance of running into Isaiah for a second time that day.

2

A Tempest in a Teacup

The setting sun cast long shadows across the beach, while the townsfolk lit torches and lamps to celebrate the dawn of peace. As they mingled with the crowds at the top of the steep shingle slope, Grace noticed how her sister's eyes lingered on the horizon where the deep indigo sea merged into a sky pricked with stars, and a fleet of lanterns shone like glow worms from the darkness.

To Grace's great disappointment, there was no sign of Isaiah. He would be serving up ale and conversation, she guessed as she planned a means of escaping from her diligent chaperone. Louisa rejected her offer to go and buy the pies for supper, and when she went to speak to one of the Roper girls, she called her straight back to offer her some brandy with a dash of warm milk that brought a rush of heat to her face.

When Jason turned up, his hair glinting gold as he removed his hat, her spirits lifted. Louisa would be relieved — and distracted by her husband's return from his spell at sea — and she would have an excuse to slip away, but it wasn't to be because he had company.

'Albert, allow me to introduce my wife and

sister-in-law, Mrs Witherall and Miss Grace Lennicker,' he said, and a young man stepped forward. He was exceptionally tall and well-built, not run to fat, but big boned, reminding Grace of one of Uncle Laxton's bullocks. With brown hair, hazel eyes and broad shoulders, she acknowledged that some might consider him dashing, but to her, he looked like any other young man eager to impress, in his blue shirt with a red bandanna tied about his neck.

'Ladies, this is Lieutenant Albert Enderby.'

'It's wonderful to meet you at last,' Louisa said. 'My husband has spoken very favourably of your achievements. You may call me Louisa.'

'Oh no, that wouldn't be right. I'll address you as Mrs Witherall, if you don't mind.'

'Grace, how about you?' Louisa pressed her.

'Grace or Miss Lennicker.' She almost added, *or the Queen of Sheba.* 'It makes no difference to me.'

'Then Grace it is,' Albert said, beaming.

She smiled back, but she was still thinking of Isaiah.

'We heard the news of Wellington's victory while cruisin' between Deal and Dunkirk,' Jason said. 'We were on the return leg when we caught a glimpse of a lugger in the moonlight. We gave chase, but she stayed ahead until the *Legacy*, havin' got the wind on her quarter, reeled off eight knots and ran straight past. I fired a warnin' shot and ordered her to heave to, but she carried on, leavin' us in her wake. I could have ordered an attack with all guns blazin', but . . . there's always another day.'

18

'I thought we'd got them this time.' Albert looked towards Grace with a doleful expression on his face. She smiled again, out of relief from knowing that Isaiah was safely ashore, not with the other smugglers. 'I wish that we had,' he went on.

'We won't cease huntin' them down until we've caught every damned one of them and put a stop to the free trade altogether,' Jason said. 'But now let us be merry for a while. Louisa, will you forgive your husband for his two left feet and join him for a dance?'

'Of course, my love,' she replied coquettishly before he took her hand and led her away towards the Waterman's Arms where the dancing had spilled out on to the street, leaving Grace with Albert, *alone*, she realised with some discomfort. This wasn't what she had planned, but she knew very well it was exactly what Jason had intended, for he had spoken many times of his lieutenant's intelligence, good manners and prospects. His virtues made him seem terribly ordinary.

'Well, it's — ' she began, thinking to excuse herself, but he interrupted her.

'May I have the pleasure of dancing with you?' A pink flush spread across his cheeks. 'Or is it 'the honour'? May I have the honour?'

'Shouldn't it be both a pleasure *and* an honour?' Grace teased.

'I do think you're right about that,' he said seriously. Apparently taking this as her consent, he offered her his arm. She took it and walked with him to where the band of pipers and fiddlers were playing their instruments as though their lives

19

depended on it and began to dance. He was a good dancer, energetic and light on his feet, not showy but allowing his partner to shine. As she grew slightly breathless, she became aware that Mary Roper was watching them — in fact, as the music died away, all eyes were on her and Lieutenant Enderby.

'My oh my, they make a handsome couple,' she heard someone say as Albert stood awkwardly in front of her.

'My commander has told me much about you,' he said.

'All good, I hope.'

'Mainly,' he replied after a long pause, apparently unable to bring himself to utter a white lie, even for the sake of propriety. 'I've heard that you have a way with animals.' For the first time, she heard a flicker of humour in his voice as he went on, 'Especially ponies.'

She knew what he was referring to: Jason must have mentioned how she and her sisters used to fetch the ponies from the mill and take them down to the beach to meet the boats when they were running goods inland.

'I'm sorry. I hope I haven't caused offence,' he said, growing serious again.

'It's all right. You spoke your mind.' She smiled. 'I like that.'

'I'm glad . . . and I should be delighted if the . . . prettiest young lady here would honour me with another dance.'

'You flatter me,' she said as the band, having drained the tankards of ale that Mrs Causton from the Waterman's Arms had delivered to them, struck up once more.

'It's the truth.' He hesitated. 'You haven't given me your answer?'

'Let's dance,' she said decisively, and they went to join a longways set of couples to strip the willow. They danced another reel and Grace began to wonder how she was going to excuse herself, because it seemed that Jason was determined to keep her in Albert's way.

'You aren't stoppin' dancin' already,' he kept saying.

As she moved to the music, she could almost forget she was with Albert, not Isaiah, and then out of the corner of her eye, she saw the latter talking to a woman, a young woman whom she didn't recognise.

'Grace,' Albert said, laughing as he took her arm and swept her back to her place in the set.

'I'm sorry — I'd quite forgotten where I was.' She giggled, a little embarrassed. 'You must think I'm slightly touched.'

'Not at all,' he smiled back.

'I thought I saw a friend in the crowd, someone I haven't seen for a long time.' The woman had her hand on Isaiah's arm, the sight giving Grace a frisson of envy as the music faded.

'I hope that we might become better acquainted. Perhaps you'll permit me to call on you when I return from my next spell on duty. You wouldn't find it unacceptable?'

'No, no,' she said, not wanting to hurt his feelings.

'Then I'll look forward to it.'

Before she could enlighten him as to what she'd

21

meant by her answer, Jason interrupted their conversation.

'I'm going to sit the next one out — I can't keep up with you youngsters,' he jested while the musicians drank a tot of brandy.

'You are not yet five and twenty,' she chuckled. 'I had hoped you would entertain Albert.'

'It would be selfish of me to keep the best dancer here to myself,' she said. 'Poor Mary's standing over there like a wallflower. I wonder if you might introduce them, Jason.'

He turned to Albert, saying, 'Very generously, I think, Grace has suggested that you might like to dance with one of her friends who is without a partner.'

Grace noticed how Albert's face fell — very briefly — before he smiled and nodded.

Mary Roper, whom Grace had known since they were littluns, spending time with their mothers and siblings on the beach, seemed surprised but pleased to have been included.

'What did you do that for?' Louisa whispered when Albert led Mary off to dance. 'Oh, never mind. Mary's dancing can hardly be described as graceful — look, she's gone the wrong way.'

Her dress — a pale cotton gown patterned with sprays of roses — was not flattering, and her light brown hair — braided and piled on top of her head — lacked lustre, Grace thought, watching as Albert kindly led his blushing partner back to her place in the set.

If only she could shake off Louisa, she could escape, but her sister had other ideas, insisting on partnering her with Old Mr Witherall who managed a few turns before she had to fetch him a chair from the Waterman's Arms. As she left him to recover, she felt a tap on her shoulder.

'It must be my turn by now. May I 'ave the pleasure of the next dance?'

'Isaiah,' she exclaimed, turning to face him.

'Well?' he said.

'Yes . . . I'll dance with you.'

'We can go for a walk if you prefer. I can 'ardly 'ear myself speak with all this noise. What do you think?'

'As long as we don't go too far.'

'We'll go as far as you decide and no further.' Grinning, he offered her his arm, but she declined, and they walked side by side at what she considered to be a respectable distance, away from the music and crowds.

'To whom were you speaking?' she asked.

'That was one of the barmaids from the Three Kings, askin' if I 'ad any work. I said I'd keep 'er in mind. Who was that boy you were dancin' with?'

'Boy?' She smiled. 'Oh, you mean Lieutenant Enderby. He's a Revenue officer — one of Jason's men and a recent addition to his crew.'

'I see. I didn't like the way 'e couldn't take 'is eyes off you.'

'Really? I didn't notice that he was paying me any special attention . . .' *Maybe I was thinking of someone else.* She bit her lip, then regretted not expressing a hint of her feelings for Isaiah, as they headed towards a fire that was alight further along the beach. One of several figures wearing dark clothing threw fresh logs and straw on to it, sending embers high into the night sky.

23

'There's the proof that the free trade stops for nothin',' Isaiah said, pausing to face her. 'That's part of the old gang over there: Lawless, Awful Doins and company. The rest are somewhere between 'ere and Dunkirk with the lugger, and good luck to 'em, I say.'

As Grace heard the smugglers muttering amongst themselves, their tone suggesting that their plans had gone asprawl, she remembered the fear that used to bite into the back of her neck and hang there with its jaws tightly clamped, until her part in a run was over.

'Surely they won't land their goods here tonight,' she said, as the acrid smoke reached her nostrils.

'I wouldn't risk it,' Isiah agreed, 'although some might, seein' that everyone is otherwise engaged in drinkin' and dancin'. They're usin' the fire to signal to the lugger — they'll stand well offshore until the party's over and the coast is clear.'

'Why aren't you out there with them?'

He raised one eyebrow. 'You're very frank.'

'Perhaps I shouldn't have . . . '

'No, you're right to question me. I 'ave nothin' to 'ide from you — unless Marlin 'as asked you to spy on me.'

'I'm not doing his work for him,' she said quickly.

'I'm glad to 'ear it. I've been wonderin' whose side you're on: Marlin's now that 'e's joined the Revenue, or that of the ordinary man like myself who gives cheer to 'is friends and acquaintances, riskin' 'is skin to sell the essentials — baccy, wine, tea and spirits — that make life worth livin'.' He gazed at her fixedly. 'Your silence tells me that

24

you're sittin' on the fence. It's all right. I don't blame you, but you should think about it, because one day you might be forced to choose. Goin' back to your question — I 'ave more pressin' business at the tavern.

'And 'ere, on the beach . . .' Isaiah cleared his throat. 'Let me say that you're a strikin' young woman.'

Not a girl, she thought as a gust of wind fanned the fire, sending the flames leaping into the sky and the embers drifting over their heads.

'I 'ave a reputation for villainy and associatin' with wrong 'uns, but I've never been a womaniser. I'm not the best lookin' and I don't always mind my manners as I should, but I've taken a fancy to you . . . Grace, don't just stand there lookin' like you've swallowed a lemon. Say somethin'.'

'I am dumbfounded.' She had been dreaming of the moment that Isaiah would declare his affection for her and now that he had, she didn't know how to react. She tried to read the expression on his shadowed features, but it was unfathomable. 'I won't have you toying with me,' she said sharply.

'I don't know why this 'as taken you by surprise — I've always 'ad a soft spot for you. You must 'ave noticed,' he said, half smiling. 'I mean what I say. Cross my 'eart and 'ope to die. And I will die of a broken 'eart if you turn me down.' His gruff voice tore at her heartstrings as he went on, 'I know I've done wrong in the past and your sisters 'ate my guts, but it doesn't alter my feelin's for you. Haven't I always looked out for you?'

She nodded, becoming aware of the faintest scent of singed fabric, then to her bewilderment,

Isaiah spat on his fingers and pressed them to her shoulder.

'What are you doing?' she squealed, as she twisted her neck to look at the mark on her gown.

'Whist! You were alight,' he said. 'Does it 'urt?'

'It stings a little,' she responded, her heart pounding when he grasped her hand and leaned closer.

'Grace, I'm mightily fond of you. Always 'ave been. You're what I call a diamond of the first water . . .' His warm breath caressed her cheek as the waves rushed back and forth across the shingle.

'Isaiah . . . no . . .' She placed the palm of her free hand on his chest, but she didn't try to push him away as he sought to kiss her mouth.

'Grace! Grace, is that you?' At the sound of Louisa's voice, Grace jumped, and Isaiah swore softly. They stepped swiftly apart. 'Thank the Lord. I've been looking for you everywhere!' Louisa held up a lantern, making Grace blink. 'Isaiah, what are you doing here . . . ? Grace, what are you doing here with him?'

'I saw the fire — I came to investigate,' she stammered.

'I insisted on walkin' with 'er,' Isaiah joined in.

'He saved my life. Look. A stray ember set my dress alight — I could have burned to death.'

'I thought you'd come to harm.' Grace felt Louisa's fingers pinching her flesh as she attempted to drag her away by the arm. 'Come on. It's long past midnight and time we went home.'

'Aren't you goin' to thank me for lookin' after your sister?' Isaiah asked dryly.

26

'You shouldn't be anywhere near her. Leave her alone in future.'

'Louisa, please don't. I'm not a child.'

'You're behaving like one. Hurry. Jason is waiting for us.'

'I'll wish you good night,' Isaiah said.

'Oh no. You may walk with us,' Grace called out, but he had already retreated into the darkness, leaving her bereft. Aware that Louisa was glaring at her, she looked away.

'I don't understand,' her sister said in a low voice. 'Why — when you could have your pick from the likes of Albert Enderby — would you associate with the son of the man who murdered our father?'

* * *

Grace returned home in high dudgeon, leaving the music and dancing on the beach behind. She was being selfish, but all she could think of was how Louisa had humiliated her in front of Isaiah and the injustice of her suggestion that it was somehow his fault that he had been born to a villain. If he'd had anything to do with it, or One Eye — his father and leader of the Rattlers at the time — had really murdered dear Pa, she wouldn't have dreamt of putting herself in his way.

Mr Lennicker had been a cheerful character with bushy eyebrows and a craggy complexion. When he hadn't been hiding in the herring hang from his household of women, singing 'The Saucy Sailor Boy' and 'Hanging Johnny' at the top of his bellows, he'd have been out fishing, or at one of the taverns, planning operations with his fellow free traders. She thought he might have had mixed feelings about the end of the war — he'd used to remark that they had much to thank old Boney for, because without war and taxes, they'd never have a sixpence to scratch with.

They were fond memories. Her recollection of his last days less so.

★ ★ ★

One night before Jason began courting Louisa, Pa had dressed up and gone out, leaving Grace and her sisters to get on with letting down the cognac. They were busy making it ready to sell by adding caramel to give it colour and diluting it down to suit the English taste when Jason called on them out of the blue, telling them to go straight to the Rattling Cat. Filled with dread, Grace had been crying even before she followed Louisa and Winnie into the tavern, where they found Pa lying in the arms of a Mrs Stickles as his blood crept across the taproom floor, staining the sawdust.

She had hardly been able to take in what was happening as Louisa tried to help Mrs Stickles, whom Grace had understood to be a woman of ill-repute back then, to stem the flow of blood from Pa's shoulder. 'You shouldn't be 'ere,' Pa muttered gruffly. 'You shouldn't 'ave to see this.'

One Eye was leaning against the counter, his good eye oddly marbled, the other covered with a patch. Greasy locks of grey hair stuck out from under his cloth bandanna, and the sleeves of his scruffy brown linen shirt were rolled up to reveal

28

tattoos of an anchor on one arm and a mermaid on the other.

'You shot him!' Louisa accused him, which Grace had thought was remarkably brave of her, considering that he was holding a pistol and the scent of gunpowder was hanging in the air. 'Somebody, fetch the constable, the army . . . do something.'

A young man staggered forward from the crowd of smugglers who had paused their drinking and games of cards to watch the drama unfolding in front of them. 'Constable Pocket at yer disposal. My apologies for bein' a trifle disguised, but I weren't expectin' no trouble tonight.'

'Give the young ladies the full and true version of events,' One Eye said. 'There's an 'alf-anker in it for you.'

'There's been a terr'ble accident,' the constable said nervously. 'As far as I'm given to understand . . . I mean, so far as I understand it, Mr Lennicker entered the inn by way of the back door, armed with a pistol and demandin' to speak privately with Mrs Stickles 'ere, but she was unavailable, bein' employed servin' be'ind the bar. Mr Feasey told 'im to go 'ome, but Mr Lennicker forced 'is way past, and bein' keen to disarm 'im, there bein' a large number of his loyal patrons present, Mr Feasey took the pistol from 'im. 'As 'e did so, it went off, 'itting Mr Lennicker in the arm.'

'If I 'adn't got it off 'im, who knows what would 'ave 'appened.' One Eye turned as one of the cats on the counter, the bones rattling on its collar, leapt on to his shoulder at the sound of horses' hooves and voices outside.

29

'It's Doctor Audley,' Awful Doins murmured, and the physician took over, ordering the men to stretcher Pa home before attending to him.

'It was an accident,' Pa maintained, going along with the constable's tale, but this wasn't the only version of the story of what had occurred at the Rattling Cat on that fateful night.

Billy — their lodger and now Winnie's husband — had been present at the time. He had confided in Louisa that Mr Lennicker had arrived with his pistol in his hand and a grievance on his lips. One Eye, having taken offence at what he'd said, took his piece from under the counter and shot him in the arm.

As it was, Pa might have survived, had not gangrene set in and carried him off a few days later.

* * *

Falling behind, Grace followed Louisa around the corner into Cockle Swamp Alley.

'Aren't you speaking to me any more?' Louisa asked, unlocking the cottage door and holding it open for her.

'Isaiah isn't like his father,' Grace blurted out. 'It isn't fair that you tar him with the same brush.'

'He's always been mean — even as a boy, he used to go out of his way to scare the little children on the beach with his tall tales.'

'That was a long time ago. He isn't as black as he's been painted.'

'Grace, you hardly know him.'

'We acknowledge each other when he's out walking with his dog. He always has time for me.'

30

'One has to ask why?'

'Because he's fond of me . . . .' Grace chewed on her lip as they walked inside.

'If he were such a paragon of virtue, he would have stood up to his father and not let him get away with cheating us out of our goods.' Grace opened her mouth to argue, but Louisa continued fiercely, 'You're forgetting how the Rattlers set the Revenue on to us, ending up in Jason's arrest, and how they kidnapped me to get me out of the way. I thought I was going to die that night.'

'I know . . . I'm sorry, but— '

'Let's say no more about it,' Louisa interrupted, her tone brooking no further argument. 'Jason is following along behind us. Be warned, I'll be telling him about this.'

'I'm innocent,' Grace pleaded.

'People will have seen you sneaking off along the beach — I have no doubt that you'll be the talk of the town on the morrow. Our only hope is that Albert didn't notice or if he did, Jason can give him a plausible excuse for it.'

Grace refrained from voicing her opinion that it wouldn't hurt if Albert found out that she'd slipped away with Isaiah, rather than having to tell him herself, knowing that his feelings might well be a little bruised by her rejection. She didn't like to think that she'd inadvertently encouraged him in his pursuit by her choice of words when he'd asked if he could call on her.

'Ah, talk of the devil. Here he is.' Louisa looked towards her husband who was walking through the door. 'We've had a little bit of an upset — that's why I had to rush away.'

31

'Black Dog lured our Grace into a compromising situation,' he sighed, referring to Isaiah by his nickname. 'My mother told me. I explained that she was mistaken — she agreed to correct her version of events. Grace, what do you have to say for yourself?'

'I'm not going to apologise,' she said stubbornly.

'As I expected.' He grinned, at which Louisa nudged him in the ribs, making him frown instead.

'I swear you are three sheets to the wind,' she said.

'I had some ale to quench my thirst,' he said, half laughing. 'My dear wife, let's go to bed. We can talk about it in the mornin'. Grace made a mistake — we all make them — and learn from them. I reckon this is what you would term a tempest in a teacup. It will soon blow over.'

Grace refrained from arguing that he was wrong. Thanks to Louisa's disapproval of her growing friendship with Isaiah, there were bound to be more storms ahead, and whether Louisa liked it or not, Grace would weather them to find out if she and Isaiah had a future together.

3

Shrewd is the One who has Seen the Calamity and Proceeds to Conceal Himself

Grace found her sister in a better mood the next morning when she went down to the kitchen, where the faintest scent of bloaters emanated from the hang where Winnie had smoked herring in the past.

Jason was sitting at the kitchen table, cutting himself two pieces of pie: one to eat straight away and one to put in his pocket. Louisa poured boiling water from the copper kettle on to the tea leaves in the pot and waited for them to stew, while Grace fetched a bowl and started peeling and chopping potatoes and scallions ready for supper.

'You aren't hungry?' Louisa commented.

'I'll have something later.' She couldn't eat a thing for thinking of Isaiah and what had passed between them. She had to see him. She would die if she didn't.

'Albert's a handsome young man,' Louisa said.

'I'm surprised you noticed when you're always sayin' that you only have eyes for your husband?' Jason chuckled. 'Perhaps you're goin' to make a cuckold of me?'

'He has lovely manners. Didn't you tell me that his parents have a house in Upper Walmer?'

'That's right, my love. His father is a chandler — he owns a warehouse in Dover, sellin' nautical supplies,' Jason replied. 'He has prospects. His willingness and aptitude for learnin' the ropes have impressed me.'

'I can see what you're trying to do,' Grace sighed. 'You can't sell him to me like he's a piece of lace. I'm not interested. He's a moon calf.' She was being a little unfair on him, she realised. She probably wouldn't have been able to resist flirting with him for her own amusement, if it hadn't been for Isaiah. Although nothing had been settled between them, she would have felt disloyal.

'He's a little backward in comin' forward, but so was I at his age,' Jason added.

Albert wasn't as shy as Jason imagined, Grace thought. 'I can tell you now that your feeble attempt at matchmaking isn't going to work — I could never love him.'

'Don't be too hasty,' Louisa cut in. 'So many men have been lost to the wars that finding a husband in future will be like finding water in the desert. A large proportion of young ladies will end up left on the shelf, condemned never to experience the joys — ' she glanced at Jason with a wicked glint in her eye '— and trials of marriage.'

'When I marry, I want my husband to be swarthy and rebellious.'

'You are young and foolish.' Louisa smiled fondly. 'A husband should be like mine, handsome and brave, but above all kind. I maintain that love without kindness isn't love.' She stood up and moved behind him, resting her hands lightly on his shoulders. 'Jason and I have decided that you

34

should go and stay with Winnie for a while.'

'I beg your pardon?' Grace said, but she hadn't misheard.

'I shall write to her today to tell her you'll arrive after Jason returns later this sennight — I'm sure she'll have no objection.'

'She'll appreciate your help with the children,' Jason contributed. 'I'll speak to Abel about borrowin' a cart to carry your luggage.'

There was the sound of knocking on the door and Grace was pleased to escape their lecture on love and their plans for her, going to answer it.

'Albert?' she said, finding him on the doorstep, hat in hand, hair brushed and boots shining.

'I-I-I've come to call for Jason,' he stammered. 'I hope I'm not too early.'

'Come in,' she said. 'I'll fetch him.'

'I'd like a moment with you first, if I may,' he said, following her into the hall where Kitty eyed him from the basket on top of the shelf.

He sounded so stern that she wondered if he'd heard about her and Isaiah, but he went on, 'It's an excuse — I had to see you before I leave. I hope you don't mind, but I didn't sleep a wink last night and it wasn't because of the noise at the Waterman's Arms. I wanted to say that your answer pleased me very much. Perhaps we can agree a time when I might call on you when I get back.'

'Oh Albert.' Her heart sank. She hadn't realised that his feelings ran that deep. 'I'm sorry — '

'Albert!' Jason emerged from the kitchen. 'You're keen.'

'I am indeed.'

35

'We'd better go and chase up the rest of the men — I reckon there'll be a few sore heads today.' Jason stopped abruptly. 'Am I interruptin' somethin'?'

'No,' Grace said, and Albert gave her a charming, lopsided smile as though complicit in some great secret.

'Grace and I were — '

'Passing the time of day,' she said quickly. 'You'd better be off to do your duty. Goodbye, Albert.'

'Until we meet again,' he said as she stepped back to let Louisa join Jason in the hall.

Taking his wife into his arms, he kissed her. 'Grace will look after you for me. Won't you, Grace?'

'I know,' Louisa said, looking tearful. 'You take care.'

'Oh, I shall. I promise.'

When Jason and Albert had gone, dressed in their uniforms, and carrying cutlasses and pistols, Louisa confirmed what Grace had already suspected, that she was in the family way.

'I'm very pleased for you,' Grace said as she cleared the table.

'There's no need to say any more on the subject.' Louisa turned away and took a sheet of paper, pen and ink from the dresser.

'You know, you don't have to write to Winnie,' Grace began.

'It's no use arguing with me about this,' Louisa said severely. 'It's a fait accompli. When you've finished your chores, you can start on the pile of mending that's been building up for weeks. There are buttons to sew on and rents to repair. Don't worry, I'll sit with you to keep you company.' *And keep an eye on you.* She left the words unsaid.

Winnie's house at Westcliffe was four miles from Deal, far enough to keep Grace out of Isaiah's way. When she and Billy — Mr and Mrs Fleet — had moved there, Grace had been surprised at her sister's choice, remembering how she'd always said that she wanted a cottage in Deal. Instead, they lived in a gentleman's residence with the usual offices, five bedrooms and servants' quarters. There was an attic and cellar, secret passageways and plenty of hiding holes for stashing away contraband, but the Fleets, like Jason and Louisa, had given up the free trade when they came into their fortune, thanks to Winnie's enterprise in breaking a spy ring and helping to return a pair of escaped French prisoners of war to their home country.

Winnie was the last person anyone would have expected to be involved in espionage, but that was why she had been picked to carry despatches. She was the quiet one of the three sisters, thoughtful and charitable, almost to a fault.

Although she had sprained her ankle, falling for a child out of wedlock, all had ended well when her lover had returned from a stint in the service of the King's Navy, having been pressed into 'volunteering' just before she had found out she was pregnant. Billy lost part of his leg in the fighting and for a while he also lost his way, but having sunk to his lowest ebb through drunkenness, he managed to turn his life around. He married Winnie and devoted himself tirelessly to his growing family and creating false limbs for returning soldiers and sailors.

If Winnie had invited her even a sennight ago, Grace would have been over the moon at the idea of spending time with her beloved nephew and nieces, but the bond she had with Isaiah had anchored her firmly in Deal. He wouldn't forget her if she was away for a month — that would be ridiculous, she thought — but she was afraid that his affection for her might fade rather than grow stronger in her absence. She worried about Albert too, that thanks to Jason's untimely interruption, she hadn't yet been able to set him straight. Recognising him for a sensitive young man, not an oafish boor, she wanted to let him down gently, not embarrass him in front of his commander.

Having hurried through her chores, she went into the hall and put on her boots.

'Where do you think you're going?' Louisa said, emerging from the parlour.

'I'm going to see Mary to let her know I'll be away for a while.' The lie slipped like quicksilver from Grace's tongue.

'Oh no, you are not.' Louisa frowned. 'I'll speak to her when I see her.'

'You can't stop me.' Grace watched her sister lock the front door, remove the key and slip it into her pocket.

'This is an outrage,' Grace cried. 'How dare you! I'm seventeen, not seven. Louisa, unlock the door and let me pass.'

'No. I'm doing this for you — I can't stand by and watch you wreck your life.'

'You won't be able to keep me indoors — I'll fetch the spare key.' Grace ran out to the kitchen and pulled the drawers in the dresser open one by

38

one, turfing out the contents.

'You won't find it,' she heard Louisa's voice from behind her, her tone cold and condescending. 'And you can put all that away, or there's no supper for you tonight.'

In tears, Grace took a seat at the table. Kitty leapt on to her lap and purred, oblivious to her mistress's distress at the thought of not being able to see Isaiah to let him know that she was being sent away to Winnie's, because it would make her look like she didn't care, that she hadn't given him a second thought.

There was no solution. As the days passed, Grace remained a prisoner in the gaol of her sister's creation. She wasn't allowed to accompany Louisa to the market and post office, or linger on the doorstep, chatting with the neighbours in the mornings.

★ ★ ★

Sitting in the parlour with her needle and thread a few days into her imprisonment that was both unwanted and unwarranted in her opinion, Grace still found it strange that the hiding hole beside the fireplace was empty and that she could pull a chair up to the table without banging her shins on a half-anker of cognac. Louisa was silent, knitting a gansey for Jason, so Grace let her mind drift, recalling how not long after they'd buried their father, Isaiah had found her crying among the tools, floats and leaky buckets inside the hut Pa had built on the beach.

'I thought I 'eard a damsel in distress,' she heard

him mutter as he pushed the door open.

'Go away,' she said roughly.

'I'm not leavin' until I know you're goin' to be all right. Oh Grace . . . ' She'd looked up to find him silhouetted against the morning sun. 'I'm so very sorry. I saw you at the church.'

'Did you?'

'I waited outside — at a distance because I knew I wouldn't be welcome — to watch the . . . to pay my respects when they put Mr Lennicker in the ground.'

She stifled a fresh sob of grief because she and her sisters, forbidden by virtue of their sex to stand on consecrated ground, had had to remain inside the church for the burial.

'I'm even more sorry now — I've made it worse for you.'

'Oh, it can't be any worse that it is already.' She glared at him. 'Who was there? Who was at the graveside?'

'Billy Fleet, another gentleman, the vicar and sexton. Do you really think I'd lie to you about bein' there?' he went on gruffly.

'While we were saying our goodbyes, the Rattlers stole our boat,' she told him. 'I have no idea what we'll do without her — we rely on her for going out fishing and provisioning . . . '

She remembered leaving St George's, walking along the passage and crossing into Oak Street, where they heard the sound of a commotion from the beach. Winnie had assumed that the Frenchies had invaded and Grace had fainted.

'I 'ad nothin' to do with it, I swear. When I told my father that I wouldn't be party to it, he gave

40

me this for my trouble.' He tilted his head to one side. The light glancing off his cheek revealed a purple bruise and half-closed eye. 'And these.' He showed her the cuts and scratches on his hands.

'Oh, you poor thing,' she said softly. 'How could he?'

''E won't touch me again. I've made sure of it. I've put 'im in fear of his life if 'e ever lays so much as one finger on me.'

'I can get you some witch hazel for your wounds — Winnie swears by it.'

'I can't expect you to 'elp the likes of me,' he sighed.

'I've been brought up to offer assistance to anyone who's in need — ' she smiled briefly through her tears '— even a villain such as you.'

'Thanks, but these'll 'eal — they always do.'

'If you're sure . . .'

'About Mr Lennicker's boat,' he said. 'I'll let you know where she is when I find out. It won't be easy. She could be anywhere — 'auled up in the marshes down Romney way, or 'idden in the Sands or moored up past Sandwich — and she'll be re-caulked, altered and 'ave 'er name painted over with another.'

Isaiah did find out where the Pamela was, but he told Jason, not Grace, that she was for sale at one of the boatyards. Although Grace had desperately wanted Louisa to buy her father's precious boat back, she refused to line the Feaseys' pockets, which is why they'd bought the *Curlew* instead.

A sharp stab from her needle brought her back to the present. Sucking the blood from her thumb, she placed her sewing on her lap and extricated a

41

skein of thread from Kitty's playful paws.

'You seem distracted,' Louisa observed. 'And look at me — I've dropped yet another stitch. I'll have to leave this for another day.'

'Do you miss the free trade?' Grace asked politely, having decided to take a different tack with her sister to give herself a chance of seeing Isaiah. The tears and scowls, and her claims that she was dying from a lack of exercise and fresh air, hadn't worked, which was fair enough — she'd realised that she was being childish and that Louisa would soon see through her ruses.

'A little.' Louisa rolled up her knitting and put it aside. 'I believe that Jason does too, although he'd never admit it.' The shadow of a smile crossed her features. 'Every run was different. Exciting. You never knew what was going to happen next. I remember how we'd wait on the beach or in the sandhills for the boats to land the goods.' Louisa had specialised in running the finest French lace, selling it direct to the draper in Walmer, or passing it on to agents who sold it in Canterbury and London. She'd also dealt with some of the local law-abiding society ladies who would throw caution to the wind for a length of galloon or a piece of black silk lace from Chantilly. 'I'd assumed that giving it up would keep us safe, but I worry about Jason because the smugglers are getting more desperate and no longer have any respect for the Revenue men.'

'Did we ever have any respect for the gobblers?' Grace said, thinking back.

'We used to take great delight in gammoning them whenever the opportunity presented itself,'

42

Louisa said. 'I recall how we gave them false information about the landings, concealed the goods under our cloaks, knowing that they'd never rummage a woman, and kept them talking so that others could get away.'

'You're making out that it was one great party, but I remember being scared out of my wits. You were too.'

'We had one or two narrow squeaks,' Louisa admitted. 'Oh, I wish Jason was back. It's been six days — he should be home by now.'

'Please don't fret,' Grace urged her. 'You should be resting as much as possible.'

'You're right.' With a wistful smile, Louisa laid her palm on her belly. 'I think I'll retire to my room for an hour or two. You have plenty to keep you occupied.'

Grace nodded. Perhaps this was her chance . . .

She waited until she thought Louisa was asleep before going across to open the window, hoping to squeeze feet first through the narrow aperture and slither out on to the cobbles. 'What are you doin'?' She looked across the alley to find Cromwell staring at her.

'Nothing,' she said quickly.

'It don't look like nothin'.' He broke into a smile. 'I won't tell anybody you're runnin' away if you'll give me a shillin'.'

'I'll give you a farthing to keep your mouth shut.'

'Two farthin's . . .'

'You drive a hard bargain. All right, I'll pay you later. Don't breathe a word of this to a soul or I'll have your guts for garters.' Grace hurried towards the beach and made her way to the Rattling Cat. It was six o'clock and the tavern was nearly empty, apart from a couple of elderly men playing cards in the corner beside the fireplace, three black cats patrolling the floor, and the short, rather buxom barmaid who was wiping the counter with a greasy cloth. The smell of tripe and stale beer, and a sudden attack of nerves made Grace feel a little sick. Would Isaiah think she was being too forward, too immodest, turning up to see him?

'What do you want?' the girl asked rudely.

'I've come to see Mr Feasey.' Grace noted her unkempt ringlets of straw-coloured hair, her faded puce dress and stained apron with distaste. She guessed that she was younger than she appeared, about twenty years old, if that.

''E isn't 'ere.' She dropped the cloth into a bucket of suds. 'And before you ask, I 'ave no idea where to find 'im.' The girl showed a sudden interest. 'Who shall I say is lookin' for 'im?'

'Grace,' she said.

'Ah, Grace Lennicker. I'm new 'ere, but I've 'eard of you. You're Black Dog's fancy woman. All I can say is, I wish you luck. You're too good for 'im.'

Thinking her most impertinent, Grace bade her farewell and returned outside. Louisa would be asleep for at least another hour, giving her time to walk as far as the capstan grounds where the shore boys were skimming stones and a pair of elderly boatmen were dragging on their pipes.

Noticing that the *Good Intent II* wasn't in her usual spot on the beach, or among the vessels in the Downs, Grace assumed that she had found the answer to Isaiah's whereabouts. Disappointed, she stopped where the *Curlew*, covered with a sheet of tarpaulin, was beached in her usual place, and turned to walk back. Despite talking of selling her, Louisa hadn't been able to part with the boat.

'Psst! Over 'ere!' A gull flew up from among the lobster pots and Grace almost leapt out of her skin. 'Don't faint. Don't make any fuss.'

'Isaiah,' she hissed. 'I've been looking for you.'

'Ah, my angel of mercy, lift the corner of the tarp . . . I need to talk to you.'

'I'll make a pretence of searching the shore for driftwood and shells,' she said, pulling a small section of the tarpaulin away and reaching inside where she felt Isaiah's hand grabbing hers and briefly caressing it. 'Pass me a bucket or something.'

'There's a pie dish 'ere,' he said, placing it in her hand.

'It belongs to Molly's pot house. We used to use it for bailing out.' She moved a few steps from the boat and picked up a mermaid's purse and a cuttlebone to start her collection.

'I'm in a spot o' bother,' she heard him say. 'I'm in dire need of your 'elp.'

'Anything,' she said.

'You'd better 'ear me out first.' She could tell from the tone of his voice that he was smiling. 'Oh, I shouldn't ask you — I'm puttin' you in an impossible situation. I will 'ave to accept my punishment on this occasion. I can only 'ope that the judge 'as mercy on me and I don't end up 'angin' from the three-legged mare.'

'What have you done?'

45

'Nothin' more than usual. We took the lugger to France, collected the goods and on our way back, Marlin gave chase. It was just as I'd expected — 'e gave 'is old foes no quarter.'

'You must have given him good reason,' she said.

'Maybe we did,' he said grudgingly. 'There were a few shots fired both ways if I remember rightly. They wrecked our mast and put an 'ole through our canvas. Anyway, seein' we were in danger, I ordered my men to lower the galley and row for it. It was pitch dark and they had no lanterns, no wittles . . . . I 'id myself be'ind the false boards in the bulkhead on the lugger, thinkin' I might be able to snatch her back from Marlin and 'is crew. 'E put a few of them onboard and sailed her in towards the shore, but I was growin' more and more afeared of bein' discovered, so I jumped and swam for it. It's a miracle that ol' briny didn't drag me down by my boots. It was the thought of you, Grace, that kept me goin'. If it 'adn't been for you, I'd have surely drowned.'

'You are well — you aren't hurt?' she asked.

'My bellows are filled with brine, but I'm 'ere to fight another day. As for the men — if they make it back, I'm 'ere to grease the wheels o' justice should they be arrested and charged.'

'You're going to bribe the magistrates, you mean?'

'If a tub of brandy is the price of freedom, I'm willin' to pay it.'

'I don't see how I can help. You seem to have your defence all sewn up.'

'I need an alibi for the night that the lugger

46

went out — last Tuesday. I could ask Sarah — she works for me — but who will take 'er word for it when she's recently married Digger Brown?'

Grace knew of Digger — he was one of the Rattlers.

'No one would suspect you of lyin', Grace,' Isaiah went on. 'If I'm arrested, you can say I was with you. We're courtin', aren't we?'

'Are we?' The waves seemed to pause for a moment, the sea holding her breath.

'You said you came lookin' for me? I meant what I said when I told you I 'ad a fancy for you.'

'You aren't just saying it because you want me to perjure myself?' she said doubtfully.

'I'm all yours if you'll 'ave me.' The water rushed in again and broke into a flurry of foaming spume. Her joy began to bubble over as he went on, 'I'm askin' a lot of you, but there's a chance that you can save my skin.' When she didn't respond, he continued, 'I know I've done wrong and I'm mightily sorry, but I can't alter it now. Perhaps you'll be a good influence and 'elp me change my ways — if they allow me to go on livin'.'

'I'll do it. I'll speak for you if it becomes necessary, out of compassion and for my own sake because I'm fond of you too.' Smiling, she went on, 'There, I didn't think I could do it — I've admitted my feelings. It is such a relief that we can be open with each other from now on. What will you do next? Are you planning to hide for ever?'

'Only until dark when I'll make my way back to the tavern.'

'When Jason comes back, I'll be going away for a while,' she said. 'That's what I was coming to tell you.'

'I'm surprised you're allowed out. I thought Louisa would 'ave 'ad you under lock and key after the other night.'

'She has — she's had me locked indoors ever since.' She heard him chuckling. 'Where are you goin'?'

'Louisa and Jason are sending me to Westcliffe to help Winnie with the children. It won't be for long, a month or so, but I thought . . . .'

'I might miss you,' he finished for her.

'I didn't want you to think that I was avoiding you.'

'I see. Is this part of the ugly sisters' plot to keep us apart? Well, it does seem that you are their little Cinderella, workin' your fingers to the bone for them. That's the trouble when folks come into money — they think they're bettermost.'

'They've been good to me,' Grace said. 'Winnie is kindness personified.'

'When you've been a dyed-in-the-wool smuggler, though, the stain never quite washes out.'

'She's adopted two orphans and paid towards the poorhouse children's education. And she's set up a trust fund in my name — I'll be entitled to the money when I'm eighteen. Maybe I shouldn't have mentioned it — it's a private arrangement.' She recalled how Louisa used to have to remind her to keep her mouth shut on certain matters, such as their plans for various smuggling runs in the past. 'Promise me you won't tell anyone.'

48

'I'll do anythin' you ask. I'd rather this — ' he lifted the tarpaulin, raised his head and ran his hand across his throat '— than blab.' He gazed at her softly and her heart gave a dangerous lurch. 'You can trust me.'

'Even though thousands of others don't?'

'I don't know where you 'eard that from.' He grinned back at her before suddenly ducking back into the hull of the boat. Glancing along the top of the beach, she spotted Old Mr Witherall limping along with his stick. 'Until we meet again — shall we say, tomorrer noontime, circumstances permittin'?'

'I'll be here. At least, I'll do my best to get away.' Elated, she stowed the dish away in Pa's hut, then hurried away, hoping that their neighbour hadn't noticed her, because as the bell of St George's struck seven, she calculated that she could get home before Louisa realised she'd gone. Once in the alley, she took a run at the window, grabbed the ledge and hauled herself over the top into the parlour where she dusted herself down and returned to her sewing.

She had managed to sew on three buttons by the time Louisa made an appearance.

'Did you sleep well?' Grace asked.

'I feel much better, thank you. Shall we make a start on cooking supper?'

'Let me do it,' Grace offered.

'I'm glad to see you're looking more cheerful.' Louisa had a particular stare that made Grace feel exposed, like an onion stripped of its outer layers. 'Oh, I wish I knew what was going on in your head sometimes.'

Bowing her head as she secured the end of her thread and snipped it off close to the knot, she was glad at that moment that Louisa did not.

4

You Cannot Hold with the Hare and Run with the Hounds

At dawn, Grace hurried downstairs at the sound of someone's knuckles beating a tattoo on the door.

'Who goes around disturbing people at this unearthly hour?' she grumbled as she stood waiting for Louisa to bring the key. Louisa unlocked and opened the door to reveal Cromwell on the doorstep.

'I 'ave news,' he said brightly, 'and I'd like that money you promised me.'

'What money?' Louisa said.

Hiding behind her sister, Grace pressed her finger to her lips and shook her head violently.

'Oh, I see. Nothin', Mrs Witherall.'

Grace could have hugged him — almost.

'Your shamming doesn't wash with me,' Louisa said sternly. 'You must try harder to find work like everyone else. I see you hanging around on the beach with the other boys, hoping something will turn up, when you should be out looking for it. But what is your news?' Louisa's voice assumed a darker tone as the bell sounded from the capstan grounds. 'What's gone wrong?

51

Where is my husband?'

'Marlin and the gobblers 'ave seized the Rattlers' boat. Come and see for yourselves.' Before they could question him further, he was off, heading back to the beach. Grace and Louisa threw their cloaks over their shoulders, put on their boots without tying the laces and ran after him. Joining the lines of people waiting on the shingle, Grace saw two vessels sailing towards them through a shimmering mist. The first one, HMS *Legacy*, furled her sails and dropped anchor a little way from the shore. Her crew lowered one of her gigs and four men scrambled in.

'I wish I'd brought the spyglass.' Louisa was referring to the one Winnie had 'borrowed' from a Riding officer and never given back. 'Oh, where is Jason?'

'There he is.' Catching sight of a glint of blond hair as a man in the gig raised his hat, Grace pointed towards him. 'He's safe,' she confirmed as the crew picked up their oars and began to row towards the shore, but Louisa had gone, sliding down the shelving slope to await his arrival.

Grace turned her attention to the second boat, a giant lugger with a black hull, her mast broken in half and her sail torn to ribbons.

'It's the *Good Intent II*,' she heard Old Mr Witherall say from her side. 'My boy — I mean, Commander Witherall — will 'ave 'ad 'er crew locked away in the cabin on the forepeak.'

'Oh, I do 'ope so,' his wife said anxiously.

Grace watched the prize crew whom Jason had chosen to sail the lugger back to Deal stand her up nearby while a pair of Riding officers and a small detachment of dragoons came riding down the beach. Jason, wearing a red flannel shirt, blue trousers and tarpaulin petticoats, disembarked from the gig, splashing through the water to greet Louisa and start walking up the beach. He'd only taken a few strides before a dozen women came running to intercept him, demanding news of their menfolk.

He held up his hands begging for calm.

'Where are they? What 'ave you done with 'em?' One of the women spat at his feet. 'We don't like dirty little turncoats. By rights, we should 'ave 'ad you killed. Who's the wrong 'un now?'

'Don't you go down there.' Mrs Witherall grasped her husband's sleeve to stop him going to defend his son. 'They'll rip you to shreds.'

'What about my boy?' he retorted as Jason ordered his officers to remove the goods from the lugger and row them across to the beach.

''E's a Revenue man— 'e 'as the protection of the law . . . and all them soldiers.'

The captain of the dragoons had a pistol at the ready, his presence seeming to have the desired effect, because when Jason said something that Grace couldn't hear from her vantage point, the women fell to crying and wailing. He corroborated Isaiah's story, that when the *Legacy* had engaged with the *Good Intent*, her crew had taken to a galley and rowed off into the darkness. Jason and his men had stayed out for three days and nights looking for them.

'We thought we caught sight of them a couple of times on the first day, but whoever was in the galley, rowed it into the Sands where we couldn't

53

follow,' Jason added. 'We haven't seen hide nor hair of them since.'

The distraught women blamed the Revenue men for forcing their husbands and lovers into terrible danger. When one — Lawless's wife — began to throw punches at Jason, the captain of the dragoons threatened her with arrest if she continued to obstruct the Revenue in the course of their duty. Jason's men rowed back and forth from the lugger, carrying numerous tubs and bales of contraband to the shore where they piled them into carts to be taken to the Customs House.

'I can't stop thinkin' about those poor souls lost at sea,' Mrs Witherall sighed as her husband chewed his pipe, unconcerned, and Grace fretted over whether or not Jason was going to arrest Isaiah.

After a while, Jason spoke to Albert whom he'd made temporary captain of the smuggling vessel. Having concluded that there were no more goods on board, he ordered him to bring the *Good Intent II* in stern-first on to the shingle as was the custom. The crew disembarked and the remaining boatmen put down their tankards of ale to help the shore boys haul her up the rollers to the top of the beach.

Albert led the crew across to join Jason and the rest of his men. Awaiting further orders, the young lieutenant looked towards Grace and smiled.

She smiled stiffly back, wondering how soon it would be before she got the chance to extricate herself from the pickle she was in. She had to let him down before she left for Winnie's the next day, even though the shameful idea of leaving without

54

telling him that she had fallen for someone else had crossed her mind.

Mrs Witherall retreated to speak to Louisa, leaving Grace with Old Mr Witherall.

'The weather's set fair, the sea's as calm as you like, and the Rattlers are a wily lot,' he said. 'What do you think, Grace?'

'I shall pray for them,' she said primly, wondering what he knew.

'Like the rest of us, they 'ave a strong instinct for self-preservation. It isn't really any of my business, but I'd advise you to watch your step, young lady. 'Ave some respect for yourself and your family.' He paused and looked up the beach. 'Ah, here he is. Talk of the Devil.'

'Black Dog, where are our menfolk?' The women crowded around him as he sauntered down the beach. 'They've been reported missin' at sea.'

'Ladies, ladies! It seems somewhat careless on your part that you admit to losin' them, if they're as precious to you as you claim.'

'Where are they? Where is my 'usband? You must know where he is — you set out for France with 'im.'

'I'm afraid you're mistaken. I've been 'ere in Deal, doin' business at the tavern.'

'Liar!'

Isaiah bowed his head. 'You 'ave me wrong, missus.'

'Make way for the officer!' The women parted to allow Jason to pass. He and Isaiah stood face-to-face.

'Mr Feasey — also known as Black Dog — of the Rattlin' Cat, I'm arrestin' you for organisin' or allowin' the illegal import of contraband, namely over three hundred barrels of cognac and the same of geneva, along with two hundred pounds of tea. Furthermore, I charge you with the crime of ownership or part ownership of a vessel of the type used by smugglers along this coast.' He paused, the muscle in his cheek tautening, while Isaiah folded his arms and smiled. 'Don't worry. You'll soon be laughin' on the other side of your face. I'm seizin' this boat and her spoils, and accordin' to the law of the land, I have the authority to order her destruction, havin' her cut into three parts. What do you have to say for yourself?'

'That you are wrong . . . sir.'

'It's well known that you own the greater share in this vessel.'

'Not any more. You can check.'

Jason nodded towards Albert who fetched the chest containing the lugger's papers. Together, he and Jason perused them as the last cartload of tubs headed into town.

'There is no mention of this villain's name,' Jason said, disgruntled. 'He's falsified the transaction, a not uncommon occurrence.'

'I've sold my share to the gentleman named in 'er papers.' Isaiah glowered at him.

'One George Minnis of Snargate,' Albert contributed.

'Another rogue,' Jason said. 'Black Dog, you can't hold with the hare and run with the hounds. I'm not satisfied with the evidence you've put forward. Enderby, arrest him!'

Grace felt sick when Isaiah turned to her, his eyes wide in entreaty.

'You can't do that,' she exclaimed as Albert clapped him in irons. 'He's innocent.'

'Don't make a scene,' Louisa hissed, pulling her back. 'Stand here at my side and hold your tongue. Albert's watching. Everyone's eyes are on you.'

'I don't care. I won't stand by to see a man wronged.'

'Isaiah's lying through his teeth — he has hoodwinked you good and proper.'

'He has done nothing of the sort.' She had wrestled with her conscience all night, asking herself how far she would go for love, and she had come to a single conclusion. Putting aside her loyalty to Jason and her family, the realisation that she could lose Isaiah to a lengthy spell in gaol, or transportation, or worse, just as he had expressed his feelings for her — and a desire to change his ways — was too painful for words.

She tore herself from her sister's grasp and pushed through the crowd, stopping in front of Jason who stood resting his hand on his cutlass, beside Albert and Isaiah.

'Mr Feasey didn't travel to France,' she said, refusing to quail under Jason's gaze and Albert's expression of confusion. 'I was with him on Tuesday . . . from midnight until dawn.' The onlookers gasped in unison.

'This can't be right,' Albert murmured.

'Grace, I'm givin' you a chance,' Jason said. 'Retract this lie of yours and we'll say no more about it.'

'I can't because it's the truth.'

'Let me reason with her, Jason,' Albert said,

57

stepping in. 'Grace, it's but a few days since you gave me your permission to call on you . . . to court you.' His cheeks coloured. 'I don't know what motive you can have to risk sullying your reputation to protect this . . . gentleman.'

'Gentleman?' Jason laughed sarcastically. 'You are too polite, Albert. He is a blackguard and evil-doer.'

'I like to think the best of people until proven otherwise,' Albert said. 'Oh dear. I fear that there's been a misunderstanding.'

'I'm sorry,' Grace said as, biting his lip, he glared at his prisoner.

'You are prepared to swear this on the Bible?' Jason asked her gently.

She nodded.

'Speak up!' he said.

'Yes,' she said, deeply regretting her fall from grace and the cruelty she had inflicted on Albert, because it was clear that she had upset and embarrassed him through her thoughtlessness. Clinging on to the one person who could save her from infamy, she stepped round to face Isaiah who was smiling and nodding in complete agreement with her cooked-up version of events.

'I took the key from my sister's pocket — she left it in her coat that day. And then I slipped out of the house when she was asleep to go and sit up with Isaiah after closing time. I am not ashamed of what I did. I'm not the only young woman in this town to have disobeyed her elders and betters to meet her betrothed.' She took a deep breath as she watched the consternation in Isaiah's eyes and the slight shake of his head, and undeterred, she went on, 'We are engaged to be married.' Holding out her hands, palms up, she spun round to face Jason and the rest of the onlookers. 'Isn't anyone going to congratulate us?'

Clearly not, she realised as Jason conferred with Albert and the captain of the dragoons. After some discussion, he ordered his men to search the tavern for contraband.

Before Grace could hear Isaiah's response, Louisa marched her away, the shingle scattering furiously beneath her feet and her silence more threatening than the torrent of words she let loose when they were back at home with the door closed behind them.

'Wipe that smirk off your face, young lady, and listen to me.' Louisa's face was the colour of beetroot, her lip dotted with spittle. 'I'm shocked and appalled that you would go against me, although — ' her tone softened slightly '— I do understand that fancying oneself in love can make one lose all sense of reason and rational thought.'

'I don't fancy myself in love,' Grace said adamantly. 'I am in love.'

'I fear that the more we point out Black Dog's flaws, the more fiercely you defend him, so I'm not going to say any more on that particular point. You can do much better for yourself. Let me appeal to your common sense. Did you . . . I mean, have you . . . ?'

'Kissed him? He tried it on with me, but I don't think that counts. I haven't done anything . . . untoward.'

'But you claim to have spent the night with him.'

59

'I'm not like Winnie. I'd never do that kind of thing before I was married.'

'Don't bring Winnie into it. Her situation was different — she was already promised to Billy when she found out she was carrying his child.'

'It's hurtful, finding out that you have such a low opinion of my character.'

Louisa paused, rubbing at her temple. 'It isn't so bad. If nothing happened, then it isn't the end of the world. An engagement can be broken. He's done it before.'

'You're making that up,' Grace hissed.

'Oh, perhaps I am mistaken,' she conceded.

'You've never taken any interest in whom he's courting. I've only ever seen Isaiah with Faith.'

'Mr Jackson's daughter?'

Grace nodded. 'They were in the tavern one afternoon — he asked me in . . . to chaperone, he said aside to me. He was afraid that the young lady in question was trying to force him into a compromising situation and then he'd have to marry her . . . or answer some awkward questions at the very least.'

'You! You've been sneaking about, going in and out of the Rattling Cat. How could you?'

'He asked me. For goodness' sake, I've been in there many times.'

'You shouldn't be anywhere near him — he's a reckless and dangerous criminal.'

'He's brave, like Jason, and I feel perfectly safe in his company. He wouldn't hurt a hair on my head and I'm going to marry him with or without your blessing.'

'You'll have to lie with him every night for the

rest of your life.'

'I know.'

'And he's only marrying you out of revenge against the Lennickers for past insults and injuries, real and imagined.

Or maybe he wants you to bend Jason's ear so he can find out where he'll be when the Rattlers are landing their goods. Oh, I wish Ma had been here to guide you. You'd have listened to her.'

Grace wished their mother had still been alive too — she felt that she of all people would have understood.

'This is how it's going to be,' Louisa said. 'You're going to stay with Winnie for a while. When you come home, there'll be no more talk of marriage. I shall call on Isaiah and explain that you made a mistake. I'll tell him you're promised to Albert if I have to, although you've cooked your goose when it comes to marrying him. Fancy leading him on like that. It was a mean thing to do.'

'I know and I'm sorry, but I didn't intend for it to happen. And I'm not going to Winnie's,' Grace said stubbornly. 'You can't make me. You'll have to drag me there kicking and screaming.'

'Go to your room! Go on. Get out of my sight!'

Grace turned and left the parlour, and went flying up the stairs, accidentally stumbling over Kitty, making her yowl and disappear under the cupboard, compounding Grace's upset. She entered her room, slammed the door behind her and threw herself down on the bed, her heart pounding with anger, hurt and insecurity.

Had Jason's men found run goods at the Rattling Cat? Had they taken Isaiah to the gaol? Was Louisa right? Had Grace made a mistake? As far as she was concerned, from Isaiah expressing his feelings for her and leaning in for a kiss, it was only a small step to an engagement, but if she was wrong about that, which she acknowledged she might be, then she had put herself in an unenviable situation. She could just about bear the shame of admitting that she had spent a night with Isaiah if they were to marry. If he thought otherwise, that it was a mere dalliance, how would she ever be able to show her face in Deal again?

She lay there for hours, hardly moving. Louisa knocked on the door twice, leaving food and drink on the landing for her, but she refused to get up and fetch it.

Much later, as dusk fell, she heard Jason return, then voices from the kitchen below as he and Louisa discussed the events of the day.

'My love, this isn't doin' you any good.' There was a pause before Jason went on, 'I'm sorry I'm so late. We did our best, but although we rummaged the tavern, we found nothin'. I reckon Black Dog had cleared the place out ready to take the goods that we intercepted this mornin'. On this occasion, I've had to accept defeat, but I will bring him to justice one day, even if it's the last thing I do.'

'He's a thoroughly detestable man,' Louisa sobbed.

'He's a shrockled apple, rotten to the core,' Jason agreed. 'I don't know how the Rattlers got away from us this time, but I won't let it happen again. I had my crew lower one of the galleys to

62

row across to the lugger, but the smugglers also got into a smaller boat. It was then that I recognised their voices and realised who they were.

'I shouted at them to come back, or I'd fire at them. I could hear Awful Doins yellin' that they'd turned about, but they couldn't find their rowlocks in the dark, and they only had three oars, one on one side and two on the other. Even though there was a lot of splashin', I couldn't tell exactly where they were. It didn't help that the moon had disappeared behind the clouds.

'My men secured the lugger while we went after them, but we found no sign of them — I assume that the boat must have foundered with all lives lost. I feel very sore about it. It's hard to see their loved ones not knowin' whether to grieve or keep prayin' for a miracle.' Jason fell silent.

He knew the smugglers well, Grace thought, having grown up and worked with them, carrying out daring rescues in the worst of storms when no one but a Deal boatman would dare to go out. Before he'd turned his coat, he'd schemed and plotted with them to carry thousands of pounds' worth of gold and contraband across the Channel.

'What about Isaiah?' Louisa asked. 'What did he have to say for himself?'

'I'm afraid he corroborated Grace's story — they are engaged.'

Grace sat up quickly, her heart bursting with rapture as wedding bells rang in her mind. Her prayers had been answered. She was going to be married to the man she loved.

'Oh no, I can't bear it. I thought she was making it up to cover for him out of some misplaced sense of loyalty. We must present a united front and forbid her to have anything more to do with him. That's it. She is underage — we will withhold our permission for the marriage to go ahead.'

'I have no doubt that she would find a way to circumvent it — move to another parish or elope. My view is that we should tread carefully, because she reminds me of someone else around here — the more you back her into a corner, the more she will rebel. I feel sorry for Albert — he's quite sore about it. I wish I hadn't encouraged him now, but there you go. You never know where love will strike.'

'How am I going to tell everyone that my sister, a Lennicker, is marrying a Feasey? How will I show my face? If she goes ahead with this, I'll disown her. I'll never speak to her again. I've half a mind to turn her out on to the street now.'

'What would that achieve? This isn't about you — it's about Grace's future happiness.'

'How will she be happy with *him*? They are strangers.'

'Are you sure about that?'

'You suspect that I'm wrong? As a matter of fact, I do recall an occasion when she was late home after running an errand for Pa. Her excuse was that on her way back, Isaiah saw her and called her over to offer her a drink. She said she didn't think there'd be anything wrong in accepting, because she felt faint from the heat, and it was only a small beer, and more than likely watered down beforehand. I wonder if he's always had a liking for her.'

There had been more than one occasion, Grace thought to herself blithely as she lay back against her pillow. She had kept the rest of her visits to the tavern to herself. Isaiah had invited her indoors on many a warm summer's day for refreshment and to stroke the cats. He'd shown her how to pick the fleas from their fur, trap them between her finger and thumbnail and cut them in half. In winter, she would call in to warm herself by the fire while he regaled her with tales of how he'd smuggled goods right under the Revenue officers' noses. Despite Louisa's opinion, he had never asked her to pay for the ale she drank.

'I'm not sayin' that I like the idea, not one little bit, but I can't help feelin' that it's a case of better the devil you know than the one you don't. Don't you remember when Billy came back from his stint in the Navy?'

'How could I forget? He drank all that brandy and filled the barrel up with water, thinking we wouldn't notice. I asked him to leave, but Winnie begged me to let him stay because little Pamela was poorly.'

'He was in a bad way, but he turned over a new leaf and look at him now — he's a decent husband, lovin' father and pillar of the community.'

'Oh no, Jason. You can't compare our Billy with Isaiah. You've never taken to the man — you've said so often enough.'

'That doesn't mean that I don't respect him — he's one of us, born and bred on the spit, an impressive fore and aft sailor, cunnin' and clever. When we searched the tavern, he was cooperative. We even bantered together without malice.'

65

'You've fallen for his lies too, hook, line and sinker.'

'All I'm sayin' before we turn in, is that if we're too hard on Grace, we'll drive her straight into his arms. I suggest that in the mornin', when everyone's calmed down, you tell her she's committed to go to Winnie's and if Isaiah is the kind of man she thinks he is, he'll be more than willin' to await her return.'

'You mean that we must let the engagement stand?'

'If we can prolong it for six months, even a year, that will be plenty of time for his façade to slip, or for him to prove himself worthy of her.'

Grace was grateful, but she didn't like the thought of waiting six months to be married. Although the war against Old Boney was well and truly over, there was always going to be more conflict to colour their lives. When it came to Isaiah and her family, would there ever be peace?

5

Commiserations and Quackery

As night fell, the alley quietened, the peace broken only by the occasional cry of an infant, the barking of a dog, and a drunken Jack Tar singing as he rolled home. As she lay in bed, Grace found some irony in the truth that one lie led to another, and that a lie had altered the course of her life for the better. How had she gone from a muddle-headed seventeen-year-old girl to a young woman about to be married to her sweetheart? She found her engagement all the more romantic for being sudden, spontaneous and against convention.

She was awake, wondering if she could twist Louisa's arm for a new gown for her wedding, when Jason left the cottage at dawn, tramping down the stairs and closing the front door behind him. Gradually, the residents of Cockle Swamp Alley raised themselves and began to go about their business: the boatmen greeting their friends; the women chattering as they swept the pavement; the shore boys running by, laughing that they'd overslept.

Without having to be nagged, Grace got up and dressed, planning to change into her Sunday best before she went to meet Isaiah at noon. On her way downstairs, she caught sight of Louisa lying prone and lifeless on the hall floor. With an exclamation of shock, she took the three bottom steps in one leap, flying to her side and falling to her knees.

'Wake up!' she urged, patting Louisa's pale face. 'My dear sister, please wake up.' Recalling how Winnie had once told her how to test for the presence of life, she fetched Louisa's hand mirror from her bedroom and held it to her mouth, watching for the telltale misting of the glass. Nothing. But then she heard a soft exhalation of breath and saw the slightest fall and rise of Louisa's chest. 'Oh, thank the Lord.'

With a groan, Louisa raised her head and looked around wildly.

'You fainted. Please, don't move.' Grace collected a cushion from the parlour, but her sister pushed it away. 'What happened? Did you fall?'

'I was on my way back from the privy — I had a funny turn.'

'Perhaps you are sickening for something.' Grace thought back to the mackerel they'd eaten for supper the night before, wondering if it had upset her.

'I'm bleeding,' Louisa murmured, and then in answer to Grace's unspoken question, she added, 'I've lost it. The baby's gone. I don't know how many times— ' She broke off, crying. 'I can't see what purpose God has in denying us a child when he blesses others with more than they can provide for.'

Grace inwardly railed against Louisa's misfortune. To carry a child then suffer the pain of losing it seemed somehow crueller than never carrying one at all. Louisa was inconsolable, and as she fell into another faint, Grace realised she was also

68

very unwell.

'Wait there,' she said, in case she could hear her. 'I'll fetch help.'

She ran next door to call for Mrs Witherall who came straight away, a shawl thrown across her shoulders and her feet bare.

'What a terr'ble shame to lose another one.' Her eyes were wet. 'She must be distraught. Grace, 'aven't you given 'er a dose of smellin' salts yet?'

'I came straight to you,' Grace said, shrinking in the face of her disapproval. She fetched the vinaigrette from the parlour and held it to Louisa's nostrils, forcing her to inhale the pricklish vapours of hartshorn and ammonia.

'I'll be all right,' Louisa said, opening her eyes and smiling weakly. 'There's no need to make a fuss.'

'There's every need,' Mrs Witherall said. 'You're burnin' up.'

Grace felt sick to the pit of her stomach, recalling how Pa had suffered — and died — from a fever when his flesh had become mortified.

'Where's Jason?' Louisa whispered.

'He went out early this morning,' Grace reminded her.

'Ah yes,' she sighed.

'I'll send someone out to fetch him back.' It wasn't impossible, Grace thought. 'And I'll arrange for Doctor Audley to visit.'

At Mrs Witherall's request, Grace helped her move Louisa into the parlour where she lay shivering on the couch, wrapped in a blanket. Grace threw her shawl over her gown, put on her boots and ran down to the beach to find Cromwell who was playing knucklebones with one of the Roper boys.

'I'll pay you what I owe you and more,' she gasped. 'I need you to fetch Doctor Audley and when you've done that, go up to the mill and find Mr Brockman.'

'Marlin's cousin. The 'orse dealer?'

'Say that Grace needs him to fetch Winnie from Westcliffe. Louisa is indisposed. And then — I haven't finished yet — you must go to the Rattling Cat and tell Isaiah — '

'Tell 'im what?' Cromwell shaded his eyes, grinning. 'I've 'eard a rumour.'

'It's none of your business, but just to confirm, Mr Feasey and I are to be married.'

'It's true then?' His jaw dropped.

'Just tell him that I can't see him today as we arranged.'

'I hope Louisa's goin' to be all right,' he said soberly.

'Hurry, Cromwell. It's urgent.' As soon as he'd gone in the direction of town, Grace searched frantically along the beach, looking for someone who could convey a message to Jason. She couldn't see HMS *Legacy* among the vessels in the Downs — she must have gone out full sail, making the most of the scant breeze and retreating tide.

The only boats remaining ashore were the Curlew and the *Good Intent II* further along with two guards standing beside her, chewing baccy and looking bored, but when they realised what Grace wanted, they hollered and waved at a fishing boat that was bobbing about not far from the beach, catching the attention of her crew.

70

'What is it, miss?' It was one of Mary's brothers who shouted to her.

'I need to get a message to Commander Witherall of the cutter, HMS *Legacy*. He must come home as soon as possible: his wife has been taken ill.'

'Marlin, you mean. We'll find 'im,' the fisherman called back.

She thanked them, barely able to speak as the reality of the situation began to sink in. She didn't have much faith in the physician. What could he do, apart from offer commiserations and quackery? Both her parents — Ma, then Pa — had passed away, despite his ministrations. As she hastened home, she recalled how he'd prescribed saltwater for Ma to drink. Unfortunately, as Winnie had poured it into her mouth, she had already taken her last breath, dying with the taste of old briny on her lips, something that had given their father much comfort. The doctor had bled Pa when he was unwell, explaining that it was the last resort, but the bloodletting had drained the little life that was left inside him, and he'd expired shortly afterwards.

★ ★ ★

A couple of hours later, Grace was at Louisa's side when Mrs Witherall showed Doctor Audley into the parlour. A gentleman in his early thirties, smartly attired in a maroon coat and dark pantaloons, he exuded an air of professional confidence as he asked Louisa some questions pertaining to her illness, while opening a black leather bag filled

71

with medical paraphernalia: spatulas, scalpels and lancets.

Having examined her, checking her pulse, the whites of her eyes and her tongue, then palpating her belly through a discreetly arranged sheet, he recommended treatment for the fever and loss of blood: a fire burning in the grate, more blankets, a rich beef broth and porter, and a purge for good measure. How he knew, Grace had no idea, but he finished by giving his opinion that Louisa would never bear a live child. The latter news seemed to break both Louisa's spirit and her heart, for she lay back after the doctor had gone, closed her eyes and refused to take sustenance of any kind, let alone swallow the purgative potion he'd prescribed.

Reassured that Louisa's bleeding had almost stopped, Grace left her to sleep for a while and rather reluctantly joined Mrs Witherall in the kitchen where their neighbour gave her a hug.

'We will do our best — that's all we can do. Winnie will be 'ere soon, and Jason. She'll feel better for seeing 'im.' There was a knock at the door. 'I'll go. You make the tea — the water's 'ot. We'll 'ave a nice little chat.'

Before Grace had taken the caddy from the dresser, she heard Mrs Witherall haranguing Isaiah on the doorstep.

'Black Dog, you aren't welcome 'ere. Sling your 'ook!'

'It's imperative that I speak with Miss Lennicker,' Isaiah was saying, one foot firmly inside the door, as Grace joined them, her heart dancing with a passionate fervour at the sight of him.

72

When she saw his expression, she faltered.

'What's this about you breakin' our engagement?' he said coldly.

Her brow tightened. 'I don't understand.'

'You might as well 'ave cut me through with a knife. You could 'ave at least 'ad the courtesy to tell me to my face, not sent Cromwell to do your dirty work. I assume it 'as somethin' to do with that Enderby fellow.'

'I'll sit with Louisa while you two lovebirds finish your discussion,' Mrs Witherall interrupted in a sarcastic tone. 'Leave the door open.'

'Oh no,' Grace said, ignoring her and showing him through to the kitchen where she closed the door firmly. 'I'd never have done that. I sent Cromwell to tell you that I couldn't meet you today, that I had to break our arrangement because my sister is unwell.'

'I see. But what about Marlin's dogsbody, the lieutenant?'

'After we danced the other night, he asked me if we might become better acquainted and I told him no. As he said, there was a misunderstanding. Isaiah, you don't believe that I deliberately led him on? I'd never do such a thing.'

'Grace, don't look so worried. I was jealous when I thought you 'ad an interest in 'im, but you've put my mind at ease.' His face relaxed into a sudden smile. 'Going back to Cromwell, I'd like to box the little varmint's ears for puttin' me in a spin, but then I was in a bit of a stir about what you said . . . You took me by surprise sayin' we were betrothed, and I wasn't 'appy about it at first — a man don't like to think he's been 'ounded

73

into makin' that kind of decision.'

'It was all I could think of at the time,' she said indignantly. 'My reputation was at stake.'

'I'm not sayin' that I'm not grateful. I am. You're right — I owe it to you for takin' my side. You're beautiful, 'ardworkin' and kind, and I'll be the 'appiest man alive when I can call you my wife. What do you think, Grace? Does our engagement stand?'

'Yes, of course.' She flung her arms around his neck, making him stagger back against the table. Chuckling, he pulled her close.

'I reckon that our union will astound the whole of Deal. But you're still very young — you don't need your sister's permission?'

'I have no legal guardian as such,' she said. 'Pa didn't name anyone to take his place on his death.'

'But Louisa and Marlin 'ave taken responsibility for you since your father's passin'. Maybe I should 'ave a word with Marlin?'

'I'm seventeen — nearly eighteen — and old enough to make up my own mind.'

'I admire your fightin' talk, but there are some who will disapprove and do everythin' within their power to stop us.'

'Louisa can't keep me locked away for ever,' Grace said, and then she remembered with a pang of guilt that her sister's life was hanging by a thread.

''Ow is she? I feel bad for not askin' afore.' Isaiah took half a step back, resting his hands on the curve of her waist.

'She's very poorly according to Doctor Audley. He says we must pray for her.'

'My love.' He wiped a tear from her cheek. 'She's a tough 'un — she'll soon be back on 'er feet, especially with you to nurse 'er.'

'I hope so.'

'Sometimes I wish I'd 'ad a dotin' family,' he said wistfully. 'My mother thought so little of me that she abandoned me when I was only three or four years old. My father was a bully and I 'ave no siblin's. Your 'alf-sister — Nancy — lived at the tavern, but we didn't 'ave much to do with each other.'

Grace pictured a boy with long hair, dirty fingernails and ragged clothes impregnated with the stench of tobacco smoke, sitting alone in the sawdust by the fireside at the Rattling Cat while the drinkers sang bawdy ballads and the women of ill-repute danced on the tables, showing off their wares before leading their paying customers into darkened corners.

'Mrs Lennicker took pity on me — she offered to l'arn me my letters and numbers, but my father told her to shove off. That's enough — I don't want you feelin' sorry for me.'

'I do, though. You've been most unfortunate.'

'I feel like my luck's changin',' he smiled. 'You and me. Mr and Mrs Feasey. I can 'ardly believe it.'

'I wouldn't want a long engagement,' Grace said abruptly, recalling Jason's discussion with Louisa of a six-month wait.

'I agree — there's no point in 'angin' about. We should marry as soon as possible. I'll go and 'ave a word with the vicar, see if 'e remembers me.'

'Reverend North is partial to a nip of brandy,

and he's rather particular about the quality of the Communion wine,' she said.

He grinned. 'You go to St George's every Sunday, don't you?'

'Only on special occasions like Easter and Christmas. Pa used to say there was only so much praying one could do when there were nets to mend.'

'And goods to run,' Isaiah added. 'We should clear the air over the feud that went on between our families. There was a lot of aggravation. Your father nicked goods that belonged by rights to Mr Feasey and 'e did the same in return, tit for tat. After your father's passin', the quarrel escalated — the Lennickers and Witheralls sank my beautiful boat, the *Good Intent*, in retaliation for the Rattlers notifyin' the Revenue of their landin' place, but that's in the past.

'I've never said 'ow sorry I am for what went on between your father and mine. You'll 'ave 'eard all the stories of what 'appened. No doubt your sisters 'ave indoctrinated you with an alternative version, but the shootin' was an accident.'

'I'm sorry too. You're right that we should forgive and forget. The hostilities were not of our making.' She paused before continuing, 'I can't expect my sisters to agree, though. Nancy suffered terribly.' 'She was terrified of my father,' Isaiah concurred. ''E 'ad a nasty temper on 'im, but to be fair 'e gave Mrs Stickles a roof over 'er 'ead when she was in a bit of bother, findin' 'erself with child.'

Her father's child, Grace thought, ashamed. Poor Nancy, born out of wedlock while Pa was married to the woman he loved. Neither man could be described as pure as the driven snow.

'I try to think of it as six of one and 'alf a dozen of the other,' Isaiah went on. 'And I'm not just sayin' it to make a good impression. I mean it, Grace. I want to live a contented sort of life with a wife and children and be looked upon with respect by my fellows. It isn't much to ask, is it?'

As he pressed his lips to her cheek, the door flew open and Mrs Witherall appeared, her mouth agape. 'Grace, your sister needs you.'

Guiltily, she stepped back.

'You must go to 'er. Give 'er my best wishes for a full and speedy recovery,' Isaiah said. 'Farewell for now, my love. Good day, Mrs Witherall.'

'Does your sister give 'er blessin' to this madness?' their neighbour asked as the door closed behind him. 'No, I didn't think so. You should be mortified, making 'er ill like this. It must 'ave been the shock of it that made 'er miscarry another littlun.'

Grace felt sick at heart, knowing how Mrs Witherall shared Louisa's loss, her desire to be a grandmother thwarted yet again and with no prospect of being satisfied in the near future, because Jason's three brothers, who were away at sea, showed no sign of wanting to anchor ashore. To her relief, though, the clatter of horses' hooves meant she didn't have to find the words to defend herself.

'Winnie's here!' Grace dashed outside to help her sister down from the brougham that had drawn up in front of the cottage, attracting a crowd into the alley. 'Thank you, Abel,' she said, addressing the driver, a young man dressed in a tall hat, waistcoat and breeches.

'It's the least I could do.' He was hauling on the ribbons to restrain a lively pair of black ponies, their coats flecked with foam.

'It isn't too late? I knew it had to be serious or you wouldn't have sent for me.' Winnie, a stout personage, wearing a dark blue velvet spencer on top of a white cotton morning gown, and a cap over her guinea-blonde hair which seemed to have defied any attempt to restrain it, handed Grace her boxes and bags, and began unbuttoning her gloves as she made her way into the house.

'She's in the parlour,' Grace said as Mrs Witherall made herself scarce, returning next door.

'Louisa, it's me.' Winnie bustled in and checked the patient's forehead with the back of her hand. 'Oh, you are burning up.'

Louisa rallied a little. 'There was no need for you to come, although it's lovely to see you, but as you're here, perhaps you can make our little sister see that she's making an irretrievable error of judgement.'

'Oh Grace, what have you done?'

'She's gone against me and consented to marry Isaiah Feasey.'

'Grace, is this true?'

She nodded.

'Foolish child! Why? Why him when you could have had just about anyone?'

'Because he's good to me, and I'll be happier living with him than without him. I don't know why you're both making such a fuss — he's no longer involved in smuggling.'

78

'Then how does he expect to feed and clothe you?' Winnie asked.

'On the profits he makes from the tavern. Even if we end up below hatches, as they say, it won't matter because we'll never be short of love.' She realised that the latter sentiment sounded hollow — she was under no illusion when it came to money. It was impossible to live on love alone. 'I'm going to marry him, whatever you say.' She recalled helping Winnie prepare for her wedding to Billy. After a series of unfortunate events that had led to its postponement, it had ended up being a small ceremony, but Grace remembered it vividly, from the flowers in Winnie's posy to weeping with joy outside the church as rose petals rained down on the happy couple.

'If Grace's appearance had been more ordinary, she would never have caught his eye,' Louisa said quietly.

'It is the combined value of our family's assets that has piqued his interest.' Winnie was scathing as she stepped close to Grace and stared into her eyes. 'If you go ahead, you can be sure I will not attend the wedding. Nor will I consent to you receiving any money from the trust fund — I will not let him get his hands on a single penny. Does he know of it?'

'I might have let it slip,' Grace said, Winnie's disapproval sliding like an icicle down the back of her neck. 'There you go then. I rest my case. He is a hang-in-chains, a shabbaroon.'

With Winnie's insults ringing in her ears, Grace turned and ran to hide in the kitchen. Her eyes blurring, she pulled their cookbook from the dresser and tried to read through the recipes for foods suitable for an invalid. How dare her sisters judge her beloved so unkindly? When the tide of their fortunes had changed, they had altered the course of their lives for the better. Why shouldn't Isaiah do the same? Why wouldn't they give him a chance to redeem himself?

80

6

Rubies are Red, Sapphires are Blue

The days passed and Louisa's condition began to improve. On the eighth day of her illness, when Grace delivered her a bowl of boiled arrowroot with milk, she pushed it away, grimacing.

'No more,' she sighed. 'Bring me a beef pie from Molly's. I'm heartily sick of all these bland dishes, even though they're made with love.'

'Thank goodness you are well again.' Grace began to cry as she put her offering aside.

'What are you crying for?' Louisa said brusquely.

'I thought you were going to die.'

'I didn't, though.' A tear rolled down Louisa's cheek and Grace realised that she had been trying to restrain her emotion, as she was prone to do. 'Give me a hug, my dear sister. If it wasn't for you and Winnie . . .'

'Don't. Please don't,' Grace sobbed, embracing her. 'All is going to be well from now on. I can feel it in my bones.'

'Are you sure?' Louisa asked, her hectoring tone making Grace withdraw and walk to the window.

'I know you and Winnie have been plotting behind my back, but there's nothing anyone can say or do to prevent my marriage. Isaiah has called every day to ask after you. He's arranged for the

81

banns to be read and set the date for the wedding.'

'Then you have made your bed— '

'Yes,' she cut in. 'The one in which I wish to lie. I love him, Louisa.'

At the sound of raised voices, Winnie came scurrying upstairs and entered the room. 'Grace, you mustn't upset our sister.'

'No, Winnie. She's had her final word. I have other, deeper sorrows to contend with.' Louisa lowered her gaze and picked at a loose thread on the coverlet, before looking up again. 'I've kept you for far too long. You must go back to Billy and the children.'

'Not yet. Not until you're back on your feet.'

'I'm going to the pot house to fetch a pie for the invalid,' Grace said.

'Less of the 'invalid',' Louisa said. 'I'm going to rise and dress later.'

Glad to escape the confines of the sickroom, Grace made her way to Molly's on Middle Street. The sound of the bell ringing as she pushed the door open summoned a female figure dressed in white from the kitchen at the back. Her apron was stained with spatters of gravy and her face covered as always by a veil.

'I've burnt myself again, gettin' the pies out of the oven,' Nancy said, blowing on her fingers. 'My mother's gone to the market. She's worried about the lack of business — it's been very quiet.'

Grace looked around at the empty tables laid with gingham cloths and porcelain cruet sets. 'It isn't much, but I'd like to buy a beef and kidney pie for Louisa.'

'She's feelin' better then? Winnie mentioned

she'd taken a bad turn.'

Grace nodded, handing over a clean cloth from her basket. Nancy fetched a pie and wrapped it to keep it warm.

'Have you heard that Isaiah and I are engaged . . . ' Grace began, wondering why Nancy hadn't congratulated her.

'Winnie said so. Oh dear, I told myself not to interfere, but are you sure you'll be 'appy with 'im? Black Dog is as black as 'e's been painted . . . blacker, perhaps, and I've dreamed up an 'undred grisly deaths for 'im in the past for what 'e and 'is father did to me.'

'One Eye bullied him into doing things he shouldn't, and I believe that he truly repents of his sins. He's changed, Nancy.'

'You aren't goin' to listen to me all the while you 'ave a fancy for 'im,' Nancy sighed. 'I 'ope you're right and it works out for you.'

Grace didn't bandy words with her, not wanting to hurt her feelings. What on earth did a young woman condemned to remain on the shelf by the pox that had cruelly scarred her, know about love? She took her purse from her basket.

'No, it's all right. You don't 'ave to pay for that one. We're family, aren't we?'

'Thank you. Give my regards to Mrs Stickles.' As Grace left Molly's, determined not to let Nancy's opinion dampen her cheerful spirits, she ran straight into Mary Roper.

'It's lovely to see you,' Grace smiled, but Mary seemed furtive and not of the same mind.

'I've heard you're gettin' married. Well, so am I.'

'To whom?'

'Albert Enderby.'

'Oh, that's wonderful.' Grace hoped that she hadn't sounded too surprised at her friend's revelation. It had been less than one month since Albert, then apparently unaware of Mary's charms, had expressed an interest in courting Grace. 'We'll be able to meet up with our husbands.'

'I'm afraid that won't be possible.' Mary looked down her nose. 'My Albert's a Revenue man — he can't possibly associate with smugglers and their wives. Besides, we're goin' up in the world. My fiancé's plannin' to rent a house for us in Walmer. Mr and Mrs Enderby are 'elpin' us set up 'ome.'

'I'm delighted for you,' Grace said dully, realising that her choice of husband had made her a social pariah in her friend's eyes. Mary wouldn't be the only one.

'Do excuse me,' Mary said, hurrying away.

Deep in thought, Grace rounded the corner further along the street and, having reached the Rattling Cat, stopped to cross the road.

'Hey, are you lookin' for me?' She glanced up to find Isaiah calling to her from an open window. 'Come and inspect your new 'ome. I want to see if it meets with your approval.'

Without hesitating, she met him in the taproom where the barmaid was sweeping the floor.

'You've met Sarah?' he said.

'I have,' Grace smiled, noting that his flowing white shirt was unfastened to the waist. 'I'm pleased to meet you, Sarah. And I'm sorry if you've had no news of your husband.'

84

'Digger and the gang will be keepin' out of 'arm's way,' Isaiah said.

'I wish I could believe you.' Sarah stopped sweeping and leaned on her broom.

'Don't worry about 'im— 'e'll turn up like a bad penny as 'e always does. I used to think of you as a bit of a light-skirt, but you've impressed me with your devotion to your 'usband. I wish you'd put the same dedication into scrubbin' the floors as you do in maintainin' your marriage. Grace, foller me. I'll show you the work that's been done so far.

'What are you waitin' for?' he went on when she dithered. 'You 'ave an eye for fashion. I could do with some advice from a member of the gentler sex on the finer points of choosin' linens and wall'angin's.'

'I've 'eard of gen'lemen invitin' young ladies to visit, but that's a new one on me,' Sarah said, cheering up.

'Don't embarrass the girl,' Isaiah chided. 'We're engaged — that's enough excuse for us to be alone together.'

Blushing, Grace followed him into a small inner hallway and up a rickety staircase on to a landing from which led several doors.

'The work isn't finished yet, but I 'ave the builder's word that it'll be done by the end of the month. Mr Tapping comes 'ighly recommended by a friend of mine.'

His words were drowned out by the sound of hammering and a few choice epithets.

'Oi, mind yer language in the presence of my fiancée.' The hammering stopped then resumed.

After one final bang, a door opened and a middle-aged man with a bulbous nose and purple cheeks stepped out, his grey smock and dark pantaloons shedding curls of woodshavings.

'The lad and I are stoppin' now, Mr Feasey — we've been workin' since dawn and we didn't have no sleep last night.'

'What am I payin' you for?'

'By the work done, not by the hour.' He doffed his cap, sending a puff of sawdust into the air. 'Good day, miss.'

'When will you return?' Isaiah asked.

'Tomorrer,' he said. 'I 'ave to pick up some more timber on the way. You don't 'appen to 'ave any more of that baccy you sold me?'

Grace's forehead tightened as Isaiah cast her a glance.

'It was all I 'ad left, but if some comes my way, I'll see you right. This way, Grace.' He showed her into one of the new guest rooms that contained a bed and dressing table. 'It needs a woman's touch to attract the better sort of customer.'

'I'm flattered that you think I know what I'm talking about, but I truly have no idea. We use whitewash for the walls at the cottage, and I've made a rug from scraps before. That's the limit of my expertise.'

'I thought Louisa would 'ave been more extravagant. She made a fine pot of money from sellin' lace and provisionin' ships. The men and I often speculated 'ow the Lace Maiden — as we used to call 'er — did it.'

'She took after Ma, getting up to all kinds of no good,' Grace said. 'When we were littluns, she

86

used to have us carry the lace tucked inside our dresses or wrapped around our waists. All we had to do was smile and keep silent. As for Louisa, she set a price in her head and wouldn't let the lace go for any less, whether it was a shawl to the draper, or the odd length of galloon to the ladies of the ton with their snowy faces and dark eyebrows.'

'The ones with plenty of money, you mean?' He chuckled. 'I imagine you 'ave an 'ead for business too.'

'I have some idea. When we went out provisioning, we used to carry packets of baccy hidden inside baskets of apples and potatoes, and cognac in pigs' bladders suspended beneath our clothes. I burst one in front of a gobbler once — Louisa spared me a repeat of that indignity, saying I was too careless to be trusted.'

'What 'appened?'

'There was a brig waiting for a pilot to show them into the Channel. The crew were already provisioned, but they were more than happy to send a rowing boat up alongside the *Curlew* and purchase fresh food and a bladder of spirit from us before returning to the brig. That's when we spotted one of the Revenue cutters nearby — the *Guinevere*. Louisa decided we should sit tight— '

'That's madness,' Isaiah exclaimed, shaking his head. 'They got you, did they?'

'Two of the *Guinevere*'s officers rowed across to us. One of them thought himself very much cock 'o the walk. 'Good morning, ladies,' he said, taking no notice of Billy who was with us. 'I'm Officer Groves.'

"Why, he's a handsome one,' I said in return, at

which Winnie had a go at me.'

'I would 'ave done too . . . . I worry that another man caught your eye and you saw fit to remark upon it,' Isaiah scolded.

'Are you jealous?' she teased.

'Well, yes, a little . . . .'

'You shouldn't be. There's no one who compares to you.'

'You 'aven't finished the story. Did the officer try to rummage you? Because if 'e did I'd 'ave punched 'is lights out.'

'You must know that they aren't permitted to rummage a woman.'

'I wasn't born yesterday,' he chuckled.

'He boarded the *Curlew* and searched Billy, finding nothing but a little baccy for his own use, but then he decided to poke around in our baskets. I knew we were in trouble when some of the apples went rolling across the deck. I fell to my knees and leaned across the basket, making a great drama of sobbing, 'This is our bread and butter — who will buy spoiled fruit?' The officer apologised, and believing that I'd saved us from further scrutiny, I sat back on my heels.' Giggling, she went on, 'The air filled with the scent of brandy — the officer said he could smell it, but Louisa blamed it on Billy. She said there was drink oozing from every pore of his body.

'I had a few too many last night, and now I wish I hadn't,' Billy said, belching for good measure. Luckily, the officer took his word for it and let us go. Louisa thanked Billy for lying on our behalf. 'I wasn't lying,' he said. 'I had a right skinful last night.'

'You got up to some larks, Grace. I wish I'd been there to see you gammonin' 'im. 'Ere, take my 'and and I'll show you another room. You'll 'ave to watch your step.'

Tentatively, she reached for his hand. Their fingers touched and tangled together. It seemed strange, awkward even, as he walked slightly ahead of her through another doorway where she found herself looking straight down between a set of parallel beams into the storey below.

'Don't be scared. I've got you.' Isaiah slid his arm around her back and rested his free hand on the curve of her waist. Giddy with fear and excitement, she felt as if she was falling as he inclined his head and pressed his lips to hers. She kissed him back, revelling in the moment until his hand moved from her waist to her . . .

'No,' she whispered, shocked. 'Not until we're married.'

'My dear Grace,' he said gruffly, his pupils as dark as the midnight sea, 'I'm tryin' to 'old back the feelin's I 'ave for you, but it's 'opeless. It's like a monster's caught 'old of me and won't let me go. There, I shouldn't 'ave said nothin'. I can see I've given you the frights by forcin' myself on you. I promise I'll be the perfect gentleman from now on. At least, until our weddin' night,' he added hopefully. 'Hey, don't cry, my love.'

'I'm happy, not sad.' The strength of his passion marked the moment when she had absolutely no doubt that they belonged to each other. 'There is one thing, though.'

'What is that? I'll do anythin' for you, Grace. Anythin'.'

'Tell me why you went out with the lugger the other night — when you said you'd sold your share in her.'

'They were a man down — Digger asked me to join them to make up the numbers. I did it as a favour to 'im.'

'I want you to promise me that you won't do that again. I refuse to be a smuggler's wife.'

'You know how the land lies with my money-makin' operations. I've been straight with you, 'aven't I?'

She nodded.

'Trust me,' he said. 'We'll run this place jointly and make it the most profitable tavern in Deal. Don't worry your little 'ead about it — you'll be comin' into your money soon enough.' Grace froze when he continued, 'Not that we'll need it with me lookin' after the finances and you lookin' after our guests.'

She wondered if she should say something about Winnie's change of heart, but he'd already changed the subject. 'Are you ready for the weddin'?'

She smiled, reassured that she didn't need to worry. 'I know what gown I'm going to wear, and I can recite the vows backwards, word for word. I adore weddings. I helped Winnie with the ribbons on her gown, her bridal flowers and her hair.' She had felt a little cheated when Louisa had eloped with Jason to Gretna Green.

'You aren't just sayin' you'll 'ave me because you want to be a bride?' he jested. 'We don't 'ave to get wed in church. There are other ways . . . '

'I'm not marrying you over a broomstick if

90

that's what you're suggesting.'

'Oh, you 'ave such a beautiful way of speakin'. You 'ave my word that all will be above board — you see, that don't sound like a smuggler talkin'. Wait here — I 'ave somethin' for you.' He disappeared into one of the rooms in the older part of the building and returned a short while later, his hands behind his back.

'Close your eyes.' She felt his breath against her skin as he moved behind her and fastened something at the nape of her neck. 'I'll show you 'ow you look. Don't peek.'

He guided her by the shoulders into what she guessed was another room where she almost choked on the stench of musk and bear-pit. 'Stop 'ere. Open your eyes.'

She obeyed, finding herself in front of a foxed mirror that stood lopsided on a dressing table in a bedchamber that appeared to have been thoroughly rummaged by the Revenue. The bed was unmade, a bolster and quilt lying rumpled on the floor, and there were clothes strewn everywhere. Isaiah seemed not to notice. He rubbed the mirror glass with his shirtsleeve, then stood behind her, his hands on her waist as she touched the pendant that nestled against her flushing breast.

'It isn't much,' he said. 'The stone's a sapphire, so I've been told, and the chain is gold.'

'It's beautiful,' she gasped.

'A ruby is red, a sapphire is blue, sugar is sweet, but not as sweet as you. Mrs Stickles must 'ave told me that one when I was a boy — it's odd 'ow things stick in yer mind.'

'No one's ever given me anything like this

91

before.'

'I should 'ope not,' he said, amused. 'It's precious, irreplaceable . . . just like my bride-to-be.'

'I shall treasure it for ever. Shall I wear it before the wedding?'

'It's yours to do with as you will.' He tipped his head slightly to one side. 'Until we're married, of course, when everythin' you 'ave becomes my property.'

'In the eyes of the law,' she agreed. She questioned the fairness of the principle, but the deal was that in return, marriage secured a wife's right to her husband's support.

'I'll 'ave Sarah tidy up before our weddin' night.'

'I don't think she'll take kindly to that,' Grace observed.

'She can't complain — it's what I pay 'er for. Cleanin', cookin' and servin' my customers.'

At the mention of cooking, Grace remembered the pie that was sitting in her basket on the counter in the taproom.

'Isaiah, I'd love to stay longer, but— '

'One kiss and I'll let you go,' he cut in.

It was a while before she returned home to discover Winnie's travelling boxes in the hall and Louisa sitting up in the kitchen with a blanket across her knees.

'We're waiting for Abel to turn up,' Winnie said, arranging the plates on the dresser. 'I thought I'd make myself useful until then.'

Grace unpacked her basket. 'I'll make some gravy to go with the pie.'

'It's too late now — we've shared the last of the salted pork,' Winnie chided her.

92

'You took your time,' Louisa observed, eyeing her keenly.

'You know what it's like — you can't walk more than a few steps before someone stops to talk to you. Nancy had a word with me, but you know that because you asked her to. And I spoke to Mary.'

'What's that around your neck, my girl?' Winnie asked.

Grace's hand flew to the pendant. 'Isaiah gave it to me.' 'Where did he get it from? Don't tell me — it fell off the back of a cart, or worse, he took it from the neck of some poor soul who drowned in the roadstead.' Winnie stared at it in disgust. 'It's become obvious that you aren't going to change your mind, so I'll wish you all the best. My prejudice against Isaiah runs deep. I cannot forgive or forget what he did when Billy had that problem with his drinking.' Grace's forehead tightened as Winnie went on, 'He gave him credit to encourage him to carry on when I needed him to stop. I'm sorry, Grace, but I can't have it on my conscience to attend your wedding.'

'Please, don't say that. I can't imagine walking down the aisle without you there.'

'I shall keep you in my prayers,' Winnie said. 'Listen. I can hear a carriage.'

'I'll help you with your boxes,' Grace offered, thankful for the interruption.

When she had stowed Winnie's belongings in Abel's brougham, she kissed her goodbye.

'I'll come and visit soon,' Grace added.

'I'd prefer that you didn't,' Winnie said, and as the carriage rolled away towards the town, Grace speculated about whether or not she would ever see her sister again. She thought of Mary marrying Albert, an altogether more propitious union than hers and Isaiah's, and wished very briefly that she could have fallen in love with the young Revenue officer of whom everyone approved, instead of her betrothed. No matter how much he claimed to be a reformed character, Isaiah's reputation went before him, driving her family and friends away and condemning her to a lifetime of loneliness. At least, that's how it seemed. Wiping away a few tears, she scolded herself for her moment of weakness. Her wedding day was imminent — this was no time for regrets.

7

In Sickness and in Wealth

Alone in her room with a storm brewing outside, Grace scrubbed a lingering stain from the hem of her dress and ran an iron along the primrose-yellow ribbons. It wasn't how she'd expected the morning of her wedding to be. She suspected that she and Isaiah would have to drag witnesses from the street because Billy wouldn't come if Winnie wouldn't, and she doubted that Louisa and Jason would either. She and Louisa had barely spoken since Winnie left.

The vivid orange marigolds in a pot on the dressing table were at odds with her mood, but it was no use moping, she told herself, as she sat down. Her sisters weren't willing to bend, and neither was she.

'May I speak with you?' The door opened slowly. 'I've come to make my peace. I want to apologise for giving you the cold shoulder.' Louisa walked up behind her as she gazed in the mirror. 'Winnie should never have blamed you for me losing the baby. It was God's will. When Jason and I committed to leaving the free trade, I thought it would be enough, that the Lord would see fit to absolve us of our sins, but it wasn't to be, and I can't let you continue bearing the guilt for it. That's why

95

you aren't speaking to me, isn't it?'

'The idea that my behaviour contributed to your loss does prey on my mind, but it's you who's been refusing to speak to me.'

Louisa smiled suddenly. 'Oh dear. I understand what we've been doing now, tiptoeing around each other, afraid to utter a word in case we cause offence. We have made rather a mull of it. Anyway, what I want to say, is that I'm giving you my blessing.'

'You are coming to the church?'

'I wouldn't miss it for the world.' Louisa proffered a box that she'd been hiding behind her back. 'I thought you'd like these. Mind you don't put them on the table — it's unlucky.' She opened the box on her knees and there, nestled inside, was a pair of white satin slippers. 'Don't cry — the tears will stain them,' Louisa said as Grace slipped them on. 'They are perfect, thank you,' she exclaimed, standing up and flinging her arms around her sister's neck.

'All I want is for you to be happy.' Louisa smiled as she extricated herself from Grace's embrace. 'I've been wondering if you'll take Kitty with you, only I've grown more fond of her than I care to admit, and I don't like the idea of her living at the tavern with the other cats and that dog of Isaiah's.'

'Are you saying you want to keep her?' Grace was torn because she loved Kitty, but taking her seemed tantamount to throwing her to the lions. 'For company?'

'The house will seem empty when you aren't here and Jason is away.'

'All right then, as long as you promise you'll

look after her.'

'You know I will. Let me help you dress and put your hair up.'

'I wish Ma and Pa were here,' Grace sighed as Louisa brushed her locks and plaited them.

'They'll be looking down on us from Heaven.' Louisa coiled Grace's hair on top of her head and began to pin it in place.

'Ouch!' Grace grimaced.

'I'm all fingers and thumbs this morning.' Louisa put away the rest of the pins, then selected the best blooms from the marigolds and let the water drip from the stems. 'Ma broke away from her family, marrying for love against their wishes, and according to Mrs Witherall, it was the making of her. When she found out how Pa earned his money, she put her heart into running his 'business' better than he did.'

Grace noticed how Louisa omitted to mention the fact that Pa had sired an illegitimate child while he was married to their mother and that he'd kept their half-sister a secret from his daughters. Whether or not Ma ever knew of Nancy, Grace wasn't sure.

'I don't want that for you, though,' Louisa went on. 'Are you sure this isn't a passing fancy?'

'I'm certain,' Grace assured her. 'Our cousin Beth married for convenience, not love. She did as Uncle Laxton told her and married that dreadful Mr Norris who treats her like one of his hounds.'

'He is a rather boldrumptious country fellow, and much older than her, but his heart's in the right place. Beth could have done a lot worse.' Louisa corrected her opinion. 'Well, not much worse when you think about it.'

'You and Jason married for love.'

'That's true.' Louisa pinned the last of the flowers into Grace's hair. 'You know, you look more beautiful than ever.' Her expression grew serious. 'I'm going to miss you more than I can say.'

Grace's voice tremored. 'I'll come and visit you and Kitty every day.'

'That's impossible.' Louisa smiled wryly. 'When you acquire a husband, you're obliged to wait on him, hand and foot. You'll be too busy cooking, cleaning and answering his needs in the . . .' Grace's face turned crimson in the mirror when she realised what Louisa was trying to say. '. . . marital bed. Men are simple creatures — allow them to take their pleasure freely and on a regular basis, and they are generally content. Withhold your favours at your peril, because a lack of intimacy makes a man ill-willed towards his spouse.'

'Why would a wife do that?'

'You have a lot to learn,' Louisa sighed.

'Have you any other advice for a happy marriage?' Grace asked, putting on the sapphire pendant and fastening the chain around her neck.

'Never go to sleep on an argument and avoid becoming his skivvy. Don't be a mouse. If your husband treats you disrespectfully — intentionally or otherwise — make sure you pull him up on it.'

'Isaiah would never be mean to me.'

'Oh dear. Time is passing,' Louisa said, changing the subject. 'We're due at St George's at half past nine. Where is your shawl?'

Jason accompanied them as they left the cottage

and walked along the alley, followed by a crowd of their neighbours who had emerged to wish Grace well.

'Here comes the blushin' bride,' Mrs Witherall said.

'Lamb to the slaughter, more like.'

'Bite your tongue, Mr Witherall. 'E doesn't mean it— 'e's a grumpy old toad nowadays.'

'That's 'ow marriage transforms a man,' he grumbled, 'It wears 'im down.' As his wife threatened to bring her foot down on his gout-ridden toes, he quickly changed his tune. 'Grace, my dear, you've always been a sweet girl — you deserve to be 'appy.'

As they continued, they reached the passageway where she heard other voices, Mrs Roper among them, crowing over the comparison between Grace's and Mary's prospective husbands.

'I never thought I'd see a day when a Feasey would shackle 'imself to one of the Lennicker sisters. I've 'eard it's a love match — there's no accountin' for taste. Well, she's made 'er bed, and she'll 'ave to lie in it.'

'Ignore them,' Louisa said haughtily.

'That's what I'm doing,' Grace said. 'I'm not going to let their opinions spoil my day.' Although, she mused, it did niggle her a little that Mary was marrying a well thought of young man while her bridegroom was looked down upon by many. No matter though, she told herself. With Grace at his side to guide and support him, Isaiah would soon gain the respect of her friends, neighbours and family.

'Grace, this is for you.' Nancy came running

99

towards them, waving a handkerchief. She pressed it into Grace's hand. 'Something blue . . . I've sewn a flower in coloured thread in the corner. Congratulations.'

Before Grace could thank her, she flitted back down the street like a butterfly. Grace tucked the handkerchief into her bodice and the procession moved on to St George's where a gentleman dressed in a tall hat, an embroidered coat and shoes with silver buckles was waiting outside. It wasn't until he raised his hat and came walking towards her, moving with an almost imperceptible limp, that she recognised him. The cowlick of red hair that Billy had had since he was a boy still refused to lie flat, no matter what he did with it.

Smiling, she ran to greet the man whom her father had taken in as a boy and treated as a son.

'You came!' she exclaimed.

'Winnie isn't with me,' he said, and her heart sank. 'She asked me to give you this though . . . 'Ow does it go'? He searched his pockets. 'Somethin' old, somethin' new, somethin' borrered, somethin' blue. Louisa asked Winnie to do the borrered part. 'Ere.' He pressed a package into her hand.

She opened it carefully to find a delicate lace shawl inside. 'Oh, thank you.'

'She says she'll be thinkin' of you.' Billy took her knitted shawl and gave it to Louisa who took it inside while Grace draped the lace over her arms.

'Will you give me away now that you're here, Billy?' she asked.

'Shouldn't Jason 'ave the honour?'

'I've known you for longer — you've always

100

been like a brother to me.'

'Then I'll be proud to do it, but if I'm honest, I'd prefer not to be givin' you away to the likes of 'im. Are you sure about this? It isn't too late to change your mind.'

'My mind and heart will not be altered,' she said severely as the rain began to fall from the dark clouds above.

'I'm sorry. Winnie asked me — '

'I guessed that would be so.'

'Let's forget I said anythin'. It's your weddin' day, the best day of your life — at least it was for me. When I turned and saw Winnie walkin' down the aisle towards me, I couldn't 'ave been 'appier.' He patted her hand. 'I'm honoured to be takin Mr Lennicker's place, God rest 'is soul.'

She took his arm and they diverted briefly to the graveyard to pay their respects at her parents' graveside among the headstones marking the mariners of Deal who had gone aloft, before a flash of lightning and a clap of thunder presaged a burst of heavy raindrops.

'Let's go inside,' Billy said, and they entered the church where Isaiah was waiting for her at the altar.

'I've never seen you looking so beautiful,' he whispered as the rain hammered against the windows, spilled from the gutters and gurgled down the drains.

Reverend North, wearing a cassock and a Canterbury cap over his straggly grey hair, conducted the service during which they declared their promise before God that they would love, comfort and honour each other for as long as they lived. Then

Isaiah took her right hand in his while they made their vows.

'I, Isaiah Thomas Feasey, take you, Grace Lennicker, to be my wife. To 'ave and to 'old from this day forward. For better, for worse, for richer, for poorer, in sickness and in wealth,' he intoned as the storm continued raging from the skies above.

'Health . . . it's in health,' the vicar corrected him. 'Let us continue.'

Grace gazed into her husband's eyes, his expression dancing with amusement, as the lightning flickered around them.

'To love and to cherish, till death do us part,' he said, repeating the vicar's words.

He took a ring from his pocket and placed it on the fourth finger of her left hand.

The vicar joined their right hands together, and said, 'Those whom God hath joined together, let no man put asunder. For as much as Black Dog . . . Isaiah and Grace have consented together in holy wedlock, I pronounce that they be man and wife together.'

A thunderbolt flickered and cracked like a shot from a cannon, but it was the perfect moment. Grace's joy knew no bounds as her husband's eyes met hers, his adoration and passion clear to see.

After the blessing and prayers, she walked at his side to the vestry where she sat down beside him and signed the register, Miss Grace Lennicker, with Billy and Jason as witnesses. She gave the pen to Isaiah who stared at it as if he'd never seen one before.

'Go on,' she said. 'Sign your name.'

He made his mark, blotting the parchment.

102

'What are you lookin' at me like that for, Mrs Feasey? I never 'ad no time for Mrs Lennicker's lessons. She l'arned Billy and lots of the shore boys to read and write, but I told 'er — as a matter of pride, not because I couldn't do it, you understand — that she'd never l'arn me.'

He had deviated from his story of how his father had prevented him from joining in, and it troubled her. Not only had he told her a fib, but the spidery cross in place of his signature had left an indelible mark across the image she held in her heart and mind of the perfect husband. She hadn't expected him to be an ignoramus, she thought, as he stood up and offered her his hand.

'Let's go 'ome,' he said.

'May happiness flow through your lives like rivers of the best French cognac,' Reverend North said with a twinkle in his eye when he wished them farewell, making Grace wonder what Isaiah had offered him to officiate at their wedding.

They stood briefly at the door of the church, waiting for the rain to stop, which it did, the clouds parting to allow a glimpse of the blood-red sun. Isaiah slipped his arm around her waist, then dropped his hand to her rump and squeezed her flesh, making her yelp. Laughing, he guided her through the small crowd who had waited to see the bride leave the church and shower her with rose petals, which stuck to her gown and ribbons. She brushed one from Isaiah's coat, before they hurried on to the Rattling Cat where he swept her into his arms and carried her across the threshold. When he stumbled, she tightened her grip around his neck.

'Got you!' he exclaimed in high spirits, keeping her feet off the floor. 'You didn't really think I'd drop you, did you? You'll 'ave to learn to trust me.'

'I do trust you,' she said, as he rubbed his nose against hers, then snatched a kiss.

'There's plenty of time for that later,' she heard Jason chuckle from behind them.

'Where's Billy?' she asked as Isaiah set her down.

'He sends his apologies — he has business in town.'

'I see. I wish I'd had a chance to thank him for giving me away.'

'The vicar's coming in his stead,' Louisa said.

'What about Nancy? Isn't she going to join us?' With a withering look, Louisa shook her head.

'Of course she isn't. She wouldn't.' Grace had to face the fact that no one else would be coming to celebrate the happiest day of her life. What did she expect when they were already calling her the smuggler's wife?

'Will you show me around your new home?' Louisa asked and Grace glanced towards Isaiah for permission which he gave willingly.

'Take your time, ladies. Marlin and I will chew the fat with the vicar until you're ready to eat.'

Grace took great delight in showing Louisa the guest rooms and then the new dining room where the men were sitting at one of the tables, watching Sarah adding the final touches to the wedding breakfast. Grace gently shooed a cat off the tablecloth and sat down beside her husband.

They helped themselves to the cold meats, cheeses, cherries and cake, while Sarah served ale, wine and tea. Grace could hardly eat, aware of Isaiah's thigh pressed against hers. Every so often, he would toss a piece of beef or salted pork towards the dog which stood drooling at the end of the table.

'I'm impressed by the alterations you've made,' Louisa said.

'I'm glad you approve. Perhaps you can see your way to spreadin' the word.'

'I wish you every success. It's a comfort to me to see that you've taken up an honest trade,' Louisa observed.

Grace smiled, aware of how much it must have taken for her sister to eat such a large slice of humble pie, and grateful that not only had the rift between her family and her husband begun to heal, but also that there'd been no mention of smugglers and smuggling.

They went on to talk about news of Bonaparte, who had surrendered to a Captain Maitland of the Bellerophon and been taken to Torbay to await transfer to the Northumberland.

'He'll be well on his way to St Helena,' Jason said.

'I don't know why the authorities thought it was a good idea to exile him to Elba in the first place,' the vicar said, the wine making him garrulous. 'It wasn't far for him to flee to Antibes with the six hundred men they'd let him have.'

Grace remembered how the British soldiers had been recalled to their battalions when news had arrived that the French king had backed down without a gun being fired when Old Boney had entered Paris just before Easter.

She'd watched them, a column of thirty thousand men, marching from Canterbury to Deal where they embarked on their ships and sailed off to fight in Flanders and around the Rhine.

'Enough of the war.' Jason stood up. 'Let's look to the future and toast the happy couple.'

'We'll 'ave a drop of somethin' stronger for that,' Isaiah smiled. 'Wench, where are you?'

Sarah came scurrying back from the direction of the kitchen, her cheeks flushed and eyes glittering. 'What is it?'

'Fetch a jug of that cognac that I keep be'ind the bar for emergencies and special occasions. Thank you,' he added, making Grace feel a little better about how he'd addressed the barmaid who seemed distressed, casting nervous glances towards the door as she collected and served the brandy.

'To our lovely Grace and Isaiah . . . I'm warnin' you, you'd better look after her, or I'll be after you,' Jason jested, raising his glass.

Sarah cried out at the same time as five figures dressed in black came charging through the doorway from the kitchen. Jason's glass shattered and a deep growl rumbled from the dog's throat, when the men, who were unshaven and wearing dirty smocks, bandannas and wet boots, surrounded the table.

'Why didn't you listen to me, you bumblin' clodpoles?' Sarah exclaimed. 'I'm mightily relieved to see you alive and kickin', but you must all turnabout and get out of 'ere, quick as you can.'

'I'm not goin' nowhere. I'm lookin' forward to

a kiss and cuddle with me wife.'

Grace assumed that the smuggler who embraced Sarah — a moon-faced man with ruddy cheeks — was Digger, her husband. She recognised Lawless and Awful Doins, but not the others, one of whom was especially short and stout, and the other over six feet tall, a towering, glowering character with a scar across his cheek.

When the smugglers started helping themselves to food and drink, she got to her feet.

'Excuse me, but this spread isn't for you,' she said, noticing that Jason was moving towards the front door to guard the exit on to the street while Louisa and the vicar looked on, open-mouthed. 'You have no right to come charging in here uninvited.'

'Who are you to decide who's welcome or not?' Awful Doins rested his arm around Lawless's shoulders. 'Oh, it's you, Grace.'

'What's Marlin doin' suppin' ale with Black Dog?' Lawless asked.

'You shouldn't be anywhere near 'ere, you idiots.' Isaiah drained his glass and stood up.

'We thought you'd be delighted to see us back, but it seems you've been celebratin' in our absence.'

'Never mind that — 'e's set us up,' the tall man hissed. 'This is a trap and we've walked straight into it.'

'You're all under arrest, the lot of you.' Jason glared at Isaiah. 'And you.'

'You can't do that — my husband hasn't done anything wrong,' Grace cut in.

'Quiet, my love. Let me deal with this.' Isaiah's

threatening tone brought her up short. 'What am I alleged to have done this time?'

'I'd say you've been givin' these fugitives shelter.'

'I don't know what you're talkin' about. I swear on my wife's life that I've 'ad nothin' to do with this. Marlin, would I risk missin' out on my weddin' night?'

'I have to admit that does seem unlikely, even for you,' Jason said coldly.

'Weddin'?' Digger said. 'You've married the prettiest girl on the spit? 'Ow did you do that?'

'We don't 'ave no time for chit-chat.' The tall smuggler picked Digger up by the shoulders and dragged him towards the kitchen doorway. 'Let's get out of 'ere.'

'Dunk, put me down!' Digger protested.

'Louisa, go and fetch the constable and my men who are guarding the lugger,' Jason ordered. 'Grace, put yourself in the way of these gatecrashers. Don't let them pass.'

She didn't hesitate, hastening to intercept the smugglers at the doorway into the kitchen where she turned to face them, ire rising in her breast. 'Get out of our way,' Dunk snapped.

'I will not,' she replied stubbornly.

Dunk gave her a black look while the vicar put his hands together and prayed, and Louisa disappeared out of the front door of the tavern.

'I'm just as surprised as anybody else to find them 'ere,' Isaiah said. 'Let's talk this through. Sarah, pour the commander another drink.'

'No, thank you,' Jason said. 'I'd like to keep my wits about me.'

108

Isaiah chuckled. 'I didn't know you 'ad any, wits, I mean.'

'This isn't the time for banter.'

'Oh, come on, Marlin,' Awful Doins piped up. 'Can't we let bygones be bygones?'

'Don't Marlin me. It's Commander Witherall of HMS *Legacy* to you, sir. I will do my duty as an officer of the Revenue.'

'It comes to somethin' when you 'ave to get your womenfolk to do your work for you,' Dunk sneered as he continued to hold on to Digger. 'Mrs Feasey, you're a smuggler's wife now — you're supposed to be on our side.' Her mouth ran dry and her heart pounded as he thrust his face into hers and growled, 'Woe betide anyone who goes against us.'

'Don't you dare speak to my lady like that,' Isaiah snarled.

Dunk released his hold on Digger, squared up to Isaiah and punched him on the nose. Isaiah thumped him back and a scuffle broke out, the other smugglers joining in.

'Desist or I'll shoot,' Jason bellowed. 'Desist at once!'

A pistol flashed from his hand and an ear-splitting report followed. The ball embedded itself in one of the beams in the ceiling, splintering the wood.

The smugglers froze. Isaiah and Dunk shuffled apart, the former pinching the bridge of his nose as blood dripped from his nostrils, the latter bent double. Taking advantage of his adversary's temporary incapacity, Isaiah walked up to Grace who had stayed at her post, frozen to the spot at the sight of such unexpected violence.

'I'm sorry you had to see that,' he whispered as she gave him Nancy's handkerchief to wipe his nose. 'Dunk does have a point, though. Whose side *are* you on? If your 'usband told you that 'e owes these gents a favour for services rendered in the past an' 'e pointed out that your be'aviour makes 'im appear less of a man . . . ? Do you get my drift?'

She nodded, realising what he wanted her to do.

'Let 'em go, eh.'

As she stepped aside, Dunk and Digger pushed past her and ran through the kitchen.

'Run, Rattlers, run!' Isaiah shouted.

'What are you waitin' for? Leg it, Lawless,' Awful Doins added, grabbing his arm and pulling him along with him and the remaining smuggler.

Jason fired another shot at the ceiling and chased after them. Isaiah took Grace's hand and whistled for the dog, and they followed on down to the beach with Sarah and the vicar in close pursuit. Stopping at the top of the slope, Grace stood beside her husband, watching the smugglers haring along the shingle towards the boats. They passed the *Curlew* and a couple of fishing vessels, before approaching the *Good Intent II* where Louisa was talking to Albert and the rest of Jason's men.

'They're goin' to overpower the guards and launch the lugger,' Isaiah said, grinning. 'It's to their benefit that the Revenue 'ave been tardy in decidin' 'er fate.'

'I don't like the way you're taking pleasure from

this situation, whereas I can hardly bear to look.'

'I didn't have you down as such a delicate flower,' Isaiah observed as Grace heard Jason yell a warning. Her heart in her mouth, she saw Dunk charge at Albert and tear his musket from his grip. Undeterred, Albert drew his cutlass and slashed at Dunk's arm, drawing blood and making him drop the gun which discharged with a bang towards Awful Doins's feet. He screamed and began hopping on the stones, like a cat on hot bricks.

'I want them taken alive!' Jason bellowed.

Dunk tripped and fell back. Albert jumped on him and after a struggle, clapped him in irons. Seeing their companion defeated and bleeding, Awful Doins, Lawless, Digger and the other man put their hands up.

'It's all to the good,' Isaiah commented as Jason lined them up along the shore. 'The sooner they face the music, the sooner they can get back to what they do best. What's Marlin doin' now?'

'We'll march them to the gaol,' Jason announced. 'All hands.'

'What about the lugger, sir?' Albert asked.

'She won't be goin' anywhere with this lot locked up. No, you're right to be circumspect.' As Jason turned away, Albert acknowledged Grace with a fleeting smile, his expression awash with pity, but he had no right, she thought, to judge her situation when she was happier than she'd ever been. She glanced towards her husband, whose eyes were dark with anger, then back at Albert who was attending to the prisoners, adjusting the cuffs on Awful Doins's wrists because he was complaining loudly about them cutting into his flesh. It wasn't surprising that Isaiah was in a fury. She was too. It had been most unfortunate that the smugglers had turned up when they did.

Jason arranged to leave two of his men behind to guard the boat before asking the vicar to warn his fellow magistrates that their presence would be required at a hearing in the morning. Before Reverend North left the beach, Isaiah excused himself and went to speak to him. As Grace tried to hear what they were saying, Louisa came up and tapped her on the shoulder.

'I've decided that it's best that you don't call at the cottage for the time being. I know you helped them get away — Jason told me.' Grace opened her mouth to speak but Louisa raised her hand. 'There's no need to explain — we've been over the same old ground before. It's imperative that my husband's reputation remains intact so that he can maintain his authority over his men and the criminal fraternity of Deal. He's my priority, as your husband will be for you from now on. Make sure you keep him out of trouble, or Jason will have him arrested and duly punished. That is all,' she finished abruptly.

With a heavy heart, Grace watched her walk away along the beach through the sea holly, thrift and rosemary. She would never forget the interruption and sudden explosion of violence at the tavern, Albert's bravery on the beach, and most of all, the way her loyalty had been tested. Despite her conscience telling her to act on the side of the law, she had gone along with Isaiah as a good wife should, except that he shouldn't have had to make her choose, if he'd carried out his promise and given up his links to the free trade. Her wedding day had been one to remember, but for all the wrong reasons.

8

A Bolt from the Blue

'I thought you were one of those annoyin' do-gooders, that you were too good for Black Dog, but you're all right,' Sarah said as she and Grace returned to the tavern, Isaiah having promised that he would follow soon. 'You did your best to 'elp my poor 'usband. 'E'll be goin' mad, worryin' about what might come to pass tomorrer. I wish I 'ad your good fortune. You 'ave a decent man there, a diamond, and there's a lot to be said for marryin' a gentleman who 'as property and an income and doesn't beat you black and blue when 'e's in the drink.'

Grace was shocked at her matter-of-fact manner of speaking. Pa had never raised a finger to Ma.

Sarah closed the door behind them and slipped the bolts across. 'I'll clear the table and wash the dishes before I go 'ome.'

'I'll help you,' Grace offered, not wanting to be alone.

'Not on your weddin' day. Go upstairs and wait for your 'usband.'

Grace found her way to his bedchamber where she discovered that someone had left her boxes and trunk on the floor beside the bed. She would unpack, she thought, except that there didn't seem to be anywhere for her clothes and belongings. Desultorily, she cleared a thick layer of dust from the dressing table and laid out her hairbrush, comb and scent bottle. There were dog hairs on the coverlet and an apple core lay rotting in the grate.

The apparent lack of preparation for her arrival made her feel unwelcome. Added to that, her worries about Isaiah's association with the smugglers as evidenced at the wedding breakfast made her cry. With tears drying on her cheeks, she sat on the window seat and watched the sky darken and night draw in, wondering what on earth was keeping Isaiah from her. Eventually, Sarah went home and Grace decided to turn in, but before she could undress, a clatter of stones alerted her to a commotion outside.

'Mrs Feasey! Get yourself down 'ere!'

She opened the window and leaned out. 'Isaiah, where have you been?'

He uttered a hollow laugh. 'That's for you to come and find out.'

She went downstairs, feeling her way down the narrow staircase and through the taproom in the dark. On reaching the door, she fumbled for the bolts and slid them back. Isaiah was waiting on the step. He grabbed her hand and planted a kiss on her mouth, before whisking her down the street towards the beach, heading in the direction of an eerie blazing light.

'The lugger is no more,' he said, the flames flickering and the scent of woodsmoke and tar intensifying as they grew closer.

Aghast, she turned to face him. 'What have you done?'

'It's a matter of principle. I've made sure that if

115

the Rattlers can't 'ave 'er, nobody can.'

'What about Jason, and the guards?'

''Is men were most obligin' — it didn't take much to persuade them to turn a blind eye. I know what you're thinkin', that you've married an uncommon criminal, but I did this out of the respect I 'ave for that vessel.'

She recalled Pa's fondness for the *Pamela* whom he'd named after their mother, and Louisa's comments that there were three people in her marriage, one of them being Jason's beloved boat.

'I've already lost one lugger, thanks to Marlin,' he added, and her mind flew back to the night of the legendary battle between Jason's crew and the Rattlers in the Sands.

* * *

Grace was fourteen or fifteen when she and her sisters and Old Mr Witherall were out with the *Curlew* running goods from the *Whimbrel* — Jason's lugger — to the shore at Deal. She and Winnie had dipped the lugsail and were heading home when a fight broke out between the *Whimbrel* and her sister vessel, the *Spindrift*, and Isaiah's lugger, the *Good Intent*. At the sound of a shout, a shot and a splash as a ball missed its mark, Grace had looked back towards Trinity Bay, a stretch of water inside the Sands where the ships were silhouetted against a crimson-streaked sky. The *Whimbrel* and *Spindrift* manoeuvred to sandwich the Rattlers' lugger between them before releasing volleys of cannon fire when the *Good Intent* fired back.

116

'We should leave,' Mr Witherall had said as the *Good Intent* rocked, her black lugsail dangling from a broken mast. 'If we stay 'ere, we're liable to get caught in the crossfire. The tide 'as turned.'

They made it into the channel leading away from the bay, racing to beat the rising water before it obscured the sandbanks on either side. Having safely returned to shore, they waited on the beach until Jason landed the *Whimbrel* with the Rattlers on board. It wasn't long before One Eye arrived, swearing and cursing when he learned that the *Good Intent* had sunk without trace.

'It was self-defence,' Jason said calmly. 'I gave your captain a choice: stop firin' and strike her colours, or carry on and go down with her. We took him and the crew off, but there wasn't much we could salvage and there's no point in goin' back — she'll be a good few fathoms below by now. What was your son thinkin' of, openin' fire on his fellow boatmen, men who've always worked together, savin' ships and savin' lives?'

Isaiah stood well back — he appeared to have lost his boots. Behind him, his battered and crest-fallen men, a raggle-taggle crew in torn slops, reunited with their womenfolk. Then One Eye turned on his men, some of whom enraged him further, saying they'd had enough of working for him. Finally, he turned on Isaiah.

'What kind of son goes against 'is father?' he roared, stopping a few feet in front of him.

'I did what you said to do.' Isaiah's hands balled into fists. 'When I saw the *Whimbrel* 'ad gone out, I used my initiative.'

'You should 'ave waited. Spoken to me first.

You're like your mother. Weak in the 'ead.'

'She wasn't so stupid as to stay with you, though. I remember 'ow you used to beat 'er till she was beggin' for mercy. You are a . . . .' Isaiah seemed to be struggling to find the right words '. . . a bilge rat, the lowest of the low.'

With a roar of anguish, One Eye charged at him. Isaiah swung round and barged him with his shoulder. One Eye lost his footing and fell backwards. An awful cracking sound cleaved the air as he landed, his head hitting the stones. His body lay perfectly still, then started to twitch.

Isaiah fell to his knees at his father's side.

'I didn't mean it!' he cried. 'All will be well. We'll buy another boat, and . . .' He slapped his father's cheek. 'Speak to me. Say somethin', you stupid old goat.'

Stunned, the crowd stood by while Grace and her sisters went to help.

'He's gone,' Winnie whispered.

'He's as dead as a doornail,' Grace said in wonderment, noting the foam on his lips and the blood creeping across the stones from the back of his head. She thought she could remember Louisa saying, 'I'm sorry, Isaiah,' but he took no notice. He sat back on his heels, raised his eyes to the sky and howled in pain.

When Grace had next met him pacing the beach with the dog at his heels, he told her that the coroner had given the cause of his father's death as a broken skull, the result of an accident.

'I don't know what to do with myself now 'e's gone,' he said. ''E always makes the decisions when it comes to the tavern . . . and the other business.'

'It's very sad,' Grace said, reminded of her own father's passing.

'We're united in loss, but we don't share the same depth of sorrow. I don't miss 'im or look back with any fondness. 'E treated me as 'is skivvy, and if I ever went against 'im, 'e'd beat me and tell me I was a milksop and a dunce.'

'Why did you stay with him?' she asked.

'Family's family, isn't it? Blood is thicker than water and all that. I didn't know any other way of life to follow. I was dragged up on the spit to be a landlord, boatman and free-trader, and when I threatened to move away, my father 'ad this knack of persuadin' me to change my mind. 'E said that 'e depended on me to 'elp 'im, that 'e'd kill 'imself . . .

'When a body keeps on at you, tellin' you that you're this or that, you start to believe them.'

★ ★ ★

'I 'aven't hurt no one, only Marlin's pride, maybe,' Isaiah went on, bringing her back to the present as the crowd who were assembling near the burning boat, passed round jugs of warm milk and brandy. ''Ave a drink in 'er memory, my love. And don't fret — I've done the right thing.'

The cognac hit the back of her throat, making her cough. She handed the jug to Isaiah who gave it up to the next pair of outstretched hands without taking a drop himself.

'I think I understand your attachment to the boat, but tell me, why do you still have this — '

119

she took a moment to find the right word '— comradeship with the smugglers?'

'Old 'abits die 'ard, I suppose. They've looked to me for leadership through good times and bad. What kind of man would I be if I abandoned my blood brothers in their hour of need?' He broke off, looking up towards a man who came to speak to them, dragging his foot as he moved.

'What are you doin', 'angin' around 'ere on your weddin' night, Black Dog?' he enquired. 'I'd be rollin' in the 'ay by now if I were you.'

'Not in front of my good lady, Startup,' Isaiah said gruffly as Grace's cheeks flushed hot. He slid his arm possessively around her back, before whistling his dog from the shadows and walking her back to the tavern. She let down her hair and changed into her nightgown while he locked up. When he came to her, the dog came too.

'Surely he sleeps downstairs,' she exclaimed, as a cold, wet nose nudged her shin. 'Shoo, Musket!' He jumped on to the bed, scratched his ear and settled down. 'Oh no.'

'There's no need to be jealous of 'im,' Isaiah said.

'I don't want him here.' She thought she'd had some idea of what to expect on her wedding night, but it wasn't this. 'What about fleas?'

'He don't 'ave any.' Isaiah grinned as he removed his clothes and dropped them at his feet, revealing his nakedness. 'It would break my 'eart to think of him pining outside.'

'You would put your dog's comfort before that of your wife?' she asked, dismayed.

'I'll make an exception for tonight,' he said,

giving in. 'I believe that's the first compromise I've 'ad to make as a married man. I 'ave a sinkin' feelin' that there'll be many more.' He dragged Musket from the bed and turfed him out on to the landing, closing the door again. 'Grace — ' he leapt into bed and patted the coverlet beside him as the dog whined '— come and lie with me. It's been a while since I sowed my wild oats.'

She didn't like to ask with whom as she crept slowly on to the bed and stretched out alongside him, her chest tight with anticipation and nerves, but for a rough man he was a gentle lover, and when she lay in his arms afterwards, she felt more-affection for him than she ever thought possible.

★ ★ ★

When she awoke with daylight streaming through the window, casting a pattern of diamonds across the crumpled quilt, it took her a moment to recall where she was.

'It's time we were dressed, sleepy'ead,' Isaiah said, smiling from beside her.

'What shall I do today?' she mumbled, feeling a pang of homesickness as the gulls cried from the roof.

'You'll attend the 'earin' with your 'usband. I'm lookin' forward to showin' you off. You'll wear the necklace I gave you and dress modestly, like a young lady, not a whore.'

'I've never dressed like a— ' she retorted.

'What I mean is, you'll keep your . . . . assets covered with a piece of lace or suchlike.'

She sank back against the pillow. 'Is it wise for

121

us to be seen at the hearing?'

'Oh Grace.' His eyes twinkled with amusement. 'I'm a respectable gen'leman, a pillar of the community. Wasn't that what you wanted, or are you one of those contrary women who are always changin' their minds?'

'Men change their minds too,' she said, a little irritated that he'd seen fit to advise her about her mode of dress, because it appeared that having been freed from following Louisa's orders, she was now subject to her husband's. 'I think I should decide which gown to put on and how to wear it. What do you know about ladies' fashion?'

'You aren't goin' to start givin' me curtain lectures, tellin' me off in private?' he sighed. 'I thought you'd be different from other wives.'

'How many have you had?' she teased.

'Just the one, and she's more than enough for me.' He kissed her again and her good cheer returned.

Within the hour, Grace walked into the courtroom at Deal gaol on Isaiah's arm.

Louisa, who was already seated, pointedly refused to meet Grace's eye, while Old Mr and Mrs Witherall who were beside her, turned away when Isaiah showed her to the last remaining seat. He stood behind her as she sat down, flashing the ring on her finger and rearranging her fichu.

'Look at 'er. She was such a sweet little thing as a child.'

Grace stared fixedly ahead as she heard whispering from nearby. These people, she thought, were envious of her good fortune. They wanted a reaction, but she refused to rise to the bait.

''E's bought 'er with that sapphire round 'er neck.'

''Ow can you tell it's a sapphire when you've never seen one afore?'

'I'm makin' an eddicated guess. I'll never 'ave anythin' like it, thanks to my skinflinty 'usband.'

The vicar, who was acting as one of the magistrates, brought the crowd to order.

'Sundry gentlemen of Deal — ' he read the names and addresses of the prisoners from the Bench in the crowded courtroom. 'You are charged that between the eleventh and eighteenth day of June, you were in possession of goods being illegally carried from France, and that you evaded being brought to justice by the Revenue officers of the cutter HMS *Legacy* while they were carrying out their duties in accordance with the law.'

The five men were in the dock, including Digger who was staring at his feet, his arms behind his back. Awful Doins and Lawless were white-faced and trembling, while Dunk smirked and whispered behind his hands with the fifth smuggler, known as Cut-throat, apparently convinced that they were going to be let off.

Grace glanced from the vicar to his fellow magistrates, Mr Norris who was married to her cousin, and Mr Causton, landlord of the Waterman's Arms. Standing to their left was Jason, who was bringing the case against the prisoners on behalf of the Revenue.

'Haven't all these people watching these proceedings got anything better to do, Vicar?' Mr Norris, a portly figure with a florid complexion, enquired as the stench of sweat and filthy clothes cut through the perfume of rosewater and lavender that had been scattered across the floor.

'I don't believe they have packs of hounds and farms to manage, Mr Norris. Many are unemployed,' the vicar replied. 'How do you plead? One at a time, sirs.'

'Not guilty,' Digger said. 'I speak on be'alf of all the prisoners. We were comin' back from a fishin' trip when the commander of HMS *Legacy* fired on us without warnin'. We jumped straight into a boat and rowed away as any right-thinkin' gen'lemen would do when they're about to be shot out of the water.'

'That isn't how the Revenue sees it.' Reverend North gave a weary sigh. 'Commander Witherall, I have read your statement. Would you like to confirm your version of events?'

'Don't listen to 'im — 'e gets paid extra if we get locked up,' Digger said.

'Pray, silence. Commander, what do you have to say on the matter?'

'I gave warnin'. My lieutenant here, Enderby, will vouch for it. As for the sham that it was a fishin' trip — there were no fish nor means of catchin' any on board the lugger. We did however find a fine haul of run goods.'

'We 'ave no knowledge of these goods you mention,' Digger argued. 'The gobblers set us up — they 'ad every opportunity to 'ide the goods themselves.'

'Commander Witherall, did you see the prisoners place the goods in the lugger?'

'No, but the urgency and means of their escape tells me they are guilty.'

124

'The law relies on evidence, supported by witness statements, not your perceptions,' Reverend North said. 'All must be proven beyond reasonable doubt.'

'The prisoner's lie is a bag of moonshine,' Jason said.

Grace glanced towards Isaiah who was staring fixedly ahead. She knew whom she believed, and it wasn't Digger.

'What is your opinion, Mr Causton?' The vicar addressed the third magistrate.

'The statements from the Revenue claim that they found run goods stashed in hidden cavities behind false boards and in a hollow inside the mast. It's feasible that the prisoners weren't aware of them.'

'Don't bite the 'and that feeds you, Mr Causton. Very wise,' one of the wives said. 'Tell the truth and they'll be back suppin' your ale before you know it — as long as you drop the price.'

When Albert had given his view of events which supported Jason's, Jason began to argue with the magistrates.

'These are capital offences that should be tried at the assizes,' he said, infuriated. 'Why quibble with my statement?'

'Because,' said the vicar, 'you have failed to make the charges stick.'

'Somethin' tells me that you — a man of the cloth — have been got at,' Jason said furiously. 'This hearin' is a disgrace. You fail to follow the law or employ any logic.'

'Where is the evidence, incontrovertible proof that these men loaded those goods on to the

125

lugger? Bring it to me, Commander, and I will willingly reconsider.'

'I will not be gammoned by these scoundrels — they have led the Revenue a merry dance for years. When I joined up, I thought I could make a difference. My orders are to arrest those responsible for importin' contraband, yet no matter how many times I bring prisoners in front of the magistrates in this town, they get away with their crimes. It's the same for the other lines of defence that the Revenue have put in place to stamp on this smugglin'. The Riding officers ashore, the Revenue cruisers at sea, and the crews of the Waterguard inshore who patrol their sections of coast from the watch houses, cannot obtain a single conviction, no matter how hard they try.'

The vicar shrugged. 'I shall confer with Mr Causton and Mr Norris.'

The magistrates left the courtroom, returning a while later as the audience was beginning to grow restive. Reverend North called for silence before summarising their findings.

'We find the prisoners guilty of evading arrest and jointly for the possession of a bag of baccy, a half-anker of cognac and three silver snuffboxes. These are summary offences that can be dealt with quickly and quietly by the Bench here. I sentence you . . . ' he listed their names again '. . . to four months' confinement at His Majesty's pleasure and a fine of seventy pounds each.'

'I will pay it.' Taking Grace by surprise, Isaiah moved towards the Bench. 'Five times seventy — that's at least three 'undred pounds— '

'Three hundred and fifty to be precise,' the

vicar cut in. 'I'm sorry. Do go on.'

'I do this out of charity for these poor desperate men and their families.'

Grace felt her heart would burst with pride at her husband's magnanimous gesture that proved him to be kindly as well as a man of considerable means, because the total amount was enough to keep an English gentleman in comfort for a whole year.

'You're goin' up in the world, Black Dog,' Mr Causton observed from the Bench. 'Business must be good.'

'It's Mr Feasey to you, sir,' Isaiah smiled, playing to the crowd as he touched the rim of his hat before turning and offering Grace his arm. 'Come along with me, missus.'

Grace walked out of the courtroom with him, her feelings mixed: a sense of superiority at her newfound position as the wife of a man of influence and fortune; an ocean of regret over her split with Louisa.

* * *

'I don't understand why the vicar changed 'is mind when 'e promised me that 'e'd see 'em right,' Isaiah said when they were walking back to the Rattling Cat. ''E won't be 'avin' nothin' else from me after that performance.'

'You think that the smugglers have suffered an injustice?' Grace asked.

'That North fellow must 'ave 'ad second thoughts about lettin' them off this time. You win some, you lose some. It's all part of the game.'

Stopping at the tavern door where the rusty sign squealed on its hooks in the wind, he added, 'Run along then, Grace. I 'ave business in town.'

'What sort of business?' she asked, disappointed. 'What shall I do?' she went on when he didn't respond.

'I don't know.' He shrugged. 'What did you used to do?'

'Cook and clean . . . ' she faltered.

'All I ask is that you keep the bed warm for me, my love.' He leaned in and kissed her before walking back into town. Finding herself at a loss, Grace went indoors and waited in the taproom for Sarah to return from the hearing, when she offered to help her with the chores.

'Are you sure?' Sarah said suspiciously. 'Black Dog 'asn't asked you to check up on me?'

'No, I want to find out exactly what it takes to run the tavern,' she said. 'I'd find it tedious being a kept woman.'

'Are you sure?' Sarah raised an eyebrow. 'Well, if you insist. Many 'ands make light work — we'll be done in a trice.'

They cleaned the guest rooms, emptied the pisspots and stripped the beds, piling the sheets into a giant wicker basket. Sarah sat on the top so that Grace could pull the leather straps tight and fasten the buckles.

'We send the laundry out, thank goodness. Don't make it look too clean and tidy, or 'e'll expect the same every time,' Sarah warned.

'Great minds think alike.' Grace stopped mid-giggle. What was she thinking of? This was their living on which she and Isaiah depended

128

— she wasn't at home with Louisa any more, challenging herself to do as little as possible without being found out. 'On second thoughts, we ought to make a proper job of it. We should buy fresh flowers and scented soap for the rooms to impress the guests.'

'I expect you want to impress your new 'usband too — I did when I married Digger, but it soon wore off. It's a terr'ble shame 'e's been locked up. We've only been married for three months.'

'Where are you living?'

'We rent an attic room in Golden Street — it's above the pawnbroker's.' Sarah smiled wistfully. 'Digger says 'e's going to make our fortune one day, but the evidence so far suggests that 'e's pretty useless at smugglin', unlike Black Dog.'

'Isaiah's given it up. He's promised me.'

'Far be it from me to cast aspersions on my employer's character when 'e's proved 'imself a gen'leman of honour, payin' my 'usband's fine like that. 'Elp me drag the basket downstairs and then we'll open up. It must be close to noon and the usual crowd will be waiting for their nuncheon.'

'Why aren't they at work?' Grace whispered as she stood behind the counter where Sarah showed her how to serve ale and take orders for cold meats and pickles from the customers who had trailed in after she'd unbolted the door.

'Elson's boatyard 'as closed— 'e's laid off his carpenters and their apprentices. There's nothin' for them to do except get under their wives' feet or come 'ere to play cards over a drink or two. This is the way we record the tabs. Each person 'as a cup marked with their initials, into which

129

you 'ave to remember to drop a pebble for every drink they 'ave on credit.'

'It seems remarkably generous,' Grace observed, noting that many of the cups were filled to overflowing.

'They settle up in the end, one way or another. One poor chap 'ad to give up a tooth by way of payment.'

Grace winced at the thought as Sarah continued, 'Another gave up 'is boots and 'at.'

'Oh dear.' Grace smiled ruefully. 'I knew that some of Isaiah's customers were ruffians, but I'm just beginning to realise what I've let myself in for.'

'You'll get used to it.'

'I'll have to,' she said. 'I'm sorry. I interrupted you. I'm very grateful for your advice.'

'It's quite simple. They'll play up if they think you're lookin' down your nose at them,' Sarah said wisely before addressing a man in his fifties, whom Grace vaguely recognised as one of her father's former landsmen. 'What will you 'ave, my darlin'?'

'Ah . . . I told you what I really wanted the last time, but I got short shrift.' The man leered. 'Knowin' you're 'appily shackled, I'll ask for a pint of ale, and whatever you're drinkin'. Where's Digger, the old bastard?'

'In gaol,' Sarah replied curtly.

Their customer was already a few sheets to the wind, Grace thought disapprovingly when he turned to her. 'Who's this pretty lady?'

'Mrs Feasey,' Sarah said. 'Mind your language.'

'Black Dog's married?' he said in wonder. 'Well

130

I never. Good for 'im. You was worth waitin' for.'

She didn't like his lecherous tone.

'You 'ave to stand up to them,' Sarah said later. 'Let their attentions be like water off a duck's back. They like to flirt, so you flirt back — it's part of the job.'

'How do you put up with it? It makes my skin crawl.'

'I enjoy it. All right, you're on your feet all day, and some of the punters fancy their chances of a kiss and a grope, but all you 'ave to do is slap them straight down. Nip it in the bud, or they'll always be tryin' it on with you. They can look but not touch. That's my rule.'

Grace was used to men staring at her in an acquisitive way, but thiswasdifferent. They were gruff. Argumentative. The more they drank, the ruder and cruder they became. As the afternoon went on, some fell asleep while others became uppity, demanding more drink, more credit and even more attention.

When Sarah rang the bell for closing time, Isaiah — having returned in time for supper — was compelled to help her and Grace drag Mr Startup outside because he was as drunk as a wheelbarrow.

'Are you going to leave him there?' Grace asked when she saw Isaiah throw a bucket of cold water over him and leave him on the doorstep. 'Will he be all right?'

' 'E'll 'ave sobered up by dawn,' Isaiah replied. ' 'E won't come to no 'arm — it's the beginnin' of August and plenty warm enough.'

'Goodnight,' Sarah said. 'I'll be in tomorrer.'

'Thank you for the advice earlier,' Grace said.

'It's nice to 'ave another girl to talk to. I know you're in charge 'ere with Black Dog, but I'm 'opin' we'll become firm friends.'

'I'm sure we will — you've been very patient with me, showing me how to pour my first pint. Sarah, should you be walking home alone?' Grace worried.

'I carry this for my protection.' She pulled a lady's pistol from her pocket, making Grace step back. 'Don't be alarmed. Digger gave it to me — it isn't loaded, but the sight of it is enough to give any footpad the frights.' She kept it in her hand as she left the tavern. 'Oh, Mr Minnis,' Grace heard her say from outside. 'Watch where you're goin'.'

There was a bang as the door flew open and hit the wall inside the taproom, bringing down a shower of plaster. 'Black Dog, where are you?'

Was this the Mr Minnis of Snargate to whom Isaiah had sold his share of the boat, and whom Jason had described as a rogue? Grace wondered as a middle-aged man — she couldn't describe him as a gentleman — walked in, his boots clacking across the stone floor, the heel segs glinting as he moved. He sounded affable, but his manner was impatient as he shook Isaiah's hand, his hairy forearms revealed as his sleeves fell back. He wore a dark coat over a grey smock, and his thighs like tree trunks rippled beneath his breeches. He was someone who could turn in an instant, she felt. 'Oh, who's this pretty one? I didn't know you 'ad a new barmaid.'

'She's my wife,' Isaiah said.

'You kept that under your 'at, didn't you? Well,

Mrs Feasey, may you be very 'appy together.'

'Thank you,' Grace said stiffly.

'Black Dog, I'd like a word. *In private.*'

To Grace's consternation, the two men disappeared into the back room. Their conversation was heated, their voices raised, so she couldn't be accused of prying, she reasoned as she pressed her ear to the door.

'I 'ear my property's gorn up in smoke. I 'ad a major investment in that wessel and I 'old you personally responsible for my losses,' George Minnis said roughly.

'You paid for 'er — she was yours to look after,' Isaiah argued.

'Oh no. I want my money back.'

'You can't 'ave it. I've put it aside to pay Mr Tapping for the buildin' work and supplies. You recommended 'im to me, sayin' I'd get a good deal, but 'e's charged me an arm and a leg.'

'You wanted a quality job and that's what you've got. Come on, be reasonable. You took the lugger out. You were captain when Marlin captured 'er.'

'I was doin' you a favour.'

'I was doin' you a favour,' George growled. 'You said you needed a bit o' work on the side — you jumped at the opportunity I gave you. Listen, matey.' Grace held her breath. 'You owe me, but to show I 'ave no 'ard feelin's, I'll say that we share the loss, 'alf an' 'alf.'

'I can't, George. I've got to pay the brewery as well as Mr Tapping.'

'We all have our burdens to carry. My missus is sick and one of my daughters 'as come back to care for 'er. I 'ave an 'ouse'old to support, men to

133

pay. You see, we're all in this together. You scratch my back and I'll scratch yours. It's all about give and take.'

Mainly take, Grace suspected, on tenterhooks wondering if her husband would stand up to him.

'No, it's impossible. No . . . '

On hearing a muffled gasp, she pushed the door open to find George shoving Isaiah up against the wall with one hand around his throat.

'What are you doing? Unhand him,' she shouted. 'How dare you march in here and assault my husband!'

Slowly, George released him. Isaiah stroked his neck, checking for bruises.

'Don't fret, Mrs Feasey. We were just 'avin' a little ruck, a mess about.' George thumped Isaiah in the back, making him cough. 'That's right, isn't it? We are in agreement?'

Isaiah nodded. ''Alf an' 'alf.'

'That's correct, and a gallon of ale for my men who are waitin' outside.'

'As much as that?' Grace said.

'They're thirsty lads,' George responded with a chuckle.

Grace fetched his order and breathed a sigh of relief when George Minnis had left and she heard the sound of horses' hooves fading into the night. She and Isaiah retired to bed, the dog accompanying them this time, although his master made him lie on the floor just inside the bedroom door.

'You shouldn't 'ave been so sharp with George,' Isaiah said as he undressed. 'I like to make 'im feel welcome.'

'How was I to know he was such a good friend

134

of yours? I assumed you would have some disreputable acquaintances, but—'

'Did you really?' he cut in, amused. 'Oh Grace, he's all right.'

'He's a smuggler, isn't he?'

'If you must know, George 'as many interests. It's no secret that 'e's runnin' a gang from Snargate in Romney Marsh, forty miles away. They call themselves the Greys for the colour of their smocks.'

'What's he doing around here?' Although she felt traitorous for doubting her husband, she wanted to know if he was prepared to tell her the truth.

''E says I should have looked after the lugger when 'e asked me to captain 'er on the last run. 'E blames me for losin' 'er to the gobblers, and wants me to pay 'im is money back.'

'Have you agreed to that?'

'I did because I'm an honourable man.'

'And Mr Minnis is not?'

'We've split the difference. I look at it as an investment. If I keep him sweet, 'e'll bring more business our way.'

'What kind of business?'

'Customers,' he said, 'travellers who'll make use of the new rooms. George has money and influence, neither of which we can afford to turn away.'

'How will you pay him when you've just spent all that
money on the smugglers' fines?'

'There's no need to worry — our ship will be comin' in soon enough.'

Assuming that he was referring to the income

135

from the tavern, Grace went on to explain the reason for her concern. 'I have a horror of debt. My father lost control of his finances after Ma's death. We were in penury when he died and it's like getting caught in a foxhole in the Sands: the harder you try to dig yourself out, the deeper you sink.' She recalled crying in private when she found out how Louisa had been hounded by the lecherous Mr Trice, while trying to keep the extent of Pa's debts from her and Winnie.

'Come 'ere, silly.' Isaiah enfolded her in his arms as they lay in bed, listening to the sound of barrels being rolled along somewhere underground, deep in the interconnecting tunnels and cellars of Deal. 'With this place full, we'll soon 'ave more money than we can spend. By the way, you and Sarah 'ave done good works, but you don't need to keep changin' the sheets — guests can use the same ones as long as they 'aven't been slept in for more than a week or two. A sprinkle of rosewater will soon put them to rights. It's a bit like washin' your entire body too often — it's ruinous to the skin. Once a month, if that, is perfectly adequate.' 'While we're talking about housekeeping, may I remind you that you should take your boots off before you come upstairs,' she said resentfully. 'And I don't want Musket in here.'

'Is there anythin' else? I didn't 'ave you down as a scold.' Quirking one eyebrow, he began to chuckle. 'Oh Grace, you're even more beautiful when you're angry. Please, don't be cross with me. I'm tryin' very 'ard to be a good 'usband.'

'I'm sorry,' she said, on the verge of tears. 'I'm finding this very strange.'

'So am I. I'm used to doin' exactly as I please, but I want to make you 'appy. I need you at my side, in my bed . . . You belong to me.'

Later, she lay awake, listening as Musket, having decided that the floor wasn't for him, jumped on to the bed and settled across her feet with a tripe-laden belch.

To find out that Isaiah was in hock to a bad'un like George Minnis had been a bolt from the blue, a surprising and unwelcome revelation on the first day of her marriage.

What was more, he had other bills to pay. What else might he be hiding from her?

It occurred to her that he wasn't a bit like Albert who had an honest face to match his character. Isaiah was much more difficult to read. His mystery was one of the reasons why she'd fallen in love with him, but what good was it if he used it to cover his deceit?

Too hot, then too cold, she tossed and turned while Isaiah slept.

What would Louisa say? That Grace was tired and overwrought, and things would look better in the light of day. Isaiah hadn't lied to her about his obligation to George — he had merely withheld the information, out of delicacy of feeling for his new wife, Grace thought. He was loyal to his friends and doing his best to cut ties with the free trade. On reflection, she had made the right choice in defying her sisters and marrying Isaiah, but even so, lying alongside him in the dark as the wind rattled the roof and blew the rain against the windows, she felt unsafe, insecure and homesick.

9

Birds of a Feather Flock Together

As summer changed to autumn, the sun remained partially obscured by a red mist that brought a distinct chill to the weather. By November, winter had arrived with a vengeance. A bitter, blusterous wind blew along the spit and it seemed to rain almost constantly. Preoccupied with running the tavern and daily bouts of a draining sickness, Grace had managed to put George Minnis and Isaiah's debts to the back of her mind.

One morning at the start of December when a gale was driving hailstones against the bedroom window, she was getting dressed when Isaiah caught her around the waist from behind and kissed the nape of her neck.

'A penny for 'em, my dearest.'

'Oh, you must know by now — my thoughts are worth more than that.' She turned and smiled archly. 'Much more.'

'I 'ad noticed. This dress of yours 'as seen better days. You should 'ave a new one made.'

'I thought we were having to restrain our spending,' she said.

'You're right to remind me to be careful not to splash my money around. It's been a time of moderate 'ardship since we wed, but it's a mere

138

hiccup in our fortunes. Thanks to your enthusiasm for the business, things are lookin' up.'

'That's true,' she said proudly. 'The rooms are full — we have people from as far as Sholden, Canterbury and Sandwich flocking here to drink our ale and sleep in our beds.'

'And it isn't long until your birthday when you'll come into your money, and then we really will be in clover.'

'My money?' A quiver of alarm darted down her spine.

'The trust fund.' He grinned. 'Winnie's gift to you will become mine. I'll let you have a little pin money from it, of course, enough to buy two or three new gowns.'

She should tell him, she panicked, except that she didn't want to disappoint him, especially now when he seemed so merry and optimistic about their future. It could wait. There were a few more weeks before she turned eighteen, plenty of time to give him the bad news.

'Takin' you as my wife 'as been the best decision I've ever made. You're my lucky charm.' He stepped back, clapped his hand against his thigh to call the dog to him and went to the door.

'Where are you going?' she asked, wishing she could spend the day with him.

'Out and about,' he said lightly. 'I'll love you and leave you, and when I return, I'll love you again . . .'

'I look forward to it,' she giggled, before a wave of nausea washed through her gullet and she had to rush past him and out to the privy in the yard.

'Are you all right?' Sarah asked when she had

139

recovered enough to go into the taproom. 'You're lookin' peaky.'

'I'm well,' she fibbed. 'Is Digger back with you yet? It must be soon.'

''E and the others should be released tomorrer,' Sarah smiled. 'In fact, I meant to ask you or Black Dog if I could take the day off.'

'It's a little inconvenient, seeing how busy we are, but yes. Yes, of course you can.'

'Thank you, Grace.'

'Have you made a start on the vegetables for today's meals?'

'Not yet. I've been run off my feet, not that I'm complainin', merely observin'.'

'Can I smell burning?' Grace retched and Sarah's expression changed from hurt to horror. 'Oh no, I clean forgot to stir the porridge. I'll 'ave to start again.'

'You're in a world of your own today,' Grace sighed, after Sarah had served a second batch of porridge to the guests who complained about the blackened sludge in their bowls.

'I'm sorry. It won't 'appen again,' Sarah reassured her.

'We can't afford to let our standards slip. I've had to offer the old couple bacon and eggs as an alternative to pacify them.' However, the bacon was too salty and the eggs chewy, and they paid only half their bill before confirming loudly that they would never return.

From then on, the day went from bad to worse. Digger and the other smugglers arrived at noon, having been released early from their incarceration.

140

'The guards were fed up with us,' Awful Doins bragged as Digger canoodled with Sarah in the corner of the taproom and Dunk, Cut-throat and Lawless crowded the bar, impatient for Grace to serve them.

'You may have one drink each and then you must leave,' she said tersely.

'They may 'ave as many as they like,' Isaiah said, grinning and holding out his arms as he strode in from the street to join them. 'The drinks are on me. It's good to 'ave you back.' Although Grace was glad that Sarah had her husband home, her ire rose as Isaiah embraced each man in turn, and when she tried to take him aside, he told her off for being a nag.

'Come and warm your cockles by the fire. Bring your drinks. Grace, make yourself useful and fetch some o' that brandy.'

Grudgingly, she kept their tankards topped up and served the food that Sarah had prepared for the guests' suppers. All she could do was pray that the smugglers would drink themselves senseless before other people arrived, looking for a bed for the night.

'I'm sorry,' Sarah said, stepping up to the counter. 'I've been neglectin' my duties.'

'I don't blame you,' Grace said more cheerfully. 'I'd do the same if it had been Isaiah who'd just been released from gaol.'

'Listen to 'em. The drink's loosenin' their tongues,' Sarah observed as snippets of the men's conversation drifted across the taproom. A spell behind bars hadn't improved their language — Awful Doins was cursing and swearing as he pontificated on the unfairness of the Corn Law that Lord Liverpool and the Tories had passed recently to protect the landowners of England.

'The rich bastards'll get their just deserts in the end,' Awful Doins said. 'Look at Sir Flinders— 'e always wanted to be Prime Minister, but 'e 'asn't made it yet.'

'I don't think 'e will now— 'e's fallen out of favour since 'e misjudged the spy, Monsieur Boule. Completely taken in, 'e was,' Lawless opined.

'Goin' back to the Corn Law and the price of bread, I reckon there'll be riots here very soon,' Digger contributed.

'What do you menfolk know about the cost of a loaf?' Sarah sang out scathingly. 'When was the last time any of you set foot in a baker's shop?'

'All right. There's no need to remind us that we've been away for a while,' Digger chuckled.

'You've never been shoppin' for anythin', not even the ring you put on my finger.'

'If you don't like it, I'll take it back and give it to a lady who'll appreciate it.' Although Digger was jesting, Grace didn't like it.

'Don't you find that disrespectful?' she asked Sarah when the men returned to their gossip.

'I can forgive 'im for it when he's showin' off in front of 'is friends, but 'e knows that if 'e ever as much as looks at another woman, I'll 'ave 'im strung up by the you-know-whats.'

'Sarah!' Grace exclaimed.

Sarah giggled. 'I've shocked you with my straight talkin'.'

'A little,' Grace admitted as the men continued to talk about how the yields of wheat and barley had been down due to the cold weather back in August and September.

'It's wrong that men come back from war, expectin' a better standard of livin' in return for the sacrifices they've made, only to face austerity. Maybe we'd 'ave been better off under old Boney. Don't look at me like that. 'E 'elped us out, didn't 'e? 'E encouraged us to continue in the free trade, settin' us up with the compound at Gravelines, the cité de smoglers,' Isaiah said, getting to his feet.

'Tis a shame about Old Boney,' Awful Doins added. 'Some say 'e was an unelected despot, but I say that 'e 'ad some good ideas, reforms that would have improved the lot of 'is countrymen: votin' rights for all men, not just the so-called great and good. Can you imagine the likes of Sir Flinders and his cronies in the government allowing that to 'appen 'ere in England?'

'I don't see 'ow that would benefit the *uncommon* man, like myself,' Isaiah said, strutting like a cockerel back and forth across the taproom. ''Ow would I know who to vote for?'

'They'd 'old rallies and print pamphlets saying 'ow they'd 'elp us,' Awful Doins replied.

'By robbin' the rich?' Cut-throat laughed sarcastically. 'That'll never 'appen. Look at you, Black Dog — your sisters-in-law are swimmin' in lard, yet they don't give you a penny.'

'Ah, but I 'ave expectations,' Isaiah said as Grace flushed, unhappy about hearing their private affairs discussed in public. 'Ladies, bring more ale.'

Sarah poured two more jugs full and Grace

143

carried them across to where the smugglers had paused their game of cards to listen to Isaiah's suggestion that the unemployed men of Deal should take up with the free trade.

'What's this? What are you talking about?' she asked, although she knew perfectly well.

'Smugglin', my love,' Isaiah said cheerfully. 'My lovely wife 'as an aversion to the business that used to sustain this town.' He laid careful emphasis on the word, used, she noticed. 'We were just observin' that it's all but died a death since the end of the war with Napoleon. Don't worry your little 'ead about it, though. This is man's talk.' He grinned and looked around at his companions who chuckled and nodded in agreement.

Pained by her husband's dismissal but understanding that the men generally came to the tavern to escape their wives and womenfolk, she returned to the counter.

''Ave you 'eard about this proposal from Floggin' Joe?' Dunk said.

'McCulloch?' Cut-throat asked.

'That's 'im. 'E's plannin' to unite the three separate sections of the Revenue — the cruisers, the Ridin' officers between North Foreland and Dungeness, and the Waterguard — under 'is command, and call it the Coastal Blockade Service. I reckon that'll 'it the free trade 'ard because it makes it nigh impossible to move goods without being intercepted.'

'There's always a way round it,' Isaiah contributed. 'Always.'

'Tell us what you'd do, Black Dog. For old times' sake,' Awful Doins said.

144

Leaning against the counter at Sarah's side, Grace listened to her husband explain how he would evade Flogging Joe and his men, if he was still involved in running goods, which he wasn't, but she could tell from the tone of his voice that he missed the challenge and excitement of lawbreaking. She delivered yet more ale, and then Isaiah stood up again, inviting the men to join him in a singsong. With one easy movement, he jumped on to the table, tankard in hand.

'Come all ye gallant seamen . . . gather round . . .'

They sang 'The Jolly Young Waterman' and 'Married to a Mermaid', before Awful Doins and Lawless joined Isaiah and linked arms with him, regaling the others with the ballad of the pirate, Captain Ward, and his fight with the crew of the *Rainbow*.

Their voices filled with sorrow when they came to the verse where Ward slew the *Rainbow*'s men.

'Go 'ome, go 'ome, says Captain Ward, and tell your king for me,' Isaiah sang.

Awful Doins and Lawless took up the strain. 'If he reigns king all on the land, Ward will reign king on the sea.'

Isaiah raised his tankard to his lips. The men did the same, gulping their ale then wiping their mouths with their sleeves.

'They drink an awful lot,' Grace observed in wonder.

'Like fish,' Sarah agreed. 'It makes them feel better, givin' them the chance to recall past triumphs and wipe out bad memories. For the present, they are like Captain Ward, kings of the sea, yet when

145

they stagger 'ome and fall into their beds, or when they wake in the mornin', the bleak reality of their lot sets in again. Which is why they keep comin' back for more.'

The sound of the door closing alerted Grace to the presence of a well-dressed gentleman and his wife — at least, Grace assumed that the couple were married — approaching the counter with a young postilion in uniform, struggling along behind them with a trunk and a hatbox.

'I'll see to these people,' Grace said.

'Have you a room for the night?' the man enquired as his wife stared nervously towards the smugglers' table.

'We do indeed,' Grace smiled. 'We have one with a sea view. Would you like supper and breakfast included?' She picked up a menu from beneath the counter and placed it in front of him, but he seemed distracted as well he might be, she thought crossly, because Dunk had picked a fight with Lawless who had blood pouring from his nose, and Awful Doins was crawling towards the fireplace where he slumped half-cut in the hearth.

The gentleman's wife jabbed her finger at them. 'I'm not staying here. I don't know why your brother recommended a house of ill-repute to us.'

'I'm sorry, my dear.' He tried to put his hands across her eyes. 'This is an outrage. We're leaving.'

'Oh no. You must stay,' Grace said. 'I can tell them to keep the noise down.'

'I will not have my wife exposed to this display of vice and drunkenness. We'll go and try the Three Kings which is what I should have done in the first place.' He took the lady's arm and left the

146

tavern, the postilion following along behind them, at which point George Minnis arrived.

'Evenin' all. You win some, you lose some, Mrs Feasey. I see that the lady and gentleman have taken their custom elsewhere, which means — I hope — that there is a bed available for your good friend, George.' He placed his hat on the counter as Isaiah approached. 'Good day to you, Sarah. I see that the Rattlers are back.'

'We're celebratin',' Isaiah said. 'Grace, get the man a drink.'

'Black Dog, I need you to stash some goods for me — it's only a temporary measure, but the gobblers are out in force on the marshes, searching the churches, ruins and taverns. One of my wife's relations, a great aunt, died of fright when they broke into her house.'

Isaiah stroked his chin. 'I don't like the sound of it, but— '

'My husband can't help you,' Grace cut in.

With a supercilious smirk, George looked her up and down.

'It isn't your place to say so. If you were my wife, I'd take you aside and give you a good 'idin'.'

She wheeled round to Isaiah, anger pulsing in her throat, because she guessed that his yearning for George's acceptance and respect would make him weaken. 'Don't. You promised me . . .'

'I know,' George said, good-humouredly. 'Out of consideration for your wife's feelin's, I'll withdraw my request.' She turned back and thought she saw him mouth, for the present, but she couldn't be sure. At least she had won the battle this time. 'I'm stayin' the night. I'll join you and

147

the lads if there's no objection.'

The men welcomed him. Digger and Sarah wished everyone goodnight and went home, leaving the rest to continue drinking until long past midnight, when Grace gave in to a wave of exhaustion, bolted the tavern door and retired to bed.

The next morning, having served George devilled kidneys, bread and butter, and seen him on his way, she cleared up after the smugglers, noticing how Isaiah's tankard was still full to the brim. Plucking up the courage to broach the subject of how much ale he wasted, because she'd noticed how her questions sometimes seemed to irritate him, she asked, 'Why don't you ever drink what I bring you?'

'I never touch a drop, apart from takin' a little milk and brandy on special occasions,' he replied, warming his hands at the fire. 'I like to make out that I'm one of them. I make them feel good — that tempts them to buy me a drink and drink more themselves. After that, they might 'ave a bite of supper — a piece of salted pork is a marvellous stimulus to a man's thirst . . .'

'Didn't you declare that the drinks were on the house last night?'

'Only the first ones — they know that. They aren't stupid.'

'I didn't keep track of how many they had.'

'It's no problem.' He wandered across to the counter, took a handful of stones from his pocket and dropped them into the cups. 'That'll be about right.'

Grace felt uncomfortable about Isaiah's deceit in inducing his friends to keep drinking, especially

148

when she thought of their wives and children going hungry at home.

'I know what you're thinkin'.' He spoke softly into her ear. 'But we need the money ourselves.'

'I wish there was another way.'

'There was, but I seem to remember that you rejected it. You could do with something to cheer you up — why don't you go and see your sister tomorrow when Sarah's back? Maybe you can settle your quarrel with Louisa now that a decent length of time 'as elapsed.'

'That's very thoughtful of you.' She turned and threw her arms around his neck. 'Will you be here, though? We're expecting a delivery from the brewery and I don't want to leave it to Sarah.'

'I'd better get in touch with 'em and ask 'em to send another couple of casks since our friends drank the place dry last night. Yes, I'll be around to receive it.'

'This isn't a trick to get me out of the way?'

'Why would I do that?' His brow furrowed. 'Oh, I see. You think I've broken my promise and done a deal with George? You know I 'aven't — you were there when we were talkin' about it.' She didn't know how to answer when he went on, 'Would I lie to you?', so she kissed him instead.

★ ★ ★

The following morning, having dressed in her navy gown, cloak and felt bonnet, Grace went into the kitchen where she found Sarah finishing off the preparations for the noon repast. The steam from the pot on the fire had condensed on the windows

149

and was running down the glass, a contrast with the ice that had formed on the upstairs windows on what was one of the coldest December days Grace could remember.

'Where are you off to?' Sarah slurped from the spoon she was using to stir the pot.

'I'm going to call on my sister, fully prepared for her to send me straight back with a flea in my ear.' Grace had seen Louisa and Jason around Deal, but neither of them had rushed over to her to offer her an olive branch.

The stew bubbled up and boiled over, sizzling into the fire.

'Sarah, you need to pay closer attention . . .'

'Oops,' she exclaimed, before lifting the pan away with a thick cloth and putting it on the table. 'You know, I can't help thinkin' that you're goin' to come down here one mornin' and send me packin' for bein' so careless.'

'What on earth would I do that for? Sarah, I'm not giving up our friendship over a handful of oats and a couple of pounds of burnt turnips. I'm not saying that I couldn't look after this place without you, but I really wouldn't want to. I'd miss you.'

'Well, thank you. You might not know it, but you were a real comfort to me while Digger was locked up. Go on. Off you go. I'll be all right here.'

'I feel much better,' Grace smiled, but it was with some trepidation that she left the Rattling Cat to walk the short distance to Cockle Swamp Alley. She hesitated outside the familiar green door, her chest tight with yearning for the years when Compass Cottage was home, and she was a young girl without a care in the world, not a wife with a troublesome husband. She knocked on the door.

Louisa opened it.

'Oh, it's you,' she said, as Kitty ran out and began winding herself around Grace's ankles, holding her tail like a shepherd's crook.

'I'm sorry — I shouldn't have disturbed you . . .'

'No, not at all. Grace, it's wonderful to see you. Come in! Jason's out with the cutter.'

'I wasn't sure if I'd be welcome.' Grace hesitated, then followed Louisa into the parlour and removed her outdoor clothes.

'I don't know what I was thinking. When I realised that by refusing to see you after the wedding, I was punishing myself, I was too proud to come round to make amends. I've missed you these past months.'

They settled on the chaise with Kitty lying between them and talked as if they'd never been apart.

'I think it's best that Jason doesn't know you called — he's still pretty sore about what happened with the Rattlers at your wedding breakfast.'

'It was my fault.'

'He thinks he should have realised that your loyalties would lie with your husband. Never mind . . . Tell me how you're getting on. Tell me everything.'

Grace talked about her friendship with Sarah, how they took delight in gammoning the elbow-crookers who tried to take advantage of them, and told her a few tales about their guests and the items, including a wig, glove stretcher and

151

jar of limes, that they left behind.

'I'm glad you're happy,' Louisa said. 'You are happy?'

Grace smiled. 'Isaiah is the best husband anyone could have . . .'

'Jason excepted,' Louisa smiled. 'And Winnie would say the same about Billy, of course. You're with child, aren't you? You have that look about you.'

'I think it's likely — I've been sick every morning for weeks. Oh dear. Perhaps I shouldn't have come . . .'

'I'm pleased for you.' Louisa stood up and wandered across to the window. 'I've tried to come to terms with my situation, but I never will — I'll always long to be a mother. You don't know this, but soon after your wedding, Jason and I applied to adopt an orphaned infant from the poorhouse. Just before we were due to bring her home, she passed away.'

'I'm so sorry,' Grace said in a small voice.

'We decided not to risk breaking our hearts all over again. We've had to accept that we'll never experience the joys of parenthood, but it hasn't stopped me hoping and praying that one day I'll find a motherless infant left for me in a basket on the doorstep.' After a pause, Louisa gasped, 'Jason and Albert are coming this way.'

Grace jumped up. 'I thought they were out. Shall I hide?'

'Don't be silly,' Louisa said as she went to greet them.

'We're back sooner than we thought,' Grace heard Jason say from the hallway. 'Albert's with

152

to defend the three hundred or so landsmen who turn up when they're runnin' goods.

They're armed and more than willin' to use violence against the Revenue on land and at sea. We have orders to clamp down on them and close them down, but we're against a powerful and intelligent gentleman, a George Minnis of Snargate who bought Black Dog's share in the lugger. He calls himself the Captain.'

Grace almost choked on her tea. Louisa patted her on the back.

'A gentleman, did you say?' Grace asked, clearing her throat.

'That's how he likes to present himself,' Jason answered. 'Have you met him?' He held her gaze.

She didn't flinch or blink as she said, 'No, I don't believe that I have.'

'He owns a farm on the marshes where he rears sheep and cattle, but it's rumoured that not long ago, he found a stash of contraband buried behind a derelict barn. He sold it to buy a house in Snargate which he's turned into an unlicensed beerhouse, reputed to be a place where anything goes, if you know what I mean. He's the devil in disguise, charmin' yet dangerous, not the kind of man you'd want to meet on the marshes on a winter's night.'

'Or a summer's one at that,' Albert added brightly, laying down his knife and fork. Grace couldn't help contrasting his manners with those of her husband, acknowledging that she and Albert might have made a reasonable match, if it hadn't been for the irresistible attraction of Isaiah's dark and handsome appearance and his dangerous reputation.

Within the cosy confines of the cottage kitchen, she felt safe and warm, and reluctant to leave her sister and Kitty behind, but eventually she excused herself and made her way back to the Rattling Cat, having promised Louisa that she would see her again soon.

'Isaiah's been waitin' for you,' Sarah said, meeting her at the tavern door.

'He knows I was at my sister's — it was his suggestion. I told him I wouldn't be back until after noon. He treats my words like flies, batting them away without acknowledgement,' Grace sighed.

'It would be a rare 'usband who truly listens to 'is wife.'

'My ears are burnin'.' Isaiah climbed up the steps from the cellar. 'You should 'ave warned me that you weren't plannin' to return in time to 'elp Sarah open up.'

'Am I not free to come and go as I please?' she said hotly.

'You're my wife and you answer to me now.' He took her hand, chafing her skin. 'When your ma died, God rest 'er soul, everyone said that your father allowed you and your sisters too much freedom. 'Avin' reflected on my decision, I'd prefer that you don't go and see Louisa again.'

'Why ever not?' Great walms of annoyance rose in her breast like a school of herring bubbling across the surface of the sea.

'Because I say so. No reason, except that you 'ave to look after yourself and the babe that's growin' inside you.'

'How do you— '

156

'It's only natural that an attentive 'usband becomes familiar with the pattern of 'is wife's courses.' Ignoring Sarah's presence, Isaiah took Grace in his arms and kissed her. 'I'm pleased about the baby. I'll buy a new boat one day for goin' out fishin' with my sons.'

'What if it's a girl?' She tousled his hair, running her fingers through his curls.

'I don't mind — we'll 'ave more.'

'Not too many more,' she said. 'I remember when Winnie was in labour with Pamela — it gave me the frights.'

'I always wished I'd 'ad brothers and sisters — I led a lonely life as an only child. I'm an 'usband and now I'm goin' to be a father — it's a ruddy miracle. The lads said I'd never win you — in fact they 'ad a bet on it.'

'They didn't!' she exclaimed.

'It was nothing major.'

'I should hope not,' she said, offended by the thought of the gang of smugglers egging him on in his pursuit. It was as if they had invaded her marriage, rather spoiling her illusion that Isaiah had chosen her purely out of love and his own volition. 'I presume that the delivery arrived.'

'It did, and everythin's stowed away shipshape and Bristol fashion. Grace, you are a good wife to me, and although I don't like to bare my heart, I love you more every day . . . ' he grinned ' . . . and night. Especially night.'

She pulled away from him, relieved that she hadn't felt obliged to explain how she'd also met Jason and Albert. Not only would he be annoyed to learn that they'd talked disparagingly of George

Minnis, but she suspected that he'd be upset about his wife having spent time in the company of the young lieutenant. She sensed too from the way he'd deftly changed the topic of conversation from the delivery to his deepening affection for her that he was hiding something, and she was determined to find out what it was.

10

Hope for the Best, Prepare for the Worst

When Isaiah had been about fifteen, he had rounded up the younger children on the beach to recount the tale of the Fey Lady who haunted the cellars and alleyways of the town. The mere mention of the name had sent shivers down Grace's spine, and being only seven years old at the time, she had buried her face in Louisa's skirts.

'It's a story,' one of the boys had said, 'nothin' but a load of hogwash.'

'I can prove it,' Isaiah had bragged. 'An acquaintance of Mr Jackson — you know 'im.'

'Mr Jackson's a boatman,' one of the Roper boys had piped up.

'Anyway, 'e broke into the cellar at the Rattlin' Cat — when my father dragged 'is dead body up the steps, 'e said 'is eyes were fixed wide open like 'e'd seen a ghost.'

'What did the coroner say?' Louisa had asked. 'There must have been an inquest.'

'I don't know. I don't remember. I was only a little lad.'

'So you can't prove the existence of this ghost,' she'd mocked.

'Oh, there's more. 'E wasn't the only victim.'

Grace had dared to look up when he uttered a bloodcurdling laugh. There was a bone on the ground that he claimed was from a pile that they'd found at the tavern.

'I took the best lookin' one, not wanting to disturb anyone's peace of mind more than I 'ave to. Somebody needs to l'arn you that girls are supposed to keep their mouths shut.'

Louisa had called Winnie to her, taken hold of Grace's hand and walked away.

If Isaiah's plan had been to frighten them, he had succeeded, but Grace hadn't thought any more of it, until now as she went snooping down the steps into the cellar. Holding up her lantern, she looked towards the heap of fresh sawdust at one end that came in through the trapdoor from the street above, then examined the few barrels of ale that were neatly lined up along the wall. There were two half-ankers of spirits, that was all. Dissatisfied with the outcome of her search, she climbed the steps into the taproom to find Sarah at the counter, looking at her with an air of suspicion.

'What were you doin' down there? I almost shut you in.'

'Sarah, do you know if the Rattlers are running goods again?'

'Your 'usband, you mean, or the gang in gen'ral?'

'Both,' she replied.

'I know Digger's plannin' 'ow best to get in with George and the Greys. I don't like the idea one little bit, but 'e won't listen to me. The gang used to do a bit of labourin' 'ere and there, but they can't find work durin' the winter, and without the boat,

160

they're scuppered. They can't even go out fishin'.'

'What about Isaiah?'

'I can't speak for 'im.' Sarah leaned towards her and lowered her voice. 'I'd advise you to watch your back when it comes to Mr Minnis. Rumour 'as it that when one of 'is men complained that 'e 'adn't paid 'im what 'e promised for a night's work, 'e went missin'. No one's seen 'im since.'

Were Sarah's words a threat or a warning? Grace wondered, deciding to err on the side of caution and delay her search of the tavern until her friend had left to buy provisions at the market, and Isaiah was out with the dog.

When they'd gone, she lit a candle and carried it over to the corner of the dining room, where there was a second trapdoor. She hauled it open, pausing briefly as the hinges squealed before gazing down at the steep steps that led into the void. She almost changed her mind, but her desire to find out exactly what Isaiah was up to drove her on.

Treading carefully, she made her way into the bowels of the building, where the pungent odour of rodents, brandy and tobacco assaulted her nostrils. A shiver ran down her spine as something scrambled across her foot while she walked slowly along a passageway, the candlelight playing on the stone walls that were oozing moisture and mould. Was this where One Eye had kept Nancy locked away?

Within a few more paces, she found her way barred by a number of tubs stacked floor to ceiling. Her heart sank.

This was the evidence that she'd been looking

161

for — she knew he'd been up to something. His behaviour had been very suspicious, too smoky by half.

She held her breath, sensing a malign presence within the passageway. It was too late to run and there was nowhere to go as a pair of hands settled heavily on her waist.

'Gotcha!'

'Isaiah!' The candle went out when she spun round to face him.

'What are you doin', sneakin' about down 'ere? If you wanted to come and see where Nancy 'id 'erself away, you only 'ad to ask. Out of the goodness of 'er 'eart, she did a bit of 'auntin' for us as the Fey Lady, to earn 'er keep and keep nosy parkers like you out of 'ere. She did the same for your family, I should point out. 'Ave you seen enough, my love?'

'I've seen more than enough,' she said, trying to force her way past him.

'Then you must unsee it,' he replied sternly.

'You've returned to the free trade. You've gone in with Mr Minnis behind my back. Why did you let him bully you into it?'

'He needed a favour from a friend — I did it willin'ly. I'm not scared of the likes of 'im.' He took a step back, his expression flickering from appeasement to anger.

'I hold the view that it would be prudent to regard Mr Minnis with a degree of chariness, but if you're so cocksure about where you stand with him, you must tell him to get his stash moved by morning, and we'll say no more about it.'

'George is taking some money off what I owe

162

'im for this. It isn't doin' any 'arm down 'ere.'

Ignoring him, she went on, 'And I want you to tell the Rattlers that they aren't welcome here.'

'I beg your pardon.'

'You saw what happened the other night. That couple left because of them. What's the point of spending money on improving the rooms to attract a better class of customer when the tap-room is a smugglers' den?'

'There's no need to be snooty about it,' he said, smirking.

'It's business,' she pointed out, infuriated because he wasn't taking her seriously. 'We need people with money in their pockets, ones who will pay for the extras — meals and drinks — and offer generous tips. They won't come if they think the gobblers will be knocking at our door. You've disappointed me. This isn't what you promised.'

'Hey, let's not fight.' He stood against the wall to allow her to pass. She whisked up the steps and took a gulp of fresh air before shouting at him, 'We wouldn't have to fight, if you weren't so . . . unreliable. You lied to me, Isaiah. You've ruined everything.'

She spun on her heels and headed into the tap-room.

'Where are you goin'?'

'Upstairs!' she yelled. 'I want to be on my own.' She ran into their room and flung herself down on the bed, sobbing. As well as being her husband and lover, Isaiah was turning out to be a complex character and his response to her complaint made her uneasy. She wondered how he would respond if she really crossed him and berated herself for

163

marrying in haste. If she'd taken the time — gone along with Jason and Louisa's idea of a six-month engagement — she'd have discovered his flaws and foibles in advance and used that knowledge to decide whether or not to go through with the wedding. Would she still have married him? At this very moment, she wasn't sure.

The next time she looked in the dining room, Isaiah had nailed the trapdoor down.

* * *

Although she and Isaiah kissed and made up, Grace remained on edge, expecting the Revenue to call, or George to turn up, wanting his goods and his money. She managed to sweet-talk Mr Tapping into waiting another month for his payment and put their prices up when she discovered that the cost of ale was the same as when One Eye had been running the tavern.

One evening on Sarah's day off, George called at closing time.

'You're too late, Mr Minnis,' Grace said formally.

'Grace, you will serve our friend,' Isaiah said. 'What will you have, George?'

'Some ale and whatever you 'ave on for supper.' He moved up to the counter and leaned against it. 'This isn't a social call. I've been askin' myself when I'll get my money back.'

'I've told you. I 'ave a little investment that's about to bear fruit. I'll settle up with you soon, by the middle of January at the latest. You can rely on me — I'm a man of my word.'

164

'I sincerely hope so, because I'd 'ate to think that my judgement had let me down. Instinct tells me that you're the genuine article, one of the old-style smugglers, bold and honest with the cunnin' of a fox.'

'You flatter me,' Isaiah beamed.

'I speak the truth.'

'Grace, give George a nip of brandy on the house and fetch some of that cold beef we 'ave left.' She did as he asked, returning from the kitchen with a platter of meats and pickles which she put on the counter.

'That's a fine serving of wittles,' George said before turning back to Isaiah. 'Did I mention that I need your 'elp?'

'I'll do my best for you,' Isaiah responded.

'He's got some of my men, that Commander Witherall — Ol' Witherin', I call him. He didn't find any goods on them, but he took them on to his vessel and carried them off to Dover on some trumped-up charges. I wonder if you can — ' he slipped his paw around Isaiah's shoulders, crushing them gently together like a vice '— use your influence and apply some kind of pressure on Marlin, whatever it takes without actually killin' 'im.'

Isaiah grimaced. 'Let me see.'

Grace noticed George's long yellow fingernails, more like claws . . . . a bear's claws.

'I hope you 'aven't 'ad a change of 'eart, my friend. My lads are in trouble. As their leader, it's up to me to extricate them from their situation. It's a simple case of wrongful arrest — I'm sure if you 'ad his ear, as you claim, you can 'ave

165

a little word in it and persuade 'im to drop the charges.' He released his grip and Isaiah shook himself off like a wet dog while Musket looked on, seemingly unwilling to offer a growl or bare his teeth in defence of his master. 'Or if you don't think he'll listen to you, your pretty wife could twist 'is arm over it.' George looked straight at her, and although her instinct was to turn away, she stared him out. 'She's an asset to you, Black Dog, in more ways than one, I should opine. It seems odd that you didn't mention to your friend that your wife was a Lennicker before marriage and calls Marlin 'er brother-in-law, but perhaps it slipped your mind. I've done a little diggin', liking to know everything about the people I'm dealing with, so as not to have any nasty surprises.'

Not for the first time, Grace realised how clever George was, changing his manner of speech and demeanour to fit in with whomsoever he was speaking to, gentleman, merchant or smuggler.

Whatever he was suggesting, though, she wasn't going to do it, and that's what she told Isaiah after midnight when the tavern closed and George had gone, leaving stone-cold sober despite drinking an impressive amount of liquor.

'You'll do this one favour to your lovin' husband, to get 'im out of an 'ole.'

'Another one? It seems to me that you are either very careless or incredibly unfortunate.'

'You'll go round to your sister's immediately and catch Marlin before 'e goes on his way to Dover for the 'earin' in the mornin'.'

'I will not. I will not lurk around furtively in dark alleyways, running errands for George Minnis,' she spat.

'It isn't for 'im — it's for me. Don't you listen, cloth ears?' He moved round and pulled her close. Her spine stiffened.

'Nothing you can do or say will change my mind. Jason is incorruptible.'

'Please, my darlin' . . . '

'No!' She stamped her foot. 'I won't do it. And far be it from me to advise my husband in his wisdom— ' she challenged him furiously.

'I have a feelin' you're going to,' he interrupted.

'He should cut all ties with Minnis.' She faltered, knowing that at present it was asking the impossible.

'And I will do, my love, as soon as I come into the money.' Isaiah's shoulders slumped. He looked weary, even afraid, she thought. 'I didn't tell 'im who you were because I knew somethin' like this would 'appen. I didn't want him involvin' you in his schemes.'

'You wanted to protect me?'

'Yes,' he said softly. 'I love you — I don't want to see you get 'urt.'

'You're afraid of Mr Minnis?'

''E doesn't scare me.'

'Then you won't make me go to see Jason.'

'When you were fetchin' 'is supper, George and I agreed that you'd do it.'

'Without consulting me?'

'When we got married, you vowed to obey me. Nothin's changed.' He paused for a moment. 'I shall tell 'im that you went round to the cottage, but Marlin was out with 'is men. It was too late. Yes, that will do. A little white lie never 'urts no

167

one.'

'I'm going to bed,' she said, still angry with him, but remembering Louisa's advice not to go to sleep on an argument, she apologised. 'I'm sorry for arguing with you.' She had a sense that George Minnis wasn't the problem — it was Isaiah. He was his own worst enemy, blagging his way into corners whence he couldn't escape. His irritation seemed to dissipate as they prepared to retire, and she did her best to forgive him over their first major disagreement. However, she felt that it was important not to forget it. Marriage was like sailing on the open ocean and she would not risk disaster by acting the meek, unthinking wife.

As she lay in bed, cocooned in Isaiah's arms, she listened to the regular thudding of his heart-beat and the dog snoring lightly at the end of the bed. She never had got her way over the dog, but she had grown used to its presence.

'Marlin did the dirty on me — everyone forgets that,' Isaiah said suddenly. 'When the gangers got 'im that time, 'e set me up to take the fall. 'E told the press officer who was 'volunteerin' 'im for the King's shillin', that 'e was a boatman by the name of Isaiah Feasey. That meant that when 'e escaped from them, it would be my name that would be marked with an R for run, not 'is.'

'I didn't know he'd done that,' Grace observed.

'It didn't 'ave any consequence for me — I 'ad a letter from Doctor Audley to show anyone who threatened to deprive me of my liberty that I was too incapacitated by illness to work ashore, let alone serve on one of 'is Majesty's ships. But

168

Marlin, 'e's always 'ad more than 'is fair share of luck. I don't understand it.'

'I don't think you can say that.'

'It's true. Everythin' he touches turns to gold, whereas for me, it crumbles to dust. I'll always remember 'ow 'e came up smellin' of roses on the night the *White 'ind* was lost.'

'I remember it well.' She didn't like to add that it had been exactly a year after One Eye had injured Pa when the worst storm in living memory had started to rage. Grace had run down to the shore that evening with her sisters, following the sound of alarm bells and whistles. An apocalyptic wind blasted across the sea, raising a furious swell and ripping tiles from the roofs of the houses along the shore.

The *Whimbrel* and *Good Intent* were side by side on the shingle, the boatmen assembled near one of the capstans. Somewhere across the roadstead, a schooner had been ripped from her moorings and blown on to the Sands.

Isaiah came marching across to confer with Jason.

'You will agree that neither one of us goes out tonight,' he said. 'We can't possibly launch the luggers in this — they'll be blown back and smashed to smithereens on the beach.'

'There are women and children on that vessel — of course we're goin'. Oh, I see.' Jason brushed raindrops from his nose. 'You're runnin' scared, and afraid we'll get there first and take the spoils. I don't care what you and your crew decide to do. This is my callin' — I'm not going to stand by and let them perish.'

169

'Then you're even more stupid than I thought.' Isaiah frowned at Jason, then shook his head. 'Go out, and your men will die.'

Although Jason gave his crew the option of remaining ashore, they were determined to try. To Grace's horror, Louisa said she would go with them, adding that her presence would reassure the women and children on board the stricken schooner. After a brief argument over the wisdom of having a woman on board, Louisa left with the lugger as the sea flared and lightning flashed.

A giant wave came ashore as the *Whimbrel* flew down the beach. The roller burst into a towering mass of foam, enveloping the lugger completely as she crashed into the water with an ear-splitting bang.

'She's lost — the *Whimbrel*'s gorn,' the crowd screamed from the beach.

Grace held her breath, waiting for the boat to rise again on the crest of the following wave. After what seemed like an eternity, the *Whimbrel* bobbed up to cheering and crying, before she began to thrash through the seething water and spindrift towards the deadly Sands while Isaiah and his crew looked on, shaking their heads and making grim predictions.

'It's all very well, but you 'ave to make 'ard decisions as a captain,' Grace heard Isaiah say above the whistling wind. 'Why should I risk my comrades' lives? I'm doin' right by my men and their families, the wives and children who depend on them.'

Grace waited on tenterhooks, not knowing who was right and who was wrong, and eventually, the

Whimbrel returned through the spray. It was a quiet triumph on Jason's part — some of the crew and passengers of the schooner were saved while others were missing, presumed drowned.

When Louisa had told them the full story of the grim rescue, Grace had realised how easily it could have gone the other way, that the crew of the *Whimbrel*, Jason and Louisa could have succumbed to a watery grave.

She shivered at the memory. Isaiah held her tighter and tucked the quilt around her shoulders. 'You're cold,' he murmured.

'A little,' Grace admitted. 'You mustn't keep blaming yourself for the decision you made,' she told him. 'Who is the braver man? Jason for risking more lives to save others? Or you for being strong enough to say no?'

'Marlin took a chance and came out an 'ero,' Isaiah concluded.

'That's as maybe, but you are going to have the one thing that he desires beyond all else, something he'd give up his home, even his boat for.'

'What's that?'

'A child.' She touched the slight curve of her belly, praying that she wouldn't lose her babies as Louisa had done.

Isaiah grunted. 'Well I never. Why don't Marlin let Louisa take another man into her bed?'

'Because it's Louisa who's barren — when she was ill, she lost the infant she was carrying. Doctor Audley is of the opinion that she'll never bear a live child. And before you suggest it, Jason wouldn't dream of asking another woman to carry his child for them.'

171

'Your father never 'ad such scruples when it came to marital fidelity.'

'That was different,' she said sharply.

'I shouldn't 'ave said that. It was wrong of me.'

'It was,' she scolded him. 'Mind you, it's a lesson to any husband who's tempted to stray.'

''E always feared bein' caught out. My father used to blackmail 'im out of the odd tub of brandy now and again.'

Grace closed her eyes, picturing Ma and her sisters on a sunlit beach, laughing and singing as they helped Pa and Billy unload buckets of silvery fish from the Pamela, and lug them back to the cottage. Perhaps life would be different when her baby came, more joyous and carefree. Maybe when Isaiah's investment came to fruition, they would be able to pay off their debts and concentrate on running the tavern. She didn't like to ask what it was exactly, suspecting that it had something to do with the free trade and George's property, which remained, as far as she was aware, piled up in the passageway beneath the dining room. As Musket continued to snore, she cuddled against her husband, thinking it best to let sleeping dogs lie.

11

More Gristle than Meat

The weather grew colder and bleaker, and on a snowy Christmas Eve, Grace and Isaiah attended the service with Sarah and Digger at St George's Chapel. Even though Grace wore gloves, an extra petticoat and two pairs of woollen stockings, she was frozen to the bone.

'I'm surprised you agreed to join me,' she whispered, her breath turning to mist as they made their way outside afterwards.

'I thought it would be cosier in church than at 'ome — I was wrong. 'Ere, 'ave a nip o' brandy.' Grinning, Isaiah pulled a flask from his great-coat pocket. 'No, not here,' she said firmly. 'Put it away.'

'I wouldn't say no to a drop of liquor,' Digger said, his nose blue with cold.

'I wasn't offerin' it to you.'

'Share and share alike — that's my motto.' Digger put his arm around Isaiah's shoulders.

'Well, it isn't mine,' Isaiah jested, shaking him off. 'Marlin, season's greetin's to you and your loved ones,' he called across to Jason who was in conversation with Reverend North and Louisa, the snow slowly turning their umbrellas white.

Having excused themselves to the vicar, the couple walked along the path to join them, their footprints rapidly disappearing behind them.

Grace embraced her sister. 'How are you?'

'All the better for seeing you.' Louisa took a step back as Jason addressed Isaiah.

'I've heard that you've become acquainted with Mr Minnis. I'd be grateful if you'd let me know when he's next in town. As a law-abidin' citizen, I'm sure you'd wish to see him put away.'

'I'm not and never will be a snake in the grass,' Isaiah said as Grace held his arm. 'Not that I'm particularly familiar with this gentleman of whom you speak.'

'Gentleman? He's a free trader,' Jason smiled.

'What's 'e supposed to 'ave done?'

'That's the problem. I don't know, only that his name keeps croppin' up whenever there's a run in the offin'. It's no secret that we've had some success in intercepting a couple of large consignments of contraband at sea recently, but we haven't been able to identify the brains behind the operation — not yet, but we will.'

'I don't know much about 'im, not bein' in that line of business any more. I've given it up out of respect for my missus.'

'So I wouldn't find anythin' untoward if I ordered my men to search the tavern?'

Grace noticed how Isaiah's body stiffened. 'I'd 'ope that you wouldn't disturb us during the next sennight. It's the season of goodwill and my wife's birthday.'

'On the last day of December,' Louisa contributed. 'Grace, I can't believe that you'll be eighteen.

174

Would you like to join us for a light supper before you go home?'

'Oh yes,' Grace said, but Isaiah interrupted her.

'It's kind of you, but no, we're goin' straight back — my wife needs 'er sleep.'

Louisa and Jason wished them farewell and they began to make their way back to the tavern through driving snow that stung Grace's face and seeped into her clothes.

'Why did you say that? Why didn't you let me speak for myself?'

'Because I know what's best for you . . . and the baby that's growin' inside you. 'Urry up, or you'll catch a chill. You should be grateful that you 'ave an attentive husband. It's better than 'avin' one who doesn't care.'

'I know — I shouldn't grumble,' she sighed. 'What are you going to do about George's property?'

'What are you talkin' about?'

'You know very well.'

'Now I'm aware that the gobblers are sniffin' about, I'll make sure it's gone afore you can say Jack Robinson.'

He was as good as his word. When George sent his men to collect the goods from the hiding hole, it was as if a great weight had fallen from his shoulders because he made unusually merry with Grace, Sarah and the customers. On Grace's birthday, he closed the tavern when the church-bells struck five and sent Sarah home.

'I'm honoured,' Grace said as she snuffed out the candles in the taproom and placed the guard in front of the fire where the logs had been reduced to glowing skeletons.

'It isn't every day that you turn eighteen. I thought we should mark the occasion. 'Ere, I 'ave a surprise for you.' He took her hand. 'Close yer peepers. No cheatin'.'

Squeezing her eyes almost shut so she could still peer through her lashes, she let him lead her into the dining room.

'You can open them now. What do you think?'

One of the tables had been laid for two, with a white cloth, a pair of balloon glasses and a centre-piece of pink silk roses.

'You did this for me?'

'For my darlin' wife, who loves me more than I deserve.' Isaiah pulled a chair up for her and, with a flourish, pretended to dust it down before she took her seat. 'I shall see if the maid is ready for us to dine.'

While he disappeared into the kitchen, Grace picked up one of the knives and examined her reflection in the polished surface.

'I would have dressed for dinner, if I'd known,' she called.

'What was that?'

'Never mind. It doesn't matter.' She smiled to herself — it was Isaiah who had cloth ears, not her.

He returned from the kitchen with an apron tied around his lean middle, a maid's cap on his head and two platters of pie and gravy balanced precariously in his hands.

'Oh, you are a picture,' she giggled as he placed them on the table. 'Does 'er ladyship require any condiments? Mustard? Salt?'

176

'I don't think so,' she smiled, touched by his efforts.

'You're spoiling me.'

'Oh, I almost forgot. I 'ave a gift for you.' He hurried off, strewing the apron and cap behind him, and came back with a box from the side table. He pulled a chair up close to hers and gave her the box in exchange for several kisses.

'Open it,' he said eventually.

She raised the lid and looked inside. 'It's a box inside a box,' she said, delighted with the contents: a jewellery casket made of rosewood and inset with mother-of-pearl flowers. She took it out and opened it, finding a silver brooch nestling in the blue velvet lining. As she made to pick it up, Isaiah snatched it and pinned it to her dress.

'I knew it would suit you — it brings out the colour of your eyes,' he said gruffly, leaning in for another kiss.

At that instant, her life was perfect and everything she had dreamt it would be. She had a loving husband who had changed his ways and occupation, she'd renewed ties with Louisa and Jason, and she had a belly swelling with child. She tried to forget George Minnis — he was the dead fly in the ointment of the apothecary.

Isaiah poured some wine and they began to eat.

'When do you think you'll 'ear from your sister?' he asked, wiping gravy from his chin.

'Louisa? We saw her outside the church on Christmas Eve.'

'The other one, Winnie.'

'I'm not expecting to,' she said sadly.

'She's bound to be in touch — you come into

177

the money today. Your trust fund . . . ' With an avaricious smile, he reached across the table and stroked her hand. 'You're entitled to receive it when you turn eighteen.'

'That?' Her pulse fluttered with panic. Isaiah's generosity marking the occasion of her birthday, and the 'investment' that he'd told George about suddenly made sense. 'Oh dear. When I said I was marrying you, Winnie told me that she'd give the benefit of it to the poorhouse children. I had no choice but to give up my interest in it.'

'Oh Grace, why didn't you tell me?' Isaiah jumped to his feet and strode across the room, before turning around with both hands on his head, his fingers buried in his hair as if he was trying to crush his own skull.

'I didn't think it mattered,' she stammered.

'Of course, it — ' he swore '— does.'

'I was going to tell you, but it was never the right time, and then you started talking about some investment you were about to receive and I assumed that you had no longer had need of Winnie's money.'

'I've been bankin' on it to pay off my debts.' He spun round again and punched the wall, leaving the imprint of his fist and a sickening ache in Grace's chest. Silenced, she laid down her knife and fork.

'I should have guessed,' she said when he pivoted back to her, rubbing his knuckles.

'If I'd known, I wouldn't 'ave let you run riot spendin' on linens for the beds and fresh flowers every day.' Anger, like a series of daggers, flashed from his eyes.

178

'You said you were doing well . . .' she faltered. 'The money never was really mine. Winnie
intended it for a rainy day.'

'If this isn't a rainy day, I don't know what is.'

Naively, she hadn't mentioned the trust since
before their wedding, confident that her husband
would support her. Considering his optimism
about making more money from the tavern and
guest rooms, she'd felt that she had no need to
concern herself with his financial position, and
like a fool, she had ignored Louisa's advice. Ma
had used to deal with the Lennickers' accounts.
When she died, Pa ignored them and left Grace
and her sisters neck-deep in debt. It had been
Louisa who had suffered the most, being exposed
to the threat of losing her virtue and the roof over
their heads to Pa's attorney, if she didn't obtain
the means of paying him back.

Now it was Grace's turn to suffer as she sat
meekly, wondering how to deal with Isaiah's continued haranguing.

'It was a dowry as such. 'Ow could your sister
cut you off like that? And 'ow did I end up with a
spendthrift of a wife?'

'You gave me permission to purchase whatever
I wanted, anything that would set the Rattling Cat
above all others.'

'I told you that all a traveller needs are a bed
and pisspot. I didn't say you could spend the
'ousekeepin' like water,' he insisted. 'Your memory is like a sieve.'

'It is not,' she countered, not wanting to inflame
his irritation, but determined to stand her ground.
'It's your memory that's gone awry, and the way

179

you do your sums in your head.'

She got up from the table and began to clear the plates, not caring that neither of them had finished.

'Leave those,' Isaiah snapped. 'Sit down.'

'I have no desire to remain in your presence for a moment longer,' she snapped back.

'I learn more about my wife with every passin' day. You are too outspoken for my likin'.'

'If you'd wanted meek and mild, you should have married a meaker!'

He stared at her, the tension between them beginning to dissipate as a smile spread across his face. He began to fumble with the apron ties behind his back.

'It looks like you need some help,' she said, as he yanked at the knot.

'I can do it.' Eventually, he gave in.

'I wish you would talk freely with me,' she said later, when they were retiring to bed. 'If I'd known about your debt— '

'It's our debt now,' he interrupted as Musket wandered into the bedroom, his claws clacking across the floor, before he paused then leapt on to the bed.

'That's what I mean — if you'd shared this with me, I wouldn't have spent the money — ' she hesitated before going on '— oh, it's no use crying over spilt milk. It's done and we have to find our path out of it.'

'There's only one way I know,' he said softly.

'Not that,' she said, removing the brooch and putting it away in the box which she left in pride of place on the dressing table. 'For the sake of our unborn child, not that. I will not be a smuggler's wife.'

'Then I'll 'ave to 'ave a word with George to see if we can come to some other arrangement.'

'How much exactly do we owe?' She stroked the curve of her belly as their baby quickened.

'Several 'undred pounds,' Isaiah said, his tone one of misery.

'As much as that.' She touched her throat, afraid for a moment that she was about to faint. 'We are in deep then,' she said, recovering her wits.

'I'd say we're in danger of drowning in it. It's a disaster.' Isaiah got into bed and turned to face the other way when she joined him.

'Don't you love me any more?' she asked in a small voice.

He rolled over. 'I love you more than anythin', Grace. I just wish you'd told me about Winnie's change of 'eart afore, but let's not go over that again. I'll deal with George.'

Isaiah was awake all night, and Grace could feel him tossing and turning, and when he went out with Musket in the morning, his expression was one of a man who had eaten a pie containing more gristle than meat. Married life wasn't turning out as Grace had anticipated and she couldn't stop brooding over what she had got herself into. The best she could hope for was that it would be different when the baby came, but that wouldn't be until at least May, and Mr Minnis was expecting Isaiah to settle the debt in the New Year.

★ ★ ★

181

Early on a freezing mid-January morning, when Grace opened the window to shake out her duster, she noticed a gaggle of urchins, including some of the shore boys whom she recognised from the capstan grounds, wandering along the street. Their sombre expressions and silence matched the pall of grey fog that had drifted in from the sea. Their eyes glittered from their pinched faces as they looked up.

'Where are you going?' she called, as she peered past the icicles that had formed from the over-flowing gutter above.

Several walked on, ignoring her, but the boy taking up the rear stopped and looked up, shading his eyes with his hand.

'Mornin', missus,' he called back.

'Cromwell, how are you?' she responded, recognising him.

'Not so good. You 'aven't got any work for me? I'd be more than 'appy to run an errand or two.' He rolled up the sleeve of his tattered jacket to show off the wiry muscle in his arm. 'I'm a strong un — look. I can fetch and carry just about anythin'.'

'We don't have any vacancies presently, but I'll keep you in mind.'

'That's what they all say. My family rely on me to 'elp keep the roof over our 'eads. I don't know what we're goin' to do. Everyone's scratchin' around for paid work.'

One of his friends came back and tugged on his arm. 'Make 'aste or you'll miss out on yer wittles. There weren't enough to go around afore. Mrs Fleet tried to make it fair, but the gen'ral rule is

182

first come, first served.'

'Mrs Fleet, did you say?'

A flicker of a smile crossed Cromwell's face. 'You know 'er, your sister. She's been organisin' the extra meals at the poor'ouse.'

'Whist! Don't say nothin',' his friend hissed. 'Your ma doesn't want everyone knowin' 'er business.'

'Grace — I mean Mrs Feasey — is aware that Mrs Fleet is a patron of the poor'ouse. She isn't stupid,' Cromwell said, affronted. 'There's no shame in acceptin' charity when you can't afford to buy a loaf of bread.'

Grace felt a little sheepish about not knowing that Winnie was helping to provide the poor children of Deal with food. She had been too wrapped up in Isaiah, running their business and worrying about George Minnis to notice what was going on beyond their own front door.

'Good day, missus,' Cromwell said, as his friend dragged him away.

She watched the boys hurrying to catch up with the rest of the group before disappearing around the corner. Cromwell's revelation had left a bitter taste in her mouth. The poorer families were suffering from the deprivation brought about by the end of the war, the scant harvest and the price-fixing applied to the corn market. What had the fighting been for? she wondered. What good had it done?

'Grace,' she heard Isaiah call. 'You're wanted down 'ere.'

With a sigh, she made her way downstairs to the taproom.

'Sarah isn't in till later, and the guests are drummin' their fingers on the tables, waitin' for their breakfasts. One of them's gettin' quite uppity, but I reckon that if you give 'im one of your smiles, he'll soon calm down. Don't look so worried. 'E won't bite you.'

She steeled herself before entering the dining room to greet the guests, a travelling salesman and a gentleman who was en route to Dover, having visited his elderly mother in Deal the day before.

'Did you sleep well, Mr Orwell?' she asked.

'Like a log,' the salesman smiled.

'Those brutes who were drinking in here kept me awake,' the other man — Doctor Aldington — said, his moustache twitching. Was it a tic or was he in a temper?

'I'd like the huffkins and cherry jam, and a copy of *The Times*.'

'I'm exceedingly sorry that you had a disturbed night. The items you've requested aren't available, but I can thoroughly recommend the bacon and eggs,' she said hopefully.

'Then send out for them. What kind of establishment is this?'

'I'll see what I can do.'

'Not wanting to put our lovely hostess to any trouble, I will have the bacon and eggs, with tea,' Mr Orwell said.

'I'll get to it right away.' She rushed out to the taproom, closing the door behind her. 'Isaiah, I need you to prepare Mr Orwell's breakfast while I run out to buy huffkins for that doctor fellow.'

'I 'aven't done much cookin' afore.'

'The tea is stewing in the pot. All you need to

184

do is melt some lard in a pan, break a couple of eggs into it and add some bacon. You know I don't want to be here alone should George turn up.' She walked up to him and placed her arms around his neck. 'Please, my love. You said you would do anything for me. This is your chance to prove it.'

'Go on then. I'll step into the breach.'

'Thank you.'

Having bought four huffkins from the bakery, she headed back to the tavern via Cockle Swamp Alley, hoping to catch Jason at home.

'I'm afraid he's out,' Louisa said. 'Is this something to do with Isaiah?'

'No, it's about Cromwell. He's looking for work and I wondered if Jason knew of anything that he could turn his hand to.'

'Why this sudden concern for Cromwell?'

'I saw him on his way to the poorhouse this morning — he's having to take his meals there. I remembered how he used to crew the *Curlew* for us, and I thought that he could do with a little help.'

'I'll have a word with Jason later. How are you, Grace?'

'I can't stop,' she said, deeply regretting that she couldn't stay and talk.

'Another time then,' Louisa said wistfully. 'Come back soon.'

'I will.' She hastened to the end of the alley then turned to wave goodbye, but as she spun round again, she came up against an immovable object in the form of George Minnis. As she reeled backwards, he grasped her by the shoulders.

'Hey, what's the hurry, Grace?' He held on to

her for an inordinately long time, inclining his head towards her, his eyes bloodshot, his expression challenging.

'You were talking to Mrs Witherall. Seeing you together, the family resemblance is striking. My dear, you're trembling — are you cold, or is it a sign of a guilty conscience?' She didn't reply and he went on, 'You're always in the tavern, earwigging on conversations that a gobbler would give his eye teeth to listen to. 'Ave you been speaking out of turn?'

'No, Mr Minnis,' she said, forcing a smile.

'I'm sure that your 'usband's made you aware of the consequences of such treachery.' Grace recoiled as he released her, having an idea that they involved murder.

'You won't mention this to Isaiah,' she said. 'He doesn't approve of me seeing my sister.'

'I don't blame 'im — I'd be concerned that you might let somethin' slip.'

'He isn't involved in smuggling any more.' How many times did she have to repeat it?

'If you say so, Grace.' He was laughing at her. 'Now I'm the gentlemanly sort, so let me assure you that I'll keep the details of your outin' under my 'at. It'll be our little secret. Tell Black Dog that I'll be along in an hour or two.'

★ ★ ★

When she arrived at the tavern, Isaiah was in a temper because Mr Orwell had sent his rubbery eggs and tainted bacon back to the kitchen, while Doctor Aldington had left without paying his bill.

186

'I don't see what's wrong with these,' he said, sitting at the table in the dining room, eating the offending leftovers along with some from the night before, noisily with his mouth open, a habit she was beginning to find jarring.

'Never mind that. I've seen Mr Minnis — he's coming here between eleven and noon.'

Isaiah's jaw dropped and a slug of yolk crawled down his chin. 'You told 'im I wasn't 'ere, I 'ope? You didn't. I can't believe 'ow negligent you are when it comes to lookin' after your 'usband.'

'I didn't think quickly enough,' she said, taking hold of the back of the chair on the other side of the table from him. 'You're going to have to face him sooner or later.'

He stood up.

'Where are you going?'

'Out.'

'Oh no, you're not.' She ran across to the door and stood in his way. Reaching out and running her hand down his arm, she added, 'I know how anxious you've been, but you'll feel better if you get it over and done with.'

'Look who I've found,' she heard Sarah calling from the taproom. 'George, let me take your coat for you.'

'Thank you, my darlin'.'

'Less of that. You're forgettin' that I'm a married woman.'

''Ow's Digger? I've 'eard that 'e's 'avin' doubts about switchin' 'is allegiance to the Greys?'

'Mr Minnis, I don't know what you mean.' Sarah's tone was haughty. 'My husband is a Rattler through and through.'

187

'It's a universally acknowledged fact that a man's loyalty can be bought — for a price.'

'Not my Digger's.'

'We'll see,' George said lightly, walking through to the dining room.

'George, come on in!' Isaiah exclaimed. 'Where 'ave you been, stranger?'

'Out and about,' George replied, taking a seat. 'I'll 'ave what you've been 'avin'.'

'The bacon and eggs are off,' Grace said. 'You can have huffkins and jam.'

'I 'ave an achin' tooth for eggs and bacon,' George replied stubbornly.

Not wanting to upset him, Grace interrupted Sarah who was sweeping the floor in the taproom to ask her to go out and buy the ingredients for George's breakfast.

'What's going on?' Sarah asked in a low voice as she leaned her broom against the bar. 'Why's George here at this time of day?'

'You must promise me that this will go no further.'

'Your secrets are safe with me. You know that.'

'Isaiah owes Mr Minnis a large sum of money. He's come to collect it, but we haven't got it. I don't know what we're going to do.'

'What a pickle. I'd never 'ave guessed that you were on the rocks when it came to money. Oh dear, I don't like the thought of your 'usband comin' to 'arm because 'e's set up George's bristles over it.'

'That's why I'm making sure that he has his eggs and bacon — to keep him sweet while Isaiah thinks up some excuse as to why he hasn't got the payment together yet.'

188

'I'll be back as soon as I can,' Sarah promised.

As soon as she'd left, George began to enquire about the whereabouts of his money.

'I regret that there's a short delay, thanks to my attorney,' Isaiah said as Grace walked back into the dining room.

'I see,' George said. 'I must introduce you to mine, Mr Houghton-White of Sandwich.' He pronounced it Hoffton. 'He's a good fellow who doesn't pussyfoot around.'

'I don't want to start all over again — the matter is proceedin', but at a snail's pace.'

'Then this is an inheritance, or monies from a trust rather than an investment?' George probed. 'It's all rather mysterious.' He banged his stick against the floor. 'Will you not be a little more transparent with me?'

Isaiah wiped his brow with the back of his hand. 'I did some work for a gentleman in the past, involvin' the transport of salt. We fell out over the deal, and I'm suin' 'im for what 'e owes me.'

Grace wished he wouldn't elaborate. The more complicated the lie, the easier it was to trip over the detail.

'The case isn't settled then?' George said, cogitating.

'As good as . . .'

'You should never count your chickens before they 'atch. Anyway, out of respect for our friendship, and reassured that you 'ave property to fall back on, I'm willin' to wait until next quarter. You'll be flush in the pocket by the beginnin' of April?'

'Without doubt,' Isaiah smiled, but his smile

189

didn't quite reach his eyes.

''Ow are the gang? Digger and the rest?' George asked, changing the subject.

'They're lyin' low for a while, not wantin' to go back to gaol in an 'urry.'

'I don't blame them. Let them know that while you're keeping your nose clean, playin' landlord, George Minnis always has opportunities available for men with experience of runnin' goods. Naturally, that includes you.' He smiled towards Grace, taunting her. 'I trust that your wife will permit you to follow whatever trade is necessary to pay off your debts and provide a good livin'.'

'Ah, you are such a joker.' Isaiah's laughter rang hollow. 'I don't 'ave to answer to my wife.'

'I've always found that a thorough beatin' knocks any tendency for a wife to order her husband about right on the 'ead.'

'Then I feel very sorry for Mrs Minnis,' Grace said, unable to hold her tongue any longer.

'Oh, don't worry about 'er. I 'aven't raised a finger to her for a long time — she's a quick learner.'

Aware of Isaiah's glowering expression and George's mocking grin, Grace picked up the pot of cold tea from the table and went into the kitchen to refresh it. She had never hated anyone as much as she hated George Minnis.

After he left, she spent her days on tenterhooks, expecting him to turn up again, demanding his money. Sometimes she imagined him prowling up and down the street like a hungry lion, but far less noble. He was more of a threat than Old Boney had ever been.

190

12

Up the Creek without a Paddle

February and March went by, then April whisked in, bringing frost and snow showers. The skies remained dark, day and night, the sun obscured by a dense red fog.

No matter how hard Grace worked, they made little money. In fact, they were lucky to break even at times. She tried standing outside the tavern in the cold, like a whore touting for business, intercepting anyone and everyone who passed by to ask them if they required a bed and board for the night. The Rattlers continued to drink and make merry at their expense, and her belly continued to swell.

Each time she raised her concerns about how they were going to pay George, Isaiah dismissed them. He was burying his head in the sand, she thought. The longer they waited for their creditor to return, the more anxious she became.

One morning, heavy with child, she was in the taproom, tidying up from the night before. She swept the floor and mopped it, then fetched a bucket of fresh sawdust to sprinkle across the flagstones to absorb any spills.

'Are you all right, Grace?' Sarah asked as she

finished blacking the grate, ready to relight the fire. 'You're very quiet. Is something troublin' you? You can speak — our menfolk are out and there's no tellin' when they'll be back. Do you think the baby's on its way?'

'I don't know — I've had a few pains.' Grace stroked her belly, wishing that she could ask Winnie's advice.

'I'd like children,' Sarah said, 'lots of them, and soon, I hope. If I 'ad a choice, I'd 'ave a pigeon pair, a girl then a boy, but what if I should end up givin' birth every year, like Mrs Roper?'

'I've heard that the longer you keep a child on the breast, the more you delay the onset of the next pregnancy.'

Sarah gave a wicked grin. 'There are other ways, like makin' sure your husband don't come near you in the first place.'

'It's too late for that,' Grace said wryly. She dusted the counter then wiped down the shelves beneath it. Hidden behind a row of pewter tankards, she found a sheaf of letters. Pulling them out to examine them, she discovered several with the address written in the same hand, marked *For the Urgent Attention of Mr I. Feasey*. All were unopened. She guessed why — Isaiah must have found the idea of asking her to read them too humiliating.

'Sarah, I'll be upstairs,' she said.

'I'm glad you're goin' to put your feet up for a while,' she smiled.

Grace headed up to the landing where she opened the letters: bills and invoices from the brewery and butcher; and several notes from J. Tapping

Esquire, detailing the outstanding amounts over-
due for goods and services rendered, plus interest.
The builder had also sent a final demand in an
uneven hand, the paper flecked with angry blots.

*Pay up, or else. If the money isn't in my hand
by midnight on the 30th day of April, 1816,
I can't be held accountable for what happens
to you and your lady wife.*

Grace slumped to the floor, hot salt tears on her
lips. It was hopeless. Today was the last day of
April and they were up the creek without a pad-
dle, as Pa used to say. Would she ever have any
peace?

On hearing Isaiah's voice, she looked up.

'Grace, I 'eard you cryin'. What's wrong?'

'This.' She held up the letter. 'Mr Tapping is
gunning for us. We are obliged to pay off our debt
in full by midnight.'

'Don't upset yourself.' He knelt and slipped his
arm around her, and she rested her head against
his chest. 'All this waitin' for our son to be born
don't 'elp.'

'It has nothing to do with it,' she exclaimed,
pulling away from him. 'Don't you understand
the gravity of our situation?'

''E's just trying to put the frighteners on us. I'll
talk to 'im if 'e turns up.'

'I'm afraid that the time for talking is over.'

''E's a friend of George's— 'e won't 'urt us,
especially not with you bein' in the family way.'
Isaiah rubbed her back. 'You'll stand by me, won't
you, Grace? Promise me you'll never leave me . . .

193

I'd die without you.'

'I'm not going anywhere,' she said, astonished by the tears that sprang to his eyes. 'We're married. For richer, for poorer . . . '

He pressed his forehead to hers. 'I won't let no 'arm come to you — I promise.'

Even so, Grace was pleased to see Digger and the gang at the tavern that evening, thinking that there was safety in numbers, in case the builder and his men turned up for his money. She even allowed them a free drink to encourage them to stay on after closing time when Isaiah locked them in.

'He isn't comin', my love,' Isaiah said, but as Digger and Dunk, Lawless and Awful Doins started to play Canterbury Fours with Cut-throat looking on, the cats who were sitting on the counter suddenly fled, the bones on their collars rattling. Musket growled, the fur on his throat vibrating as he bared his teeth.

'Hush!' Isaiah warned. 'We 'ave visitors and they aren't welcome.'

'Who is it, Black Dog?' Lawless slurred.

'Let me in, or I'll batter the door down and smash all yer winders!'

'It's Tapping wantin' 'is money,' Isaiah said, panicking.

'Go, Digger,' Sarah urged him. 'I don't want you gettin' involved in business that doesn't concern you.'

'Aren't you goin' to stand by your leader, the one you've always relied on to get you out of a sticky situation?' Isaiah cut in as Digger flung down his cards.

194

'Open up!'

'I dunno, Black Dog. By rights, we're no longer obliged to put our lives on the line for you.'

'Once a Rattler, always a Rattler,' Isaiah argued. 'That's how it's always been.'

'That's it. I'm not waiting any longer, you lily-livered mongrel.' There was a pause then a splintering sound. The bolts held fast as the windows rattled.

'I don't know about the rest of you, but I'm off.' Dunk got to his feet and the rest of the gang followed suit.

'Please stay!' Isaiah entreated. 'I'll pay you.'

Digger laughed dryly. 'It's clear that you're already in quite deep. Now, out of respect for my wife, I'm keepin' out of this. Come with me, Sarah.'

'I'm not leavin' Grace, not in 'er condition,' she said quietly, her words cut short by another ear-splitting crash, at which one of the bolts snapped from its fastenings. 'Don't argue with me, Digger.' She nodded towards the tip of a rusty pickaxe blade that had pierced through the door. 'I know Mr Tapping— 'e wouldn't 'arm a woman. Go!'

Obeying his wife, Digger and the gang made their way out through the dining room and kitchen, and that was the last Grace heard of them. The would-be intruders managed to extract the pickaxe and renew their attack on the door with fresh vigour.

'Ladies, you must 'ide,' Isaiah said. 'Quick, foller me.'

Taking Sarah's hand, Grace hurried after him to

the corner of the dining room where he grabbed a knife and used it to lever the trapdoor open.

'Get yourselves down there — there's a chest in the passageway. It 'as everythin' you need: a candle, flint and steel to light it, a pistol and pouch of powder. Keep goin' all the way to the end and you'll find the exit. Use the ladder to get over the wall into the neighbour's garden. Go left and through the gate, and you'll be in the alley. Turn right after that, or you'll finish up in the dead end.'

'What about you? Aren't you coming?' Grace asked, a pain niggling low in her belly.

In answer, he pushed her towards the steps. 'If I don't see you again, remember that I love you an' always will.'

'You'd better not let him kill you, or — '

'Or what? Oh Grace, just do as I tell you . . . .' His voice was drowned out by another loud crack of cleaving wood.

'They're in,' Sarah hissed.

Grace waddled down the steps with Sarah breathing heavily behind her. The trapdoor slammed shut above their heads, plunging them into darkness.

'Put your hands on my waist and I'll guide you,' Grace whispered, waiting for Sarah to catch up before they made their way along the passageway where she found the chest and lifted the lid, then fumbled for the candle.

'Hold that,' she said, giving it to Sarah. Having lit it, creating a measly, smoking flame, she picked up and loaded the pistol, pouring a little powder from the pouch into the muzzle. She wrapped one of the lead balls in a piece of cloth and used the ramrod to push it down towards the powder, making sure not to pack it too tightly. She primed it, putting a small amount of powder in the pan while listening to the sound of men's voices.

'Let's get out of 'ere, like Black Dog said,' Sarah whispered.

'I'm glad of your offer to stay with me, but I want you to leave — keep walking along the passageway and you'll find the way out.'

'What kind of friend would I be if I left you in the lurch?'

'I couldn't live with myself if you got hurt — or worse,' Grace said darkly, turning back the way they'd come in. 'Isaiah got us into this mess — there's no need for you to be involved.'

She heard the hesitation in Sarah's tone as she said, 'Where are you goin'?'

'Back to defend my 'usband, of course.' Sarah's eyes glinted in defiance and Grace went on, 'You'd do the same for yours. Wish me luck and let me pass. Look after yourself, Sarah.'

Sarah stepped aside with her head bowed.

'Thank you.' Grace returned to the foot of the staircase and crawled up the steps, stopping mid-way. The only light was a faint strip coming through the gap between two planks in the trapdoor. She heard a scuffle and a hard slap, followed by a wretched, animal-like groan.

'You are the worst kind of villain.' Mr Tapping's voice rang out loud and clear. 'You make out you're a gen'leman of means, and then I find out — too late — that you've been lyin' through your teeth. Well, I tell you, if you don't give me that money you owe me, or goods in kind, you won't

197

'ave any teeth left to lie through.'

'I 'aven't got it,' Isaiah yelped. 'There's ale in the cellar and some brandy be'ind the counter. You can 'ave what's in the till, my watch and my wife's jewellery as security.'

Grace touched the pendant at her throat — there was no way Mr Tapping would be getting his hands on it, if she had her way. Moving slowly, she pushed the trapdoor up just a fraction and peered out. The dining room was empty, but she could see four pairs of feet through the doorway into the taproom. It took her a moment to work out that Isaiah was tied to a chair with the builder leaning over him, his fists tensing around an iron bar, while two men holding ash staves stood back, watching.

Much as she had occasionally wished her husband ill, she hadn't meant it. Seeing him there with his face bruised, his mouth bleeding and his expression tortured, her heart flooded with compassion.

'Where do you keep your stash?' Mr Tapping growled.

'I don't 'ave any run goods — I'm a respectable landlord, not a smuggler,' Isaiah muttered. 'If you'll just wait another month or two, I'll 'ave your money.'

'You've used that excuse too many times before. It's too late.'

'My wife's with child. Please . . . let me go.'

'I 'ave five daughters and I say that I 'ave four sons, although only one came back alive from the war, thanks to Old Boney. The other three left their wives and children for me to take care of.

198

You see, we all 'ave our crosses to bear.' He nodded to one of his men. 'What do you say we make a start? The pliers if you will.'

At the sound of the iron bar falling to the ground, Grace cocked the pistol and with a surge of strength, shoved the trapdoor open. The echo as it slammed against the floor still ringing in her ears, she climbed the last few steps and moved as quickly as she could, rushing into the taproom, aiming the pistol towards Mr Tapping.

'Don't move, or I'll fire,' she shouted, stepping between him and Isaiah as one of his men raised his piece and pointed it in her direction.

'You won't,' the builder sighed, his face scarlet and lips adorned with spittle. 'You'll put that firearm down and we'll talk. You understand why I'm 'ere. I'm entitled to that money — I've earned it. It isn't right to deprive a man of his livelihood, especially when 'e 'as a family who depend on 'im.'

'Tell your men to drop their weapons — ' All she had to do was pull the trigger and send the ball on its way.

'What shall I do, mister? I can't bring meself to shoot at a woman who's about to drop. Look at 'er. You didn't mention that this chap 'ad a wife who was in the family way.'

'Drop them,' she urged, trembling. 'Leave it,' she added when the builder made to pick up the iron bar. 'Step away, or I'll . . .'

It appeared that she sounded braver than she felt, because he shuffled back a few paces, his eyes narrowed, his brow dripping with sweat.

'Mr Tappin', this is one of them occasions when

199

discretion is the better part of valour.' The man stowed his pistol in his belt. 'I can't 'ave the petrification of an innocent woman on my conscience, and I couldn't forgive myself if anythin' bad should 'appen to the littlun that's growin' inside 'er.'

'She isn't innocent — she's a smuggler's wife,' Mr Tapping exploded, rushing towards her as his men made a rapid escape through the shattered door on to the street. Closing her eyes, she pulled the trigger. As the shot faded, she opened her eyes again to see the builder clutching his leg in pain. 'I'll be back,' he grimaced. 'I'll see you and the babe dead next time.'

With that, he hobbled away after his men, but as Grace breathed a sigh of relief, a dull ache dragged through her loins, gradually intensifying until she was bent double, clutching her belly and only vaguely aware of Isaiah screaming, 'My wife — she's been shot.'

'Your wife is in labour — the babe's on its way,' Sarah's voice cut into her consciousness.

'You didn't leave,' Grace said, but she wasn't sure that Sarah heard her.

'Are you sure she isn't 'urt? She's makin' an awful racket. Fetch a knife and cut away these ropes, will you?'

Having released Isaiah from his bonds, Sarah arrived at Grace's side while Isaiah fell to his knees in front of her and grasped her hands.

'My darlin',' he breathed as her pain began to pass. 'You saved my skin — I thought I was a goner.'

'They'll be back — you heard what he said.'

'Never mind that now. Tell me what to do.'

'In normal circumstances,' Sarah said, 'you should go off nidgetin', callin' on the midwife and perhaps Grace's sister, but it's too dangerous for you to go outside. Tapping's men could be waitin' to 'ave another go. I wish my 'usband 'adn't done a runner — we could do with 'im and the gang to stand guard.'

'You'll 'ave to deliver the child,' Isaiah said urgently.

'That's askin' too much.'

'You're my wife's loyal friend — she trusts you.'

'Will you not talk about me as if I'm not here?' A fresh pain began to grow inside Grace's belly, like a sea anemone spreading its tentacles to deliver a vicious sting. 'Ow,' she gasped.

'I wish I could take the pain for you,' Isaiah said. 'I love you that much and more, Grace.'

'Go away,' she snapped. 'I can't stand to have you near me.'

'Please, don't say that. Don't push me away.'

'She doesn't mean it — she isn't 'erself. 'Elp me get 'er upstairs,' Sarah said as the door burst open, sending the bolts flying. Grace froze, watching Isaiah spring from the floor and put himself between her and Sarah and the intruders, but it was only Digger and the gang.

'Why didn't you knock?' Isaiah exclaimed.

'We did and not receivin' any response, we were about to leave when we 'eard the most terrible screams,' Digger said.

'Most terrible,' Awful Doins echoed, 'like someone was stranglin' a cat.'

'We thought Tapping and 'is men 'ad come back to finish you off. We 'id behind the lobster pots and watched them leave, but didn't see where they went,' Lawless said.

'It's ale all round, I reckon, and some brandy to steady our nerves. Come on, ladies. We're dyin' of thirst 'ere.' Digger stopped abruptly, his eyes on Grace. 'What's goin' on?'

''Elp yourself to drinks,' Isaiah said. 'My wife's about to drop.'

'I'll fetch the midwife, Mrs Kesby,' Awful Doins offered.

Grace managed to crawl up to bed where she sat on the edge of the mattress, touching her taut smuggler's tub of a belly as the pains came and went, and returned again while the Rattlers continued drinking in the taproom below. The hours passed and she began to wonder if she'd be lucky enough to cheat death for a second time that night.

'Will it ever stop?' she moaned as Sarah and the midwife, a middle-aged woman with large hands, dirty fingernails and a constellation of hairy warts on her cheek, attended to her.

'You're doin' well, ducks,' Mrs Kesby kept saying. 'Sarah, mop 'er brow.'

'No, leave me alone,' Grace grunted, her gown soaked with perspiration.

'I'm not one for confinin' a woman to a birthin' chair or tyin' her legs up in stirrups,' Mrs Kesby said abrasively when Sarah began to question her competence. 'I lets my ladies move about, accordin' to how Nature directs 'em. I like the winders wide open to let in the sound and sight of the sea— 'ow else will a littlun get ol' briny into its soul otherwise? Where's the brandy? We make a caudle — the old traditions are there for a reason.

Make it thick and sweet with milk and eggs.'

Sarah opened the door at the sound of knocking.

'What is it?' Grace heard her say.

'I've 'ad enough of listenin' to 'er sufferin',' Isaiah said.

'I've sent for Doctor Audley.'

'You 'aven't? You shouldn't 'ave done that without consultin' me. I don't want 'im interferin',' Mrs Kesby sneered as Grace lay back on the bed, her hand on her forehead, the pain driving through her . . . and suddenly, it was gone and a single sharp cry pierced her ears.

After a minute or two, Mrs Kesby dropped a wriggling puce bundle on to Grace's chest, saying, 'It's a little girl, Mrs Feasey. That's the easy part done — you just 'ave to bring 'er up for the next fourteen, fifteen years.'

Weak with relief, Grace gazed down at the baby, admiring her black curls and her eyes that were the colour of the sea on a bright summer's day.

'Is it over? Is all well?' Isaiah couldn't contain himself any longer. He pushed past the midwife to reach the bedside, despite her angry protestations.

'This is most irreg'lar, 'avin' a father in the lyin'-in chamber,' Mrs Kesby said, shaking her head. 'Sarah, find a blanket for the baby. Yes, somethin' to swaddle 'er in.'

Grace was too besotted to take much notice of anything except for her newborn daughter, and for Isaiah too, it appeared to be a case of love at first sight.

'I thank the Lord for sparin' my wife and child.

I thought you were gorn, Grace. And the littlun
. . .'

'I'm still here,' she said softly, inhaling the baby's
sweet, milky scent as she stroked her cheek. 'Isn't
she beautiful?'

'Like her ma,' he said. 'Look at 'er dainty fingers. She's tiny.'

'I reckon she came early,' Mrs Kesby opined.
'That can 'appen when Mama's 'ad a shock, and
I've 'eard you 'ad a nasty one. Sarah told me. Mr
Feasey, you really must leave your wife to rest.
Have you chosen a name for the littlun?'

'I'd settled on Robert.' Isaiah grinned as Mrs
Kesby scolded him.

'That won't do, will it?' she said huffily.

'How about Agatha, Agatha Grace Feasey?' he
suggested.

'I think that will suit her down to the ground.'
Grace smiled, delighted that he didn't seem to
care that she was a girl, not the boy that he'd
wished for.

'I'll be off then. If my wife needs anythin', anythin' at all, she must 'ave it. I'll see you soon, my
love.' He leaned down and kissed her, then pressed
his lips to the baby's head before backing out of
the room, hardly able to keep his eyes off them.

'Take care,' Grace whispered.

'I've never seen Black Dog like this,' she heard
Mrs Kesby saying. 'The love of a good woman 'as
changed 'im for the better. It's a miracle, but will
it last? That's what I'm askin' myself.'

Despite how close Isaiah had been to losing
his teeth, and despite the mess that Tapping and
his men had left behind, Grace wasn't ready to

countenance Isaiah's return to the free trade, but for how much longer could she cling — like a shipwrecked sailor to the sinking timbers of his ship — to her dreams of respectability when the likes of Mr Tapping and George Minnis were on Isaiah's back?

★ ★ ★

Over the next few days, Isaiah and the Rattlers repaired the damage that Mr Tapping and his men had inflicted, while Sarah supported Grace, who'd refused to take any more than forty-eight hours of bedrest, in running the tavern and caring for the baby. Isaiah borrowed a cradle with rockers from a friend and Lawless's wife gave them some hand-me-downs for the littlun. The evidence of their conflict with the builder was still evident in the fading bruises on Isaiah's face and Digger's constant presence as an armed guard at the tavern, Grace having insisted that he and Sarah should have board and lodgings in return for their services.

When Aggie was a sennight old, Grace left her to sleep in the cradle while she caught up with some of the chores. She was changing the linen in one of the guest rooms when she heard Isaiah's footsteps creeping up the stairs. She paused to listen.

'Hello, little Miss Feasey,' he said in a low voice as he entered the adjacent bedroom where the baby was sleeping.

Please don't wake her, Grace prayed. She plumped up the pillows and folded the coverlet

205

back, leaving a lavender bag on top to keep bad odours at bay, then went to see what her husband was up to.

'Oh, be careful,' she exclaimed, watching him bundle Aggie awkwardly into his arms and carry her to the bed where he perched on the edge of the mattress.

'Don't fret. I won't drop her,' he grinned, keeping his eyes on the baby. 'Get back to work. Go on!'

She moved away and hid behind the door, listening to Isaiah talk to their daughter.

'Forgive me if I've been rough with you — I've never 'eld a littlun in my arms. I wouldn't 'ave believed that you could be so tiny and perfect. And innocent. I'm makin' you this solemn promise — that I'll keep you safe, my dear girl, and I shall l'arn you everythin' I know, how to fish, hovel and run a tavern. I'll advise you on choosin' a suitable 'usband, not some reprobate like me. I'll correct that. I'm doin' my best to stay on the straight and narrer for you and your ma.'

If only her sisters could see Isaiah now, Grace mused fondly, her heart aching with love for him. His admission of his past wickedness and his expression of his intent to keep out of trouble in future, refreshed her sometimes flagging opinion that she had chosen well in marrying him. 'She needs 'er ma.' Isaiah looked up in alarm when

Aggie snuffled and uttered a small cry. 'Grace, you 'ave 'er. I don't know what to do.'

She walked over and took the baby from him, then carried her to the nursing chair where she fed her discreetly under a shawl while Isaiah remained in the room, staring out of the window towards the horizon where a storm was brewing, anvil clouds towering over the sea.

'I've been thinking,' she said eventually. 'What about asking for a loan from a bank?'

'Men like me don't make that kind of application. The manager would laugh in my face.'

'We have the tavern as collateral. Is there no one else you can ask?'

'You could go beggin' to your sisters.'

'They won't throw good money after bad. They'd consider us profligate if they knew the whole story.'

'You mean they think I'm the irresponsible one, not you. They 'ate me. Everyone 'ates me!'

Biting her tongue, she laid the baby against her shoulder and patted her back. If Isaiah wanted to wallow in self-pity, that was up to him. Lieutenant Enderby would never mope about his lot, not that he was the kind of man who would have got himself into debt in the first place. Unsure why Albert had suddenly come to mind when it had been a few months since they'd last spoken, she chastened herself for thinking of him. He was Mary's sensible, dependable husband and nothing to do with Grace, except that there were times when she yearned for the peace of mind and security that on reflection she might have had if she'd married Albert. She would never talk of how she felt, though, not even to Sarah.

By noon, a south-easterly wind had begun to blow, Isaiah had stacked some hessian sacks of sand outside the tavern doors, and the smugglers had started to drink. Lightning flashed and thunder reverberated over the town, presaging a shower of hailstones the size of eggs followed by heavy rain. By six o'clock, the wind had become a gale and the tide was running up the beach, breaking over the top of the slope and washing into the streets, filling the gutters, bringing up shingle, leaving it littering the gardens and pavements as the water retreated, only to surge again. When Grace was upstairs putting Aggie in her cradle to sleep for a while, she heard people shouting and screaming outside, as they helped neighbours rescue their valuables and block the ingress of water as well as they could.

The roof tiles rattled and the cats retreated indoors, hiding under the tables. Musket was drying off by the fire, his steaming coat sending a strong odour of dog into the air. Grace went down to the taproom then jumped as a sudden hammering came at the door.

'Who's that?' Her blood running cold, she looked around the room and did a quick head count. All present and correct, which meant that whoever it was at the door, wasn't welcome.

Digger got up to unbolt the door, a large cutlass in his hand.

'Don't open it,' Grace said, afraid that it was Mr Tapping coming back to have another go at collecting his money.

'What if it's some poor traveller who's been forced by the weather to seek shelter?' Sarah asked from behind the counter.

'Go on then,' Grace said, changing her mind. Seeing that her husband wasn't going to move from his place at the smugglers' table, she grabbed the pistol from its place beneath the counter. 'Let them in.'

'Mr Minnis— ' she exclaimed as he came stumbling into the bar, wiping the rain from his eyes. Grace tucked the pistol into her pocket.

' 'Ere, take this.' He unbuttoned his sodden coat and handed it to Sarah, before striding across the taproom as if he owned the place, to stand in front of the fire.

'Evenin', George,' Isaiah said, walking over to greet him. 'Whatever induced you to travel abroad tonight?'

'I 'eard you'd 'ad a bit of a ruckus with Mr Tapping. I presume that you never did get that inheritance or investment or whatever it was, so I thought I'd see if you were ready to accept my offer in your hour of need.'

'Why me? Why us?' Isaiah asked.

'Because the Rattlers have been workin' this section of the coast for generations. You 'ave the contacts, willin' and able men — on the whole — with a range of skills that can be called upon. You know of the best landin' places and hidin' holes, you're familiar with the gobblers' movements, and you can call on a network of experienced landsmen . . . Your father's reputation for toughness and a willingness to threaten violence — and use it, if necessary — goes before you.'

Grace noticed how Isaiah's manner transformed as George puffed him up with praise and attention.

'The Greys have access to various vessels for carryin' goods — I can see an opportunity for you to make a few fishin' trips yourself. Marlin's always been acknowledged as the best fore and aft sailor in the county, but I know from 'istory that you're as good, if not better.' George paused before going on, 'I 'ave an achin' tooth for a draught of geneva, if you have some?'

'I'll 'ave a look in the cellar,' Isaiah said.

Grace couldn't stand to see George and her husband fawning over each other any longer, knowing that the former would have some ulterior motive for his excessive friendliness.

'Come through to the dining room — we'll find you some refreshment,' she said. 'There are some bloaters left over.' George wrinkled his nose. 'I'd prefer beef or mutton.'

'We've had to cut our cloth,' Grace said sharply. She was sick of bloaters herself — the deceptive beauty of the smoked fish's golden skin betrayed the soft pungency of its flesh, but it was plentiful and cheap, especially when it was on the turn.

'There may be a portion of salted pork left,' Sarah offered as he made his way to one of the tables in the dining room and leaned his stick — a bough of polished chestnut, the end carved into the shape of a ram's head — against it. Grace hadn't seen him carrying a stick before and wondered if it was an affectation or weapon. 'I'll go and see.'

Returning from the kitchen, Sarah placed a tray of meat, potatoes and pickles in front of him.

'Thank you, Sarah. That will be all,' Grace said.

When Sarah had left the dining room to check on Aggie for Grace, and Isaiah had gone down to the cellar, George rested his hairy forearms on the tablecloth, his eyes on Grace's pendant.

'A loyal and obedient wife is worth more than all the sapphires in the world,' he said. 'You're a lovely-lookin' woman, but 'andsome is as 'andsome does. You're an asset to 'im and you could be a great 'elp to me with your connection to the Revenue.'

Forcing a smile, she leaned towards him until his breath ruffled the lace at her breast. 'Whatever you've come to discuss with my husband, say your piece and go. I know what you're about and we don't want any part in it. Mr Feasey is a changed man.'

'I don't see 'ow 'e can afford to keep to the moral 'igh ground.'

'I will not have you putting temptation in his way,' she warned as Isaiah came back from the cellar with a jug brimming with gin.

'There you are, George,' he said. ' 'Elp yourself to the best Holland gin, genuine Crowlink.'

'If you say so. You know, I'd rather like your lady to pour it for me,' George said with a sly smile.

'Of course,' Grace said through gritted teeth. Having slammed the jug down on the table, she turned and grasped Isaiah by his jerkin and dragged him into the taproom.

'What are you doin', woman?' he protested.

'That geneva — where did it come from?'

'It was originally from 'olland then imported through Crowlink Gap in the county of Sussex,' he said, smirking. 'At least, that's what I've told George.'

'You haven't answered the question,' she said coldly.

'It's from the last run I was involved in — it was

211

ages ago. Don't fret about it.'

'But I do worry, and it would make me happy if you didn't speak to me as if I'm an inconsequential flibbertigibbet.'

'I'll speak to you how I like— ' He was grinning, but there was an edge to his tone that vexed her, as he grabbed her by the waist and pulled her against him. 'I'm your 'usband. Now, George will be wonderin' where we are— 'e's expectin' us to entertain 'im.'

Reluctantly, she followed Isaiah back into the dining room.

'Sit down, Black Dog.' George patted the chair beside him. ''Aven't I always done my best for you? Come on. 'Umour me.'

Isaiah sat down.

'This unpleasantness with Mr Tapping . . . I can solve it for you. I can pay 'im off on your behalf in one fell swoop. You won't even 'ave to deal with 'im. What do you think?'

'It's temptin', but I'm not in a position to pay you back. You know that.'

'You 'ave property, a valuable piece of real estate. I'll ask my attorney to write up a bond stating that the tavern is surety for the settlement of your debt to me in full.' George glanced towards Grace. 'I can tell that this suggestion of mine doesn't please your wife, but it's the only way out. You keep the roof over your 'eads and I get my money back, one way or another. How you obtain it, is up to you. My offer of work still stands.'

'I'll take the loan, but I'll 'ave to think about the other,' Isaiah said.

'That's all right. Take your time. I know you'll

come to the right decision in the end.'

'There's water comin' under the door,' Digger interrupted from the taproom. 'It won't be long afore the tavern's six feet under.'

Isaiah leapt up, shouting, 'All 'ands on deck. Get bailin'.'

'Sarah, fetch the buckets and mop,' Grace called as George sat glued to his seat, draining the jug of gin. 'I'll find some cloths. Isaiah, get the men to bring the barrels up from the cellar and put them upstairs. The sawdust can be left. Are there any more sandbags?'

No number of sandbags could have stemmed the tide that came swirling in around their ankles and pouring into the cellar, but it was insignificant compared to the rising tide of debt that threatened her family's lives, Grace thought as she headed upstairs to check on Aggie. The seaweed and dead fish floating on top of the water and the tidemark left on the walls could be cleaned away, but there was nothing she could do about their financial predicament.

13

The Year Without a Summer, 1816

Aggie was two months old. Musket had wearied of giving her predatory looks whenever she cried and Grace had made one of the guest rooms into a nursery. The cellar was empty but for a single barrel of ale and the brewery had failed to make a delivery for three weeks.

If Isaiah had agreed to work for George, there was no evidence of it, apart from the fact that he spent much of his time away from the tavern. Grace had learned not to ask him too many questions, but she feared the worst. What else was he doing in Deal where most of the shops were shuttered and the businesses closed, and a desperation had crept into the cries of the fishwives? It was Sarah's day off and Grace was in the kitchen boiling up some stock when Isaiah appeared, having been out for the morning. He stepped up beside her, took one of the cod heads from the pot and tossed it to the three cats that were waiting in hope. Mewling and hissing, they fought over it, one escaping with the prize.

He didn't kiss her, she noticed. He hadn't shown her any affection for some time, his interest in her in 'that way' having waned since Aggie was born.

She didn't blame him — they were constantly on edge, being in hock to the brewery, the butcher and the baker, as well as George. Forsooth, she felt that there was hardly anyone in Deal to whom they didn't owe money.

Their situation had aged him: he had dark circles under his eyes, hollow cheeks and a salting of silver hairs at his temples.

'I was under the impression that the gen'leman who took a room last night was extendin' 'is visit by a sennight.'

'He was recuperating from a brief illness and came to Deal to spend some time beside the sea, according to his doctor's orders. Unfortunately, he said the mattress was lumpy and the tavern too noisy for a convalescent.'

'Why didn't you use your charms to persuade him to stay?'

'I did try,' she argued, stung by his criticism.

'Not hard enough, obviously.'

'Please, stop harrumphing at me like that.'

''Arrumphin'? What kind of talk is that?' Despite their problems, he started to chuckle.

'You're laughing at me now.'

He slipped his arm around her shoulders. 'I'm sorry, but that tickled me. Grace, I want to laugh with you, not at you, but you don't smile any more, not like you used to.'

'That's because nothing that I do is ever good enough for you. I can't do right for doing wrong and it's breaking my heart. Do you not desire me any more?' she asked sadly.

'I still 'ave a strong fancy for you, but I 'ave a lot on my mind. I 'ave a feelin' we're in for more

215

stormy weather.'

'I believe it's set fair for at least a sennight.'

'I mean, metaphorically speakin'. You know, I don't think anybody could 'ave worked harder at not doing somethin' than I 'ave.'

'I don't know what you mean.'

'I've been to see Mr Salisbury — the owner of the brewery, in case you don't know — and it's bad news.' Her heart sank as he went on, 'The brewery won't deliver until the debt is settled in full. Grace, I don't know what to do.' He placed his hands on her hips and buried his face in her hair. 'I 'ad the best of intentions, but circumstances are forcin' my 'and.'

'No, Isaiah. You can't do this.' She knew exactly what he was thinking. 'George is a crook of the worst kind. You mustn't ask him to lend you any more money.' She could see the problem, though — a tavern wasn't a tavern without ale.

'Before I married you, I was ridin' the crest of the wave and then before I knew it, the wave broke and my fortunes crashed with it. The worst part of it is, that I know I could turn it around again, if I could just find the money to settle up with George. You don't want me to go in with 'im and I respect you for that, but you leave me with no alternative . . . unless . . .'

'I won't do it,' she said. 'Winnie will not bend — I know my sister.'

Isaiah stepped away, chewed on his fingernail, tore it off with his teeth and spat it out, making her grimace.

'Don't look at me like that,' he grunted. 'I've already called in all the favours I'm owed, and

216

George's patience is runnin' out. If you were a truly lovin' wife with 'er 'usband's best interests at 'eart, you'd go and ask Winnie to reconsider 'er decision about the trust, or borrer a bit from Louisa. Blood's thicker than water and they 'ave more money than they can spend. Tell them the baby's ailin'.'

'I can't do that — it would upset them terribly.'

'Something else then. That you need medicine.'

She touched her neck, seeking the familiar shape of her pendant.

'I could pawn this.'

'No, not that.' He began to laugh, then stopped abruptly. 'Do you know what it's worth?'

'I have an idea that it is of value, but I'll ask Mr Turner what he thinks.' She'd never been to a pawnbroker before, but she'd seen his customers queuing outside his shop on Golden Street.

' 'E'll offer you a couple of shillin's for it, if that.'

Grace looked up, shocked. 'That can't be right. You've always said that it was special, that I should look after it because it's expensive, irreplaceable . . .' She recalled the words that had spilled from his mouth when he'd presented her with the pendant and chain.

'It's just a trinket.' He shrugged his shoulders. 'Paste and pinchbeck.' How could he? She would rather he had confessed to infidelity than this betrayal — he'd been lying to her from the beginning. 'Tomorrer you'll go and see Winnie,' he added. 'Leave Aggie with Sarah. She's supposed to be sick, remember. You need to tug at Winnie's 'eartstrings, if she 'as an 'eart, that is.'

'I can't leave the baby behind when I'm feeding

her. I don't want Sarah giving her cow's milk and pap — she'll get the gripes.'

'Take her with you then, but make 'er look poorly.'

'How?'

'Oh, come on. You might not be a smuggler's wife, but you are a smuggler's daughter. You know the sort of thing — rub a little soot around 'er eyes and use some currant juice to give the impression of a rash.'

'Isaiah, how much do you owe George now? You have to tell me the exact amount, so I know what to ask Winnie for.'

'It's as I've said before: several 'undred pounds, and the rest,' he confessed. 'I didn't realise 'ow much interest 'e'd charge. You see, 'ow can I pay back that kind of sum when my wife forbids me to enter into the free trade? I can't see any other way out, unless you can convince your sisters to give us the money. Billy Fleet fell on his feet — who would 'ave thought that the little squirt would 'ave done so very well for 'imself, livin' out of his wife's purse?' Isaiah went on bitterly, blaming his lack of success on everyone but himself, when it was his fault that he had failed to capitalise on the advantages his father had left to him. 'Winnie pretends that she's prim and proper, and 'olier than thou, yet she made 'er money through nefarious activities. Louisa's the same — she and Marlin made their fortune from runnin' gold. They took the lion's share of that business by virtue of their relationship with that agent, Mr Cork. 'E was a villain too as it turned out.'

'You can't say that you couldn't have had a

piece of that particular pie,' Grace said. 'You and the Rattlers could have set yourselves up with a guinea boat and done the same. In fact, I don't know why you didn't.'

'Because I didn't 'ave the connections, or the forty guineas to buy a suitable vessel. I've been thinkin' that if I'd buried my head in books as a boy, I could have made somethin' of myself. I could have been an attorney-at-law or a farmer with an 'erd of fat cattle and a flock o' sheep. Just think of that. Imagine me, sittin' on the Bench wearin' a wig and bangin' a gavel.' His manner changed abruptly. 'All this talk is wearin' me out. We're agreed that you'll go to Westcliffe tomorrer.'

She nodded, but his request rankled with Grace. She felt as if he blamed her for his failures when at the root of the matter it had been his lackadaisical approach to the accounts and running the tavern that had started the rot.

However, she would do what she was told. What choice did she have?

★ ★ ★

The next morning, Grace fed Aggie, then joined Sarah downstairs.

'Where's my husband?' she asked.

'I 'aven't seen 'im. I expect 'e's gone down to the beach with Digger and the gang, and Musket. May I 'old Aggie for you? They say that if you 'old an infant in your arms, you'll 'ave your own by the time the year is out.'

'Of course you can — she can go in her cradle when you've had a cuddle.' Grace had asked

219

Isaiah to bring it downstairs. 'I'm going to visit my sister at Westcliffe today. I'll give you a hand with the rooms before I go.'

Having eaten poached eggs for breakfast, she kissed Aggie's soft cheek as she was sleeping in her cradle, then followed Sarah upstairs to strip the muddy sheets from the beds, the recent guests having apparently slept in their boots. They dragged the linen basket down to the taproom and intercepted two of the shore boys who were ambling along the street to ask them to take it to the laundry. They returned the basket soon afterwards, saying that the laundrywoman had refused to accept it.

'She says she won't do it unless she's paid in advance,' one of the boys said helpfully. 'I told 'er there must 'ave been a misunderstandin'.'

'That's right. There must be . . . ' Grace's voice trailed off. 'How's Cromwell by the way? I haven't seen him recently.'

'He's gone over to the other side. Marlin — I mean, Commander Witherall— 'as taken 'im on. 'E's a ruddy gobbler. Who'd 'ave believed it?'

'I'm happy for him.' Grace dropped a few coins into his palm. 'Thank you for running that errand for us.'

'Anytime, missus.' He saluted, clapped his heels together, then ran off.

'I reckon they'll all be turnin' their coats soon,' Sarah observed as they dragged the basket inside. 'Grace, you've been good to me and I consider you a friend, my only friend. I want to let you know — in confidence — that George has been talking to Digger and the men behind Mr Feasey's back, asking them to go in with the Greys.'

'I see. Isaiah won't be happy about that.'

'I wish I 'adn't mentioned it now.'

'You were right to. I won't say anything, I promise.'

'George 'as asked Digger to be 'is second-in-command. 'E said 'e'd been tryin' to persuade Black Dog to join 'im, thinkin' that it would 'elp you out, but 'e refused, bein' tied to 'is wife's apron strings. Digger and the gang are minded to accept George's offer. They can't buy meat or bread — some days, they're scratchin' around like chickens for a morsel to eat. They blame Black Dog for leavin' them in the lurch. They relied on 'im, and 'e's let them down.'

'What makes them think that? He's been giving them credit for months.'

'They 'aven't 'ad much work since Black Dog dropped out and sold 'is share in the boat. They would 'ave crewed for the Greys, if the lugger 'adn't gone up in flames. Bein' on the straight and narrer 'asn't done you and your 'usband any favours.'

'The truth hurts,' Grace murmured.

'I respect you for stickin' to your principles, but is it worth puttin' yourself and your family through all this pain and sufferin' for the sake of your conscience?'

She had thought that it was, but she was beginning to doubt herself.

'I don't know. Have you seen my bonnet?' she said, changing the subject.

Grace dabbed a little soot and some pickled beetroot juice on Aggie's cheeks, then wiped it

221

off, knowing that it wouldn't fool Winnie.

Having bade farewell to Sarah, she left the tavern with Aggie slung across her breast and her shopping basket over her arm, and set out to cover the four miles to Westcliffe. Being accustomed to long walks, it didn't occur to her to ask for a lift. Walking into the countryside, she let her mind drift back to the days when she would have come to pick a posy of soldier's buttons, buttercups and daisies from the hedgerow and run home to give them to her mother. She had never envisaged that she would have to endure the shame of having to beg from her sister.

When she reached her destination, she walked on up to the big white house that was set back from the country road. She passed through the lawned garden at the front where the flowerbeds were filled with rose bushes, geraniums and hollyhocks, then walked up the steps and rang the bell. No one answered, but it was such a grand house that it would take a sennight to get from one end to the other, Grace thought, ringing it for a second and third time.

Eventually, a maid came to the door. 'If you're 'awkin' goods, go away and don't come back.'

'I've come to see Mrs Fleet. I'm her sister,' Grace said firmly.

'Oh? I'll see if she'll receive you.'

Shortly afterwards, Winnie appeared.

'Well I never . . . You could have knocked me down with a feather when Ann announced that you were here. Grace, you're so thin — you look like a ghost. What am I doing? Come on in.' Winnie stepped aside as the baby in her arms

222

tugged at her dress.

'Hello.' Grace gently pinched the chubby red-haired boy's cheek.

'This is Tommy — he's six months old now. I wasn't certain at the time, but it turns out that I was carrying him when I last saw you.' Winnie eyed her curiously. 'Oh, who is this?'

'This is Aggie,' Grace said, bursting with maternal pride.

'Louisa hasn't mentioned her.'

'I haven't seen Louisa for ages.'

'You didn't invite us to the christening.'

'She isn't — we haven't— '

'Oh Grace . . . I despair. What has become of you?' Winnie took a step back. 'I don't know why you've come, but on reflection, I don't want you here unsettling the girls. You must go back where you belong.' It was too late. Three little girls came out of the drawing room — two running and one toddling behind them — along with a scruffy grey dog with a red ribbon around its neck. 'Ann, take the children outside. Let them choose some flowers for the table.'

'Yes, ma'am,' the maid said, gathering them together as Winnie shooed Grace on to the steps.

'Why will you not allow me to speak to them?' Grace asked sadly.

'I have my reasons,' Winnie said. 'What really brings you here? Did that husband of yours send you?'

'I came of my own accord.' She couldn't do it, she realised. She couldn't bring herself to stoop so low as to beg her sister for money, even though she was afraid of what Isaiah would say — or do —

223

to her when she returned home empty-handed. 'I wanted to . . . ' she shrugged as she heard shrieks of laughter coming from outside. 'I'm glad to see that you and the children are well and happy. And you're right, I should go.'

Winnie's manner softened a little. 'Grace, has he hurt you? Are you scared of him?' When she didn't respond, she went on, 'It must be hard for you to discuss what goes on behind closed doors, but if you fear for your life, then you must speak up. You know that anything you say to me will be in confidence.'

'He isn't unkind to me,' Grace said uncertainly. 'We argue, but it's no different from any other married couple.'

'Then if it isn't about love, it's about money,' Winnie said. 'I'm sorry, but it's no use coming to me. I've told you before that I'll never let that wastrel get his hands on a single penny.'

'It isn't his fault that we're struggling.'

'I've heard rumours that he lets his old gang use the tavern as a rondy as he did in the past, that he overstretched himself when he had the place extended . . . Grace, I can't help him — he is beyond it, but I can help you. Don't go back to him. Stay here — you and the baby — with me, Billy and the children, and I'll see you right. We're in need of a nanny — you'd be perfect for the role.'

'No, Winnie.' Grace's eyes blurred with tears. 'I'm very grateful, but I can't leave my husband.' She recalled him saying in the past how he couldn't live without her, and her heart clenched with pain as she thought of his desolation should she not

224

return. 'He adores this little one. He'd be broken if I took her away.'

'Don't be too hasty. If you want to stay with him out of love and mutual affection — ' Winnie emphasised the word 'mutual' '— so be it, but if it's out of duty or wishing to keep up appearances in society, then you must steel yourself and leave him. If he comes here to drag you back, Billy and I will protect you.'

'He isn't a bad man. He doesn't drink much or gamble, and he's doing his best to keep away from smuggling.'

'Then he is the bee's knees and you should count yourself lucky.' Winnie gave her a searching look. 'Grace, it's your decision.'

Torn, she took time to think. She was sorely tempted by the prospect of being nanny to the children and living in comfort at Westcliffe, away from the predatory George Minnis and the onslaught of Isaiah's creditors, never knowing when someone was going to turn up demanding money. However, her sense of duty and loyalty ran too deep. She could never leave him.

'I have to go home,' she said simply. 'I'm sorry to have bothered you.'

'I don't understand you, but there we go. We're all different,' Winnie sighed. 'Let me ask Cook if there's anything you can take home with you.' She held out her hand for the basket, went inside and came back a few minutes later, the basket heavier with a bundle of rhubarb sticks lying across the top.

'Thank you,' Grace said. 'Give my love to Billy.'

'Convey my regards to your husband in return,'

Winnie said stiffly. 'And Grace—'

'Yes?' Halfway down the steps, she looked back.

'Take care of yourself and the baby.'

'I will.'

As Grace walked the four miles back to Deal, she noticed a leather purse hidden within the stalks of rhubarb which had been tied together with twine. She stopped and opened it. Inside, she found four crowns and a note in Winnie's handwriting: *For a rainy day*. Biting back tears, she tucked them inside her bodice.

Despite it being the end of June, there was a distinct chill in the air as she walked through Hawksdown and Walmer back to town. The bells of St Leonard's chimed noon as she went past, yet the sun at its zenith was partially obscured by a haze like dust drifting across a brickfield.

Carrying on along the Dover road, she passed the North Barracks, a three-storey building with a clock tower, then the great walls of the castle, and the Shutter Station on the seafront, where the glassmen watched day and night, sending coded signals via its octagonal shutters that could be flipped upright and sideways, all the way to the Admiralty in London via a series of similar towers.

There were only a hundred or so ships in the roadstead and Beach Street was oddly quiet — the men at the remaining boatyard appeared to have laid down tools. The fishing boats were out, as were the luggers, and a handful of the shore boys were kicking a pig's bladder around.

''Ave you got a penny to spare for a man who's down on 'is luck?'

She stopped and looked down towards a heap

of lobster pots and discarded nets where an old Jack Tar was sitting on the ground with a couple of his mates. Grace recoiled when she noticed the filthy state of their dress, the rents in their brown linen shirts and the holes in their boots.

'I wouldn't normally ask, missus, but you 'ave a kind face, and my pockets are empty.' The sailor's forearm was adorned with the tattoo of a serpent and one of his fingers was missing.

'We 'aven't eaten a morsel since Wednesday,' one of the others contributed. 'We've been lookin' for work, but there's none to be 'ad. We're bold men who fought for our country — now they've thrown us away, like the contents of a pisspot. Who'd 'ave thought, eh? When I volunteered for the King's shillin', I did it by choice, riskin' losin' my life to save my fellow countrymen.'

'You joined up because you was told the navy were never short 'o rum and wittles,' their companion jested. A wracking cough caught him up short.

'I haven't got much.' Grace extracted one of the crowns.

'You will share it,' she said, dropping it into the first sailor's palm. His eyes lit up in wonder.

'Who'd rabbit it? A piece o' silver. Of course, missus. God bless you.'

'I wish I had more to spare.'

'This and the sight of your lovely smile is enough.'

'You flatter me,' she smiled wryly before leaving them to talk of their good fortune and made her way into Golden Street. She pulled her bonnet down to shade her face and took her place at the

227

end of the small queue waiting outside the pawn-broker's.

The baby opened her eyes and yawned.

'Hush, my sweet,' Grace whispered. 'Please, don't open your lungs. It wasn't long ago that I fed you.' She'd stopped in the shelter of a hedge to attend to her. Aggie's face creased, her cheeks grew pink, her mouth opened wide and she screamed. 'There, there, my little darling.' Grace rocked and jiggled her, aware that all eyes were on her, a terrible mother who couldn't soothe her child.

'Mine were like him . . . her,' the woman behind her in the queue commented. 'Don't worry about everyone else. She'll quieten down soon enough.'

Not soon enough for some, Grace thought as the old man ahead of her put his hands over his ears. Trying not to cry, she kissed Aggie on her forehead and hummed a lullaby until she fell asleep again, just before the pawnbroker called her inside and introduced himself.

'What do you think, Mr Turner?' she asked, handing him the pendant and chain.

'It isn't worth much.' He examined the stone with his eyeglass and looked for a hallmark on the yellow metal clasp, shaking his head and tugging at his moustache, but his act was too late. Grace had noticed the avaricious glint in his eye and the glimmer of appreciation when he first laid eyes on the jewel, and it was enough to convince her not to pawn it, at least not yet.

Whose opinion did she believe? Her husband's or Mr Turner's?

'I can give you four shillings for it on my customary terms or I can buy it from you outright for

228

seven.'

'I'll think about it.' If he wasn't going to lend her enough money to make a difference, then she had a reason to keep it. Once she had loved it for its sentimental value, but now she recognised it as a reminder to take everything her husband said with a pinch of salt. 'Thank you for your time.'

On arriving back at the tavern, she went inside, hoping to avoid Isaiah, but he was in the taproom, sitting at the counter and sharpening his knife over a pigeon carcase while the dog sat drooling at his feet.

'What did they say?'

'Louisa sent me away,' she lied. 'And Winnie refused to allow me into her house.'

He spat on the knife and wiped it, then tested the sharpness, shaving the tiniest curl of skin from his palm. 'Then it is decided — there is only one way out. Hey, where are you goin'?'

'To leave this in the kitchen for Sarah — she can stew the rhubarb for later.' Supporting Aggie in the sling across her breast, Grace nodded towards the basket. 'Then I'm going upstairs to feed the baby.' She needed time alone to digest the fact that she and Isaiah were never going to be thought of as a respectable, law-abiding couple like Louisa and Jason, and Winnie and Billy. She was devastated. How would she face her sisters, and former friends and acquaintances like Mary and Albert, when they found out that she had ended up — as they had warned her — a smuggler's wife?

229

14

Heads or Tails?

'I've 'eard through the grapevine that you want to see me.'

Smiling, George took off his coat and gave it to Grace when he arrived at the Rattling Cat one evening a few days later.

'Ah yes. Welcome!' Isaiah said, swaggering across to shake his hand.

'I'm expectin' good news.'

'I prefer to discuss our business in private.' Isaiah nodded towards the corner of the taproom where Digger and the rest of the smugglers — Dunk, Cutthroat, Awful Doins and Lawless — were playing cards.

'You can say what you 'ave to say in front of them — they're workin' for me now. I'm proud to call them Greys and delighted to introduce Digger as my right'and man, the position havin' been vacant since my father-in-law met with an accident, his skull crushed when he wandered into a bull pen one night.'

Isaiah's bluster vanished. 'Yes. Yes, George. I too look forward to playin' my part.'

'Is your wife willin' to support you in pledgin' her loyalty to the Greys?'

'I speak for Mrs Feasey. She does as I bid her.' Isaiah glared at Grace, warning her not to speak.

Defeated, she kept her mouth shut and her head bowed. Her dreams had been shattered. The moniker of the smuggler's wife would be with her for the rest of her life, an accurate portrayal of who she was and would be, because she couldn't see how on earth Isaiah would be persuaded to leave the free trade for a second time.

'Ah, then I'm cock-a-hoop. We all are, aren't we, lads? Let's drink to the Greys and a prosperous future. The drinks are on me.'

'There's no ale,' Sarah interrupted. 'I've just poured the last pint.'

George frowned. 'How can you 'ave a tavern without ale? Digger, my man, run along to Causton's place.' He took a purse from his pocket and poured coins into Digger's palm. 'Fetch some jugs of ale.'

'Aye, Captain,' Digger said, grinning.

'You go too, Black Dog,' George said.

'I'm the landlord, not an errand boy,' Isaiah glowered, then apparently remembering that he couldn't afford to offend the man who had the potential to save him and his family from penury, he curled his lips into a half-smile, half-snarl and said, 'I'll go. Sarah, some wittles for our honoured guest.'

Sarah scurried into the kitchen and the men went to buy ale, leaving Grace alone with George.

'Aren't you goin' to thank me?' he asked.

'As you know, my husband speaks for me. I have no voice with which to express my gratitude.'

'That's the cleverest answer I've heard in a long

231

time,' he said, amused. 'Your 'usband is neither a drinker nor a gambler, but I don't mind wagerin' that by the end of this evening, 'e'll be both.'

'Isaiah has made mistakes, but he's no fool and you're wrong to play him for one. For your information, neither of us gamble.'

'We'll see,' he grinned. ''Ow's the littlun?'

'She's well, thank you,' she said, resenting the intrusion and praying that the men would be back soon.

'Hey, lads. This is on George.' Digger and Isaiah came hurrying in from the street, sploshing ale across the sawdust as they carried their jugs to the counter. Grace poured the drinks and Isaiah and the smugglers went to sit down with George in the dining room where he regaled them with stories of the Greys' exploits.

'One of our number is what I'd call an 'ard drinker — when he's 'alf cut, 'e's 'elpless, not quarrelsome at all. Anyway, last winter, we were on a run when 'e and 'is companion, on 'earin' there were some soldiers nearby, 'id be'ind an 'edge. Seein' they were stuck there for the duration, they tapped one of the tubs they 'ad with them and drank themselves senseless. It took their minds off their troubles, I suppose, but they ended up lyin' outside all night in the frost.

'Next mornin', I went to look for them and I found one dead drunk and the other dead as a doornail. When I asked the livin' one 'ow 'is friend 'ad met 'is end, 'e replied that 'e'd died of what 'e loved.' George took a small dagger from his belt and stabbed at the hunk of pork that Sarah had served him. 'I like my lads to 'ave a drink now and

232

then, but I can't 'ave them stealin' my property.'

'Did the gentleman l'arn his lesson?' Awful Doins asked, wide-eyed.

'Oh yes. He had a dunkin' in the Royal Military Canal before he agreed to pay me back in full for what he'd drunk.'

A little unnerved at George's methods of dealing with his wayward smugglers, Grace topped up their tankards while he was finishing his meal.

'That was what I'd call acceptable. I see that there are some improvements to be made to this establishment, both materially and to the level of service, the quality of the food and the like, but there are the bones of a business 'ere,' he said, wiping his mouth. 'If I employ the right landlord to run the place, I believe I will do very well.'

All eyes turned to Isaiah.

'You've sold out to George?' Awful Doins said.

'You might as well know — I signed the tavern over as part of the settlement of my debt,' Isaiah said, downcast. Grace moved round and rested her hand on his shoulder. He covered her hand with his. 'The Rattlin' Cat doesn't belong to the Feaseys any longer — I'll be workin' for George from now on. As for where my wife and I shall live . . .'

'Black Dog, to show you that your superior, the Captain of the Greys, is a reasonable and fair man, I'd like to give you the option to win the tavern back.'

Isaiah got to his feet and clasped his hands together. 'You would give me that chance? But 'ow?'

Grace didn't share his expectation that George

meant what he said.

'Isaiah, it's a trick,' she whispered into his ear. 'He has no intention of letting you keep your birthright.'

''E's a man of 'is word.' Isaiah moved back to the table. 'George, what are you proposin'?'

'A duel,' Dunk suggested.

'A game of cards,' said Lawless.

'Neither of those,' George beamed. 'I thought that we'd settle it with the toss of a coin.'

'Then it is a wager, not a competition of skill or intelligence?' Grace cut in.

'That's right, my dear,' George said condescendingly. 'The whole of life is a gamble.'

'Lady Luck 'as never smiled on me.' Isaiah faded. 'Perhaps this time, she will.'

'Isaiah, come with me. I need to say something,' Grace said.

'Whatever you 'ave to say, you can say it in front of our friends.'

'Why do you never listen to me?' she snapped. 'You mustn't agree to this.' If George won, the Rattling Cat was his and there was no going back. As it was, there was still the faintest chance that they would find a way of paying him back and keeping the tavern. 'We could lose everything.'

'That's right: lock, stock and barrel,' George said. 'All fixtures and fittin's pertaining to the business of runnin' the tavern, includin' the cats because they're part of it, but not the dog. He lowers the tone of the place, scratchin' 'is ears and lickin' his nether parts in front of all and sundry. But you could win, Black Dog . . . and your debt to me will be settled.'

'By the toss of a coin, you say?' Isaiah confirmed, as George wiped his plate clean with a hunk of bread, then ate it in two bites. Then he reached down and unlaced his left boot, reached inside and extracted a gold coin. Having put his boot back on, keeping the coin in his palm, he proceeded to wave it in front of Isaiah's nose.

'While we're on the subject of gamblin', I'll bet you 'aven't seen one of these for a long time; a guinea, the 1813 military issue no less.'

'I w-w-wouldn't know,' Isaiah said, discombobulated.

'You aren't going to do this.' Grace tugged on his sleeve, but he brushed her off. 'How do we know that this isn't a trick, a sham? Let me see the coin at least.'

'Oh? Don't you trust old George? I'd be showin' 'im a little more gratitude for 'is patience and generosity, if I was you. You'd 'ave been out on the street a long time ago, if it 'adn't been for my intervention.' He was teasing her, she thought. If he didn't show her the coin, she could be sure he was out to cheat her husband of his last remaining claim to his property. 'I could foreclose on our deal at any time.'

'The coin,' she said firmly, refusing to allow George to dupe Isaiah out of his property.

'Stop mitherin' the gen'leman. He's tryin' to 'elp us.'

'He's trying to help himself . . . Why can't you see it?'

'Ah, Grace. You're more of a lioness than the pussycat I judged you to be,' George mocked. 'Your villainous husband could l'arn a few lessons

235

from you. Here . . . Come closer.'

Reluctantly, she took a step towards him. He held out his fist, and repeatedly hooked his index finger in her direction, drawing her closer. Shuddering with revulsion, she let him take her hand, caging her fingers for far longer than necessary before dropping the coin into her palm.

'That is the King's 'ead, I believe,' he said.

She turned the coin over.

'You agree that that is the spade shield design on the reverse?'

She nodded, giving the coin back.

'Then it is a fair competition, relyin' only on luck, nothin' else.' George stood up and called Digger over to him. 'Digger, my man, I shall ask you to do the honours. As a friend to us both, no one could possibly question your impartiality.'

Grace found that she couldn't argue on that point.

'See for yourself that the coin is good,' George went on, handing it over to his deputy.

Digger held it up to the lanternlight and studied both sides, then ran it across his teeth.

'Well?'

Was she imagining it or was there an extra element of challenge in George's voice? Or was he nervous, realising that he was on the verge of winning or losing the tavern, a property of considerable worth in Deal?

'It's good, George,' Digger said, keeping his eyes averted.

'Then we will start . . . shall we say, best of three? I choose 'Heads' as the captain of the Greys.'

'Just get on with it,' Isaiah muttered. He took Grace's hand, unable to disguise the tremor in his fingers and the sweat leaking into his palm.

Digger flicked the coin from his thumb, sending it flipping through the air. It fell back into his hand. "'Eads,' he said gruffly, showing Isaiah and Grace, who could hardly bear to look. He repeated the process a second time, and the coin clattered across the flagstones. Grace knelt to examine it, her lifeblood draining away when she saw the King's regal profile staring towards the table-leg.

'Help her up — she's come over all funny,' George said abruptly.

'I'm all right.' She reached for the coin, but George's boot landed on it before she could get hold of it.

'You can't 'ave that, my dear. It's my lucky guinea.'

'And the agent of our misfortune,' she cried. Her head spinning, she dragged herself up and sat on a chair, keeping her eyes on her husband who stared back, white as a ghost and unseeing.

'I'm sorry,' Digger murmured.

'We have lost everything!'

'Let me help you.' George tucked the coin back inside his boot.

'I reckon you've given us more than enough help already,' Grace spat.

He held up his hand.

'As an esteemed member of the Greys, you and your husband — and the littlun,' he added as Aggie started to cry from her cradle upstairs, 'are entitled to receive certain benefits, such as access to a physician and attorney when required.

237

There's a cottage available for a peppercorn rent in Snargate — it's small but adequate for a family of three.' He grinned. 'Beggars can't be choosers, can they? I'll send a cart to collect you and your personal belongin's at first light the day after tomorrow.' He moved around behind Isaiah and patted him on the back. 'Never let it be said that George Minnis doesn't look after the men — and women — who pledge their loyalty to 'im.'

'Don't expect the streets of Snargate to be paved with gold,' Digger said. 'I've been there and it's a tiddly little place with a church and a few 'ouses, a bakery and shop, a forge . . . and a wheelwright's.'

'It's all right. I'd 'ad enough of the tavern anyway. It's been a millstone around our necks — constantly kowtowin' to this one and that, the guests fussin' about the strength of the ale and quality of the beef. I'm glad to be out of it. I'm ready for pastures new. If only my wife's sisters could 'ave found it in their 'earts to assist us in our time of need . . . Mind you, I do 'ave my pride. If they 'ad offered, I'd 'ave struggled to accept it.' In a rare moment of insight, he went on, 'Grace, I'm sorry to 'ave dragged you into this, but I can feel it in my bones — Snargate is where we're goin' to make our fortune.'

Dashing tears from her eyes, Grace ran upstairs to comfort Aggie, leaving Sarah to look after the men.

In the morning, she took the baby downstairs to the taproom where she found Isaiah slumped on the floor in front of the fireplace with Musket. Several empty tankards lying on their sides were

238

scattered around him. She walked across and stooped to shake his shoulder.

'Isaiah,' she said.

He answered her with a loud snore.

'Wake up. Ugh, you stink of drink.' Disgusted and upset that George's predictions had come to pass, she stood up and went into the kitchen where the pots and pans were piled up in the sink, untouched from the night before. She fished one out and rinsed it, then lit the fire and used up the last of the oats from the pantry to make porridge. She had been too kind, thoughtful and accommodating in the past, and far too gullible. As an act of rebellion — against George and Isaiah, the men who had brought her down — she cooked enough for herself, and no one else, and took it into the dining room. 'Mornin', Grace. I've come to say goodbye for now.'

Sarah was carrying a carpetbag and a box.

'Where are you going?' Grace asked, feeling bereft.

'I'm sorry for leavin' you like this, but it isn't our responsibility any more. The tavern belongs to George.'

'You don't have to remind me,' Grace sighed. 'I haven't thought of anything else all night.'

'Digger and I are goin' to Folkestone to see my family on our way to Snargate where George has offered us board and lodgin' at his house in return for me lookin' after his poorly wife.' Sarah moved round and touched Grace's arm. 'It isn't all bad. We'll still be able to see each other, livin' in the same village and our 'usbands bein' in the same line of business. I'll call on you as soon as I can.'

239

Having lost her appetite, Grace dropped her spoon and swept Aggie into her arms, then went to the taproom window to watch Sarah and Digger leave.

'Why didn't you wake me?' Isaiah grumbled, rubbing at his temple when he staggered to his feet just before noon. 'My 'ead 'urts.'

I have no sympathy, was on the tip of her tongue, but he looked so unwell and dejected that she returned to her task of packing up their belongings in silence.

* * *

'There's quite a stir outside,' Isaiah said, tying his cravat as he dressed on the morning they were due to leave for Snargate. 'It looks like most of Deal 'ave come to wave the town's most notorious free trader off on 'is journey to a fortune. It'll be quite a tale to tell their children and gran'children.'

'Is that why you're dressing up?' Grace asked, listening to the sound of voices outside on the street.

'That's right, and you must too. We're goin' to walk out there with our 'eads 'eld 'igh, because we 'ave nothin' to be ashamed of. Put on the gown you wore for our weddin' and the jewellery I've given you.' At the sound of a knock on the door, he added, 'There's no need to rush. They can wait for us.'

Ignoring him, she went to answer it.

'Good morning, missus. My name's Mr Paddick. Mr Minnis sent me.' The young man on the doorstep bowed his head.

'Oh, we aren't ready,' she stammered.

'I'll wait. You've been cryin'.' She was about to tell him off for being impertinent, but there was something about his gentle manner that stopped her. He was about twenty-three or twenty-four, she guessed, and had a fair countenance, ruddy cheeks, eyes the colour of cobnuts and a quiff of blond hair. 'Your transport's around the corner — I left it there, assumin' that you would wish to leave quietly and discreetly, but I see that that's impossible.' He waved his arm towards the crowd outside. 'Look at all these people, more than if Farmer George was leaving Buckin'am Palace.

'I'll fetch the 'orse and cart. Bring a tarpaulin to cover your boxes if you 'ave any — the rain's settin' in.'

Grace went back upstairs to dress and prepare Aggie for the journey while Isaiah and the carter loaded the cart. She took one last look around the tavern, her heart aching as she recalled the occasion not so long ago when Isaiah had carried her over the threshold and another when she first held the baby in her arms.

When it was time to leave, Isaiah helped her into the cart where she sat on one of their boxes cradling Aggie, feeling like a goldfish in a bowl as people stared and pointed their fingers.

'Who'd 'ave thought they'd have come to this?' Old Mr Witherall was saying.

'I knew all along that this would 'appen. I told 'er so, but would she listen?' Mrs Witherall said, her face half hidden under a large black umbrella. 'Why 'aven't you been to see your sister, Grace? That's right — you 'ang your 'ead in shame. You

241

brought this on yourself, marryin' a villain.'

Her spine stiffened. 'I'm not ashamed,' she snapped back. 'Upset and sorry, but not ashamed because this situation is not of my making.'

'That don't explain why you 'aven't told Louisa where you're off to. Where are you goin'?'

'If you must know, we're moving to a popular village in Romney Marsh,' Grace said through gritted teeth. 'We have a beautiful home ready and waiting for us. Tell my sister that I'll write to her with our new address.' She wished she could tell her herself, but Mrs Witherall was right: she couldn't face letting her know how far they had sunk.

'You'll 'ate livin' there,' Mrs Witherall said, unconvinced. 'Them marshfolk are backward and be'ind the times. You'll recognise them by the way they walk about with straw 'angin' from their mouths and carryin' pitchforks.'

'Hush, the carter'll hear you,' Old Mr Witherall warned.

'No, he can't.'

'Oh yes, I can,' the young man called cheerfully. 'No offence taken.'

Trying to console Aggie who wouldn't stop crying, Grace turned away as the carter flicked his whip and sent the horse and cart lurching forward, scattering the crowd.

Isaiah whistled for Musket who followed at a lope behind them. 'I don't want to go to Snargate,' Grace said when the baby began to settle, thanks to the movement of the cart. 'We belong in Deal — this is our home. This is where we've chosen to bring up our daughter, within sight and

242

sound of the sea.'

'Stop grumblin'. I know this isn't what you dreamed of, but your 'usband's done his best. My father was right when 'e said that I'd turn out to be a square peg in a round 'ole. I 'ate havin' to hob-nob with strangers. I'm good at smugglin', and in partnership with George, there's no limit to what we can earn.'

She didn't contradict him, certain that George saw him as an employee or servant, not an equal. If George said, fetch ale, Isaiah would. If George said, jump, Isaiah would ask, how high? If George said, shoot that officer . . . she brought her thoughts up short. Would he do it?

'We're going to 'ave a roof over our 'eads and an occupation that's better rewarded than the 'ospitality trade. We 'ave our daughter, and each other.' He rested his hand on her knee as the cart trundled on. 'What more could we wish for?'

That they could make their living from honest means, she thought. Looking back, she'd been so naive and in love when she'd married him, that she'd managed to convince herself that he wasn't a villain. Since then she'd had to accept that he was indeed a wrongdoer, but he was her wrongdoer and she loved him. If it meant keeping her family off the streets, she would play her part as a smuggler's wife.

As they continued on their journey in the rain, Aggie fell asleep and Isaiah began to converse with the carter.

'My wife 'as a way with 'orses,' he said. 'She 'as many 'idden talents. Do you do much work for George?'

''E's always callin' on me for transport, but I never ask 'im what it's for, if you know what I mean. I won't say that I know the gentleman. See no evil, 'ear no evil, speak no evil: that's my motto.'

'Do you 'ave a wife and children?'

'No . . . I'm a widow.'

'I wish I 'adn't pried,' Isaiah said.

'I brought my Clary from Dover six months ago, and she died within three . . . from marsh fever.' He fell silent before continuing, 'My brother keeps tellin' me to go and find another young lady, but I'm not goin' to be like the rest who bring four or five brides to the marshes, each one dyin' after the other. I loved Clary and I miss 'er. And there's nothin' I'd like more than the company of a wife, but I won't let another woman suffer like she did.'

'Is there any way of avoiding it?' Grace wondered aloud.

'We did everythin' — kept our doors and winders closed, and made sure she was home by early evenin'. As for a cure, the 'erbs, white wine, vinegar and rosewater didn't work.' He smiled ruefully. 'The only way of keepin' it at bay is to stay away from the marsh.' Aggie howled for a while as though sympathising for Mr Paddick's loss.

'She 'as a great pair of lungs on 'er,' Isaiah said proudly as if he was the only man in the world to have a daughter.

Grace fed her, winded her and let her lie in her arms, watching the world go by as they journeyed through Ringwould and Dover, Folkestone and Hythe, and Dymchurch. Mr Paddick's mention of his sad loss had filled her with alarm. How would she ever sleep for worrying about the mysterious

244

marsh fever that could make her child sicken and die, or leave her without a mother? Why hadn't she thought more carefully about Winnie's offer for her to be nanny to her children? She didn't want to lose Aggie or die here on the lonely marsh.

'Grace, you aren't listening to me.' Isaiah's voice cut into her thoughts. 'I said, it would behove you to mark the lie of the land for future reference.' He slid his arm around her back when the carter took the road through New and Old Romney, but his touch didn't make her feel any less homesick for Deal.

The rainclouds were clearing to the east, allowing the sun to make a brief appearance. A rainbow arced overhead, one end curving into a windswept clump of stunted trees, the other disappearing into thin air — where the pot of gold should be, she observed wryly — when a shepherd emerged from his hut to wave his crook and wish them a safe journey.

The marshes seemed like a foreign country, the green and fertile flatlands ringing with buzzing flies, the grasshopper's rattling trill and the bleating of a thousand sheep. There were a few sleek cattle grazing near Old Romney, some fighting for shade beneath a handful of willow trees, the rest stamping their feet and licking their hides.

'You won't get through this way at times in winter,' the carter said, pointing out the vast expanse of Walland Marsh, more flatland overgrown with rushes and purple thistle, and criss-crossed by lanes and ditches. 'This area lies lower than Romney Marsh, makin' it very swampy. If you don't sink in a bog or fall into a sewer — that's what we call the ditches around 'ere — and drown, the bad air will kill you.' He fell silent again.

Having reached the crossroads at Brenzett, he ignored the left turn towards Brookland and Camber, and drove straight ahead.

'Is it much further, Mr Paddick?' Grace asked, beginning to wonder if their journey would ever end.

'A couple of miles, that's all. To avoid confusion, you can call me Peter — the gentleman who's lettin' the cottage is my brother, Mr John Paddick. He's the blacksmith who owns the forge and cottage opposite yours.' He chuckled. 'You're going to be marsh folk, the people who are charged with servin' God and honourin' the King . . . or his spendthrift son, Prinny . . . but only after maintainin' the wall. That's the priority of the landowners 'ere, because without it, the sea will swallow us up.'

They stopped at the Red Lion in Snargate — George had an account with the proprietor which meant that they didn't have to pay the bill for their refreshments — before they took a lane from the centre of the village and followed it for a few hundred yards.

'This is it. This is your new abode,' Mr Paddick said enthusiastically, pulling the horse up in front of a pair of attached cottages. 'If there's anythin' I can do, anythin' . . . '

'You could give us an 'and with this lot.' Isaiah waved towards the cart. They hadn't brought much, Grace thought: Aggie's cradle; a mattress and linen; plates and cutlery, and a couple of pans; her jewellery box; their clothes. Isaiah had wanted

246

to take one of the tables, but she'd forbidden it, not wanting to have George accuse them of stealing his fixtures and fittings.

While the men were unloading the contents of the cart just inside the gate and Musket was exploring the overgrown garden, Grace took a closer look at their new home, a timber-framed hovel. It was worse than she'd thought. The chimney was leaning precariously to one side and the cowl was missing. Several roof tiles had fallen off, the door appeared to be off its hinges and the path leading up to it was overgrown with brambles.

'Are we at the right place?' she asked.

'This is Hazel Cottage. The one to your left is Beech Cottage — it's derelict at present, but my brother has plans to do it up. If you look across the lane, you'll see Forge Cottage where he lives with his family.'

Grace followed his gaze, looking towards the substantial house built in Kentish ragstone, a cobbled yard in front of it. A horse was standing tied to a ring in the wall and she could see a figure moving about in the attached building, a blacksmith in a leather apron, taking a shoe from a glowing furnace. He stepped outside with the shoe on a pritchel, gave them a wave and shouted to his brother, before attending to the horse.

Grace turned back towards the cottage. If she hadn't been so hasty in settling for Isaiah, she could have been in Mary's shoes, living in a generously proportioned house in the desirable area of Walmer. For that, she would have had to marry Albert and live quietly, without danger or excitement. There was a time when the idea would have repelled her, but now she could see its appeal.

'I'm sorry if it isn't what you're expectin', missus,' Peter said. 'The previous tenant left in rather an 'urry.'

'Why? What happened?' Grace asked.

Peter thought for a moment. 'All things considered it's probably better you don't find out. Anyway, my brother 'asn't 'ad time to tidy it up — he'll knock a bit off the rent for the inconvenience of 'avin' to clear it up yourselves.' He left the last of their boxes on the ground. 'I wish you all the best,' he said, touching his cap. 'I expect we'll meet again — as you're workin' for Mr Minnis.'

'Workin' with 'im,' Isaiah bragged.

Smiling sagely, Peter returned to the cart and drove off, leaving Grace to walk slowly up the path, Isaiah picking the brambles away from her skirt as she went. A chill began to seep into her bones as she entered the cottage: a one-up-one-down that smelled like a pigsty. The floor was covered with dust and stones, and a dead rat, baring its yellow teeth in welcome, lay in the fireplace.

'We can't bring up Aggie here,' she said, holding her shawl across the baby's face to protect her from the stench of damp.

'It'll be all right with a bit of a clean. I can fix the door and cut the brambles back.' Isaiah, for all his earlier bravado, looked defeated without an audience. He had gambled everything and lost. 'This time it will work out, my love. One day, we'll 'ave an 'ouse like Winnie's, but in Deal and we'll never 'ave to work again, just lounge about idle from dawn till dusk. Let me fetch our things before we see the rest of it.'

Grace perched on the bench seat under the window in the kitchen area to feed Aggie before settling her in her cradle downstairs and looking around with Isaiah. There wasn't much to see, just an upstairs room for sleeping and a garden with an earth privy at the rear.

'It's horrid,' Grace exclaimed as they returned down the rickety staircase, the walls and ceilings seeming to press in on her. 'You let George steal our property and our livelihood from right under our noses. How are you going to protect and support your wife now?' Bitter bile fluxed into her throat. 'By rights, I should leave you for breaking your promises to me.'

'You wouldn't!' His eyes narrowed; his pupils flared.

'I should walk out of here with Aggie and not come back.'

'Don't say that!' he growled.

'I'll say and do as I wish,' she retorted.

He walked over and grabbed her by the throat, taking her by surprise.

'Don't you dare leave me, or I'll— '

'Stop! Let me go!' she gasped, as the pressure on her windpipe grew, and she scrabbled to grasp his hands. His blood had rushed to his face, and as she began to lose consciousness, his skin seemed to turn black as if the Devil had taken over his soul. She tried to scream, but no sound came out of her mouth. She was dying . . .

She closed her eyes and began to pray for Aggie's future.

Suddenly, he released her and pushed her away. She fell to the floor, panting and gulping air into her bellows. Her chest hurt, but it was nothing compared with the pain in her heart that he'd inflicted by his violent action.

'No one has ever done anything like that to me before.' She looked up at him accusingly as he stared down at her, his eyes wet, his expression contrite. 'You almost throttled me to death.'

'I'm sorry, but you drove me to it,' he said, his voice rasping, as he offered his hand. Looking away, she stood up, touching the tender flesh on either side of her neck.

'You said you were goin' to leave me and take the baby with you. I saw red . . . You won't go, will you? We're promised to each other until death do us part.' A smile touched his lips. 'You see, I've remembered the vows we made. Grace, please . . .'

'I should walk away after what you've just done to me. I might be my husband's chattel, but I'm not staying with a wife beater.'

He knelt in front of her, took her hands and kissed them, making her flesh crawl.

'I'll never do it again. I swear on Aggie's life . . . Look,' he went on when she remained silent, 'it wasn't meant to be like this. I wanted to give you everythin', my sweet, but we've ended up with nothin'.' She watched the muscle in his cheek twitching as he waited for her to give in to him. 'If you do leave me, you'll be goin' without the baby. Could you do that? Could you bring yourself to foller in my mother's footsteps?'

A tear rolled down her cheek at the thought of being parted from Aggie.

'Don't cry, my love. We're both exhausted,' he

250

said. 'Neither of us are in our right minds.'

'I'll stay,' she said, her heart softening. 'I do love you, but if that ever happens again, I will walk away and never come back. And I will take Aggie with me.'

'Thank you,' he said, pulling himself up and holding out his arms. 'Thank you,' he repeated over and over as she steeled herself to receive his embrace. Whether she liked it or not, they were in the mire together. Somehow, they had to find the strength to dig themselves out of it and make a different kind of life on the marsh. She wasn't sure that they could be happy again after what he'd done — she doubted that she could forgive or forget.

15

Slops for the Duffers

The sound of birdsong and Isaiah whistling
'Greensleeves' woke Grace from a fitful sleep the
next morning. Yawning, she tipped Musket off the
end of the bed, dressed and fed Aggie and then
went downstairs to find Isaiah pouring two tankards of ale at the rickety table. He pushed one
across to her and handed her a plate of minted
cheese, an apple and a hunk of bread.

'What's this?' she asked, bemused.

'I'm trying to make it up to you.'

'Well, thank you.'

'I've picked the mould off,' he added.

'You seem more cheerful today.'

'Alas, my love, I did you wrong,' he sang, changing the lyrics to the song. 'Let me take the babe
and I'll show 'er what I've been doin' in the garden.'

She handed Aggie to him and sat on the bench,
supping ale and picking at the food while she
watched father and daughter through the open
door. Aggie was far too young to understand, she
observed, smiling as he carried her through a for-
est of weeds to the vegetable patch beyond.

'I've been doin' some diggin' for your ma so she

can try 'er 'and at growin' fruit and veg. Maybe she'll turn out to 'ave green fingers. She's a clever lady, quick-witted and good with letters and numbers, and maybe in retrospect, your old pa should 'ave taken a bit more notice of what she 'ad to say.'

Grace swallowed hard as a lump caught in her throat. A year had passed since their marriage, yet this was the first time she'd heard him praise her and confess that he might have made a mistake. It reassured her that he did care for her, but it wasn't enough to absolve him of his loss of temper the day before.

He walked about, rocking the baby and telling her the story of the gingerbread man, while the dog looked on and the sun tried to break through the sheet of grey cloud that covered the sky.

'Run, run as fast as you can, you can't catch me, I'm the gingerbread man . . . don't fret, Aggie. The real gingerbread man got caught and gobbled up by the wily fox, but your pa's not like 'im. 'E's goin' to keep 'imself out of trouble— 'e won't let Marlin get 'im, and 'e won't let old George gobble 'im up.'

Surprised at his view of George Minnis, Grace stood up and moved to the door.

'You are the apple of my eye, littlun. I'm goin' to make our fortune. Trust me.'

When Grace stepped outside, he looked up, abashed.

'You must think I'm goin' soft.'

'Aggie's lucky to have such a loving father.' She smiled, looking up at the ivy and honeysuckle that clothed the rear of the cottage, a little more optimistic that they would make something of

253

their new life on the marsh after all, although she desperately missed the sea. Her senses sought its salty tang, its everchanging colours and the way it heaved and rolled back and forth along the shore.

Walking across to the window of the adjacent cottage, she peered into the window.

'Why does no one live here?' she asked.

'It's fallin' down,' Isaiah replied, moving up beside her. 'The roof is beyond repair, the beams rotten — should anyone enter, it'll all come tumblin' down on their 'ead. At least, that's the story that the Greys have put about — I've 'ad a chat with John across the road this mornin'. 'E told me that George uses it as an 'idin' 'ole.'

'I don't like it.' A sense of unease crept across the back of her neck. 'If the gobblers come to search the area and find us living next door to a stash of tubs, they'll arrest us without question.' When she saw his face fall, she added, 'I'm sorry. I know you're doing your best.'

'Mornin'! I could hear voices, so I thought I'd introduce myself.' A woman appeared at the side gate. With long grey hair and a thin, lined face, she looked about forty, but when she moved swiftly towards them, she seemed younger. 'I'm Mrs Paddick, but you can call me Myrtle. I hope you're the neighbourly sort, not like Mr and Mrs Jones before. They're the ones who left the place in a state. They had some kind of a fallin'-out with George and did a moonlight flit. Anyway — ' she wouldn't let them get a word in edgewise '— I have a trio of layin' hens you can have — a gift from George. Next week's rent's been settled. After that, he expects you to pay your own way.

Oh, you have a littlun. What's her name?'

'Aggie,' Grace said. 'She's two and a half months old.'

'I have three boys under seven.' Smiling, Myrtle rolled her eyes. 'They're a right handful, but I wouldn't be without them. Come over later, after noon. You can meet them then. And there's work for you, Grace. It is Grace, isn't it?'

She nodded as Myrtle continued, almost breathless, 'George has put in an order for some clothin'. Can you sew? Of course you can. Right, I'd best hurry — I don't know what the boys'll get up to while I'm away.' With that, she disappeared.

'I think our neighbour may be slightly touched,' Isaiah whispered when Myrtle was out of earshot. 'She's a gabster, can't stop talkin'.'

'I don't know what to think. It seems that George has set us up good and proper, sending us here where Myrtle and John can spy on us on his behalf. I feel like we're under surveillance, as though he doesn't trust you.'

'You're wrong, but I'm not going to argue over it. If they're watchin' us and reportin' back to 'im, that's all to the good. When 'e realises that I do know what I'm doin' when it comes to the free trade, 'e'll put me above Digger. I 'ave to prove myself, and that's what I shall do, startin' this mornin' when John's taking me to meet some of George's men.'

Grace calculated that Digger had been promoted because George knew that he would do what he was told, whereas her husband was more opinionated and forceful. Isaiah and George would clash if Isaiah started throwing his weight around.

255

She hoped that her husband would restrain his ambition, suspecting that he would be better off being one of George's subalterns than his second in command.

* * *

Isaiah went out, leaving her with Aggie. She swept the kitchen floor, washed the windows and chased the spiders out, before making a closer inspection of the vegetable patch. There were some raspberry canes (the birds had taken all the fruit), a few runner beans that had been mauled by slugs, and lastly three potato plants. Curious, she dug one of them up, but all she found nestling in the soil was a harvest of potatoes the size of peas.

'Those aren't going to fill your pa's belly, are they?'

Aggie smiled and gurgled, then chewed on her fist.

'You're like a baby sparrow,' Grace chuckled. 'Always hungry.'

Feeling virtuous after her morning's efforts, she made her way across the road to the forge where she found Myrtle receiving another visitor.

'I didn't expect to see you today, Sarah,' Grace said, delighted to see her friend.

'We're only up the road.' Sarah took Aggie from her and cuddled her. 'I 'ave to be back in time to give Mrs Minnis her supper at seven, so I'm available to 'elp out until then. George said there was some work for us.'

'Come on in.' Myrtle showed them into a spacious kitchen where she had a pile of linen cut out

256

according to a pattern, some needles and thread, and scithers on the scrubbed pine table. There was a baby lying in a cradle, and two boys playing with saucepans and wooden spoons. 'These are my little soldiers,' Myrtle said fondly as they pretended to march to the drums. 'Abraham, Joseph and Neddie. I pray that I have a girl next time. Where are my manners? Do sit down. Can I get you some refreshment? Don't be shy. Put the littlun in the pram outside the back door — we'll hear her if she cries.'

Aggie was so distracted by the way the breeze was rustling the leaves on the apple boughs overhead that she didn't make a fuss when Sarah put her down in the homemade contraption consisting of a large, shell-shaped wicker basket on wheels, leaving Grace free to enjoy tea and cherry cake before the women settled down to sew.

'You know what these are?' Myrtle said.

'Yes,' Sarah said as Grace nodded.

'I don't know if you want to sew one complete outfit each, or have one doin' the crowns, another doin' the aprons, and another the thigh pockets.'

'You decide,' Grace suggested.

Myrtle gave Grace the crowns to work on while she and Sarah sewed the other sections. Grace threaded a needle and made a knot in the end, ready to join two pieces of material together to create a cap with pockets, into which a duffer — a landsman who carried tea — could stuff a dollop, or bag of leaves. Smiling to herself, she recalled seeing the duffers looking like fat puffs who'd eaten too many dinners, waddling up the beaches and making their way to the merchants waiting for them in Canterbury and London.

As she pushed the needle into the cloth, another memory came into her head: the day at Compass Cottage when she and her sisters had received a visit from Aunt Mary and their cousin Beth. Grace could recall every last detail as if it were yesterday, even down to Beth's dress: a grey bonnet and gown with a pink redingcote over the top that made her green with envy. Beth was two years older than Louisa, her appearance and manner more refined.

Having been invited in to the kitchen, not the parlour where she thought she belonged, Aunt Mary had given her opinion on those who were 'in trade', saying that her family were but a few acres short of being able to live on the rental income from their estate.

'One should always aim high — you've all seen what happens when you don't,' she said, a barbed dig at the Lennickers. Ma's side of the family had built up their income and property by growing food for a town that had become increasingly hungry, due to the War of American Independence, followed by the wars against France. There was little love lost between her father and her mother's family, the Laxtons, considering that she had married down — which was what Grace had done, too, marrying Isaiah against her sisters' wishes.

Winnie had snipped her thread and slid her needlework underneath a roll of linen, then fetched two chairs from the inglenook. Before Aunt Mary sat down, she moved up behind Grace and stared over her shoulder.

'Oh, let me see . . . Is it a garment of some kind?'

'You could say that, Aunt Mary,' Grace said. 'It's slops for the duffers.'

'I beg your pardon!' Her fingers were on her necklace, her eyes wide with shock.

'Not really. Of course it isn't,' Grace backtracked, thinking that her aunt was merely pearl clutching because she knew very well what trade the Lennickers followed. 'I'm making a pattern for a bustle. Mr Gigg has the most beautiful pale green muslin in his shop, and Pa has said that if I'm a dutiful daughter, he'll buy it for me to make a gown.'

'Then he is spoiling you,' their aunt said sternly. She left them a basket of fresh provisions from the farm and requested some tea to take home with her in exchange. She had some nerve, Grace thought, smiling to herself when Louisa said she could have some bloaters instead.

As they talked, Grace poured some tea made from the alleged last remnants of the leaves in the caddy, but at the sound of a thump and a door creaking, Aunt Mary was on her feet and out of the kitchen in a shot, intercepting Pa on his way along the hall.

'There you are, Robert,' she said, being one of the few people who used his given name rather than his nickname of Righteous. 'It's no use — you can't keep hiding from me,' she added as she came back into the room, sending him ahead of her with her arms held out each side as if she was driving a wayward pig into its sty. He turned, coughing and rubbing his red-rimmed eyes.

259

'What can I do for you, Mary?'

'It's about the girls. It worries me that you allow them to walk the streets unchaperoned, to come and go, and do as they please. My husband saw Grace walking alone the other day when he was supervising deliveries.'

'She was running an errand.' Pa gave Grace a look, meaning, *I'll be having a word with you later, young lady.*

'Don't smirk like that, Robert. The moral welfare of your daughters is no laughing matter. I come, not to interfere, but as my promise to my sister-in-law, to advise or chastise whenever I see fit. Tell me this — how are dear Louisa, Winnie and Grace to find suitable husbands with their reputations under scrutiny?'

'Much as I appreciate your concern, I'm 'ead of this 'ouse'old and what I say goes. I trust my daughters to keep theirselves out of trouble.' Pa beamed suddenly. 'I'm glad to see you — and you, Beth, but I reckon it's time you were gettin' back — you don't want to leave it too late with all these unruly Jacks and soldiers about, waitin' to pounce and steal a woman's virtue straight off the street.'

'Oh, you are insufferable as always,' Aunt Mary said crossly. 'Come along, Beth. We are done here. It is as I expected, my words are falling on deaf ears.'

After they'd gone, Pa turned to Grace who bowed her head.

'Far be it from me to tell anyone 'ow to bring up their daughters . . . I'm no expert, merely a father who loves 'is girls more than 'e ever thought 'e could. From the very first cry, I lost my 'eart to each one of you, which is why I 'ate to scold you for goin' against me. Where did you go, Grace? Tell me the honest truth.'

'I went for a walk along the beach,' she said, her cheeks burning as she recalled spending an afternoon helping to thread bones on to one of the cat's collars at the tavern. Isaiah claimed that the rattling sound they made when the cat moved gave the smugglers warning of any unexpected arrivals when they were discussing business.

Pa took her explanation at face value, but she wasn't sure about Louisa and Winnie.

'I'll give you a little advice. Don't go wandering the streets on your own, but if you ever find yourself in a situation where a stranger of the male persuasion pays you attention, you should turn and walk away, findin' safety in a crowd. If 'e should persist, then you know what to do . . . .' Mr Lennicker paused, his complexion scarlet as he waited for their answer.

'I have absolutely no idea,' Winnie said.

'Call for help?' Louisa suggested.

'Do tell us, Pa,' Grace urged.

'You kick 'em where it 'urts. In the nether parts. And you scream as loud as your lungs will allow it.'

There was a moment of silence. Pa looked so serious that Grace wanted to laugh. Fighting the giggle that was bubbling up in her throat, she looked away, but when Louisa's shoulders began to shake, she lost it. Soon, they were laughing together.

★ ★ ★

261

'Grace, can you hear me? Your eyes have glazed over. Oh dear, I'm borin' you already — John's always tellin' me I talk too much. Let others have their say, Myrtle. It's a good job he's the quiet sort.'

'It isn't that, Myrtle. Sitting here sewing slops reminds me of home,' Grace said, temporarily overcome by a wave of homesickness and regret.

'Of the tavern you've left behind?'

'Further back in time than that.'

'Before you were married?' There was a twinkle in Myrtle's eyes. 'The good old days.'

'Kind of. There are times when I wish I had a more docile husband.'

'You wouldn't love one of the ordinary, respectable sort,' Sarah cut in. 'You're like me in that regard. For every woman who sets her cap at a gentleman, there's another who yearns to marry a villain. My life would 'ave been very dull if I 'adn't wed Digger.'

'Can I ask you a question, Myrtle?' Grace asked, changing the subject. 'It's about potatoes.' She pulled the puny vegetables from her pocket and showed her.

'Oh no,' she chuckled. 'You're supposed to leave them until the leaves turn yellow. Don't you know anythin' about gardenin'?'

'Not really, we didn't have much of a garden in Deal,' Grace said. 'We made our living from the sea: fishing, hovelling . . . '

'And the other,' Myrtle added with a wink. 'No one likes to own up to it, but everyone round here has a hand in it, whether they like it or not. It's the only way to survive with the price of grain shootin'

262

up out of reach. There's not goin' to be much of a harvest this year because of the weather. Nothin's growin' except the grass.'

'Digger said they've 'ad snow in London this month,' Sarah contributed as she peered at her handiwork. 'I'm no seamstress — I'm glad it doesn't matter what these slops look like.'

'Oh, but it does,' Myrtle replied sharply.

'Even though the men wear them under their ordinary clothes?' Grace frowned as she watched Myrtle's expression change from affront to amusement.

'What I mean is that I care what they look like. The men aren't bothered in the slightest. Sometimes they'll only wear them once, discardin' them before they make their way home, to stop the gobblers arrestin' them for smugglin', knowin' very well the purpose of these items.'

'It seems such a waste,' Sarah sighed.

'It keeps us in clover — George pays per set,' Myrtle said. 'And speakin' of George, he and the men are rendezvousin' here tomorrow evenin', and I could do with some help cookin' and servin' the food. Would you two be interested in return for some more pin money?'

Grace would have rather been at home mothering Aggie, but Sarah persuaded her to accept Myrtle's invitation.

'George likes the women to make an effort with their appearance,' Myrtle said, her eyes on Grace's grubby apron. 'He says it inspires the menfolk to work harder.'

'It makes them lecherous,' Sarah sighed. 'Never mind. We're used to fendin' them off, aren't we,

263

Grace? When do we get paid for the slops? We're a bit short.'

'George'll lend you money — you only have to ask him. He's a good man — some address him as the Captain, but I call him King of the Marsh.'

With that, Grace bade Myrtle farewell, collected a drowsy Aggie and went back to the cottage across the road with Sarah accompanying her.

'How do you find Mrs Minnis?' Grace asked.

'Rather strange. She isn't bodily ill, as you might say. She's jumpy as a grasshopper and never utters a word, as if she's 'ad a terrible fright and never recovered from it. What do you think of this place?' Sarah went on as they stopped at the gate. 'The people?'

'I can't help feeling that I have to mind my Ps and Qs. What if Myrtle's spying on us and reporting back to George?' Grace hesitated, wondering if Sarah was in on it too. 'Oh, I'm being silly. I'm tired, that's all. The last few days have been quite a strain.'

'It's bound to feel odd, but we'll get used to it,' Sarah said. 'I'm just glad that you're nearby, because we can 'elp each other out, just as we did at the tavern. Goodnight, Grace, I'll see you tomorrow.'

* * *

'What are you wearin' that for?' Isaiah asked the following day when Grace had washed, dressed and put her hair up. It was past noon — she'd heard the church bells chime twelve.

'We have to wear our Sunday best while serving the refreshments later. I'm going over to Myrtle's

264

early to help her prepare the dishes.'

'I'd rather you stayed 'ere with me.'

'George is paying us. We need the money, Isaiah. According to Myrtle, it's too late in the season to plant anything but cabbages, and I don't want us to starve.' She was already hungry. The few provisions they'd brought from Deal hadn't stretched very far, and she didn't want to have to spend the remainder of the money Winnie had given her, except as a last resort. Aggie was red-cheeked and cross, and always crying to be fed, making Grace worry that her milk was drying up.

'It's goin' to be all right this time.' Isaiah walked across to kiss her cheek. 'Trust me.'

'I find that hard to believe. We seem to make a mull of everything we do.'

'Come on, Grace. We've agreed to make the best of it 'ere in Snargate with George and the Greys. We can 'ave another child, a brother for Aggie.'

She smiled wryly. It seemed unlikely that she would bear any more babies because Isaiah had acquired a case of brewer's droop, even though he barely drank.

'If you must go across the road dressed like that, at least wear your piece of lace to fill in the neckline. You're a temptin' armful as it is — I don't want you appearin' like a trollop in front of George's men.'

'All right. I'll put it on. Anything for some peace and quiet.'

'There's no need to be like that. I'm lookin' after you, like an 'usband should.'

Later that afternoon, wearing her lace, she

265

chopped carrots and onions and cooked rabbit stew with Sarah under Myrtle's supervision. In the evening, the men began to arrive, some on foot, some on horseback, until there were twenty of them, including John, Isaiah, Digger and George, along with Awful Doins, Lawless, Cut-throat and Dunk from the Rattlers who'd ridden from Deal, the rest being members of the Greys.

They ate and drank, then settled down to plot their way to a fortune, but not before George had banished the ladies to the kitchen. Myrtle had put her boys to bed and Aggie was sleeping in her cradle which Sarah had helped her carry over from the cottage. Sarah and Grace washed the pots and Myrtle put them away, as snippets of the smugglers' conversation drifted in from the adjacent room.

The landing was to be at Lydd, the meeting place at one of the inns en route.

'Most of the landlords of the public 'ouses from Rye to Deal and south of the Royal Military Canal are loyal to the Greys. They all know me and appreciate my generosity in bringing business their way.

'Every man must wear a grey smock and black 'is face with soot,' George added as he went through a long list of rules and regulations. The landsmen were to be guarded by eighteen armed smugglers, and there would be compulsory training sessions in the use of military tactics run by a former soldier.

'We won't initiate violence, but we will retaliate if the gobblers use weaponry against us,' George said.

266

Sarah glanced towards Grace who shook her head, not liking the sound of it.

'Are you sure that Mrs Feasey can be trusted?' she heard one of the men ask. 'Who's to say she won't inform 'er brother-in-law of our plans?'

'Why do you think I brought 'er 'ere to the middle of nowhere?' said George. 'It takes at least nine hours by shank's pony to reach Deal. What's more, I 'ave eyes and ears everywhere — I'll soon find out if anyone grasses us up.'

'Let me assure you that my wife does what I tell 'er,' Isaiah added.

'Always?' Digger said.

'Always,' Isaiah confirmed.

'Except when she doesn't,' Awful Doins chuckled, apparently pleased with his show of wit.

'Black Dog, I want your wife present at the landin' place,' George said.

'Oh, I don't know about that,' Isaiah responded. 'She 'as to be at 'ome with the littlun.'

'She's our insurance when it comes to the gobblers. If we 'ave any trouble with Commander Witherall or Lieutenant Enderby, we'll use 'er as an 'ostage. We'll threaten to kill 'er unless they cooperate.'

Grace bit her lip, feeling sick. How could George talk so lightly of her death?

''E doesn't mean it, Grace,' Myrtle whispered.

'I think he does. He'll stop at nothing to get his way,' Grace muttered hotly, imagining Jason and his men — including Cromwell, she remembered — standing on the beach while George paraded her up and down in front of them at gunpoint.

'I'm not 'avin' a woman along with us,' Dunk

267

piped up. Grace was glad to hear that chivalry wasn't dead, until he went on, 'They scream and holler at the slightest thing: the dark; spiders; rats.'

'I'll 'ave you know that my wife used to go out smugglin' with her sisters,' Isaiah said in her defence.

'Myrtle will mind the child,' George said. 'It's imperative that Grace comes with us, and Sarah too. We will not give Marlin the satisfaction of interruptin' our business. You 'ave an axe to grind with 'im as well.' George addressed Dunk. 'Didn't 'e leave you stranded in Gravelines one time?'

'And me,' Cut-throat added, joining the conversation.

'You came back to the wharf after the guinea boat 'ad left, whereas Marlin deliberately abandoned me,' Dunk said darkly. 'Mind you, I 'ad tried to start a mutiny so maybe I'm partly to blame. We were takin' a couple of Frenchies back 'ome to France. They'd escaped from their parole town in Hampshire and made their way as far as Deal where Marlin offered them passage — for a fee, of course. Anyway, 'e needed a few more men to row the boat across so I applied, not knowin' that the greedy b— was goin' to overload 'er with that many beans plus three passengers that it was like rowin' through treacle.'

'I recall that 'e claimed to 'ave thirty thousand guineas on board,' Cut-throat said.

'If I'd 'ad any idea before 'and, I'd 'ave demanded a greater share of the spoils from that enterprise, and I said so. I told 'im — halfway across the Straits of Dover — that 'e was takin' advantage, treating us like dumb asses. When 'e told me I'd 'ave to

268

like it or lump it, I suggested that we should turn back, find a place to land and unload the gold. It could 'ave been the biggest prize of our lives. But what did you do, eh, Cut-throat? Tell them.'

'I was one of the crew who refused to go against Marlin— 'e saved our necks many a time. You wanted to tie 'im up and throw 'im overboard. If we'd gone along with you, we'd 'ave 'ad to kill the woman, Mrs Fleet, as well. We'd 'ave 'anged for that, no question.'

Grace recognised her sister's name. Winnie had nursed one of the prisoners of war who was dying from consumption, making sure he was comfortable while he travelled home. It was obvious now that she had never revealed the whole story of her adventure.

'That's why I had to grab you — to stop you doing anythin' stupid,' Cut-throat said.

'You almost choked me to death,' Dunk growled.

'Hey, lads. Let's let bygones be bygones,' George interrupted. 'What 'appened next, Dunk?'

'He tied me up.' He jabbed his finger towards Cut-throat.

'But it was Marlin who left me behind. Look at 'im now— 'e's a traitor workin' for the other side. If I ever come across 'im alone on a dark night, I'll 'ave him.'

'We're in danger of going off on a tangent,' George broke in, and the men went on to discuss the number of carts they would need, protocols for signalling to each other, and directions to the proposed meeting place. Grace listened intently, memorising the details in case she should need them.

By midnight, the men began to leave, dispersing into the darkness. Grace and Isaiah made their way across the road with Aggie.

'You'll do it without a fuss, won't you?' Isaiah shoved the cottage door open for her. When she didn't reply, he went on, 'There was a time when you said you were so in love with your 'usband that you'd do anythin' for 'im. Would you break your word and 'is 'eart at the same time?'

'I have no choice but to go along with it,' she said in a small voice, afraid that George would have his revenge if she refused to join the run. 'It will turn out badly for us one day though, you mark my words.'

'You should 'ave more faith in me. George and I 'ave planned everythin' down to the last detail. We've left nothin' to chance.'

There was so much she wanted to say but didn't for fear of angering him. It was George and Digger who had done the planning, and no amount of organisation and paying attention to detail could account for every unforeseen circumstance that might arise when there were armed men roaming the countryside in the dark. The Greys — Dunk, in particular — were dangerous men and in her view, Isaiah was playing with fire. She was afraid of losing him through a fatal injury or arrest — and although they'd had their differences over the path he had been forced to take and his recent loss of temper, she didn't know how she'd live without him.

16

Muskets at Dawn

On the evening of the first of August as planned, Grace and Sarah walked to Medlar Farm to collect transport from Peter Paddick.

'Don't worry about the 'orse, ladies,' he said as he secured the horse's harness and hitched it to the cart. ''E's a nice little cob and 'e comes 'ighly trained.'

Grace let the black horse sniff her hand, then stroked his forehead which had a whorl of white hairs in the centre.

'He's lovely,' she said.

'You'll need some blackin',' Peter smiled. 'I've got some if you need it.'

'It's all right — we have a pot at home.'

''Is name's Bobbie. 'E 'as a sixth sense when it comes to avoidin' the boggy ground where a man or woman might disappear without trace. Look after 'im and 'e'll look after you. Let 'im 'ave a drink now and again, and some grub from 'is nosebag.'

'Thank you. We'll bring him back as soon as we can,' Grace promised before she took up the ribbons and flicked the whip, according to Peter's instructions, and drove the cart away.

''E's a lonesome kind of fellow, isn't 'e?' Sarah said.

271

'Myrtle says he's still mourning his wife.'

'I can't imagine losin' your other 'alf. I don't know what I'd do without Digger. 'E's my best friend . . . after you, of course. You always listen whereas 'e only 'ears what 'e wants to hear.'

Grace chuckled. 'That's menfolk for you.'

They returned to the cottage where they picked up Isaiah. Before they left, having decided to leave Musket behind, Grace fetched the blacking and tried to paint out the horse's white star. As soon as she approached, he flung his head in the air, and no amount of hauling on the ribbons would persuade him to lower it again.

'I'm not impressed by your intelligence — like a proud father boasting about his child's abilities, Peter has rather overegged yours.'

'He's teasin' you,' Sarah smiled.

'We 'aven't got time to mess about. Let me 'ave a go,' Isaiah said, and to Grace's chagrin, the horse stood quietly as he blacked out the star. 'Have we got everythin' we need? Wittles? Ale?'

Grace fetched a basket of provisions while Sarah loaded a tarpaulin, a stave, a lamp and a spout lantern into the cart. Isaiah fetched a large wooden box and heaved it over the side.

'What's that for?' Grace asked, puzzled.

'Weaponry: a musket; pistol; ammunition; a cutlass. Don't worry about it — it's for our own protection.'

'It seems rather excessive.'

'It isn't like the old days when your folks and the Witheralls ran a few tubs and a bale or two of lace, and the Ridin' officers could be bribed to lay off with a wad of baccy or a dollop of best Bohea

272

tea.'

'We never managed to persuade them to succumb to bribery.' She smiled briefly. 'Flattery, maybe.'

'This is a far more professional operation, a completely different kettle o' fish, and we're up against a much more organised enemy in the form of the three arms of Floggin' Joe's Coastal Blockade,' Isaiah explained. 'Are you ready? We're meetin' the Greys at Lydd. Where's Digger? Isn't 'e supposed to be with us?'

' 'E's with George,' Sarah said.

Filled with a deep sense of dread that had been building since George had revealed his plans at the rendezvous, Grace glanced towards Forge Cottage where Myrtle was minding Aggie for her, before she climbed on to the cart, took up the ribbons and drove them into the dusk. The setting sun splashed a blood-red streak of light across the darkening sky as they left Snargate and travelled southeast in the direction of Lydd.

'The littlun will be fine, my love,' Isaiah said as though reading her mind. 'We'll be 'ome before she realises we've gone.'

They carried on in silence, the horse snorting now and again as the bats swooped across the sky and the wind rattled through the reeds.

'You know what you 'ave to do, Grace?' Isaiah began as wisps of sea fret started to drift across the marsh.

'I drive the cart to Lydd, find a place to hide, wait for you to give the signal to come and collect you and the goods and bring you back to Snargate,' she replied abruptly. 'Unfortunately, I

273

wasn't privy to the discussion on the whereabouts of the hiding holes.'

'And? What else?'

'That's it.'

'You're to act like you're scared in front of Marlin and his men if they 'ave a go at arrestin' any of the Greys. George will 'old a knife to your face and threaten to disfigure you — or 'e might 'ave said disembowel. I can't remember rightly.'

'You let him talk about me like that? I have no intention of hanging about — at the merest sign of the gobblers, I'll make myself scarce.'

'You're 'ere as our insurance,' he hissed. 'You'll do exactly what I ask of you, or George will 'ave my guts for garters. I thought 'e chose me to join the Greys because of my skill and experience, but it was because of you and your relationship to Marlin — ' he swore aloud '— 'e's been the bane of my life since I was a littlun on the beach, always out to get one over on me.'

Grace glanced behind her — Sarah was asleep, wrapped in her cloak.

'Keep your voice down,' she warned. 'When did you find out about George? I thought you were bosom friends?'

'That's what 'e led me to believe. You were right about 'im and I was wrong.'

'What are we going to do?'

'Nothin'. We're stuck with 'im now. This is it, Grace. I'm sorry for not heedin' your reservations about 'im. I've been a fool, lettin' 'im flatter me with his attentions and make promises 'e 'ad no intention of keepin'. Look at me: the leader of the Rattlers reduced to a minion of the Greys.'

'Can we not walk away?' she whispered.

'It's too late for that — we're up to our necks in debt to 'im. If we left Snargate, 'e'd come lookin' for us.'

'We could go to London.'

'And live on the streets with Aggie, forever watchin' our backs, waitin' for 'is men to find us? No. I can't tell you how much I regret draggin' you into this.' Her spirits lifted at his apology. 'You're smilin'. What 'ave I said?'

'I'm grateful for your expression of penitence.' It was a loving act, she thought, because she knew how much it must have taken for him to admit that he'd misjudged George Minnis.

'For 'ow much 'umble pie I've eaten, you mean.' His teeth flashed from the darkness. 'Oh Grace, you still 'ave this lovely, refined way of speakin'. I wish I could be a better 'usband to you.'

'Stop it,' she scolded as a fingerpost loomed from the shadows. 'You are giving yourself the megrims. Which way now?'

'Take the left turn.'

'It says Lydd straight on.'

'I'm sure it's left.'

'We should be heading towards the sea,' she frowned.

'This isn't the time for a marital spat,' Sarah said crossly from behind her. 'Grace is right — carry on straight ahead.'

Grace made a clicking sound in her throat to drive the horse on, hoping that Sarah hadn't been pretending to sleep in order to eavesdrop on their conversation. The last thing they needed was for news of Isaiah's doubt and distrust to get back to

George. What was the saying? Don't bite the hand that feeds you.

As they approached the coast, they joined a stream of others, most wearing grey smocks, some in dark coats, driving carts, walking and riding horses along the road to Lydd where they assembled on the Rype, common land not far from the church that Isaiah described as the Cathedral of the Marsh. The landlord of the Dolphin Inn had jugs of ale brought outside, courtesy of George.

'This is where you leave me,' Isaiah said. 'Carry on until you get to the shore, turn right and tuck yourselves away in the scrub. Stay there until I give you the signal: three short whistles, one long.'

'Where are you going? Who will protect us?'

'You'll 'ave to look after yourselves.' Isaiah leaned across and kissed her, before grabbing the box and lantern and sliding down from the cart.

'Don't take all the weapons with you,' Grace said. 'Leave us a pistol at the very least.'

'You don't need one,' he said, and without looking back, he ran to a house set some way from the track and disappeared inside.

'I'll be having words with my husband when I see him next,' she said angrily as Sarah moved up, taking his place beside her. 'What does he think he's doing, leaving us with no means of self-defence?'

'Is it all right to talk'?' Sarah muttered. 'I find it calms my nerves.'

'As long as we keep it to a whisper,' Grace said as the mist came rolling in across their path. 'I'm glad you're here. You didn't happen to overhear the conversation Isaiah and I were having earlier?'

276

'No,' Sarah said, a little too quickly for her liking. 'I was asleep.'

'So you did hear something?'

'A little, but I promise you I'll never repeat it.' Grace saw her teeth glinting from the gloom. 'I don't want to be 'ere — I feel sick and tired because I'm with child.'

'That's wonderful news.'

'It'll be a blessin' in many ways. When my belly starts to swell, Digger will take pity on me and let me stay at 'ome, and the babe will be a playmate for Aggie. They'll grow up together on the marsh. Grace, 'ow can you see to drive in this? I can't see my 'and in front of my face.'

Grace let the horse pick his way along the track, listening to the change in his hoofbeat as the compacted earth was replaced by shingle.

'Will you pick up the spout lantern?' she asked. 'Shine the light to the front.'

It wasn't much help, the beam from the spout being too narrow to illuminate more than a strip of ground ahead of them. When Sarah turned it to the side, Grace caught sight of some leafless branches, like witches' arms, holding their twiggy fingers out to grab them. Shivering, she told herself not to be silly.

'There are some bushes over to the right,' Sarah said and Grace pulled over, manoeuvring the horse and cart as far into the scrub as she could. She gave Bobbie his nosebag as Peter had requested, then sat down with Sarah between the blackthorn bushes, where the scents of seaweed and crushed elder mingled in the air and the mist seemed to muffle the sound of the waves that were breaking across the beach.

The visibility was poor, less than twenty yards at times, but Grace was aware of a body of men, many of them dressed in grey smocks, standing in lines along the shore. Several carried lanterns, their glimmering light revealing brief glimpses of the men's weapons: the flashes of a cutlass and pistol; the shadow of an ash stave; the shape of a musket slung over a smuggler's shoulder.

They were protecting over two hundred landsmen who were running the goods from a boat — she couldn't tell what kind it was — but she could see the silhouettes of the men lugging tubs and bales of what might be baccy or silk up the beach. Some loaded the goods into waiting carts while others continued inland.

'I wish we were anywhere but 'ere,' Sarah whispered, slipping her arm through Grace's. I wish I'd never married the— '

'Hush,' Grace said softly.

It wasn't until after two o'clock that she spotted the first blue flash of a pistol to their left and heard its sharp report.

'Watch out! There's a gobbler about!' one of the tub carriers yelled, at which the smugglers who were guarding them, released a volley of musketry.

'There's a lot more of them than that,' someone else added.

'Not enough to trouble us. Keep your 'eads down, lads, and your pistols primed. We'll see them off.'

'I've seen a galley load rowin' over from the cutter — the *Legacy* — and there's another group from the watch 'ouse. This is excessive 'arassment, if you ask me.'

'I'm afraid we are sunk.'

'Shut your gob and keep movin'. We'll spirit the goods away right under their noses, just as we always do.'

Naively, Grace had imagined the run was going to be straightforward. Hadn't George, Digger and Isaiah insisted that they were more organised, better trained and practised than any gang had been before? Yet with the number of landsmen, it had been impossible to keep their enterprise completely secret and the gobblers had got wind of their plans — she prayed that George wouldn't point the finger at her.

'They're comin' closer,' Sarah said, panicking.

'Get in the cart and hide under the tarpaulin,' Grace ordered.

'Aren't you goin' to join me?'

'I'll keep watch. Go on.' Sarah clambered into the cart and pulled the cover over her head while Grace moved to the other side of the horse, wishing that she was carrying a pistol because there was nothing she could do to protect herself and Sarah without one. Peering over the horse's withers, she spotted several smugglers carrying muskets, and two men in dark clothing running towards the group.

'Who are you?' the gang called.

'Commander Witherall and Seaman Appleton, officers of the Revenue!' said one of the pair. 'Come quietly — you're all under arrest.' She recognised Dunk from his evil laughter. 'You'll 'ave to catch us first.'

She guessed from the cut of his jib that it was

279

Cromwell who fired his pistol. Dunk returned fire, a ball striking Cromwell on the stomach, sending him flying.

'There the dunder'ead drops,' Dunk shouted in triumph, but Jason ran at him, yelling, 'Enderby, I need your 'elp.'

'I'm right behind you, Commander,' Albert responded, his appearance confusing Grace for a moment, because as he emerged from the mist, she realised that he was dressed in a grey smock, posing as a smuggler. Cromwell was still down and Jason was wrestling Dunk for his musket. Something went wrong. Jason lost his footing and ended up on the ground with Dunk's musket aiming at his head.

'I've been lookin' forward to this,' Dunk growled as Albert's gun went off, the ball hitting Dunk in the chest with a soft thud, sending him sinking to his knees, then slumping on to his front. 'I'm dyin',' he groaned. 'You are shamming,' Albert replied, drawing his cutlass. 'No . . . ' Albert checked the smuggler for signs of life. 'He's gone. Cromwell, you're bleeding.'

'It's nothing,' he said.

'As long as you're sure. Commander, are you . . . ?'

Jason was on his feet, brushing himself down. 'I'm well, thanks to you. I owe you, Albert. You saved my life.'

'Everything I do is in the name of duty,' he responded.

'I see that you're as modest and unassuming as ever,' Jason observed. 'Keep your wits about you — I hear voices.'

280

Trembling and in fear of being discovered, Grace forced herself to continue watching as two more figures came running up from the beach, one carrying a tub, the other firing shots randomly into the air. More shots echoed from the distance until she wasn't sure who was shooting at whom. In the chaos and confusion, she made out Digger's figure running down towards the Revenue men.

'What's he doing?' she breathed, hoping that Sarah wasn't looking on when her husband shoved a musket into Albert's hand.

'Shoot that gobbler . . . ' he swore, pointing at Cromwell. 'Shoot 'im.'

Albert grabbed Digger by the hem of his smock. 'I'm arresting you. If you resist, I'll blow your brains out.'

An agitated Digger held his hands up in surrender as Cromwell and Jason clapped Digger and his companion in irons.

'I'm done. I've 'ad enough tonight,' Digger exclaimed.

'What the 'ell did you do that for?' his companion shouted.

Isaiah? Grace's heart sank as Albert handed both men into Jason's custody, suggesting that he and Cromwell take them to the watch house while he searched for the tub that Isaiah had abandoned somewhere nearby. She was worried sick because she didn't see how George or anyone else could prevent her husband and Sarah's going to trial when they had been caught on the beach after midnight in the throes of a run.

'Sarah,' she hissed as Albert moved closer,

281

using a stick to search through the blackthorn and brambles. 'We must make our way back. I'll explain what's happened when we're out of earshot. Stay as you are.' She took the horse's ribbons and encouraged him to move further into the scrub, the blackthorn tearing at her arms and pricking her finger, but it was too late.

She twisted her neck when she heard the soft click of a pistol.

'Don't make a sound,' Albert said. 'Hold your hands above your head.'

As she raised her hands, the hood on her cloak slipped back.

'Grace? Is that you?'

'Yes . . . '

Her head was light and her knees quaking as he went on, 'We are ill-met. I have orders to arrest and interrogate anyone I find out and about tonight.'

'Then arrest me,' she said softly. 'But on what charge?'

'Smuggling, of course,' he replied, his voice laced with humour. 'What else would you be doing out here in the dark?'

'You have my permission to rummage the cart. You won't find anything.'

'I believe you, even if thousands of others wouldn't. We're after George Minnis and the men who are the brains and brawn behind his operation, not their wives and mothers of their children. On this occasion, I will let you go on your way unhindered, but I can't guarantee your liberty in future, or that others, such as Commander Witherall, will deal with you so generously.'

'Thank you, Albert. I don't deserve your

compassion after the way I treated you.'

'You behaved very badly, leading me on when you were engaged to Black Dog,' he said honestly. 'If you'd been a man, I'd have called you out.' She thought she saw him smile. 'I've forgiven you. Go straight home. The men who were abed at the watch house have been sent to intercept any stragglers they may come across. Take care, Grace.' With that, his figure melted away towards the beach and disappeared.

Grace led the horse on to the road. She was aware that she'd had two strokes of luck that night, the first being that Isaiah had abandoned her so that George couldn't possibly carry out his threat to hold her hostage, and the second that it had been Albert who had come across her in the dark, not Jason who wouldn't have dealt with her so leniently. She climbed into the cart and flicked the whip, not that Bobbie needed any encouragement as he was in a hurry to get home. When she was sure that the coast was clear, she lifted the tarpaulin. Sarah crawled out and sat alongside her, huddled beneath her cloak, tears in her eyes.

'The gobblers 'ave got our menfolk,' she said, distraught. 'And we've 'ada close call, thanks to that officer recognisin' you. You've 'ad a far more colourful life than you've led me to believe.'

'Oh no, he was never my lover, just a young man who had a passing fancy for me. No, I'm doing him an injustice — I didn't recognise it at the time, but it turns out that he's an exceptional person, the kind you might meet once in a life-time.'

'You make him sound like an angel.'

283

'He is,' she confirmed, reflecting on how he had saved Jason's life, thus sparing Louisa the pain of losing her beloved husband. 'It was a bit of luck that he let us go on our way, but it doesn't help Digger and Isaiah.'

'George will get them off,' Sarah said more cheerfully. ''E'll persuade the magistrates to let them go. It isn't as if they 'ad any goods on them.'

'We'll see,' Grace said pessimistically. 'It's been a terrible night all round — Dunk is dead.'

Sarah's mouth formed an 'o'. 'That's terrible. 'E's one of us.'

'I never took to the man myself, but he didn't deserve to die. It does mean that the Revenue and the magistrates will be more inclined to pursue a conviction, to make an example of them, if nothing else. We should be grateful for small mercies, Sarah. It could have been our husbands lying there.' Thanks to the Greys' tendency to violence, a smuggler had been killed and at least one Revenue officer injured. What Grace had seen changed everything.

An ominous silence descended as they made their way back towards Snargate. A few landsmen appeared on their route, some carrying pairs of tubs fastened together by a small cord and slung over their shoulders and chests. Further along, someone had abandoned their haul. Spotting a tub in the grass, Grace pulled the horse up and jumped down to search the verge, finding three half-ankers, one of which was leaking through a crack between two of its staves.

'Help me pick these up, Sarah,' she said, glancing along the road to check that no one was watching.

'What if we should come across a gobbler? Or George?'

'It's a risk I'm prepared to take. We can sell them or use them to barter with, but you mustn't breathe a word of this.'

'You're right. With our husbands away, we might need a little extra.'

'We'll take the good ones, not the stinkibus — I'm not going to lose my liberty over a tub of seawater. If George asks, we'll say we were looking after them for him.'

The tubs were heavy, about sixty pounds in weight, but between them they managed to roll them to the roadside and lift them into the cart where Sarah covered them with the tarpaulin.

'We'll hide them on the way,' Grace said, glancing back at the orb of the sun that was rising behind them, painting the reeds and ditches crimson. 'Red sky in the morning, shepherd's warning.'

'Do you think the sun's goin' out, like a dyin' fire?' Sarah asked. 'I'm afraid that it's God's punishment for our sins, because no matter how you look at it, we must share the guilt for what 'appened to Dunk.'

Stopping to hide the tubs in the ruins of a former cottage, covering them with grass and foliage, Grace wondered if there was some truth in what Sarah was saying. She couldn't hear the birds singing, nor could she remember when she'd last seen a wasp or dumbledore buzzing amongst the flowers and the spindly corn.

Driving on, they returned the horse and cart to Peter, then walked back into Snargate, following the sound of hammering: iron against iron.

'Come home with me,' Grace begged. 'I don't want to be alone, just me and Aggie. Will Mrs Minnis be needing you?'

'I'll come back for a while,' Sarah said. 'As long as I'm home in time to make 'er supper as usual.'

As they turned the corner, Grace noticed a chestnut mare tied up outside the forge. John was testing the fit of a shoe, pressing it to the horse's hoof and sending a flurry of yellow smoke into the air while Myrtle, who was cuddling Aggie, was talking to George. Apparently satisfied with his handiwork, John dropped the shoe into a bucket of water, making it steam and hiss.

Grace paused outside the house, Sarah at her side.

'There you are.' Myrtle brought Aggie to her. 'She's been as good as gold while you've been gone.'

'Oh, I'm never going to leave you again,' Grace murmured as the baby smiled broadly at being back in her mother's arms. Grace smiled back and stroked her curls, the traumas of the night receding into the background until Myrtle said, 'George says there's been some trouble.'

'I'd like a word with these two ladies,' he said, pushing in. 'My horse cast a shoe, but I was on my way 'ere anyway. I don't know 'ow much you know, but Digger and Black Dog 'ave been captured by the gobblers, Marlin's crew, and taken to New Hall in Dymchurch for a preliminary 'earin' this afternoon.'

'We had an inkling that something had gone awry when we lost sight of them on the beach,'

Grace said, giving Sarah a warning glance.

'It is remarkably careless of you both to lose your 'usbands.' He moved closer and pinched the baby's cheek. His words stung and the baby wailed as he went on, 'Aren't you goin' to invite me in to your 'umble abode? I'd prefer to speak with you in private.'

Reluctantly, Grace nodded. George opened the gate, letting her and Sarah through before following them up the path and into the cottage. Noticing that there was no sign of Musket, Grace showed George to the bench where he sat down at one end, Sarah at the other.

''Ave you any wittles while I'm waitin'?'

The hens had gone off lay because of the cool, unseasonal weather, and the cupboard was bare. All she had was a little milk souring in a jug.

'There's tea, but the fire isn't lit,' she said, remembering they'd left the basket of provisions behind in the cart. 'George, we can't stop here — Sarah and I have to go to Dymchurch.'

'It's a three-hour walk,' he said. 'The 'earin' will be over by the time you get there. No, it's better that you wait 'ere. I'll go on 'orseback and ride back triumphant, bringin' your 'usbands home.' He tipped his head to one side. 'Unless they've been up to somethin' they shouldn't 'ave, some-thin' more serious than carryin' a few tubs.'

He was a sly devil, Grace thought as he contin-ued, 'I'd like to ask Black Dog why 'e went against my instructions, leavin' your side like that.'

'My husband was with me all the time.'

'You think you're so clever . . . That blabber-mouth Awful Doins said 'e left you and went to

287

join the rest of my men in the house near the inn.'

'He met with us after that,' was Grace's instant response. 'He was dropping off the box of weapons.'

'I see.' George rubbed his nose, deep in thought. 'We heard a man cry out that he was dying, then Digger's voice calling for help. Isaiah ran off to assist him against the gobblers without a thought for his own safety — he was a hero.' She swallowed hard. 'I haven't seen him since. Having heard the gunshots, Sarah and I took the cart back towards the town and hid in a field until the skirmish died down. We were scared witless and the horse wasn't too happy either — he dragged us through some blackthorn. My arms are scratched to pieces and I have a thorn in my finger.'

'Black Dog saved my 'usband's life,' Sarah contributed to Grace's tale.

'Then I won't judge 'im too 'arshly for goin' against my orders. He stuck by 'is fellow Greys and that's good enough for me.' George stood up, almost bumping his head on a beam. 'I must go and see if my 'orse is ready. I bid you ladies good day.'

Shortly after he left, on hearing the sound of hooves clattering at a gallop along the road, Grace breathed a sigh of relief that he'd gone. She wasn't as happy about the dog being missing, knowing how upset Isaiah would be if Musket didn't come back.

She left Aggie with Sarah, breaking into the money that Winnie had given her to buy a loaf, eggs and scallions, along with a quart of porter, pouring some out for Sarah on her return. 'Drink

288

this — it'll put some colour back in your cheeks.' Sarah took one sip and ran outside, retching. 'You were right about being in the family way,' Grace

said, allowing herself a brief smile. 'It was holding Aggie in your arms that did it.'

'I'm regretting it now,' Sarah cried. 'How will I manage with another mouth to feed, another body to clothe, without my 'usband?'

'You heard what George said — he'll be bringing Digger and Isaiah home with him tonight.'

Sarah gazed at her. 'You lied to George. If he ever finds out . . .'

'He won't though, will he?' Grace challenged her.

'I'd never blab. I thought you knew me better than that.'

'I'm sorry. I never thought I'd hear myself say this, but I wish we were emptying pisspots and changing the beds back in Deal.' She pinched her finger trying to remove the niggling thorn, aware that George Minnis was very much a thorn in her side, and one that she would have great difficulty removing, unless she and Isaiah could revive the Feaseys' fortunes. 'Why don't you have a lie-down upstairs?' she suggested. 'You look worn out.'

'Oh, I don't know,' Sarah said.

'I'll wake you as soon as George is back.' 'Thank you. You're a good friend to me . . . the best.'

Grace watched from the upstairs window with Aggie in her arms, looking out for both George and the dog, as Sarah slept on the bed. The baby had the gripes and wouldn't settle, even after a spoonful of rosehip syrup, a remedy that Myrtle had suggested for soothing a digestive disturbance

289

caused by the goat's milk and pap that Myrtle had fed her while Grace had been away. The afternoon sun began to sink in the sky as the church bells marked the passing of the hours since George had left. Four o'clock, five o'clock, then six, before a horse and rider appeared in the distance.

'He's back.' Having shaken Sarah by the shoulder to wake her from a deep slumber, Grace hurried downstairs to meet George on the doorstep. Leaving his mare tied up at the gate, her ribbons looped over the gatepost, he walked up the path, his mouth set in a grim straight line.

'It isn't the best of news, I'm afraid. The magistrates at Dymchurch aren't sympathetic to the plight of the common man, one who's so desperate to feed his family in these times of terrible 'ardship that he'll do anythin' to make a bit of money. They refused to take account of the fact that the crimes of which your 'usbands are accused took place at a time when the visibility was so poor that even one of the gobblers — Witherall's lieutenant — was moved to admit that he couldn't see the back of his hand. I've 'eard that Enderby's a good chap — honest, fair and likeable. Apparently, he was chasin' a suspicious character along the clifftop the other night, when this chap went over the edge, landing on a ledge twenty feet down. Enderby fetched a rope and at great risk to himself, managed to haul him back up. It's a pity he isn't on our side.

'Goin' back to the 'earin', the outcome's a travesty of justice in my opinion, but suffice to say, your menfolk are bein' held at Dymchurch until they're committed for trial in front of a judge and

290

jury at the Trinity Assizes in Maidstone. They won't be locked up for long — the trial is set for the end of the second sennight of August, merely two weeks away. I've arranged for you to borrow a cart from Peter so you can pay them a visit in the next few days, and I'll be askin' my attorney, Mr Houghton-White, to defend them. Be reassured that I'm doin' everything possible to get them 'ome.

'And talkin' of which, my wife's sister is arrivin' in Snargate today, which means that I can spare you, Sarah. Bein' a gentleman of a chivalrous nature, I'd suggest that you stay here to keep Grace company while your menfolk are away.' He didn't give her a chance to answer, wishing them farewell and walking back down the path, but before he'd taken more than a couple of steps, he stopped.

'There's a question that's been troublin' me, Grace,' he said, turning back to her. ''Ow did the gobblers know where we were landin' the goods last night? It isn't unusual for them to turn up on occasion, but accordin' to witnesses at the hearin', Enderby was wearin' a grey smock as if he'd dressed to deceive us, knowin' in advance that we'd be there.'

'I have no idea.' Even though she was telling the truth, perspiration began to trickle down her back just as surely as if she was lying.

'Never mind. I shall find out soon enough.' He smiled. 'There is a sayin': keep your friends close and your enemies closer. I'll be seein' you again soon, ladies.'

'What was that all about? Why was he talkin' in

291

riddles?' Sarah asked after George had gone.

'Because he doesn't believe me,' Grace explained. 'And the feeling is mutual, because I don't trust him, not in the slightest, but if he can extricate our husbands from their predicament, then I'll have to go along with him. His benefi-cence troubles me, though.'

'You're right— 'is good deeds and charity 'ave a purpose: to make you feel obliged to 'im. It's 'is way of controllin' 'is men and their families. I used to think of 'im as bein' fairly 'armless, but 'e's the most dangerous person I know. Our fate is in 'is 'ands.' Sarah began to cry again while Grace tried to put on a brave face for Aggie's sake.

Over the next few days, news came of Dunk's burial in Deal. George Minnis had paid for a headstone and given a lump sum to Dunk's com-mon-law wife and five children. Grace and Sarah visited their husbands in Dymchurch, when Grace had to tell Isaiah that she hadn't seen Musket since they'd left Snargate for Lydd. He cried and so did she. No matter how difficult things were between them and no matter what he'd done, he was her husband and Aggie's father, and she needed him home.

17

The Trinity Assizes

As George had confirmed, Isaiah and Digger were set to face the Assize Grand Jury at Maidstone in the middle of August. George paid for the hire of a carriage, and rooms for Grace and Sarah at the Marquis of Granby in Maidstone High Street. Grace had left Aggie with Myrtle, despite fearing that she would end up suffering another attack of the gripes.

'George must 'ave done very well out of the free trade— 'e's splashin' 'is money about like water,' Sarah observed when they were walking to the courthouse on the morning of the trial. Grace didn't respond, wondering how much Isaiah was enjoying his notoriety compared with the loss of his freedom.

Having entered the courtroom, they took their seats in the crowded gallery.

'There's Marlin,' Sarah said, nudging Grace's elbow. Gazing along the rows of people below, Grace saw Jason glance in her direction then turn his back, a gesture that cut her to the quick. Albert and Cromwell sat flanking their commander, waiting to give evidence, and George was present too, nodding and smiling to many of the other Greys who had come to attend the trial.

The judge and court officials took their places

293

and the guards led the prisoners into the dock: Digger muttered something to Isaiah before the clerk of the court read out the charges.

'The two prisoners are indicted on several counts. That they did assemble unlawfully and feloniously to aid and assist in the illegal running, landing and carrying away of three hundred gallons of foreign brandy and the same of foreign geneva, on which duties had not been paid. That they did maliciously discharge divers guns and pistols, shooting at officers of His Majesty's Navy and of His Majesty's Customs in the execution of their duties. And that they did dangerously wound those officers.'

Neither Digger nor Isaiah, standing behind the railings with their heads held high, looked particularly unhappy at their situation, and Grace wondered if they knew something that she didn't. Even so, she wished that they'd show a little more humility in front of the judge, who was resplendent in a wig, black scarf, tippet and scarlet robe.

Suddenly, Isaiah looked straight at her. She gave him a small wave.

'How do you plead?' the clerk asked.

'Not guilty,' the prisoners said, one at a time.

The case proceeded with the prosecution first to speak their case, followed by the defence. As it dragged into the afternoon, Grace began to wonder if it would ever end.

As far as she could work out, Jason had received information that the smugglers would be landing goods at Lydd that night, which was why Albert had dressed up in the grey smock, hoping to blend in with the gang on the beach. When questioned further about the source of his information, Jason revealed that the free-trader known as Awful Doins had been bragging about joining the Greys when he'd let slip details of the run to one of the shore boys in Deal, a friend of Cromwell's. It was a weight off Grace's mind — it was Awful Doins who would have to worry about George now, not her.

Following the inquest that had been held previously into Dunk's death, the coroner had decided that Dunk had threatened to kill Commander Witherall, and Lieutenant Enderby had fired at him in self-defence. Having addressed that, the judge made it clear that the jury were trying Digger and Isaiah for the events which followed.

Cromwell and Albert had taken Digger to Jew's Gut watch house after his arrest, but because he was in his cups, Albert had given him a ducking in one of the sewers to sober him up. Marlin had taken Isaiah directly to the watch house where he undertook a search of both prisoners. He stated that he'd taken a knife from inside Digger's smock, and some wet powder and a few grains of swan shot from Isaiah's pockets, before commenting that Isaiah's clothes were wet.

'Was it not raining, Commander?' Mr Houghton-White asked. In his forties, he was tall and slender, and partial to ending his sentences with a flourish of his right hand, flashing a crystal cufflink and gold ring.

'Not at that time,' Jason said. 'I had the impression he'd been in the sea, bein' wet up to his middle.'

'Or down to it,' someone added.

'Proof that a situation may be interpreted in many different ways, Commander Witherall — or shall we call you Marlin?' The attorney smiled at his audience, letting his point sink in. 'You are a former boatman of Deal and partner in the free trade . . . How can we take you at your word when you have been on the wrong side of the law in the past?'

'We are not here to address the character of an officer of the Revenue,' the judge spoke out. 'Please keep to the facts of the case. I will not have idle speculation in this court.'

'Your honour, I shall continue.' He recapped Jason's answers to his earlier questions, and Grace wondered if he was trying to send the jury to sleep: three gentlemen who appeared to have partaken of a liquid nuncheon kept nodding off, then jerking awake, seemingly oblivious to the fact that there were men's lives at stake.

'Commander Witherall, you say in your statement that Mr Feasey's hands and face were black with gunpowder and that he had a fowling-piece flint on his person.'

'That's correct. The assistant surgeon of HMS *Legacy* was present — he tasted the black powder on his fingers.

'What have you been doing with this?' he enquired, and Mr Feasey answered that he'd been shootin' rooks on a friend's farm in the afternoon. He had been bitin' the cartridges as was his custom.'

'It is a perfectly reasonable, rational and honest explanation of Mr Feasey's condition,' the attorney said. 'No further questions.'

Smirking, Isaiah caught Grace's eye. Cautiously, she shook her head. Whatever he thought, he wasn't off the hook, because another of the gobblers had already claimed to have brought a gun that he'd found discarded in the marsh to the watch house. The charge inside it had been gunpowder and swan shot, and the obvious conclusion was that the gun belonged to Isaiah. There were statements from the other Revenue officers before the warehouse keeper at the custom house in New Romney said that Cromwell had brought him some casks the following afternoon, one of which contained four gallons of foreign gin.

Digger gave his side of the story, how — carrying a gun with him for protection — he was out drinking when he'd met the smugglers at the Dolphin Inn.

They invited him to join them on their tour of the taverns on the road to Lydd. More drinks followed before he started to make his way home, knowing that his dear wife — he looked up at Sarah in the gallery — would be waiting for him.

'I found myself surrounded by landsmen carryin' tubs and smugglers brandishin' weapons, and I told myself, Digger, you've got to get away from 'ere,' he went on, addressing the judge and jury. 'I stopped at the next public 'ouse — The Flyin' Duck, if I remember rightly, which I might not because I'd 'ad a right skinful. Anyway, I 'ad beer and a pipe of tobacco to smoke on the road, but I took the wrong footpath and ended up in the middle of an affray. It was dark and the fog was like pea-soup. I could 'ear men runnin' this way and that, guns goin' off . . . I stumbled across a personage who shouted that 'e was in a pickle and could 'e borrow my musket? I gave it to 'im and made to run away, but I was caught, arrested and taken to the watch 'ouse.'

'You are saying this is a case of mistaken identity, that you were arrested in error?' the attorney for the prosecution asked.

'Exactly.' Digger grinned and held out his arms, as if he was regaling the smugglers with a tale of his daring exploits back on a cosy evening at the Rattling Cat. 'I did a man a favour and got arrested for it.'

'Let us recall the allegation that you handed the gentleman a gun and shouted, shoot the . . .!'

'I don't remember sayin' that, but I wouldn't because I was three sheets to the wind, if not four.'

'So, there is a possibility that those words did cross your lips?'

He was well and truly caught out, Grace thought. Digger was in trouble and seeing Sarah bury her head in her hands, her friend knew it too.

When the defence questioned Isaiah about the gunpowder and rook shooting, he explained how he was in the habit of going out with a gun to shoot rooks on Peter's land.

'I carry ammunition for that purpose,' he added.

'Where did you obtain the powder and shot?'

Isaiah explained, and their neighbour, John, affirmed that he had given them to him and that he'd seen him take the powder in a paper and roll it up before putting it in his waistcoat pocket. He didn't use a flask.

The trial went on, until the judge summed up the evidence and asked the jury to consider their

298

verdict. Sarah put her arm through Grace's, and they waited with bated breath.

'Gentlemen of the jury, is it possible that these two men, loving husbands and one a father, are capable of carrying out the crimes of which they've been accused? Take a good long look at them, members of the jury. Are they vicious criminals or ordinary men who have fallen victim to circumstances? Mr Brown — also known as Digger — has explained how he gave up his gun at great risk to his person to help another, while Mr Feasey is also another innocent bystander. I would remind the jury that the marsh was alive with people that night. It was dark and foggy. Many have stated that they 'couldn't see their hands in front of their faces'. However, a smuggler ended up dead, and several Revenue officers injured. I leave the issues of fact for the jury to determine.'

The twelve good men retired, returning an hour later for the foreman to give their verdicts.

'How do you find the defendant, Mr Brown?' the judge asked.

'We, the jury, find him guilty of all charges— '

'No! That's wrong,' Sarah gasped.

'Silence in Court,' the judge warned, and Sarah broke down sobbing.

'And the defendant, Mr Feasey? How do you find him?'

Grace perched on the edge of her seat. 'Not guilty, your honour.' Grace sat back, relieved but unsmiling. Jason wasn't smiling either, glowering at Isaiah with his fist clenched around the handle of his cutlass.

'I shall return to sentence the unfortunate Mr

Brown after a short recess,' the judge said.

'George said it would be all right, that 'is attorney would 'ave both our 'usbands freed,' Sarah cried. 'Digger wouldn't 'urt a fly.'

It seemed that there was no room for appeal. Digger had been apprehended as he handed over a loaded gun, urging Albert whom he mistakenly assumed was a smuggler because he was wearing a smock, to use it on Cromwell, so his guilt wasn't in doubt. Isaiah had been lucky this time. Found on the beach without a gun or tubs, the case against him couldn't be proven since the evidence in the form of the gunpowder and swan shot was circumstantial.

'For the crime of murder, Mr Brown, I sentence you to death by hanging. You will be taken to Penenden Heath where you will be hanged by the neck until . . . '

As the smugglers gasped in horror and the Revenue cheered, Sarah slumped forward and slid from her seat.

'She's fainted. Please, keep back. Let her have some air,' Grace exclaimed as a well-dressed middle-aged lady with a powdered face and beauty spot painted on her upper lip offered to help, taking a vinaigrette from her purse and holding it under Sarah's nose.

'Breathe in, ducky. That's right.'

Sarah opened her eyes. 'Am I dyin'? I wish I was dead.'

'My dear friend,' Grace said. 'You must summon all your strength and dignity. It's imperative that we speak to the attorney and the guards, and see if you can have a moment with Digger before

. . . ' She swallowed hard, unable to continue, as the lady helped Sarah to her feet and brushed the dust from her skirts. Having thanked her, Grace took Sarah's hand and led her down to find someone whom they could ask. Instead, they met with Mr Houghton-White who was being talked at by George Minnis.

'I'm not 'appy about the verdicts,' George was saying. 'What went wrong?'

'I cannot fabricate evidence, no matter how fat a fee you offer me,' the attorney glowered. 'The outcomes were as I advised you — one guilty, the other innocent. I have no power to influence the judge when it comes to sentencing, and you heard what he said about the futility of appealing against it. Mr Brown's only hope of a reprieve is for him to reconsider turning King's evidence, because we all know he wasn't the only guilty party that night.'

'That would help 'im, but not certain others,' George said, glancing towards Sarah. 'It puts 'im between the Devil and the deep blue sea: turning others in for them to 'ang in 'is place. If 'e goes down that route, there's sure to be repercussions — '

'I wish to see 'im,' Sarah interrupted, 'before it's too late.'

'There'll be a delay of at least one sennight,' the attorney said.

'Arrange for Mrs Brown to see 'er 'usband before she returns to Snargate,' George said. 'Ah, Mr Feasey . . . ' He shook hands with Isaiah whom the guards had released. 'I'm glad the judge and jury saw sense — it seems that Commander

301

Witherall and 'is crew overstepped the mark in arrestin' you. It comes to somethin' when a man can't wander the marsh in the middle of the night for a bit of peace and fresh air, without bein' captured and thrown into gaol.'

'I'm very grateful for what you've done for me.'

George put his arm around Isaiah's shoulder.

'You'll 'ave to be more careful. Next time, it might not work out so well for you,' he said in a low voice. 'Marlin's lost face — he'll be gunnin' for you. Go 'ome with your wife. I'll be in touch.'

Isaiah turned to Grace. 'I'm glad to see you, my love, but you needn't 'ave come. I knew the judge would see sense and let me off. That's not to say that I didn't miss you, or 'ave a few dark moments when I thought I might never see you and the littlun again.'

'I've missed you too.' Grace took his hand.

''As there been any news of Musket?' he asked, his voice quavering slightly.

'No, I'm afraid not. It's strange not having the dog around — I'd grown used to him, in spite of his fleas.'

Isaiah's shoulders sagged and Grace changed the subject. 'Let's wait for Sarah at the tavern. Our transport will be along soon.'

On their way to the Marquis of Granby, she reassured him that Aggie was well, but Isaiah kept harking back to the trial.

'It was Marlin's fault that I got thrown into gaol. He could 'ave arrested anyone that night, but 'e picked on me. 'E got 'is just deserts, though — George's attorney made 'im look like an ass in court.'

'Have you no feelings? You haven't mentioned Digger. Or Dunk.'

'Digger's a fool. Who in 'is right mind 'ands 'is gun over to a gobbler?'

'He made a mistake and he's paying for it with his life. Sarah — who is carrying his child — will be a widow before she's twenty-one. I want her to come and stay with us until Digger's fate is settled, one way or the other.'

'Are you askin' me, or tellin' me?' A smile played on his lips.

'I'm telling you,' she said crossly. 'I don't think she should be on her own at a time like this.' She didn't trust George, and if any of the other smugglers thought that Digger was going to turn against them, Sarah would be in danger of reprisals.

'You aren't goin' to tell me that I 'ave to cut ties with the Greys?'

She shook her head. What was the point when the court case had only put them under more obligation to George than ever? She had no doubt that the cost of the attorney, transport and her stay in Maidstone had been added to their debt, and as Isaiah had earned nothing from the run, they couldn't even begin to pay it off.

'Ah, you're beginnin' to come round to it,' Isaiah crowed. 'I knew you would. What 'appened was a one-off. The next run's going to be bigger and better, and we're goin' to make our fortune and pay George in full to get 'im off our backs.'

What could she say? Dunk had been killed and Revenue officers injured. Next time, the outcome could only be worse with the men on both sides fired up for revenge.

303

When Sarah found them at the tavern, she had been crying.

'I've lost everythin',' she said. 'My 'usband won't go against 'is conscience and turn King's evidence to save 'is life, even though I begged 'im to change 'is mind for the sake of 'is unborn child.'

'Give him time,' Grace murmured. 'He'll look at it differently in the morning.'

'You don't know my Digger— 'e's a stubborn fellow. Oh Grace, to add insult to injury, that lady — the one who revived me with the smellin' salts — it turns out that she's a known thief who 'angs around the court'ouse, takin' advantage of the vulnerable. She's picked my purse out of my pocket. It's gorn.'

18

Keep your Friends Close,
Keep your Enemies Closer

A couple of weeks after the trial, a letter addressed to Sarah arrived at the Minnises' house in Snargate. Grace was in the front garden hoeing the weeds while Aggie lay on a blanket, kicking her legs, when one of the village lads delivered it to Hazel Cottage.

Grace called for Sarah, who appeared on the doorstep, wiping her hands on her apron.

'Would you read it for me, Grace?' Her eyes were red from crying. 'Is it good news, or . . . the worst?'

'Let's go inside.' Grace took Aggie indoors and put her in her cradle downstairs for a nap before she opened the letter. 'Sit down, Sarah.'

'Has 'e done it? Has 'e agreed to turn the others in? Dear Lord, I pray that my 'usband 'as seen sense at last and found it in 'is conscience to do whatever it takes, so that 'e can come 'ome to his lovin' wife.'

Grace began to read, her heart in her mouth.

'Dear Sarah,
    I've been told that, although I crave one last sight of you, it's best that you don't come to the hanging itself. The chaplain says it will

305

be too upsetting and the last thing I want is
for my good and kind wife to suffer.'

Sarah stifled a sob, stuffing her handkerchief into
her mouth.

'Then 'e 'asn't changed his mind,' she said,
recovering herself a little. 'Read on. There is more?'

Grace nodded. She could hardly bring herself to continue. Digger had shown himself to be
an honourable man, but was he more scared of
George Minnis than the noose?

'He says he is quite prepared to meet his end.

*We eat and drink today, and tomorrow, we
die. Looking on the bright side, I've learned
the Lord's Prayer from beginning to end
while in prison. It's giving me much comfort.
I'm resigned to my punishment, feeling confident of mercy in the afterlife.'*

Grace paused and reached out to hold Sarah's
hand.

*'I wish that you — my dearest Sarah — will
not grieve any more than necessary, knowing
that we will have happier times together in
Heaven. I'm sorry I can't make amends.'*

'My dear 'usband . . . ' Sarah broke down completely, and Grace cried with her. ''E's only
thirty years old. If 'e 'adn't been caught up with
the Greys, like a fish in a net, we would 'ave 'ad
another twenty years of 'appiness at least, maybe
more.'

306

'Are you ready for me to continue?' Grace said softly.

Sarah nodded.

'I have a confession to make — I wish you to convey my deepest regrets to Mr and Mrs Feasey for going along with our friend G — 's ruse regarding the wager that went on for the Rattling Cat. If you recall, G —, knowing that Mr Feasey trusted me, asked me to confirm that the coin was a good 'un. It was a test. The coin he gave me was the same each side: two heads. G— whispered that if I betrayed him, he'd have my head cut off. I'm not sure to this day if he was joking or not.'

'You must 'ate us now,' Sarah said uneasily.

'Did you know about this?'

'I'd 'ave made 'im apologise before if I 'ad.'

'I won't allow this revelation to alter our friendship, nor will I mention it to Isaiah,' Grace assured her. 'It's too late for recriminations. The papers had already been drawn up, making George the legal owner. He made a great show of his largesse to impress the Rattlers and diminish Isaiah in their eyes, because he didn't want my husband challenging his leadership of the Greys. He's devious, manipulative, and I detest him.'

'I wish there was some way of takin' George Minnis down.'

'There is a note added in another hand . . . oh, this is . . . ' She didn't read the rest: that Digger's body was to be hung in chains near the site of his capture on the bleak wasteland of Walland Marsh.

307

'What is it?'

'Nothing,' Grace said.

'Please, don't keep it from me . . . I need to know the worst.'

'I suppose you will have to know in the end.' Grace explained the addendum.

'That's cruel, the final insult to a gentleman smuggler who's goin' to 'is death, loyal to 'is friends to the last.'

'Perhaps there is something we can do to prevent it.' Digger might have chosen to put his principles above his wife and unborn child, but Grace couldn't let his mortal remains be treated with such a lack of respect, left exposed to the gawping masses, boys lobbing stones and jeering crowds. 'I'm going to take this letter to a magistrate to ask him to intercede on your behalf. It is you who will suffer if this is permitted to go ahead. Despite his transgressions, he's been a loving husband and you should be able to give him a decent burial.'

'You would do that for us?' Sarah said.

'For you, Sarah. I'm not sure how I feel about Digger and his role in letting George have the tavern.'

'Don't you think we should ask George first? I don't want to offend 'im by goin' behind his back.'

'You're right. We'll call on him straight away to ask his advice.'

'Shouldn't you ask Isaiah's permission first?' Sarah said doubtfully.

'I would if I knew where he was. He's gone with the Greys to shoot ducks on the marsh for target practice. This can't wait . . . ' She faltered.

She'd been about to say that Digger's demise was imminent, his death confirmed for the end of the sennight.

Pushing Aggie in a pram that Myrtle had borrowed from her sister, they walked past the church to the Minnises' residence, a rambling two-storey red-brick house with a tiled roof.

'It's deceptive,' Sarah said. 'The west side of the 'ouse contains the livin' quarters. If you go round the back, there's another entrance that leads into a taproom of sorts. That's where the smugglers drink and make merry, and where George stores 'is——'

'Enough said,' Grace cut in, but Sarah hadn't finished.

' 'E sells up to one hundred tubs of liquor from 'ere every week. Imagine that. There's a well and pear trees, and outbuildin's behind the house. I've 'eard it said that there's an underground tunnel that leads from George's barn into the church where there's a ship painted on one of the walls to show that it's a place of safety for smugglers. Myrtle told me that the vicar of St Dunstan's can find 'is way back in the dark by followin' the smell of baccy.'

Sarah rang the bell and an elderly maid wearing a white cap, starched apron and black dress answered the door. Sarah introduced her.

'This is Nell. Nell, this is my friend, Grace.'

'Black Dog's wife,' the maid said, peering at her through cloudy eyes. 'Everyone knows everyone around here. Have you come to call on Mrs Minnis? Only she's indisposed.'

'We've come to see George,' Sarah said.

'I'll ask him if it's convenient.' With that, Nell shuffled away and didn't come back.

'Do you think she's all right?' Grace whispered as Aggie began blowing raspberries from the pram.

'She takes 'er time — it's 'er lumbago.'

Eventually, the maid returned, saying, 'He's in his study — he'll receive you there. Leave the baby over there under the tree.'

'Thank you. We won't be long.' Grace left Aggie snoozing in the pram and followed Sarah across the hall where she knocked at a half-open door.

'Come in, ladies. To what do I owe this unexpected pleasure?' George stood up behind his desk. 'Do take a seat.'

'We aren't stopping,' Grace said.

'You're 'ere to ask for money. I expect you're a bit short, Grace. What was your 'usband to receive as payment for that last run? We agreed on twenty-seven shillin's if I remember correctly.' He stared at her, his eyes narrowed, his lips compressed as he picked up several coins from the dish of silver that stood on the desk and counted them into his palm.

His memory was conveniently flexible, Grace thought, because Isaiah had told her it would be at least thirty. Any amount would be a help, but with a cruel smile, George dropped the coins chinking back into the dish, saying, 'Black Dog forfeited his payment when 'e got 'imself arrested. It's a shame, but 'e's goin' to 'ave to refund me for the attorney's fees — I'll add it to the amount 'e owes me.'

Humiliated, Grace blinked back a tear, but she wouldn't go back on her promise to Sarah. 'We've

310

received a letter from Digger. Knowing of your fondness for him, singling him out in the past for his loyalty to the Greys, we've come to ask if — out of the goodness of your heart — you'll put a word in with the appropriate authority to let Sarah bring Digger's body home where he belongs.'

George strode to the window and looked out on to the garden behind the house.

'He's gone? The deed 'as been done.'

'Not yet.'

He turned back. 'Sit down — you're makin' the place look untidy.'

Reluctantly, Grace obeyed and Sarah followed suit.

'Would you deprive a grieving widow of the chance to bury her husband? You're a gentleman of influence, well respected and admired — ' the words were sticking in her craw as she went on '— for your kindness and generosity.'

Smiling, he sat down in his leather chair opposite them and leaned forward, his fingertips forming a steeple.

'We've been acquainted for a while, so I'm willin' to make an offer.' Grace's brow tensed when he addressed Sarah. 'With your 'usband gone and Mrs Minnis bein' my wife in name only, it seems to me that an 'arrangement' would suit us both. You scratch my back, I'll scratch yours.'

'Sarah, you don't have to— ' Grace began, but George interrupted.

'Let 'er answer for 'erself. It's a straightforward trade.'

Grace listened to the slow tick of the mantel clock, a Continental timepiece adorned with gold

311

leaf and a blue enamelled dial, while she awaited Sarah's decision.

'I'll do it,' Sarah said.

A moment later, Cut-throat appeared at the window, shouting and hollering and banging on the glass. His smile fading, George jumped up and lifted the sash.

'What is it?' he growled. 'Why are you 'ere makin' this racket? It's enough to wake the dead.'

'It's done, George. We've done it,' Cut-throat gasped.

George's face turned ashen.

A group of six or seven more smugglers, Isaiah included, wearing their grey smocks and with muskets slung over their shoulders, came storming into the garden, carrying a deer roped to a chestnut pole and draped with a frayed blanket. They dropped it beside the pear tree before Lawless appeared, bawling like a baby.

Aggie? Grace remembered, panicking.

'I've left the littlun outside. Sarah, we have to go,' she said, getting up and hurrying out of the room. On reaching the front door, she wrenched it open and ran to the pram where she found Aggie cooing to herself and chewing on her fist, completely unconcerned. Weak with relief, she pushed the pram back to Hazel Cottage as quickly as she could with Sarah jogging along behind her.

'We didn't see nothin' untoward, did we?' Sarah asked later, sitting on the bench by the window with her arms wrapped around her knees, while Grace stirred the pot of onion and turnip broth that she'd prepared for their supper.

'Nothing at all,' she confirmed, feeling sick

312

because she couldn't stop reliving the scene, asking herself what she'd really seen.

'It's no great sacrifice, givin' myself to that . . . that man. He might 'ave use of my body, but 'e'll never . . . ' she gave a sob ' . . . 'ave my soul. Or my heart, because that belongs to Digger.'

Grace left the spoon in the pot and walked across to comfort her, until the front door suddenly banged open, sending a shower of plaster to the floor.

'I've just swept up,' she exclaimed.

'That's a fine way to greet your 'usband when 'e's been on 'is feet all day.' Isaiah came in, yawning and stretching before he kicked off his boots. 'How's the littlun?'

'She's asleep,' Grace said, wincing as he gave her a kiss on the cheek. 'You've been drinking.'

'I took advantage of George's 'ospitality and indulged in a couple of pints.'

'And the rest,' she said wryly.

'I didn't come 'ome to be mithered. I'm sorry for airin' our dirty linen in front of you, Sarah,' he went on more gently. 'George mentioned that you'd been to see 'im — I must 'ave missed you somehow.'

'Aggie was in her pram at the front of the house — you came into the back garden with the. . . '

'Deer,' he finished for her. 'George 'as asked me to go to Maidstone with Peter when the time comes.' He moved to the fireplace and looked in the pot. 'What's this? More broth? A workin' man needs meat.'

With a shrug, Grace fetched three bowls from the cupboard and dished up. 'No money, no meat.'

On the Saturday afternoon, Peter's cart arrived outside the cottage with Isaiah, Lawless and Cut-throat following along behind with their heads bowed. A small crowd, including Myrtle and John, gathered to watch the smugglers carry Digger's body in its winding sheet into Grace's home, and lay him out on the table which John had extended with some planks of wood.

Sarah tugged at the sheet to expose her husband's head and fell to crying as she kissed and stroked his face. As Grace stood watching, unable to say or do anything to console her friend, Isaiah took her hand and held it tight.

'Tell me everythin',' Sarah said, looking up. 'I want to know . . . .'

'I saw 'im placed on a cart with 'is back to the 'orses' tails so he couldn't see where he was goin',' Isaiah responded. 'I think you would 'ave been pleased to 'ave 'eard the women remarkin' that 'e was the 'andsomest of all the prisoners that went to the 'eath that day.'

'How did 'e seem? Was 'e cryin'?'

''E was very calm and dignified when 'e went up on to the platform . . . Sarah, don't torment yourself by askin' me to say any more about it.'

'I'll suffer more not knowin' how it ended. I should 'ave been there — I should 'ave gone against 'im.'

'If you must, then . . . The 'angman tied a cord around 'is neck and fastened it to the three-legged mare while the chaplain prayed and sang psalms. I was allowed to join our old friend to give 'im your message and say farewell.' Isaiah's eyes were wet, his voice thick with grief. ''E said 'e loved you and wishes . . . wished 'e'd been a better 'usband.'

'Thank you.'

Isaiah fell silent, but Sarah hadn't finished torturing herself.

'Did he suffer at the end?'

'No,' Isaiah said firmly. ''E couldn't see anythin' because the 'angman covered 'is eyes and whipped the 'orses up to a frenzy before lettin' them go, pullin' the cart away from under 'is feet.'

Grace glanced towards Peter who was standing quietly in the corner, his hat in his hands, and then she counted the smugglers, the remaining Rattlers from Deal who used to laugh, plot, drink and sing, and generally make a nuisance of themselves at the tavern.

'Isaiah, where's Awful Doins? I thought he'd be here with the rest of you.'

'Oh, I don't know,' he said, glancing towards Lawless and Cut-throat. ''Ave you seen him recently?'

''E's ridden 'ome,' Cut-throat said. 'A member of 'is family's been taken ill, bodily ill. That's right, isn't it, Lawless?'

'That's the story,' Lawless muttered, leaving Grace feeling more uneasy than ever. Dunk and Digger were dead and she couldn't help feeling that Awful Doins had come to grief too. The Greys had to be stopped before anyone else was injured or killed. She couldn't stand by and let them continue their murderous mission to feather their own nests — George's mainly — at the expense of everyone else. George had been right to question

315

where her loyalties lay, she thought as she began to formulate a plan to find out what she could about the next run and send the information to Jason. She wasn't sure how to reach him without arousing Isaiah's suspicions, but it wasn't beyond the wit of man — she allowed herself a small smile — or woman.

She showed Peter out, thanking him for his assistance, then chased the smugglers out too, so she could help Sarah prepare Digger's body for burial.

The next morning, Grace found Sarah in the garden, dressed in the same clothes that she'd been wearing the day before.

'Aren't you going to attend the service at St Dunstan's?' she asked.

Sarah shook her head. 'Digger and I weren't what you call regular churchgoers, and bein' a woman, I'm not allowed to be there to see 'im put in the ground.' She was almost shouting as if she was going a little mad, Grace thought, but that wasn't surprising, considering what she had to look forward to when George came to collect his dues.

Grace cuddled Aggie as she watched Isaiah and the other bearers stretcher Digger's body out of the cottage and down the path. Digger's death had been a lesson to them all, but she couldn't help wondering how many of the smugglers would learn from it.

Twisting round, she found Sarah making a start on sweeping the floor.

'What are you doing? I can do that,' she said.

Thanking her, Sarah thrust the broom into

Grace's hand and rushed upstairs before running down again, her shawl flying behind her. She stopped at the door.

'I'm leavin' while I can. It'll be a while till George realises I've gone — it'll give me a 'ead start. I'm goin' 'ome to Folkestone. I'm sorry, Grace. I'll never forget you and your kindness, and the good times we've 'ad.'

'Me too,' Grace said softly.

'I 'ave one more favour to ask. Will you tend Digger's grave for me?'

'Of course I will.' Grace held out her arms and gave her a hug. 'I'll write to you, if you'll give me your address.'

'I'll send it to you, I promise — although I'll 'ave to ask my mother to screeve on my behalf. Oh dear, I'm goin' to miss you and Aggie. There, I won't say any more, or I'll start cryin',' Sarah murmured, stepping away and heading outside.

'Watch your back,' Grace said, but she was already at the gate.

In low spirits, Grace cleaned the cottage and folded the clothes that Sarah had left behind, thinking that she might be able to sell them, then dug up one of the remaining potato plants, finding three reasonably sized potatoes that she pared and added to the broth in the pot. She dreamed of hot pies from Molly's, chitterlings served with mustard and vinegar, and rich suet puddings.

With Sarah gone, she felt quite lost. Myrtle was pleasant enough, but she didn't trust her not to report back to George. She fretted over Aggie, worrying that she'd end up squinty-eyed from the hours that she spent staring at her blanket, and

317

wondering if she was feeding her enough.

Pulling herself together, she sat down to feed Aggie and wait for Isaiah to come home. Next spring, she would plant seeds and grow vegetables from scratch, she would have a few more chickens and see if she could prune the neglected apple trees to encourage them to produce fruit. Thinking about the garden and the future gave her hope and a welcome distraction.

She put Aggie to bed, but still Isaiah had not returned. Hours later, she wandered down the garden path to the front gate with a lantern to see if there was any sign of her errant husband.

'Yoo-hoo, is that you, Grace?' She heard Myrtle before she saw her, a shadowy figure crossing the lane to join her. 'You don't happen to know what's keeping our menfolk? John told me he was invited to George's. I wasn't happy when he decided to have the rendezvous at his place, not ours, but there you go. They're sworn to secrecy after what happened with the last run. They don't want anyone alertin' the gobblers this time.' Myrtle paused for breath, then carried on. 'I saw Sarah going out earlier, but I haven't seen her come back?'

'She wanted some time to herself.' Grace scolded herself inwardly for not thinking ahead and fabricating a story to allow time for Sarah to cover a good distance before the alarm was raised.

'She's gone home to Folkestone, hasn't she?' Myrtle said. 'I thought as much.'

'How did you know?'

'She talked to me about her family once or twice — I'd get away as far as I could from Snargate, if I were in her shoes. There's nothing here for her

318

now, the poor thing.'

'Myrtle, I don't think we should mention where's she's gone to George, or anyone else. We'll put it about that she took off in a distressed state — they can come to their own conclusions. I was present when George made her an offer, despite his being married to Mrs Minnis.'

'Hush,' Myrtle whispered. 'You'd be surprised how a voice carries across the marsh. Ah, listen. I can hear the men on their way home.'

'Let me do the talking,' Grace said firmly, hastening towards them. 'Isaiah, have you seen Sarah anywhere?' She gave him the story of how she'd left the cottage. 'She was upset.'

'Why didn't you go after 'er?' He was slurring as he stumbled towards her, his hands curling into fists. 'There are times when I wonder about you, you useless— '

'Hey, Black Dog, we're 'ere now — we'll raise a few of the men and send out a search party,' John cut in.

'It's pitch-dark,' Isaiah grumbled, calming down. 'We'll 'ave to go out at first light.'

'Come on indoors, John,' Myrtle said. 'You can tell me what was said at the rondy.'

'I can't tell you anythin',' John said solemnly. 'You can needle me as much as you like — my lips are sealed.' With that, he belched, apologised for his lack of manners and followed Myrtle across the lane, leaving Grace facing Isaiah who grasped her by the arm and dragged her up the path and into their cottage.

'She's drowned, I reckon. Musket's probably suffered the same fate— 'e'll 'ave wandered off

319

and fallen into one of the drains when we left 'im be'ind that night,' he said gloomily as she tore herself away and moved to the opposite side of the table. 'It's been one of those days when I've 'ad to take the rough with the smooth. George paid me a few shillin's for going to Maidstone on his behalf. I told him he was leavin' us short and 'ow my wife can't make a silk purse from a pig's ear. When I mentioned that we'd run out of credit at the bakery, 'e just shrugged and said we'd 'ave to cut our cloth. You Lennickers 'ave always 'ad it easy, but you're goin' to 'ave to toughen up.'

Little did he know how strong she was, she thought as he went on, 'I'm afraid I'm fallin' out of favour — things 'aven't been right since the run went asprawl, but I'll prove that I'm worthy of George's patronage next time. We'll 'ave our revenge on the gobblers for what they did to Dunk and Digger.'

'This thuggery has gone too far,' Grace interrupted. 'Too much blood has been spilled already. It will end in disaster.'

'I'll do whatever it takes to keep us afloat. It sounds 'arsh, but the Revenue would as soon aim fire at us as we would at them. Grace, I'm sorry for bein' in the drink — can we make our peace and go back to 'ow we were before?'

She walked across to him, put her arms around his neck and pressed her lips to his cheek. 'It's time we retired.

'Don't wake the baby,' she added as he staggered upstairs and fell into bed. She followed, checking on Aggie in her cradle next to the makeshift dressing table that Isaiah had made from some old pieces of timber and nails from the forge. Having undressed and changed into her nightgown, she lay down beside her husband.

'I haven't told you this before because I didn't want to cause any trouble between you and George, but I've hidden a couple of tubs in the ruins up the road — I came across them on the way home after the run went wrong. One of the landsmen must have dropped them, or they fell off a cart.'

'Well done, Grace,' Isaiah said. 'We aren't goin' to say nothin' to George though, are we? You were the one who held 'er nerve and picked them up. I'll move them on in the next few days, sell them before anyone stumbles across them.'

He rolled on to his back, chewing the side of his thumb. 'You know that I have to go along with whatever George wants,' he said quietly. 'I've seen what fate befalls those who don't.'

'Awful Doins?' she asked in a raw whisper, recalling the men bringing what she'd thought was a dead deer into George's garden.

'George wanted rid of 'im. We were goin' to bury 'im on Walland Marsh, but we were disturbed by some nosy higgler on 'is way to Appledore, or so 'e claimed. Panickin', we took the deceased to George's 'ouse and dropped 'im down the well.' Isaiah shuddered. 'I'm pretty sure 'e 'as company down there.

'I can't see a way out — I'm almost resigned to being bound to the Greys for the rest of my life.'

'Not necessarily,' she said, resting her arm across his chest. 'What about this run?'

'I can't say anythin' about it. You'll be comin' with me, but the less you know the better.'

321

'You could at least tell me when and where the landing will be.' She wheedled and cajoled him, but he refused to tell her, thwarting her tentative plan to send the information to Jason in a bid to prevent the run going ahead.

'I'm tryin' to protect you and the littlun. It isn't much, but it's the best I can do. I've been blamin' you and everyone else for getting' me into deep water, but I'm beginnin' to realise that some of the fault lies with me.'

What Isaiah dreamed of, was returning to Deal in triumph with enough money to buy his old life back: the Rattling Cat and a lugger. Grace felt almost as sorry for him as she did for herself, being trapped by circumstances that were beyond their control.

19

A Flash in the Pan

'We've 'ad a bit of luck recently — I made good money for those tubs you picked up,' Isaiah said when Grace was serving him an early supper of boiled tripe and potatoes on a chilly September evening.

'I wish I'd seen a little more of it,' Grace commented. 'What did you spend the rest on?'

'Ah, the landlord at the Rose and Crown in Brenzett is payin' in instalments.'

'Why did you agree to that?' she exclaimed.

'Because 'e threatened to tell George that I was sellin' liquor be'ind his back. 'Ow was I to know that they were bosom friends?'

'You should have guessed — the Devil casts a wide net. This is a bad omen for tonight,' she said sadly. 'The weather isn't right for smuggling — there isn't a cloud in the sky.'

'George won't delay — there's too much at stake. You'll look after the 'orse and cart as you did afore while Myrtle minds Aggie.' He took her hands and kissed her. 'Listen, my love. The men took a few missteps the last time when Dunk got killed — that's why Digger and I got caught. It won't 'appen again. We're far more organised — we've been trainin' all the hours that God sends, doin' target practice and the like.'

'Which is how Awful Doins got shot,' she said quietly.

'I know, but 'e asked for it. I believe what I'm told, Grace. That's the best way.'

'It isn't like it used to be when everyone knew each other.' Blinking back tears, she gazed out of the window that looked out on to their tiny patch of garden and beyond, where the few stunted trees were already acquiring the golden mantle of autumn.

'It's time you accepted that you are and always will be a smuggler's wife.' He spooned a hot potato into his mouth and instantly spat it out. 'I'm terribly sore about Digger's fate, but there's nothin' I can do about it. George says this is the big one, the run to end all runs. It could be our ticket out of 'ere.' He tipped his head back and dropped the potato into his mouth, chewed it twice then swallowed. ''Adn't you better be on your way to collect our transport?'

'I'll drop Aggie over to Myrtle's.' She left him to the rest of his meal while she dressed in her cloak, boots and felt hat, and collected Aggie's blanket and rattle. She spent a short while talking to Myrtle who was full of the news that Peter had been robbed overnight.

'He lost a set of harness and three saddles, none of which are cheap to replace.'

'Poor Peter. That's terrible — what kind of person steals the items a man needs to run his business?' Grace said.

'I think we all know the answer,' Myrtle said. 'Don't repeat this, but some of George's men are beginning to make a nuisance of themselves. Now, let me have the littlun. I'll take care of her, don't you worry.'

Reluctantly, Grace handed her over, but Aggie didn't want Grace to leave this time, holding out her arms and crying for her. Grace hesitated.

'Mama will be back,' Myrtle sang out. 'Go on, Grace. Go.'

'Bobbie's ready for you.' Peter greeted her with a smile when she arrived at the farm. 'I've given 'im an extra brush and trimmed 'is tail.'

'He looks very smart, thank you. I'll look after him.'

'Make sure you look after yourself as well,' he said. 'There are some scoundrels about.'

'I'm sorry for what happened last night — Myrtle told me.'

'There were two of them — if I 'adn't disturbed them, they would 'ave stolen every piece of tack I own.'

'Do you know who they are?'

'It doesn't make any difference whether I do or not. They 'ave the protection of a certain gen'leman who will remain nameless. Make of that what you will. Is your 'usband goin' on this jaunt with you?'

She nodded as the horse reached towards her and nuzzled her face before taking off her hat and dropping it. Apologising, Peter rushed to pick it up at the same time as she did. Their hands touched and he snatched the hat away.

'I'm sorry,' he muttered, dusting it down and transferring a muddy handprint to the black felt. 'I've made it worse. What can I do?'

'Don't worry. What's a little mud between

friends?' she said as he gave it back.

'Indeed.' Blushing, he waited for her to put her hat back on, then handed her the ribbons. As she made to drive the cart out of the yard, he added, 'Promise me you'll take care of yourself. I 'eard what 'appened last time.'

By seven, Grace and Isaiah were on their way, the box of weapons and ammunition and a basket of provisions on board, and a handful of soot wrapped in paper inside Isaiah's pocket to rub on to their faces after dark.

'Which way are we going?' she asked, pulling up at the crossroads in Snargate. 'You still haven't told me.'

'We're 'eadin' for Dover.'

'Thank you, but I don't know why you refused to let me know in advance.'

'As I said before, George and I wanted to be sure that there were no leaks this time. I didn't want you goin' the same way as a mutual friend.'

'You don't trust me?' she said, a shiver running down her spine as she recalled the fate of Awful Doins.

'I do, Grace. George doesn't. Crack your whip and make this tortoise of an 'orse step out, and remember to keep an eye out for the dog.'

'You said that you thought he'd drowned,' Grace said, ignoring his demand to make Bobbie move faster.

'He's a tough un, like his master. There's still a chance that he 'asn't come to grief, but— 'With a shrug, he went on, 'You know, I 'ave a fair achin' tooth for an 'ard-boiled egg.'

'You can't be hungry already.'

326

'I'm starvin'.' He opened the basket of provisions and ate half of them before wiping his mouth and resting his hand on Grace's waist, as they travelled through Brenzett, Ivychurch and St Mary in the Marsh to Dymchurch, where they stopped at a public house before heading on to their destination via Hythe, Sandgate and Folkestone. It was between midnight and one when they arrived on the beach, their faces smeared with soot.

Grace gave the horse his nosebag and stood him in the shadows among the bathing machines on Dover beach.

'What do we do now?' she asked.

'We wait,' Isaiah replied.

'Are you sure we're in the right place? It's very quiet.'

'It's what George and I agreed.' Isaiah nibbled his fingernails, his anxiety putting Grace on edge. 'Can you hear voices?'

'Only the sea, the waves and the whistle of the wind.' In the light of a crescent moon, the visibility not conducive to smuggling, she could make out the white horses dancing on the water and then the silhouette of a boat close by: a giant lugger, more than forty feet long, her canvas furled, her guns glinting.

'Ah, 'ere they are,' Isaiah whispered as figures armed with muskets, staves and fowling pieces began to appear between the bathing machines, until there were fifty or sixty men present, all dressed in grey smocks with dark trousers. Her heart began to pound relentlessly as Isaiah stepped out from the shadows and raised his hands to his mouth to utter three sharp barks, bringing George

327

riding across to meet him.

Bobbie whickered at George's mare as he and Isaiah exchanged a few words.

'Hush,' Grace muttered. 'What's going on?' she said, addressing Isaiah when he came sauntering back to her side.

'There's no sign of the gobblers — we'll be able to run the goods unhindered. Keep your mouth shut and listen for the signal. George 'as reiterated that I'm to stick to your side like glue.'

'You didn't look after me and Sarah last time,' she whispered.

'That's because you 'ad each other.'

The horse's ears pricked when the crew of the lugger started calling across the water. George shouted back, 'Hello, come on!' and the party of smugglers marched down towards the boat, their attention diverted by the thought of the great haul of tubs waiting for them and the fortune they were about to make.

Grace leaned against the horse's shoulder, keeping to the shadow cast by the adjacent bathing machine, a covered cart on wheels in which a lady could maintain her modesty whilst taking a dip in the waves. She couldn't understand the enthusiasm for salt-water bathing herself. The boatmen of Deal and their families had always done their utmost to avoid entering the sea.

Twenty armed men stood along the high watermark, guarding the rest who waded across to the lugger where the crew handed down the tubs that they'd brought from France. As the unloading continued, Grace suddenly noticed the outline of another boat: a cutter of an equal size with a long

328

bowsprit lurking further out.

'There's another wessel,' someone shouted. 'What is that boat?'

George, still mounted on his horse, stared through his spyglasses, then stuffed them into his coat pocket, stood in his stirrups and yelled, 'It's 'er, HMS *Legacy*. The gobblers 'ave come to watch. Keep calm and don't lose your 'eads.' He doffed his tall hat and put it back on.

'They're lowerin' their gigs! I don't think we should 'ang about.' One of the smugglers dropped his tubs and set off at a run up the beach, at which George fired a shot into the air, making Bobbie leap forward. It didn't stop the smuggler who scarpered off into the darkness. 'That's one less to share the profits with,' George announced loudly. 'Let's get this job done, then I'll treat you all to beer and brandy.'

As Grace tried to calm the horse, the remaining smugglers cheered and redoubled their efforts. They carried tubs up the beach to the waiting carts, moving stealthily and at speed, but not rapidly enough, because the first of the Revenue's gigs arrived, skimming on to the beach, her hull grating across the shingle as the gobblers threw down their oars and jumped out. When Grace turned back to look for Isaiah, he'd gone to join his fellow Greys, his desire to take part in the action apparently overcoming his concern for his wife's safety and the consequences of going against George's orders for a second time.

Grace's pulse began to throb with alarm as the second gig arrived alongside the first, the figures of several officers clearly visible in the moonlight.

329

'Where is the one who 'ad our man last time? Which one's Enderby?' she heard George yelling.

'It's 'im over there. It's 'im who killed Dunk. 'E danced with my missus once,' Isaiah shouted from the midst of the melee. 'Let me at 'im. I'll blow 'is brains out.'

She saw the flash in the pan and heard the report, but she couldn't see who was shooting whom. The landsmen continued to trudge up the beach with tubs slung across their chests and shoulders, while the guards aimed a volley of shots at the Revenue officers who threw themselves to the ground and crawled to the shelter of the bathing machines. The horse, normally stolid and calm, was getting nervier with each shot, tugging at the ribbons, and almost wrenching Grace's arms from their sockets.

She spotted two officers nearby, getting to their feet to confront one of the smugglers. The shorter officer was priming his pistol when the smuggler dashed at him, striking him with the butt of his musket.

'What are you doing?' he exclaimed, holding his hands up.

'You all right, Appleton?' she heard his fellow officer ask. Distracted, the smuggler turned slightly, giving Cromwell time to draw his cutlass and strike him across the shoulder, and again across the neck.

'Enderby, where are you?' Jason was shouting from the beach as some of his crew were trying to seize tubs from the landsmen.

'Over here,' Albert called back as he stood by Cromwell, covering him with his musket, as six or seven smugglers surrounded them. 'We need back-up!'

There was an ear-splitting bang, a cloud of smoke and the sickening thud of a body falling to the ground. The horse had had enough. He bucked and plunged, then tore himself away, the ribbons burning lines in Grace's palms as he headed off at a wild gallop, the cart bouncing along behind him.

''E's 'urt',' Cromwell screamed, still on his feet as Jason and another ten or twelve of his men came charging up, brandishing their guns and cutlasses. 'You've murdered him. We'll 'ave you all.'

Seeing that they were outnumbered, the smugglers ran like startled rats into the darkness, and the Revenue men went after them, leaving Grace on her own. Keeping to the shelter of the machines, she tiptoed towards the sound of groaning. Smuggler or gobbler? It didn't matter to her. There was a man lying injured, needing urgent help.

'Albert?' she whispered when she found him lying in the sand, his face glistening in the faint light of the moon.

'Mary? Is it you?' he gasped.

'It's Grace . . . Grace Feasey.' She knelt beside him.

'I've been shot,' he sobbed. 'I'm dyin'.'

'Let me see . . . I can put pressure on the wound to stem the bleeding until the doctor comes.' She unfastened his brass buttons and opened his jacket, revealing a gaping hole in his chest from which his life blood was trickling relentlessly into the fabric of his shirt.

'It was Black Dog who did it . . . ' he stuttered,

shivering uncontrollably. 'He was holding the gun.'

'You're cold,' she said, taking off her cloak and spreading it across his legs. 'Keep talking to me, Albert. Don't go to sleep.'

'My watch . . . will you give it to my wife? Tell her — I love her. Tell her — until we meet again.'

'Of course, but you'll be able to tell her yourself . . . ' Grace's voice faltered as his breathing stopped and his features froze, his eyes staring at the stars above. 'Oh, Albert.'

Wracked with guilt and with hot tears scoring tracks down her cheeks, she prayed for his soul and her own, because she thought she might have had a chance of saving him, if only she'd tried harder to find out where the landing was going to be. If she'd known the Greys were meeting at Dover, she could have sent word to Jason — she'd already decided how she would write him a note and enclose it in a letter addressed to Louisa to avoid detection, but it was too late.

'I promise that Mary will hear of your bravery and of your eternal love for her,' she whispered as she searched for the watch. She found it in his pocket and slipped it inside her bodice before wiping her hands on her dress. Then she heard the sound of voices again: the gobblers were coming back. She got up and ran at full tilt as far as she could until — out of breath and aching all over — she had to stop to cast up her accounts in a ditch alongside the road. She ducked down into the lee of the hedge and crawled along until she found a puddle in which to rinse her hands and bloodstained dress.

All she had to do now was make her way home across the marsh unseen, because she knew very well that if she was caught, she would be implicated in Albert's murder and never see little Aggie again.

The horse and cart had disappeared — she hoped Bobbie had had the sense to head for home. As for her, it was the longest walk she'd ever had to take. She jumped at every rustle in the hedge, every distant bellow of a cow and bleat of a sheep. On hearing footsteps, imaginary or not, she pushed her way through a clump of rushes to hide, sitting down with her arms wrapped around her knees, hardly daring to breathe as the clouds scudded across the moon. Why had Isaiah left her alone? What had he been thinking? She had no doubt that Albert had been telling the truth, that Isaiah, her once beloved husband, the man to whom she had given everything and sacrificed her relationship with her sisters for, had . . . she choked back a sob. *Oh, my love, what have you done?*

Where was he? Had the gobblers caught up with him again?

Waiting until she was sure the coast was clear, she retraced her steps to reach the road and walked on, wrapping her cloak around her and pulling the brim of her hat down to shade her eyes as dawn's soft blue light began to suffuse the landscape, turning the ditches and ponds into mirrors. She stopped to check her reflection, and before anyone could say knife, she'd splashed her face with water and rubbed the blood off.

'Good mornin', missus.'

She almost fell in. Touching her throat, she forced a chuckle. 'You startled me, sir.' Standing up, she turned to the owner of the voice: an elderly shepherd with a crook.

'What's a young lady like you doin' out here alone?' he asked.

'I'm going to collect my daughter — my neighbour's been minding her for me.' Grace wiped a tear from her eye. 'I've been away caring for my sister — she's an invalid.'

'I see. Well, you be careful — accordin' to some soldiers who came along this road not so long ago, there are some undesirable characters abroad.'

'Thank you for letting me know.'

'Are you far from your destination?'

'I'm not sure.' She surveyed the landscape. 'I think I've taken a wrong turn.' Uncertain whether or not she could trust him, she asked, 'You don't happen to know the way to Brenzett?'

Having explained how to get back to the main road, he bade her farewell and left her free to continue to Snargate. Although it was late afternoon and she was utterly exhausted, she went straight to Medlar Farm.

'I've lost Bobbie and the cart,' she confessed, meeting Peter in the yard. 'He bolted — I couldn't hold him.'

'I don't take kindly to people losin' my 'orses,' he said seriously, then, eyes twinkling, he added, ''Ave a look in the stable over there.'

As she approached, a familiar black horse put his head over the door, spilling hay from his mouth.

'I told you 'e was a clever one — 'e found 'is way home. The cart suffered a bit of damage, but

George'll pay to put that right. I was worried about you — I thought something terrible 'ad 'appened.'

It has, she wanted to say, but she held her tongue.

'I've 'eard about last night,' he said quietly. 'This will 'ave turned the tide of feelin' against the free trade. Enderby was well liked by both smugglers and his colleagues. His death won't be forgiven or forgot. There was a time when the smugglers garnered admiration and support from the local people, the farmers, shopkeepers and even the church. That 'as gone.'

'How do you know all this? Who told you?'

'A landsman came by early this morning — I caught 'im 'elpin' 'imself to water from the 'orses' trough. Despite my reservations about assistin' the Greys, I gave 'im an apple and some leftover pease puddin', in return for information.'

'He didn't happen to mention my husband? You haven't seen him?'

'I 'aven't seen any of George's men since yesterday. Mrs Feasey, if you don't mind me sayin', you look pretty rough.'

'I do mind,' she said.

'I'm sorry. I remember my mother sayin' that that wasn't the kind of sentiment that ladies appreciate. You still look beautiful . . . I shouldn't say that either, you bein' a married woman and all that. Please forgive me. I'm in the 'abit of blurtin' out what's in my 'ead without thinkin'.'

'It's all right, Peter. Worse things have happened at sea.'

'Did you see anythin' amiss?' he asked. When she hesitated, he went on, 'No matter. I shan't pry. What you don't know can't kill you. I mustn't keep you — you'll be wantin' to get 'ome to your littlun.'

Walking the short distance to the cottage, she was grateful that he understood. Peter appeared to be the kind of person who could keep a secret, but she couldn't say too much, knowing what George was capable of if he decided that a man or woman needed to be silenced.

John was already at the forge with two horses tied up outside: one saddled; the other with part of a harness draped over its loins.

'I've got a couple of strays here,' he said, greeting her. 'You 'aven't seen anyone missing 'is mount, 'ave you?'

She shook her head, unable to speak, her memory of the horror of the early hours sapping what was left of her strength. Her vision filled with coalescing black circles, her knees buckled and her spirit failed . . .

'Oh dear, ducks, you fainted,' she heard Myrtle saying. 'She's exhausted, the poor thing. John, there's no need for you to hang about indoors. I can look after her from here.'

Grace opened her eyes to find herself sitting in a chair in Myrtle's kitchen where the table was laden with a feast of hard-boiled eggs, cold bacon, potato cakes and pickles.

'What went on last night?' Myrtle asked, closing the door firmly shut behind her husband and returning to Grace's side. 'You're covered in blood and George and his men haven't arrived back in Snargate. In fact, John's been out searchin' since dawn, but he hasn't seen hide nor hair of them.

336

The militia are out, checkin' all the ditches and houses in the marsh, and the food I've prepared is going to waste.'

'Where's Aggie?'

'She's been a little angel — she's in the crib over there, sleeping soundly.'

'There was a fight — more than that, a battle — on the beach between the Greys and the gobblers. I didn't see — ' she shivered as Myrtle divested her of her cloak and dropped it on the floor '— anything. What are you doing?'

'I'm going to heat up some water so you can have a good wash. There's a tub that John uses beside the back door and you can borrow one of my old dresses. When you've done that, you'll have something to eat, then take Aggie home and burn those clothes before the Greys return. They'll be back, all of them, by nightfall if not before. Us women have to look after each other when our menfolk won't.'

Grace thanked her, grateful to find out at last that Myrtle could be trusted.

She returned to the cottage and lit a fire at the end of the garden, throwing on some extra logs that Myrtle had given her, before she took her bloodied clothing, tore it into strips and dropped it into the flames, stirring it up with a poker to make sure that every scrap burned down to ash.

Having put the baby to bed, she sat up in the upstairs room by candlelight and gazed across the lonely marsh. An owl hooted, making her spine stiffen. Was it Isaiah, or another of the Greys? It called again and she relaxed a little. It was just an owl.

If only she had listened to Louisa and Winnie. If only she had taken Isaiah's promise to leave the free trade with a pinch of salt. She had been naive and gullible, and she bitterly regretted having married a smuggler — and murderer. She was guilty of being careless with Albert's feelings and of speaking badly of Mary, a friend, and now Albert, a good and honourable man, was dead at her husband's hand.

The violence had to be stopped and she had to be the one to do it. She would do penance for her part in it, for keeping her silence when she could have spoken up before the second, even the first run. She had the means to rid the marshes of George and the Greys and end the free trade for good, and she was willing to turn her husband in to Jason to face the full force of the law, no matter what it took.

20

In Deep Water

A friend of John's who'd brought his horse to the forge to be shod reported that Albert had been buried a hero with great pomp and ceremony at St George's in Deal, while the Greys were on the run with Jason and the Revenue after them, intent on avenging Albert's death.

The effects of the tragedy spread through the community of marshfolk, some of whom wanted to take it out on the people they held responsible, which was why Grace found herself scrubbing splatters of egg from her front door one morning. She'd spotted three youths from the village throwing missiles at the cottage and chased them away.

'It's a lovely day, missus.' A labourer stopped in the lane and doffed his cap.

She looked up with a rueful smile. 'It would be, if I didn't have to clear this mess up, among other things.'

'I can guess who might 'ave done it. Shall I 'ave a word with them?'

'No, thank you. I think it's best forgotten unless they do it again.'

'That's right — least said, soonest mended.'

'Make way. Make way for Commander Witherall, officer of the Revenue.' She dropped her cloth in her bucket of suds as a young man in

339

uniform swaggered up the garden path, scattering the labourers as he brandished a cutlass.

'Quick. Scarper. The gobblers are 'ere.' The labourer who'd been speaking to Grace turned and tried to dodge past the young man who caught him by the arm, bringing him up short in front of his commander.

'Thank you, Cromwell,' Jason said. 'This is not one of the fugitives whom we seek. Let him go.' As the labourer ran away as fast as his legs could carry him, Jason looked towards the door where Grace was standing with Aggie.

'Grace?' he said. 'I knew you were livin' in Snargate, but I was under the impression . . . ' She guessed what he was going to say, that she had come down in the world, moving into what was little more than a hovel, but he stopped short and said, 'I'm glad to see that you and my niece are safe and well. Is Black Dog about?'

'I haven't seen him for a while.'

'I've been authorised to search every house in the marsh for contraband and weapons, and any other evidence linked to the gang of smugglers known as the Greys. Furthermore, my aim is to arrest anyone suspected of being involved in the murder of Lieutenant Enderby, a young man whom I held dear, a husband, father, colleague — ' he faltered slightly '— and friend.'

'I heard about that and I'm deeply sorry.'

'I remember how you danced with him once,' Jason said. 'I have no quarrel with you. All I want is to chase these villains down and rid the marsh of their malign influence, once and for all.' He addressed Cromwell. 'Take the men and go through the house top to bottom, and check the garden. When you've done that, do the same next door.'

'Yes, sir,' Cromwell said.

'I shall take Mrs Feasey aside to ask her a few questions.' They walked through the house and stood in the back garden where she could only stand and watch as his men raked through the vegetable patch, digging up the last of the potatoes.

'Please be careful,' she begged.

'I won't intervene,' Jason said softly. 'I don't want to be accused of favourin' you because we're related by marriage.

'Mrs Feasey,' he went on, his voice carrying across the garden, making his men look up. 'It would behove you to tell me the whereabouts of your husband.'

'That's one thing I'm grateful for — I can say hand on heart that I have no idea where he is.'

'What about his associates? One George Minnis, for example?'

She shook her head.

'I have to ask — did you go with them when they set off from Snargate on the evenin' of the twenty-fifth of September?' His eyes flashed with a fleeting moment of humour. 'Remember, I'll know if you're lyin'.'

There were plenty of people who would confirm that she had gone out that night.

'I fetched a horse and cart and drove Isaiah to Dover beach where we waited beside the bathing machines for the men to start landing the goods.'

341

'Did you see what happened? Were you a witness to the events on the beach?'

'I was distracted when the horse took fright and bolted.'

'I see.' He pulled a roll of paper from his pocket and unfurled it. 'Look at this.'

Grace studied the handbill:

Customs House London is offering a reward of five hundred pounds to anyone who discovers or causes to be discovered the smugglers involved in the death of Albert Enderby, a first-rate Lieutenant, and the beating and wounding of Seaman Appleton, both serving the Coast Blockade Service for the Prevention of Smuggling on HMS Legacy, and stationed at Deal.

'The marsh will soon be crawling with people lookin' for your husband, but I want to be the one who catches him.'

'I've told you — I don't know where he is,' she repeated.

'Someone does and we will find out, one way or another. You are still fond of him?'

She thought for a moment. 'I speak fondly of him.' She glanced round to see if anyone was listening — Jason's men had turned their attention to the adjoining cottage. 'It isn't the same. I want to see these thugs, including my husband, put away.'

'You would go as far as seein' him hang?'

'Yes,' she said in an agonised whisper. 'If that is what the law deems an appropriate punishment

342

for what he's done.'

'You dissembled when I asked if you'd witnessed the confrontation between the smugglers and my men. Grace, I will arrest you for being an accessory to murder, if I feel that you aren't being frank with me. One of the Greys — not a Deal man — has been captured and interviewed by the Bow Street Runners from London. He's informed on his friends and we are closin' in on them.'

'Let me show you something.' She had him wait in the kitchen while she went up to the bedroom, pulled the rug away and pulled up a loose floorboard. Taking out her jewellery box, she opened it and removed Albert's watch. Slipping it into her pocket, she returned downstairs.

'I have a favour to ask of you.' She showed him the watch. 'It's Albert's — I was there, hiding near the bathing machines. He asked me to give it to Mary as he lay dying. Before he slipped away, he said to tell her that he loved her and would meet her in Heaven. Mary will be even more devastated if the wife of her husband's murderer is the one who returns the watch to her. Will you do it, Jason?'

'You mean Black Dog killed Albert?'

'That's what Albert told me. I know that Isaiah was in the vicinity with George Minnis, and I'm prepared to testify against them both, but you have to catch them first, and I'm worried about what they might do if they find out that I've broken my silence.'

'You know you can trust me, Grace.'

'There is more. Believing that Awful Doins let slip to one of the shore boys about the time and

343

place of the previous landing, George ordered his men to shoot him, to make it look like an accident while they were doing their regular target practice. They brought his body to George's house. There's a well . . . .'

'Thank you. You know, I'd rather you didn't stay here alone. I'll have one of my men escort you and the infant to Deal where you can stay with Louisa. You'll be safe enough there.'

'No, Jason. I'm going to stay here until Isaiah shows up. If he finds out that I've left Snargate, there's no reason for him to come back. He'll just disappear.'

'You're putting yourself at risk if he finds out that you're intending to turn him in.'

'I can look after myself. I'm a smuggler's wife, after all.'

'I can't leave a man on guard, but I can request that a patrol from one of the watch houses comes this way every evening.'

'I leave a candle burning in the window upstairs every night to light his way home — if he's here, I'll snuff it out. It's the best I can do.'

'I don't like this plan of yours, but I can see I'll have to go along with it.'

'Don't tell my sister how you find me,' she said, 'but say that I send my love.'

'I'll say exactly what I like — Louisa and I don't have secrets between us, Grace. I wish you all the best, and I hope and pray that we find Black Dog before he finds you.'

* * *

344

During the days that followed, after the Revenue had left Walland Marsh to continue their search elsewhere, Grace kept herself busy, trying to take her mind off worrying about whether Isaiah was dead or alive, or if he was going to return at any moment to beg her to help him hide from the gobblers, or defend him in court. She secured the cottage as far as she could, moving the bench against the front door to act as a barricade against intruders, and keeping the back door bolted at night.

Making the most of an unusually balmy October day, she left the baby in the pram outside in the rear garden. Aggie was looking up at the bright blue sky, chuckling to herself and sucking her toes while Grace collected the eggs, finding one among the raspberry canes and another in the straw in the henhouse.

'That's better, ladies. You're beginning to earn your keep at last.' She took the eggs inside and put them in the dish on the windowsill, thinking that they were an omen of better times to come. She took in the few items of laundry that had been drying on the line, folded them and took them upstairs.

On hearing a commotion in the garden, she looked out of the rear window.

To her horror, the chickens had scattered and George Minnis was beside Aggie's pram with Cutthroat alongside him. As he whisked the baby out, Grace flew down to the garden, her heart pounding, her chest tight.

'What are you doing? Let her go!' she begged.

'Keep your voice down and talk nicely to old

George,' he said, grinning as he held a smiling Aggie facing away from him at arm's length. 'Here, Cut-throat. Catch!' Spinning on his heels, he threw the baby at his fellow fugitive. Eyes wide with surprise, Cut-throat caught her.

'Throw 'er back to me — that's right.' George snatched her as she came flying through the air. 'Grace, you can be piggy in the middle.' He gazed at her, tormenting her.

'George, stop this. It isn't funny.' The smile had faded from Aggie's face when he threw her back to Cut-throat. 'You'll hurt her.'

'To me, Cut-throat,' George chuckled. He caught her then let her go and caught her again. 'Oops, I 'ave butterfingers,' he said, before dropping her back into the pram, crying. As Grace rushed across to pick her up and console her, George approached. She backed off. Both men had shaggy, unkempt hair and smelled as if they hadn't washed for weeks.

'I enjoyed that — it's good to kick up a lark now and again. 'Owever, I'm really 'ere to find out if you've seen your 'usband recently?'

'No,' she said in a panic. 'I wish I had.'

'You're still loyal to 'im?'

'I'll stand by him through hell or high water, no matter what he's done.' As the lie spilled from her mouth, she wished she'd answered him with a simple yes, because George was immediately on alert.

'What 'as 'e done, Mrs Feasey? What exactly did you witness the other night?'

'I saw nothing of the events that you're referring to. Peter Paddick's horse took fright and bolted,

346

taking me with him.'

George stroked his beard. 'That's a good story. Excellent. Make sure you stick to it, should the gobblers pay you a visit. They 'aven't been 'ere, 'ave they?'

'No,' she lied.

'I worry about you, Grace,' he said.

'I don't want any consideration from you,' she snapped, her cheeks burning.

'I don't mean that,' he said slyly. 'What I'm sayin' is that I'm concerned that you 'ave too much of a conscience to be a good wife to a free trader like Black Dog. In addition, you 'ave other family to turn to: Witherall, for example. It would be all too easy for you to 'ave a little word in Marlin's ear, but I'm tellin' you, if you blab or I find out there's any havey-cavey business goin' on between you and your brother-in-law, I'll 'ave your tongue cut out and the littlun killed. The same goes if I find out you've been tellin' me faradiddles about Black Dog's whereabouts. Do I make myself plain?'

'Perfectly, George,' Cut-throat said.

'I wasn't talkin' to you, you dolt. I was speakin' to the young lady 'ere.'

Grace pressed her mouth to Aggie's forehead as Aggie continued to sob. 'I want you to leave now,' she said, suppressing the quiver in her voice.

''Ave you got any wittles?' George said.

'What do you think? We're living hand to mouth. The baby's six months old and ready for weaning — I'm struggling to buy the right foods for her.'

'You must 'ave somethin' indoors. Cut-throat, go and see what you can find.'

'No, it's all right. I'll do it.' There was no way

347

she was letting them have the eggs, she thought, fetching a dish of congealed porridge and some pickles.

'It's better than nothin', I suppose,' George sighed as he distributed the lion's share of the food amongst his pockets. 'You 'ave the rest,' he said, gesturing to Cut-throat who devoured the remainder, stuffing it into his mouth all at once.

'I'm sorry for disturbin' you, but it 'ad to be done.' George looked more cheerful when he wished her a pleasant day and clambered over the garden fence with his companion.

Grace waited for them to disappear into the marsh, then she brought Aggie and the pram indoors and shoved the table against the back door before collecting the pistol and gunpowder, her pendant and the change from the money Winnie had given her, from the hole under the floorboards upstairs, and putting them under her pillow.

She couldn't continue like this, living in fear of Aggie's life. As she lay on the bed, curving her body around her sobbing baby, she prayed for guidance, and by morning, having not slept a wink, she had made her decision, the only way she could think of to keep her daughter safe. She was determined: she wouldn't let George get in her way of bringing the Greys to justice, no matter how long it took or — she glanced down at Aggie's face, her eyes wide and innocent, her thumb in her mouth — how painful it was going to be.

21

Needs Must When the Devil Drives

Grace fed Aggie, washed her face and hands and dressed her warmly in a cream flannel barracoat and a knitted bonnet with ribbons that she tied under her chin, much against her will. She packed a few provisions in a basket, put her purse in her pocket and tucked the pistol into her belt. Wearing the pendant, she threw a shawl over her shoulders and left the house with the baby in her arms.

'I reckon you've put on at least three pounds in the last week, although I don't know how.' By the time she'd reached the gate, she'd decided to take the pram, whether or not it would withstand the journey along the rutted unmade byways that ran across the marsh.

'We don't want you freezing to death,' she scolded lightly as Aggie started to cry and wriggle out of the blanket that she'd wrapped her in before putting her in the pram.

'You want to see where we're going?' With a small smile, Grace propped her up against a pillow and set out, closing the gate behind her.

'Where are you off to on this fine day?' She put on a brave face as John waved her over to the forge to quiz her.

'I'm going to Deal to meet my sister so we can

put flowers on my parents' grave. I would have asked Myrtle to mind the baby, but Aggie's caught a chill and I thought that a day by the sea would do her some good. Besides, I need something to take my mind off worrying about my husband.'

'You 'aven't 'eard from 'im?'

'I'm beginning to fear that he's met with some mishap.' She broke off, not wanting to cry in front of their neighbour.

'It don't seem wise to go gallivantin' across the marsh when 'e might turn up at any time.'

'It's been three weeks since he disappeared. If he should turn up, you'll let him know where I've gone and that I'll be back very soon.'

'Myrtle didn't mention that the babe was poorly.' He was frowning as he rubbed a smear of soot across his brow. 'Oh well, I wish you a safe journey. You don't think you're goin' to travel all the way to Deal by shank's pony, do you?'

'I'm used to walking.'

'It'll take days. This is the wettest October we've ever 'ad — much of Walland Marsh is impassable on foot. You must 'ire a cart from my brother.'

'I can't,' she sighed. 'My circumstances don't allow it.'

'Tell Peter that 'is brother guarantees that George Minnis will pay for it.'

'Have you seen George?' she asked, not letting on that he and Cut-throat had paid her a visit the day before.

' 'E'll be busy primin' witnesses and payin' others to 'old their tongues, makin' sure 'is alibis are in place and 'is defence is watertight. Anyway, back to this expedition of yours. The marsh is a

350

dangerous place for anyone to be at present, least of all a defenceless woman and child.

I can't 'ave it on my conscience to let you go wanderin' off alone — Black Dog won't like it if he finds out. From what I've l'arned about him, I wouldn't be surprised if 'e punched my lights out.'

'I don't need a chaperone,' she exclaimed, feeling trapped.

'Peter or one of his labourers will go with you. Let me accompany you to the farm.'

'That isn't necessary,' she said, as he laid his pritchel and tongs across the anvil that stood just inside the forge and picked up his waistcoat. Fishing around in the pockets, he pulled out a clay pipe and tobacco. Reluctantly she followed and they walked together, John blowing rings of smoke while Grace pushed the pram.

On reaching the farm, they found Peter in the yard, fitting a saddle to a grey filly's back. He buckled a leather girth to the straps beneath the saddle-flap, moved around to the other side of her and repeated the exercise, securing the saddle, at which the filly flew into a panic, bucking and rearing, and breaking the rope by which she'd been tied up outside the stables.

'Whoa, young lady!' Peter called, his voice flat calm as the horse did a circuit of the yard, then stopped and snorted. 'Steady there.' He walked across to her, stroked her shoulder, then took hold of the remains of the rope and led her back.

'Don't ask me to put shoes on that one,' John said cheerfully.

'I thought you'd relish the challenge.' Peter was

351

grinning as he led the filly into the stable and left her there. 'What can I do for you?'

'Grace is lookin' for a lift to Deal and back to see her sister and visit her parents' grave. I need one of your lads to keep an eye on her.' Was it a slip of the tongue or had he really meant to suggest that they were keeping her under surveillance? Did they still believe, despite her attempt to convince George otherwise, that she had information that would incriminate the Greys?

'I'll take you there, Mrs Feasey,' Peter said. 'I 'ave business that way, a couple of mares to look at. They're broken-down nags but might still be good for breedin'. We'll take the shootin' brake. You'll want to spend some time with your sister, so I'll go and look at these horses, spend the night there and pick you and the littlun up in the mornin'.'

She could have sworn that when she thanked him, he blushed.

Within half an hour, John had gone back to the forge and Peter and one of his men had prepared a pair of black carriage horses, proud beasts with flowing manes and tails, and hitched them to the open brake. Wearing a battered hat and a greatcoat, breeches and long boots, Peter helped Grace climb aboard with Aggie, passed her the basket and then lifted the pram into the rear, before getting in himself and sitting down on the raised box at the front to drive the horses. They set off at an easy pace, alternating between walk and trot, before slowing down to negotiate a lake of water that lay across the marsh beyond Brenzett.

'Is it safe?' she asked.

'If it goes more than halfway up the wheels, I'll know to turn round,' he replied as the horses splashed fetlock-deep through the flood. 'I've driven this way many times afore. I'm sorry that it isn't more comfortable for you, Mrs Feasey.'

'The baby doesn't mind — she's gone to sleep. And I wish you wouldn't address me as Mrs Feasey. You can call me Grace.'

'I prefer 'Mrs Feasey' when your 'usband isn't present,' he said, rather sternly, she thought, wondering if he thought her a trollop.

The brake's wheels slipped in the mud as they reached the far side of the flood and the horses struggled to make it through to drier ground, but Peter maintained that they were making good time.

'I'm goin' to 'ave a stop for some wittles at the next public 'ouse, the Red Fox. It'll give the horses a breather.'

On one hand she wanted the journey over and done with, believing that the longer it took, the more likely she was to back out of her mission, but on the other she wished that it would last for ever.

After three stops and several hours, they reached Walmer and took the road into Deal.

'Where shall I leave you?' Peter asked as they passed the great walls of the castle.

'At the Shutter Station, just along here on the seafront, thank you.'

He pulled the horses up at the foot of the wooden tower, saying, 'I 'ope you find your sister well and the sea air does the littlun some good. Where shall I meet you in the mornin'?'

'At the same place, if you will. Deal's a veritable warren of streets and alleyways where one might easily get lost.'

'I'll be here at noon, or is that too early for you? It doesn't give you much time with your sister.'

'It will be long enough.' She forced a smile.

'It's 'ard losin' your parents,' Peter said. 'You're goin' to pay your respects,' he added when she was trying to work out what he meant. 'I lost my father ten years ago— 'e fell from an 'orse and broke 'is 'ead.'

'And your mother?'

'She's very much alive. She married a gentleman farmer and moved to Ashford.' He jumped down from the brake and helped Grace disembark. When he lifted the pram out, she lowered Aggie into it, at which she started to cry.

'Please, stay calm for your ma,' Grace begged. 'She doesn't like being restricted,' she explained to Peter.

'I don't blame 'er. She's goin' to be one of those children who want to run before they can walk,' Peter grinned.

Embarrassed at the way Aggie's screaming was attracting attention and comment from passers-by, Grace tickled her under the chin, then gave her the rattle from the basket. Nothing worked, and she had to shout her thanks to Peter and say that noon was fine for her, before wishing him a pleasant evening. Still smiling and covering his ears in jest, he returned to the brake and drove off, leaving her stranded on the seafront as dusk was falling with nowhere to go. If she went to Louisa, she'd insist that she stayed overnight, and Grace knew she wasn't capable of putting on a brave face in front of her sister. There was a certain irony in the idea that she could take a room at the Rattling Cat, but as far as she was aware, George still owned the tavern. He could be hiding there for all she knew.

'Where shall we go?' she whispered as the baby gazed at her expectantly, her tears drying on her cheeks, her fist red and covered in drool. 'I know a place where we can spend the night. I'm going to have one last cuddle before . . . I can't say it.' She gulped back a sob.

Her head bowed, she hastened along the seafront, suppressing the urge to glance along Cockle Swamp Alley as she passed it. She crossed the road, trying not to look at the Rattling Cat where, brimming with hope and dreams, she had spent the beginning of her married life with Isaiah, but she couldn't stop herself. The sound of laughter and conversation came drifting from the open windows along with the appetising aroma of roast beef. The sign above the door had been repaired and the front of the tavern repainted, the sight of which rubbed salt into the wound, because despite times being hard, George Minnis had employed a manager to make a success of the business where she and Isaiah had failed.

She had to abandon the pram at the top of the beach when its wheels caught in the shingle. Taking Aggie and the basket, she carried on walking along the shore, glancing out towards the ships in the Downs. She thought she recognised HMS *Legacy* which reminded her of Albert and how she'd been unable to save him. The sight of the sea and sound of the waves caressing the shingle soothed her a little. Albert had forgiven her for the way she'd treated him. He wouldn't have wanted her to feel guilty for thinking she hadn't done enough to stop the run going ahead.

She skirted a fishing boat that was beached alongside the *Curlew* — Louisa hadn't sold her yet and she was still in her usual place, not far from the pile of lobster pots and Pa's old hut. Checking that no one was watching, she lifted the tarpaulin that partially covered her hull and lowered the baby and basket inside, before climbing in after them. She shifted a box out of the way and spread her shawl out across the boards before lying down in the dark with Aggie.

'This is where your pa hid himself away when he was running from the gobblers,' she murmured, pressing her nose to Aggie's hair, breathing her scent of milk and soap, and imprinting it on her memory, knowing that she might never see her again. 'He should have learned his lesson back then. It's too late now — I'm afraid he's a condemned man.'

As the hours passed, the drunken Jacks came rolling down the beach, shouting and singing; the ships' bells marked the changes of watch; the waves rushed in as the tide turned. Grace was up before the rising sun brought the boatmen and shore boys to the capstan grounds. Her joints aching and her muscles sore, she hauled herself out of the *Curlew*. Having arranged her shawl to cover her nose and mouth, she carried Aggie and the basket back along the beach as the first rays of sunshine imparted an amber glow to the sea and stones. The pram had gone, but she didn't care.

She was about to carry out the greatest sacrifice of her life.

Standing at the corner of Cockle Swamp Alley and Beach Street, she watched and waited. Mrs Witherall was sweeping the pavement outside her house, unaware of Grace's presence.

'Oh Aggie, it's almost time,' she whispered. 'You'll never want for anything. My sister will adore you and care for you as much as . . .' She couldn't go on because it would have been a lie. No one could love Aggie as deeply as Grace did. Scalding tears began to stream down her face as she gave her one last kiss and let her wrap her fingers around her thumb one last time.

'I will pray for you every second, every minute, every hour of every day. You will always be in my thoughts.' Every sinew, every fibre in her being, every throbbing beat of her heart was urging her to take Aggie home, but the thought of George lying in wait to capture and torture her daughter drove her on. She could only achieve her aim of bringing the smugglers to justice if she knew that Aggie was safe. 'My pain will diminish, but my heart will never mend. I trust that you will grow into a beautiful young woman, secure in the knowledge that your ma gave you up out of love.'

On hearing Mrs Witherall knocking her broom against the doorstep, Grace glanced along the alley, making sure that her former neighbour had gone indoors before she made her way along the alley. She stopped outside Compass Cottage, wishing she could turn the clock back, as she placed the basket containing a letter detailing Aggie's likes and dislikes, how to comfort her when she cried,

357

how to feed her with goat's milk and continue weaning her, on the doorstep.

When she heard a dull thud from inside the house, she laid Aggie on a blanket beside the basket, then knocked at the door and flew down the alley. Peering back around the corner, she saw Louisa waving her fist and heard her shouting, 'It isn't funny, you little tykes . . . Oh! What's this?'

Reassured that Aggie was out of harm's way, Grace fled.

* * *

''Aven't you forgotten somethin'?' Peter asked when he jumped down to help her into the brake in front of the Shutter Station. 'The littlun? Is she . . . 'as she taken a turn for the worse? No, it can't be that — you don't strike me as the kind of mother who'd leave 'er child behind if she was at death's door . . . . I've said somethin' wrong. I'm sorry.'

'Louisa suggested that she had her for a week or two — she's going to take her out every day for the sea air.' Grace had been thinking about what she was going to tell Peter while she had been walking along the beach to fill in the hours between dawn and noon when they'd arranged to meet.

'So, she isn't poorly then?' She held his gaze, determined not to break down in front of him. Had he guessed what she'd done?

'Her condition is much improved — I agreed that she should stay to convalesce.'

'I'm glad and relieved to 'ear it,' he said. 'I was afraid she was sufferin' from the ague, the marsh

358

fever that took my Clary away from me.'

Peter seemed convinced by her story — she didn't think he would take kindly to the real reason she'd left Aggie with Louisa. As for her tears, he appeared to accept that it was nothing more than the natural distress of a mother being temporarily parted from her infant.

'Didn't you want to stay on in Deal?'

'My sister's house isn't set up for guests,' she said. 'I didn't want to inconvenience her, and I'd like to be back in Snargate in case my husband turns up. I wish I knew where he was.'

'It's said that there are up to twenty men on the run, including George Minnis, which makes me wonder why it's been impossible to spot them. I wonder if they've gone 'fishin" so to speak — taken a boat out with the idea of hoverin' at sea until the gobblers' enthusiasm for catchin' up with them has died down. Mind you, that won't 'appen for a while.'

'They'll never give up.'

'You're probably right. Enderby might have been a gobbler, but he was held in high esteem. We're all sick of it. Even John is growin' tired of George and his constant demands. He calls him Minnis the menace — not to his face, I hasten to add. George pays well, but what price is a life? The dangers are becomin' too great to countenance.

'That Commander Witherall came to the farm with his men recently, poking about in the barns and stables, and upsettin' the 'orses.'

'They called at the cottage too, looking for my husband,' she said.

Peter drove on in silence, leaving Grace to her

thoughts. As dusk crept across the marsh, he stopped at a tavern as before for food and ale, then lit the carriage lanterns before setting off again. They reached Snargate after dark, the return journey being a little faster because the floodwaters had receded and the horses were keen to get back.

'I'm goin' to drop you at your house,' Peter offered.

'I can walk from the farm,' she said. 'It isn't far.'

'I want to make sure you get home safely. Some of the chancers who are out lookin' for the Greys are willin' to take them alive for the bounty on their heads, but others will shoot them on sight as vengeance for the young officer's murder. I'll stop by and 'ave a word with my brother about shoein' a couple of my 'orses. You'd have thought he'd give me a favourable rate, but he don't, the tightfisted . . . I apologise.'

'Apology accepted,' she said.

When they reached Hazel Cottage, Peter insisted on going inside before she did, taking a lantern with him and looking upstairs and downstairs, and checking the windows and doors.

'It don't seem right, you bein' here on your own, Mrs Feasey,' he said. 'If you need another lift, anythin', you know where I am.'

'Thank you for your kindness,' Grace replied simply.

'Make sure you keep the doors locked,' he added. 'Good night.'

She watched him from the window, walking purposefully along the path to the gate, where he said something to the horses, and returned to his seat on the brake before driving it across to the forge. In his presence, she had managed to convince herself that leaving Aggie had been but a hideous nightmare, but when he'd gone, the reality of what she'd done struck her like a lightning bolt to her chest. Even the thought that she had made Louisa's dream come true did nothing to assuage her grief and guilt.

Bereft and sobbing, she barricaded the doors and trudged up the creaking stairs to light the candle on the windowsill, then threw herself on the bed. She had done right by her child. That's all that mattered. She didn't care what Isaiah might do to her if — or when — he found out what she'd done.

The next morning, Myrtle was on the doorstep.

'Peter told us you'd left Aggie with your sister. She took a sudden turn, did she? Who would 'ave thought it, as bright as ninepins one day and bodily ill the next?'

'Oh, that's an exaggeration,' Grace said. 'She was a little under the weather, that's all.'

'A neighbour's baby has had croup. It isn't croup, is it?'

'I'm more concerned about my husband.' She burst into tears.

'Oh, have a good cry — you'll feel better for it.'

She didn't though, because she was imagining Louisa and Jason on the chaise in the parlour at Compass Cottage: Aggie in Louisa's arms, freshly bathed, her belly full and her expression one of bemusement as her new parents studied her features in wonder and adoration, just as Grace had done from the day she was born.

'Why don't you come over and sit with me and

the boys?' Myrtle offered.

'No, thank you. I'm going to have a quiet day, catching up with the chores.'

'I was under the impression you didn't find much joy in housework — I don't mean to imply that you don't do any. My mother used to say that cobwebs are a good sign: it means the cottage is dry, not damp. Oh, I won't keep you. If you want me, you know where to find me.'

Later, Myrtle brought her a portion of shepherd's pie.

'Oh, you shouldn't have,' Grace said.

'You need to keep your strength up. Are you feelin' better?'

'Yes, thank you.' Holding the platter, she watched Myrtle retreat down the path and cross the lane, realising that she had grown so used to lying that the untruths kept pouring unchecked from her mouth. Tomorrow she would have to remember to mention how much she'd enjoyed her supper when she'd actually tipped it out for the hens, because she couldn't eat for crying. She returned indoors and went upstairs to light the candle before collapsing on the bed where she listened to the owls, marsh frogs and the sharp cries of a vixen, until the desire to sleep overwhelmed her.

22

A Reward of Five Hundred Pounds

Feeling lost without Aggie, the days and nights stretched out ahead of her, empty and desolate like the marsh itself, while she watched and waited for Isaiah's return. When dusk was falling on a bitter November evening, she went upstairs to light the candle as was her custom. The tallow smoked and spat, emitting a foul smell as she gazed out across the lane to the forge where John was letting the fire go out and putting away his tools. As the sun set and the stars emerged, and the lights in Forge Cottage went out, she noticed the faint orange glow of a lantern swinging along in front of the hedge.

Her heart missed a beat as the light grew closer, then disappeared and reappeared at the end of the path where it stopped, suspended in the air, illuminating the traveller's face and revealing the familiar shape of Isaiah's jawline and cheek. Grace grabbed her hairbrush and ran it through her hair, pinched her cheeks to put some colour into them and hurried downstairs to fling the door open.

'Isaiah . . . I thought you were— ' His presence sent a chill through her bones, making her doubt that she could carry off the first part of her plan.

'Dead? Never comin' back?' he cut in.

'No . . . Oh, I don't know. You're here now.' His bedraggled, thin appearance made her resolve quail further. He looked chastened and desperate with congbells dangling from his nostrils, and frost on his beard. 'Where are the others? Is there anyone with you?'

'Not now. There's a price on our 'eads.'

'I know of it.' She stepped aside to let him in before closing the door behind him.

' 'As anybody called lookin' for me?'

She nodded. 'George came to speak to me. And Jason and his men have been searching the marshes. They knocked at our door a couple of sennights ago and asked me a few questions. I told them the truth — that I hadn't seen you and I didn't know where you were.'

'Is it a lot of money then?'

'Five hundred pounds.'

He whistled through his teeth. 'I 'ad no idea our lives were worth that much.'

'I've been worried sick,' Grace said, wondering if he'd express any remorse for what he'd done. 'Oh, my love.' Bracing herself, she kissed him and took a step back. His hair was twisted into greasy locks, his face grey, his beard grown long, his clothes hanging off his frame, his boots falling apart, but worse than that, he smelled like an old dog. 'What a shame — you've missed Aggie.'

'What do you mean? Where's our daughter?'

'She's staying with Louisa — she took a chill while you were away. She's on the mend now, but I thought it wise for her to have the benefit of the sea air for a week or two.'

'How could you?'

'Remember when Peter told us about his wife dying of marsh fever?' she said quickly. 'I was afraid Aggie was going the same way.'

'You must fetch her back as soon as possible. I've broken many of the promises I made to you, and I'm deeply sorry for it, but I'm determined to renew this solemn vow in front of you and keep to it: Grace, from now on, I will love and protect you for as long as we both shall live. In return for my service and for remainin' silent, George 'as given me the means to take you and Aggie away. We'll go abroad — to Belgium or Italy, or America. The world is our oyster.' He put the lantern down and took both her hands. 'We'll buy a plot of land and start a farm.'

'What do you know about farming?'

'We'll buy a place by the sea then — it'll be good for the baby. I'll do a bit o' fishin'. I'll do anythin' to keep our little family together.'

Even though you did everything to force us apart, she thought sadly.

'When I was at my lowest ebb, I thought of endin' it, but I won't be a coward any more. Believe me when I say that I've left the free trade for good.'

'I don't believe you — you've made too many meaningless promises in the past. You'll never give it up.'

'But I 'ave.' He held out his hands, palms up. 'Look at me . . . I'm a reformed man.'

She stared into his eyes searching for a sign that he'd changed, but there wasn't even a flicker of regret, nothing to suggest that he felt any guilt for what he'd done to Albert.

'I'm proof that it's never too late to 'ave a road

365

to Damascus experience, my darlin',' he went on. 'Now I'd like to sit down and 'ave some supper.'

She wanted to tell him that it was too late, whether or not he had abandoned his smuggling ways, but she had a pretence to keep up. 'What am I thinking, keeping you talking like this? Oh dear, you must be starving. If I'd known you were coming, I'd have made sure there was food in the cupboard. It's almost bare.'

'I'll eat anythin', even broth. I've been livin' on whatever I can find in the fields or beg from an isolated farmhouse. There was a farmer's wife who took a shine to me, or so it seemed, but it turned out that she thought she recognised me as one of the wanted men and she was tryin' to sweet-talk me into 'anging around until 'er 'usband finished ploughin'. Trust me when I say I didn't reciprocate.'

'I know you wouldn't be unfaithful to me, even if you were capable,' she said cruelly. 'Sit down.' Meekly, he did as he was told, taking off his boots before slumping on the bench, resting his hands on his knees.

'You're shaking,' she observed as she served him a piece of hard cheese with the mites cut out, and a rank slice of brawn. 'Was anyone following you? Do you think someone saw you in Snargate?'

'I came in straight off the marsh and waited for our neighbours to turn in. I 'ave this — ' he showed her the knife at his belt '— and you have the pistol? If the gobblers should show up, I'll run out the back and disappear while you use your wits to convince them that I was never 'ere.'

'You should put your boots back on then,' she

366

suggested.

'I'll keep them to 'and,' he said, picking them up and tying the laces together before hanging them around his neck. ''Ave you 'eard that George and Cut-throat 'ave been arrested?'

She shook her head. 'I've hardly been out.'

'I was in the vicinity a few days ago, when I met with Cut-throat, George and Lawless at George's 'ouse. That old maid of his called out 'Warrior', a signal she'd agreed with George to warn of the gobblers' approach. Lawless and I scarpered but the other two were too slow — George isn't the athletic type. He and Cut-throat put up a fight, but the gobblers overpowered them and carried them off to Maidstone. I didn't understand why the dogs didn't bark a warnin', but I found out afterwards that the gobblers had rounded them up in advance.'

'Where's Lawless then?'

''E said 'e was goin' to 'ead for the coast and go out on his cousin's fishin' boat. Grace, I 'ave to get you and Aggie away from 'ere, away from England before they catch up with me. Is there any more of that cheese?'

'There are some cobnuts, that's all.' She fetched them from the dish on the windowsill, rather regretting that she had mentioned them, because she could have saved them for herself.

'Oh, I've just remembered — I've brought you somethin'. It isn't of any value, but I was under the impression that you miss the sea . . . ' He pulled a whelk shell from his pocket and moved behind her, his body leaning into hers as he gently tangled his fingers through her hair, drawing it back and pressing the opening of the shell to her ear.

Closing her eyes, she listened for the rush of the waves, but all she could hear was her breathing, short and sharp, as a memory she'd tried to forget came rising to the surface. Of his hands around her neck. She was a hair's breadth from screaming when she pulled herself together.

'It transports me back to Deal,' she said, at which she pictured Aggie on the doorstep of Compass Cottage and burst into tears. 'Oh, it has made me cry.'

'There, there,' Isaiah whispered. 'All will be well, I promise you. Tonight we'll put our 'eads together and work out 'ow to get to your sister's 'ouse to fetch our littlun without attracting attention.'

'Shouldn't we leave immediately?'

'It's too late now, and I 'aven't slept for days. We should be ready to set out tomorrow at dusk. That way, we'll be in Deal by the followin' day. I'll lie low while you collect Aggie, and we'll retrace our steps to Dover where we'll pay for passage to our new life.'

'What about the gobblers, the soldiers and every Tom, Dick and Harry who's intent on tracking you down for the reward?'

'I know the marshes like the back of my 'and — I've been movin' about, keepin' out of trouble for the past few weeks. We'll travel the tracks and byways by night, under the cover of darkness. Tomorrow, we'll pack what we need and you'll sew a couple of 'idden pockets inside your dress for the gold George 'as given me. It's better that you carry it . . . we all know the Revenue will

368

never rummage a member of the weaker sex.' He cracked a cobnut between his teeth and ate the kernel.

'You're a wonderful woman, far too good for the likes of me,' he said. 'Look at you, bein' lovin' and affectionate even after all I've put you through.'

'It's my duty,' she said. 'Will you bathe?'

'Another time. I need to rest. Let's go upstairs.'

When he saw the candle in the window, he spat on his finger and thumb and snuffed it out, questioning her profligacy.

'It's for Aggie,' she said, but she didn't relight it, realising that it was far too late for the gobblers to be out on a routine patrol. She changed into her nightgown and slipped into bed, her skin crawling with a mixture of revulsion, regret and guilt at her deception. Too exhausted to realise what she was doing, Isaiah was allowing himself to be led like a lamb to the slaughter. If he had been a little more attentive, he might have detected the stiffness in her manner and the ring of falsehood in the tone of her voice.

'I've been dreamin' of 'oldin' you close again.' His arms snaked around her back.

'Did you do it?' she whispered. 'Was it you who shot Enderby?'

He held his breath — she had gone too far in her questioning. He had guessed what she was planning. Could he hear the butterflies in her belly? Could he smell the sweat trickling down her chest?

'Tell me the truth. You owe it to me. George and Cut-throat came and threatened to hurt Aggie, and I've been given the cold shoulder, been spat

369

on and had eggs thrown at my door. Where were you when I needed you?'

'What did you say to Marlin when you took Aggie to Deal?'

'Nothing, because I didn't see him. Louisa doesn't talk about his work. Think on this, my love. Do you really think I'd report back to the Revenue and put Aggie's life in jeopardy? Of course not! You should be on your knees, thanking me for covering for you. You left me alone that night — it was not a kindly act.'

'I'm sorry, I'm sorry. What more can I say?' He shut his eyes, closing the conversation without answering the question about his role in Albert's death or expressing an ounce of regret over the loss of the young Revenue officer.

In the morning, having lit a fire in the grate downstairs and made tea, she fended off Myrtle who had come to see if she wanted to walk into the village with her. 'You can't stay indoors alone all day,' she said, a little affronted. 'If you are alone, that is? I said to John last night that I thought I'd seen a lantern bobbin' about outside, but he said I was imaginin' it.'

'There's no one else here — it's just me.' Grace managed a small smile.

'When are you plannin' on goin' back for Aggie?'

'My sister's going to bring her to save me another journey.'

'Well, I don't know what's goin' on, but I'll get it out of you in the end,' Myrtle said wryly.

Wishing her a good day, Grace closed the door and returned the barricade to its place, breathing a sigh of relief.

'Snargate's worse than Deal with everyone wantin' to know their neighbour's business,' Isaiah said, buttoning his shirt as he came down the stairs.

'People are the same everywhere. Let me warm some more water so you can wash. We have a few hours to kill.' She kept herself occupied, hoping in vain to calm her nerves. She packed and repacked a bag to take with her, agreeing with Isaiah's suggestion that they should travel light, then went outside to rake up the leaves in the garden. When the three speckled hens came running to be fed, she cried, remembering how Aggie would chuckle and flap her hands at the sight of them. Drying her eyes, she went indoors, found a small piece of soap and a cloth, and prepared a bowl of hot water.

Isaiah stripped off his clothes and she helped him bathe, scrubbing his back and washing his hair.

'I'm not one for sentiment, but the thought of seeing the sea again makes me nostalgic for times gone by, when I didn't 'ave a care in the world and I'd walk the beach with Musket, hoping to catch sight of you, and on a good day, you'd be there, picking up shells or talkin' to the old men in the capstan grounds, your hair streaming in the wind and your eyes lit up with joy,' he said as she rinsed the cloth, turning the water a muddy brown.

'You can't possibly show your face in Deal. You'll be arrested on sight. I propose that you lie in wait for me on the cliffs between Dover and Kingsdown while I fetch Aggie, then we can leave from Dover where you aren't as well known. It

371

makes sense,' she said when he hesitated. 'Someone is bound to recognise you.'

'I don't know.' He twisted a lock of damp curls
that had fallen over his eyes. 'I think we should
stick together.'

'So you can watch over me to check that I
don't betray you to the gobblers? It's rather ironic
when you were so quick to leave me high and dry
while we were running goods at Lydd and Dover.'
When he didn't reply, she went on, 'You have to
trust me. If you waver for a second, I will walk
away from you, taking Aggie with me.' Grimacing as she stood behind him and picked up the
comb that she'd brought downstairs, she added,
'My nerves won't stand for any more of this. If
we can't rely on each other, then our marriage is
worthless.' She dug the teeth of the comb into his
scalp and dragged it through the knots in his hair,
making him squirm. 'I love you, Isaiah, heart and
soul.'

'You 'ave a funny way of showin' it.' With a quiet
chuckle, he grasped her wrist and extracted the
comb from her fingers. 'You don't 'ave to mother
me — I'll do it.' Drying her hands, she stepped
back. 'I don't care where we go, as long as you're
with me.'

Grace went across the lane to borrow a needle
and thread from Myrtle, apologising for giving
her short shrift.

'I'm not myself,' she said, as she stood on the
doorstep.

'It's hardly a surprise — you're missin' Aggie,'
Myrtle observed kindly as she held her youngest
on one hip and tried to prevent the other boys

running outside. 'Abraham, you can't go out there. Your father's busy.'

'I want to see the soldiers,' the oldest said, grinning as he saluted her. 'I'm goin' to be one when I grow up.'

'I reckon your pa will have somethin' to say about that.' Myrtle ruffled his blond hair. 'Still, there's plenty of time to revise your plan when you're only five years old.'

'I'm six, Ma,' he countered indignantly.

'Oh, I lose track,' she chuckled.

'Soldiers?' Fear crawled across Grace's skin like a slow-moving spider. 'What are they doing here?'

'Lookin' for you know who,' Myrtle said, meaning Isaiah.

'Lookin' for the enemy,' Abraham added.

'One of their horses has gone lame — John's having a look at it. Was there anythin' else you wanted?'

'Just a needle and thread, thank you.'

'Why don't you pop along to the forge with the boys while I fetch them? Abraham, Joseph, if you want to see the soldiers, you must promise to hold Grace's hand at all times.'

The two boys jumped up and down with delight, as Grace took them by their sticky fingers and walked across to where John was standing beside a tall bay horse with a switch tail. He was talking to a uniformed officer whose brass buttons gleamed from his red coat as he tapped his whip against his palm, impatient to return to his detachment.

'Good day, madam.' He gazed at her keenly. 'I don't believe we've met.'

373

'This is Mrs— our neighbour,' John said, picking up a large set of pincers from the leather bucket that held some of his tools. 'And these are two of my sons, Abraham and Joseph. This is Captain Pelham of the dragoons.' The presence of a captain, no less, seemed to have stunned the boys into silence. They stared up at him in awe. 'I'd suggest that you take the 'orse to my brother's— 'e'll let you 'ave another suitable mount until this one's sound enough to make the journey back to the barracks.'

'Come on, boys,' Grace said. 'Let's leave your pa to his work.'

'It's been an honour to meet some Snargate folk,' the captain said. 'What did you say your name was, Mrs . . .?' A metallic clatter interrupted him as John's pincers hit the cobbles and the horse reared up in fright, scattering Myrtle's hens who had been pecking for slugs and snails nearby.

Inwardly thanking John for his quick thinking, Grace urged the boys to hurry back to their mother with her, and collected what she needed for sewing the extra pockets into the dress she would be wearing for her trip to the coast.

When she reached the cottage, she shut the door, spun round and leaned her back against it.

'What is it, love?' Isaiah said from where he was lazing on the bench, his legs stretched out in front of him. 'You look like you've seen a ghost.'

'The militia are out patrolling the marsh. Perhaps we should delay our journey for a day or two.'

'The longer I 'ang about 'ere, the more chance there is of bein' discovered. We're in peril, whichever way we turn.'

374

They left Snargate after dark, carrying as little as possible apart from some provisions, the pistol, pendant, a few coins and the gold in Grace's pocket. Isaiah carried a lamp, a flint and oil, but he kept the light hidden behind the flap of his coat until they were on the road outside the village. Their breath condensing in clouds, they cut across the marsh, making slow progress along the green lanes to Newchurch. Leaving St Peter's and St Paul's church behind them, they skirted the higher ground to the north by keeping to Lower Wall Road until they reached the hamlet of Botolph's Bridge. Stopping on the bridge over the drainage dyke as dawn was breaking, Grace stared at the fernlike patterns of ice forming over the surface of the water and shivered.

'We should stop for a while at the inn 'ere,' Isaiah said, taking her gloved hand.

'It's too risky — we should find somewhere to rest until nightfall.' Grace realised how optimistic she had been, thinking that it would take a single night to cover more than thirty miles on rough terrain that was criss-crossed by impassable drains and ditches. She was exhausted and frozen to the bone, and she could barely feel her fingers or the blisters on her feet.

'I'm not goin' to argue with you — ' Isaiah yawned '— although I'm gaspin' for a long draught of ale. We need to drop south of 'ere and pick up the Dymchurch road to avoid the canal where there are soldiers guardin' the crossin' points. George usually pays them off, but he isn't here.

375

If we keep close to the shore as far as Seabrook, we can miss the Royal Military Canal altogether. Once we reach Sandgate, we'll be 'ome and dry.'

'There's still a long way to go after that: Folkestone, Dover . . . Walmer.' For a moment, she wished that she'd had an alternative plan for delivering Isaiah into the hands of the law that didn't involve walking for miles in his company, through desolate countryside where an icy wind blew across the withered sedge grasses and scrub. With every rustle from the rushes, every crack of a twig, she almost leapt out of her skin.

'Did you 'ear that?' Isaiah said as they left the lane to cross a boggy field. 'It's the call of the seven whistlers. It's a bad omen.'

'You mustn't think that,' she said, not wanting him to slump into despondency. 'It's just a flock of curlew flying about. All we have to do is cuddle up over there in the shelter of the hedge until we're rested, then carry on, keeping our wits about us. Think of the prize, my love. You, me and Aggie, free to live our lives without fear of the law catching up with us.'

After a briefer stop than Grace had intended, because they would have frozen to death if they'd stayed any longer, they moved on in daylight, striding briskly uphill to reach the heights above Dover. Isaiah walked right up close to the edge of the sheer chalk drop, as if to test his nerve, while Grace stood well back, watching the gulls diving into the sea while the fishing boats kept away from the black flinty rocks at the foot of the cliffs.

It was mid-afternoon by the time they reached Kingsdown where Isaiah said he'd wait, having a friend there who would look after him.

'You might know 'im— 'e's a cousin of Lawless, a fisherman and fellow free trader.'

'We can't trust anyone, particularly a smuggler when money's involved,' Grace said. 'I have a better idea. You can wait in the churchyard at St Leonard's. You know where to find the entrance to the hiding hole.'

'I don't believe that I do.'

'You should — your father and the Rattlers had a hand in removing mine and my sisters' inheritance in the form of run goods from the underground chamber there.' His denial was a lie that reminded her of how, blinded by naivety, infatuation and Isaiah's attentions, she'd failed to acknowledge the evidence of his criminal character. It was no wonder that Louisa and Winnie had warned her against marrying him. Seeing that he wasn't going to admit to stealing the Lennickers' tubs and lace, she went on, 'There's a tomb the length and breadth of a man, and up to about my waist in height. The slab on top is covered in moss, but you can still see the inscription: *Here lieth Michael Kent, a mariner of Deal, gone aloft on this day 17th March 1702.* Pa made us learn it off by heart for future reference.'

'I'll wait there rather than at Kingsdown if that will put your mind at ease. 'Ow long do you think you'll be?'

'Three or four hours, no more than that.'

Having walked on along the shore as far as Walmer Castle, Grace sent him off through Walmer itself, while she continued to Deal Castle and on to Beach Street, keeping her hat pulled

377

down and her cloak wrapped around her as she diverted to the greengrocer's where she bought a couple of large swedes.

'Thank you,' she said, handing over the correct change.

'Grace? Grace Feasey? Is that you?' At the sound of Mary's voice, her confidence drained away.

'Are you talkin' to me?' she muttered gruffly.

'I thought you were — I'm sorry, I was mistaken.' As Grace fled from the shop, she heard Mary go on, 'Did you see the state that poor woman was in, her clothes in rags?'

Deeply ashamed that she'd neglected her appearance so much that Mary hadn't recognised her, she went back to the beach where, on reflection, she decided that it was probably for the best. Keeping her head down, she arrived at Pa's beach hut and shoved the door open. She dragged out the old handcart in which they used to carry the odd tub or bale of lace, then found a couple of needles for mending nets which she stabbed into the swedes, joining them together to resemble a head and body. She wrapped them in a cloth and placed them in the handcart, before hauling it up the shingle to the road, its wheels squeaking like a cornered mouse.

So far, so good, she thought, but now she had to send word to Jason as to Isaiah's whereabouts. As she stared out to sea looking for any sign of the *Legacy*, she began to wonder if her luck was about to run out.

With nightfall rapidly approaching, her spirit began to fail, but then she spotted Cromwell, who'd grown a foot taller since she'd last seen him close up, walking from the direction of the pot house.

'Hello,' she called as she crossed the street to intercept him. 'It's me, Grace.'

He stopped, frowning. 'What are you doin' 'ere?'

'I haven't got time to explain — I need to see Jason. Have you any idea where I might find him?'

'He's just leavin' Molly's. Follow me.'

'I don't want anyone to know that I'm here — I'm travelling incognito.'

'Wait 'ere then, and I'll fetch 'im.'

When Jason arrived, lantern in hand to light their way, there was no time for small talk. Grace explained how she and Isaiah had walked to Deal and Jason went straight into the details of how they were going to apprehend him, asking her if he was armed.

'He has a knife, that's all.'

'I don't want you there when we apprehend him, Grace,' Jason said. 'It's too risky for you and — you've seen Louisa?'

'No, this is . . . ' She lifted the shawl from the swede baby's face.

'You've thought this through.'

'I should come with you to St Leonard's — that's where he's in hiding. If you go in looking for him, he'll fight or flee into the warren of tunnels under the churchyard, whereas if I'm there, he'll come out quietly because he's expecting me to bring the baby. He'll listen to me.'

'Then you'd better join us, but remember that this is against my better judgement. Cromwell, push the handcart for Mrs Feasey.'

She struggled to keep up with the two men as they marched to St Leonard's, anxious to make the arrest before anyone else found him.

'Aggie is well,' Jason said. 'I thought you'd like to know.'

'I'm glad,' she said flatly. 'I decided not to disturb Louisa.'

'She'd like to see you, but returning to our strategy, it occurs to me that there is another way. I assume that Black Dog will be very upset when he finds out that you've tricked him, that you haven't brought Aggie to him, and that he won't be travellin' to Dover with you after all that he's been through.' He caught her arm as she stumbled in the dark.

'Thank you,' she muttered. 'I don't care about hurting his feelings — he doesn't have any respect for anyone else's — but I am scared that he'll blame me for the loss of his freedom, and find some way of getting back at me, through George Minnis or another of the Greys. There are no limits to their capacity for vengeance.'

'You mean that they'd threaten your life, and maybe Aggie's too?'

'I have no doubt that we'd be in mortal danger.'

'Then we must take care of you. I have a suggestion of how we can improve on your plan to sham him and keep you safe.' He kept his voice low as he enlarged on his idea. 'What do you think?'

'You are a genius,' she whispered as the handcart squeaked along behind them.

When they reached the lychgate, Cromwell stopped, letting Grace lift the lumpy bundle of swede into her arms. She hugged it to her, wishing that she was holding Aggie instead, but it was no time for the megrims.

'Wait a minute,' Jason hissed as a light flickered behind one of the stained-glass windows at the side of the church.

'The vicar's still writing his sermons. Listen, Cromwell. Grace is going to call for Black Dog when she's at the tomb, reassuring him that she has the baby and that no one has followed her up from Walmer. Grace, I'm goin' to lie in wait. Cromwell, you'll guard the gate. When you hear my signal — a simple halloo — we'll collar the — ' he swore '— who murdered Enderby. Are you ready?'

'Yes,' she whispered in a small voice as Jason used the light from his lantern to guide her way along the perimeter of the churchyard, the gravestones — old and new — looming up in front of her. When she reached the tomb, Jason disappeared into the shadow of one of the adjacent yew trees.

Noticing that the smooth slab at one side of the tomb had been moved aside, revealing the entrance to the hiding hole through which a man of Isaiah's stature would struggle to squeeze through, she called his name.

'Isaiah, my love. I'm here.'

'At last,' he called from the darkness. 'I'd almost given you up for dead. Where are you?'

'Come to me,' she urged him.

'I'm on my way.' She heard the sound of scrabbling and falling stones and hurriedly backed away to join Jason who nodded encouragingly.

'Where are you?' Isaiah repeated. 'I can't see a thing.'

'Follow the lantern,' she said, her heart fluttering in her throat.

'Ah, I see it now.'

It happened so fast that Grace wasn't sure who did what, but after a short scuffle, Isaiah was on the ground, his arms and legs clapped in irons. Jason was standing over him, holding a knife and shining his lantern in his prisoner's face. At the same time, the churchyard was overrun by soldiers and Riding officers who'd been tipped off by some of Jason's men on their way out of Deal.

'You bitch!' Isaiah exclaimed, staring at Grace, his eyes almost popping out of their sockets, the vessels in his neck bulging. 'You've taken me for a ride. I'll get you for this!'

'Mrs Feasey, you are under arrest for aidin' and abettin' your husband who is on the run from the law,' Jason said, loud and clear, much to the surprise of his men from the expressions on their faces, especially Cromwell's when he ordered him to take back the 'baby', put her in the handcart and clap Grace in irons too. 'Gently though,' he added.

'You are a turncoat! How could you do this to me?' Grace shouted, hawking and spitting at Jason's feet, at which Isaiah changed his tune.

'Leave my wife alone — she's sweet and innocent. She's done nothin' wrong.'

'She's guilty by association. Married to a villain like you, she must have been party to your schemes and activities. I'll bring her in front of the magistrates for harbourin' a fugitive, if nothin' else.'

'You'll release 'er 'ere and now,' Isaiah said.

382

'You're related by marriage — that 'as to count for somethin'. I can offer you an inducement to let my wife go. What's wrong with you? The gobblers have been willing to make deals in the past — for a price.'

'You know me well enough to realise that I do everythin' by the book,' Jason said.

'Grace, my darlin', don't say a word.' Seeing that his adversary couldn't be bribed, Isaiah kept on at her, telling her to keep her mouth shut as the iron cuffs cut into her wrists. 'Deny everythin' and they'll let you go.'

'We'll face the magistrates together,' she said bravely.

'And a judge and jury, because I have you in my clutches, and this time, I'm goin' to make the charges stick,' Jason added for good measure.

'Let me see my daughter,' Isaiah cried as Cromwell hauled him up. 'Why's she so quiet? What 'ave you done to my precious girl? Where are we goin'? Where are you takin' us?'

'Straight to gaol,' Jason said. 'Well done, men. That's been an excellent night's work.'

23

A Sea Change

Jason and his men marched Isaiah and Grace back into Deal, where Cromwell had Isaiah admitted to the gaol while Jason waited with Grace. As soon as Isaiah was out of sight and earshot, Jason removed the bonds from her wrists.

'How's Aggie? I've been wanting to ask . . .' She faltered, wondering what right she had to enquire after her health when she'd given her away without explanation.

'She's well. You can see for yourself — you're comin' home with me,' he said. 'We'll spread the rumour that you're poorly which is why you can't be held in gaol or attend the preliminary hearin' with Isaiah and the rest. To maintain the illusion that you're under guard awaitin' trial, you'll have to stay indoors. What do you think?'

When she hesitated, he added, 'I realise this is going to be difficult for you and Louisa, but you can't go back to Snargate. You could go and spend some time with Winnie, I suppose, but . . .'

'It wouldn't be fair to risk bringing trouble to her door,' Grace said, fearful of what George Minnis might do to her sister if he found out that she was intent on testifying against the Greys. 'How long do you think this is going to take?'

'I have no doubt that the magistrates will

384

commit them to a trial by judge and jury. The offences are too serious to be treated otherwise. You could be with us for six to eight weeks. Listen, it's late, we've had a long day, I'm starvin' hungry, and you must be too. Look at you shiverin' . . . ' He offered her his arm. 'Let's go home before we freeze to death.' She took his arm and limped along beside him, trying to find the words to express her gratitude for his role in arresting Isaiah and offering her shelter.

'Don't worry about it,' he said. 'It should be me who's thankin' you. Grace, this might feel like the end of it, but it's only the beginnin'. There's a long way to go.' When they turned into the alley and headed towards Compass Cottage, he added wryly, 'You'd better let me do the talkin'.'

Having shown her indoors, Jason went upstairs to find Louisa, leaving Grace sitting on the third step up, struggling to remove her gloves and boots as the blood began to pulse back into her fingers and toes. Her stockings were worn to shreds and her feet raw with blisters.

'Hello, stranger,' Louisa said, looking down from the landing, a candle burning in her hand, the flame illuminating her features. 'My husband says you're staying for a while.' Her tone was taut and barely welcoming, her mouth pinched. 'Find yourself some supper if you want any.'

'Where is Aggie?' Grace asked.

'Tucked up in her cot, as she should be at this time of night.' There was an edge to Louisa's voice. 'What kind of mother do you think I am?'

'The best, I'm sure,' Grace said softly. 'I haven't come to take her away, I promise.'

However the next morning, when she saw her daughter — not her daughter, she reminded herself — sitting in a high chair in the kitchen, happily grabbing at the spoon as Louisa fed her, every fibre in her being urged her to pick her up, tear her away and flee.

'Can I help you with the chores?' she asked, turning away to hide her pain.

'That would be helpful,' Louisa said. 'I'm going to enjoy having your company for a while — it can be lonely when Jason isn't here.'

★ ★ ★

The time crept slowly by, marked by their mutual delight over Aggie's antics. At eight months, she was already rolling from one place to another and trying to crawl. Although Louisa attempted to discourage her, she addressed everyone as 'Mama', including the attorney, Mr Spoke, and his clerk who called to go through Grace's witness statement and advise her on what to expect when the smugglers' case came to trial. He was of the opinion that her testimony was convincing enough, and that she came across as sober, sensible and well-spoken for a smuggler's wife. In his experience, that was half the battle won.

When Jason came home from a spell on duty, he brought news of Lawless. Isaiah had tried to bargain with the authorities, offering up Lawless's likely whereabouts in return for being tried on a lesser charge, but he was too late. Jason and his crew had already discovered him while searching a fishing boat in the waters off the coast north of Sandwich, and he was to be tried with Isaiah, George, Cut-throat and four others at the Maidstone quarter assizes in January.

A further bright moment in what was a series of long dull days indoors, was Christmas Eve when Louisa and Jason went to church, leaving Grace to mind Aggie.

When they returned after the service, Grace reluctantly handed the baby back and retired to her room. Lying down on the bed, she overheard Jason and Louisa talking downstairs.

'I'm incredibly proud of you for lettin' Grace stay with us,' he said. 'It's hard for me, but it's far worse for you.'

'When she first arrived, I jumped to the conclusion that she was here to take the baby away from me. It's what I've been afraid of, ever since I found the littlun on the doorstep. Perhaps that's why I've found it more difficult to mother her than I expected. Don't get me wrong — I've become inordinately fond of her . . .' Louisa's voice faded.

'We've had some very happy times during the past weeks,' Jason began, 'but Aggie is Grace's child. You can see how much Grace loves her, which is why I don't think it's right of us to keep her.'

Grace winced as Louisa sobbed, 'Oh no. I don't know if I can.'

'I'm not going to pressure you — I want you to make your own decision and I will go along with whatever you choose.'

Louisa muttered an inaudible response.

'Grace has lost everythin' — her baby, husband and home. We're the lucky ones — we have each other.'

'I couldn't wish for a better husband,' Louisa said. 'I'll think about what you've said.'

'Take your time. For Aggie's safety, I think it best that the outside world — '

'You mean the Greys?' Louisa cut in.

'I want everyone to remain under the impression that Grace has given her up — and that she's awaitin' trial herself, of course — until justice has been served. We can't have Minnis sendin' men round here to threaten and intimidate her into retractin' her witness statement.'

'She won't do that — she's determined to put her head above the parapet and speak out. If the Greys are cleared of the charges, though, she'll spend the rest of her life watching her back.'

'She knows that — I've made it clear. Her testimony is compellin', but it comes down to whom the jury believes.'

'And whether or not they've been hobbled,' Louisa added. 'Let's hope that the guilty are convicted and punished this time.'

Shivering, Grace enshrouded herself in a blanket and covered her ears, having heard enough. Jason's comment regarding Aggie had, like a stone thrown into a calm sea, sent her into a turmoil. He had held out the tiniest sliver of hope that she might one day have her daughter back, something she had tried so hard not to wish for, knowing that it would unsettle her and divert her from her single-minded purpose of destroying George Minnis, her husband and the Greys, once and for all.

It was a new year and Grace had just turned nine-teen when the day of the trial arrived. Not long after dawn broke, she left Compass Cottage for the first time since arriving on the night of Isaiah's arrest. She walked with Jason and two of the shore boys who were carrying their boxes to rendezvous on Beach Street with Cromwell and the enclosed carriage that they'd hired for the trip to Maid-stone. When they passed the Rattling Cat, she looked up to see a man gazing out of the window of the bedroom that she used to share with Isaiah. Her heart missed a beat when she noticed his dark curls, but that was where the resemblance ended. He was older and more jowly than Isaiah. She felt a pang of regret for past times when she had been happy, before the scales had fallen from her eyes, revealing her husband's true self. He'd been the villain who'd stood at her shoulder, wheedling and complaining, telling her how to dress and what to think, but never again.

Glancing away towards the sea, she found her mind drifting back to the marsh, the open skies and desolate beauty of the landscape, Myrtle's friendship and the joy she found in tending the garden. Snargate was her home now, not Deal.

'Grace, we're waitin' for you.' Jason was some way ahead of her. 'Cromwell's on time for once and Abel's along there at the corner with the coach.'

Apologising, she hastened to catch up.

Abel Brockman — Jason's cousin — was a top-sawyer when it came to handling horses, although

Grace couldn't see how he could be any more skilful than Peter Paddick. He helped them load their boxes before they embarked on the journey to Maidstone, where they took rooms at the Marquis of Granby, the place she had stayed at with Sarah. She wondered what had happened to her friend, whether her family had received her back in Folkestone with open arms and if she'd had her baby yet. If Sarah had sent a letter with her address, Grace hadn't received it before she'd left Snargate for Deal.

The next day, having hardly slept, Grace dressed in a modest gown and winter coat with a matching dark brown bonnet that Louisa had lent her for the occasion. She walked to the courthouse flanked by Jason, Cromwell and several more of the Revenue men from HMS *Legacy*, along with two constables, ostensibly a prisoner.

'That's 'er, the smuggler's wife,' she heard someone comment as a large crowd milled about in front of the building, hoping to catch a glimpse of the notorious Greys. 'They deserve to 'ang, the lot of them, for what they did to that Enderby fellow.'

Although she held her head high as she entered the building, her resolve faltered. It was hopeless. She was married to one of the smugglers. Why would a jury believe her? Would the prosecution tear her reputation to shreds? She felt numb with fear. She wanted to go home to her vegetable plot and hens, and the open space of the marsh.

But then in the distance at the end of the entrance hall, she caught sight of Mary Enderby, dressed in black and standing with her parents and one of her sisters, reminding her that it was her duty to tell the world what she'd seen on that fateful night in September.

'This way, Mrs Feasey.' A court official showed her into a private room. 'You'll stay here until you're called. You are aware of the procedure.' He went on to tell her anyway. 'The prosecution will present their case. You'll stand in the witness box, swear an oath, then give your testimony, after which the defence will have the opportunity to cross-examine you. Then the prosecution may ask you further questions to clarify any point that you may have raised during cross-examination.'

Taking what she thought was quite a liberty, he stepped up far too close to her for comfort.

'Sir, you are standing on my dress,' she said sharply, catching sight of the glint of a blade as he raised it to her neck and slid his free hand around her back, pulling her against him.

'Don't shout, don't scream, don't move!' he hissed. 'A message from George — keep your trap shut or you'll end up in some dark alley with your throat slit to the bone. You understand?'

Aware of the pressure of the blade against her flesh, she muttered that she did.

He released her, pushed her away and hurried out through the door, leaving her cowering against the wall, her mind churning as she wondered what to do.

'Mrs Feasey? Is there a Mrs Feasey about? I've been charged to look after her.' A young man stalked into the room. Tall and skinny with gangly legs and an overly large beak, he reminded her of a heron.

391

'I'm Mrs Feasey,' she said, trembling. 'Who are you?'

'Mr Jones. Commander Witherall has asked me to take special care of you. Oh, there's no need to be frightened. The idea of facing all those people in the courtroom is daunting, but it'll soon be over with.'

He seemed kindly, but she couldn't trust him. She couldn't bring herself to trust anyone. He ran back and forth to the courtroom, reporting the progress of the case without going into detail. The prisoners of which there were seven, including George Minnis and Isaiah, were charged with smuggling, the murder of Albert Enderby, and the beating and wounding of Seaman Cromwell Appleton. George Minnis and the remaining members of the gang known as the Rattlers were also charged with conspiracy to murder the smuggler known as Awful Doins and with the unlawful disposal of a body. All of them pleaded not guilty to all charges.

When the prosecution had finished detailing their case against the Greys, Mr Jones warned Grace that it would soon be her turn to be called to the witness box. Realising that she would be in danger as soon as she stepped into the courtroom as a witness for the prosecution, she panicked.

'I will not leave this room until I've spoken to the judge,' she said.

He frowned. 'That would be most . . . no, it isn't possible. It's completely out of order.'

'Please,' she begged. 'I can't go out there.'

'Are you saying that you won't take the stand, Mrs Feasey?'

'Will you fetch me a pen and ink, and a scrap of paper? If I can't speak to the judge, I must send a note to the attorney, Mr Spoke.'

There was a delay as Grace's written concerns about the threat she'd received were discussed by the judge and attorneys, but after a while, the decision was made to continue the trial behind closed doors and she found herself waiting to enter the courtroom, guarded by two armed constables. As she walked in, she saw the Revenue officers sitting in a row behind Mary and her entourage.

'I call Mrs Grace Feasey of Snargate as a witness for the prosecution,' Mr Spoke said.

There was a gasp of alarm from the dock. Isaiah's face was scarlet, his eyes flashing with fury.

'Traitor!' he exclaimed.

'I should 'ave 'ad her dealt with,' George growled. 'I knew it.'

As the judge called for order, Grace stepped into the box where she took the oath, then, at ease with her conscience, she steeled herself to answer Mr Spoke's questions as he led her gently through her statement.

He invited her to identify the men in the dock who had been on the beach that night, then asked further questions about the run itself.

'How many tubs were carried off by your reckoning?'

'I couldn't tell you, but the blockade men prevented the removal of the whole cargo. In fact, the party were obliged to leave the shore after less than five minutes.'

'Do you know their destination? Where were

they hidden'?'

'I do not.'

'Were you paid for your night's work?'

'My husband was expecting to receive twenty-three shillings a week later, but he was already heavily in debt to Mr Minnis. He didn't receive a penny for the previous run, but Mr Minnis did pay him a few shillings for completing another errand for him.'

Mr Spoke moved on to the subject of the violent acts that had been committed and the words that George had used to attract the attention of the party of smugglers. He went on to ascertain for the jury's benefit that George had incriminated himself in the actual smuggling of goods when he'd said, 'That's one less to share the profits with,' when one of his gang had scarpered, then added, 'Let's get this job done, then I'll treat you all to beer and brandy.' He'd also shouted when the second gig had arrived carrying officers from HMS *Legacy*, 'Where is the one who 'ad our man last time? Which one's Enderby?'

'How did your husband respond to that?' Mr Spoke asked.

'I . . . he said . . . 'The words seemed to stick in her gullet as she breathed in the unpleasant odour of rosemary, lavender, unwashed clothes and drains.

'Speak up, Mrs Feasey.'

'He said, 'It's him over there. He danced with my missus once. Let me at him. I'll blow his brains out.'

'Let me at him. I'll blow his brains out,' Mr Spoke repeated for the jury before turning back to

394

Grace. 'The young lieutenant told you that your husband had fired the fatal shot, and you heard George Minnis's admission that he was involved in the smuggling of goods that night.

'Furthermore, your statement also refers to another incident on the 5th of September when you witnessed several of these men' — he named them — 'arriving in the rear garden of George Minnis's property in Snargate. These men were in a distressed state and carrying what you thought at the time was a dead deer. Since then, your husband has mentioned that one of his former gang members, known as Awful Doins, was dead, having been 'got rid of' according to Mr Minnis's instructions.

'Since then, not one, but two bodies have been exhumed from a disused well at the same property, the more recently deceased being identified as the missing smuggler.'

As the jury sat in silence, digesting Mr Spoke's words, Grace dared to glance towards the dock. Isaiah was frowning and George's face had drained of colour.

'That is all,' Mr Spoke said before Mr Houghton-White, attorney for the defence, ambushed her and employed every trick in the book to rip her evidence apart and discredit her as a witness.

Her spine tingling with antipathy, she refused to drop her gaze, looking him in the eye as he tried to stare her out. She was not a naive, meek and obedient young wife any more. She would not be intimidated.

'I put it to you, Mrs Feasey — ' he kept using her name to remind the jury that she was married to one of the accused '— that you have chosen to testify against the prisoners in a clever attempt to avoid implicating yourself in the murder of Lieutenant Enderby. In addition, you are determined to see your husband put away or hanged for a crime that he didn't commit, because he is a wife beater and you see this as your only means of escape.'

'No, sir,' she said hotly. 'I'm here to see justice done.'

'Tell me once more in your own words exactly what you think you saw and heard on the night of the twenty-fifth of September.'

She repeated how she had collected the horse and cart and driven her husband from Snargate. 'It was only then that my husband told me that we were meeting with the rest of the Greys at Dover. We didn't get to the beach until between midnight and one.'

'You claim that although the visibility was poor, you could see the defendant, George Minnis, on his horse, and even the detail of what he was wearing.'

'He wasn't dressed in a grey smock like the rest of the smugglers,' Grace said. 'He stood out for that reason.'

'I would suggest that this gentleman whom you believe you saw was not in fact George Minnis, but another man who had inadvertently been caught up in the landing on his way to visit friends in Kingsdown to the north.'

'It was Mr Minnis — I'd recognise him anywhere. And he makes the rules for the Greys but doesn't follow them himself. His choice of clothing was a smokescreen. At first glance, you could easily assume that he was a blockade man in his dark coat and tall hat.'

'This is speculation,' the judge interrupted. 'Please, keep to the facts of this case.'

'What happened next? Remind us,' Mr Houghton-White said.

'There was a fight between the Revenue officers and the smugglers. The shots sent the horse bolting away with the cart. The smugglers ran into the darkness and the officers went after them. I was alone. I heard the sound of groaning and went to investigate, which is when I found Lieutenant Enderby.' She paused before continuing, 'He was lying mortally injured.'

'How did you recognise him? I mean, had you met him before?'

'I suppose you could describe him as my brother-in-law's protégée. I was introduced to him when I was living in Deal. We danced together on one occasion — it was when we were celebrating the end of the war with Old Boney.' She corrected herself. 'I mean, Mr Bonaparte.'

'What did you do when you found Lieutenant Enderby? Did you raise the alarm?'

'No.'

'I would suggest that you didn't call for assistance because you were afraid of being discovered and arrested for being party to this crime. You were part of this enterprise, Mrs Feasey, out to make a profit from what is euphemistically called the 'free trade'.'

'No!' she exclaimed. 'I tried to stem the bleeding and keep him talking, but it was too late. He died shortly afterwards.'

'In this — by your own admission — brief moment, you claim that there was time for him to tell you that it was your husband who'd shot at him, and request that you take his watch and a message to his wife.'

'Yes.'

'And then you ran away with the property that you had removed from the dead man's coat, and later, having had a crisis of conscience, arranged for Commander Witherall here to return it to Lieutenant Enderby's widow?'

'You are putting words into my mouth,' she said angrily. 'That isn't how it happened.'

Mr Houghton-White smiled at her. He actually smiled before he dismissed her.

Grace waited with Mr Jones and a guard until the remaining witnesses for the prosecution and defence had been examined and cross-examined, when she was called back in to hear the judge's summing up. The jury retired briefly before they returned to the courtroom for the foreman to read out their verdicts.

'We find the defendant, George Minnis, guilty of all charges: inciting the murders of Lieutenant Enderby and the smuggler known as Awful Doins, along with the unlawful disposal of the mortal remains of the latter gentleman and another, identity unknown; unlawfully and feloniously assisting the illegal running of uncustomed goods.

'We find the defendant, Isaiah Feasey — 'Grace took a deep breath as the foreman continued '— guilty of all charges: the murder of Lieutenant Enderby and the smuggler . . . '

398

They'd done it. She glanced towards Jason who smiled and punched the air, but she didn't share his jubilation. The Greys were finished and about to receive their sentences, but she couldn't celebrate. The struggles that she'd had to go through to bring them to this point had brought her to her knees.

The smugglers stood hunched and trembling in the dock as the judge promptly sentenced them to death by hanging.

'No.' She heard Isaiah's strangulated cry, followed by uproar in the dock because George and his men had no intention of going quietly. 'It's lies, all lies.'

'It's your wife who's dropped us in it.' George had Isaiah by the neck, throttling him. 'She's a turncoat, a duplicitous, double-dealin', faithless woman.'

'Take the prisoners down!' The judge struck his gavel, and the guards leapt into action, separating the pair and marching them off to the cells, George still shouting, 'The gobblers 'ave got to 'er. They've filled 'er 'ead with false'oods . . .'

As the prisoners' voices faded and several doors slammed shut, Mr Houghton-White addressed the judge.

'M'lord, I wish to appeal against the unduly harsh sentence.'

'On what grounds?'

'There is a precedent that has been set: that if a murder is carried out in the hours of darkness, the punishment should be the lesser sentence of transportation, not death. Admittedly, it's possible although not proven that the killing of the smuggler known as Awful Doins occurred in daylight, but there is no evidence as to which of the prisoners was holding the gun.'

'There will be a short recess while I consider your challenge, Mr Houghton-White,' the judge said and within the hour, he had overturned the prisoners' sentence, commuting the death penalty to transportation for life to one of His Majesty's colonies.

With that, Grace's ordeal was almost over, except that she needed to see her husband one last time, not wanting to close the book on her marriage without reading the final page.

Mr Jones arranged a brief reunion in the presence of a guard who was watching Isaiah like a hawk, suspecting that it was a plot to spring him from his bonds.

''Ow could you be so cruel as to testify against me?'

Isaiah sobbed. 'Doesn't the affection that we 'ave for each other mean anythin' to you?'

'Stand back, Mrs Feasey,' the guard snapped. 'No touchin'.'

'You might as well 'ave given me a death sentence. George is goin' to kill me, maybe not straight away, but when I'm on that miserable stinkin' hulk awaitin' transport, I won't be able to sleep for wonderin' when he'll choose to lay 'is 'ands around my neck.

'Where's the littlun? I thought you'd bring 'er to see 'er pa.'

'Why would I expose her to the bad air inside a courtroom?' It gave her no pleasure to deliver the final blow. 'You won't be seeing Aggie again and this is the last time we shall meet.' She bit back tears of grief and regret as she went on, 'Our marriage is over in all but name. My love for you died when I found out that you were responsible for Albert's death.

'Tell me why you would risk everything to avenge Dunk's killing? He was the aggressor. Albert killed him in self-defence, to protect himself and Jason. I don't understand . . . .'

'George told me to do it. 'E said he'd have you and the littlun dealt with if I didn't go along with it. I did it to protect you and Aggie. I've given up my liberty for you.'

'You could have spoken to me about it,' Grace said fiercely, 'then we could have gone to Jason and prevented it. Isaiah, we should have saved Albert's life.'

'George would 'ave found out,' Isaiah insisted. ''E owns me, Grace. I'm 'is puppet. Besides, Enderby isn't any great loss to the world — people warmed to 'im, but 'e wasn't that special.'

Grace looked at him in disbelief. 'How dare you denigrate his memory — he was a lovely man who was worth ten of you. You were jealous . . . that's what it was all about. You were jealous of his success and popularity with the gobblers and smugglers alike.'

'I remember seein' you dancin' with 'im once,' Isaiah said feebly, 'and then you tellin' me that he had taken an interest in you. It's always rankled with me.'

'You know, I can't remember why I married you.' She stared at him, a stranger with silvering hair, fading looks and lacking spirit. 'You're

401

a weak and foolish man, damaged, deluded, desperately wanting to impress . . . You've lied to me, played on my naivety and inexperience . . . I can see clearly now how you've dragged me down. But I'm free of you now, as the marshfolk and those living along the coast are free of George Minnis and the Greys. I am proud of what I've done. It's me who is walking away with her head held high, while you, a common criminal, are leaving in chains.'

He was a broken man, she mused. He hadn't even asked her about the fate of the dog, or his gold.

She left the court to shouting and jeering, applause and cheering. Jason and Cromwell spirited her through the jostling crowds of reporters, locals and souvenir hunters.

'Missus, an 'andkerchief, a garter or scrap of your petticoat for a poor penniless widow with seven mouths to feed.' The beggarwoman whose hands were on Grace's coat and pockets seemed familiar: although in a different guise, she was the lady who'd stolen Sarah's purse.

'Stop, thief!' she cried as the woman ran off.

'Stay with us,' Jason said as Cromwell made to chase after her. 'It's more important that we get Grace home in one piece. Ah, one of the constables has caught her. Keep walkin'.'

* * *

On their way back to Deal the following morning, having stayed overnight to avoid travelling in the dark, Grace thanked Jason for his assistance.

'It's the least I could do,' he said. 'By removin''

the Greys, we've effectively stopped organised smugglin' in this part of Kent — it's quite an achievement. Best of all, I have my man at last. I'm sorry though, Grace, because I remember how besotted you were with Isaiah at the beginnin'. He's your husband and that must count for somethin'.'

She wasn't sure that it did — she'd wasted over a year being married to a liar and a bully, but she had learned much about human nature. No longer a naive seventeen-year-old girl, but a grown nineteen-year-old, she wouldn't make the same mistake again.

She sat back in the coach, watching the snow starting to fall. The year of 1817 looked as if it was going to be similar to the previous one: cold, dull and holding out little hope of any comfort.

24

Home Sweet Home

Ten hours passed before they entered Deal, thanks to the snow, mud and ice. They disembarked from the carriage after dark, thanking Abel for looking after them, and bidding farewell to Cromwell who went straight home while Grace walked along Cockle Swamp Alley with Jason. He let them into Compass Cottage and called for Louisa.

'I'm in the kitchen,' she called back as Grace took off her gloves and boots and placed her hat and coat on one of the hooks in the hall.

'I'm goin' up to change,' Jason said, leaving her to join her sister who was standing beside the fire with Aggie in her arms. A candle was burning on the table next to the baby's rattle and a rag doll.

'She's getting too heavy for this.' Louisa smiled through tears as Aggie chuckled and squirmed, trying to escape. 'I can't put her down — she never stays where she's put. She's forever crawling after Kitty and pulling on her tail. Anyway, how was the trial? Is it good news?'

Grace explained that Isaiah, George and the rest of the smugglers had been sentenced to transportation.

'I wouldn't say I was happy about it. I'm relieved,' Grace concluded. As far as she was concerned, it was a quiet triumph, but for Jason and his crew, it was an excuse to celebrate. She'd heard him and Cromwell planning how they'd have a few drinks at the Waterman's Arms in honour of their friend, Albert, and to mark their role in bringing the Greys to justice.

'Aggie, your mama's here,' Louisa said, her voice breaking. Gathering herself together, she continued, 'I told you that she'd be back.'

'Did I hear you right?' Grace whispered, tears springing to her eyes. 'Louisa, I've told you that I didn't come back to take her away from you and Jason.'

'I know. You made my dream come true, leaving her on the doorstep for me, and I've loved every minute of playing mother to her, but . . .' Louisa paused.

The candle on the table flickered and almost died, then flickered back into life, like the hope that flared in Grace's breast when Louisa spoke again, 'Every time I look at her, I see you, and I'm reminded that she isn't mine and never will be.'

Grace opened her mouth to speak, but Louisa shook her head.

'You and Aggie are safe now. Minnis and his men will soon be thousands of miles away, so the predicament that forced you to bring her here no longer exists.' Louisa moved towards her and lowered Aggie into Grace's outstretched arms.

'Thank you, thank you, thank you,' she said, hugging and kissing her beautiful daughter, half crying, half laughing. Aggie stared at her. Her face crumpled and she burst into tears. 'Oh, my darling, I'm sorry. I'm scaring you.'

Louisa picked up the rattle and shook it, then

held it within Aggie's reach. Distracted, the baby took it and dropped it, beaming when it skittered across the floor.

'What will you do with yourself?' Grace asked, watching Louisa pick the rattle up again and hand it back to Aggie.

'I'm going to enjoy being an auntie to her and the rest of our nieces and our nephew. Winnie has another on the way — I'm going to stay with her for a few days when Jason's on his next round of duty, and of course, I'll mind Aggie for you whenever you need me to. Jason and I will help you find a suitable house in Deal — '

'There's no need. I'm planning on going back to Snargate,' Grace cut in. 'I hope you aren't disappointed, but Deal doesn't feel like home to me any more. You'll always be welcome.'

'I do understand,' Louisa said eventually. 'How will you live?'

'I'll rent a cottage with a garden where I'll grow fruit and vegetables, tend a flock of hens and take in sewing. I have a little money behind me.' Strictly speaking, it was in the form of the gold that Isaiah had asked her to carry for him, along with the pendant and chain, and the brooch he had given her, sourced from his smuggling activities, she guessed. It was more than enough to tide her over for a considerable time.

'It sounds idyllic, but won't you be lonely?'

'I have a good friend and neighbour, Myrtle Paddick, and the marshfolk — ' she found herself thinking of Peter '— are not as backward and behind the times as Mrs Witherall would have you believe.' She smiled as Aggie dropped the rattle

406

again. 'You'd love it there.'

'I'll reserve judgement until after I've paid you a visit.' Louisa returned Aggie's rattle for a second time then wrapped her arms around the two of them.

'What do you think Winnie will say?'

'After she's said, 'I told you so,' you mean, because she's bound to pass comment?' Grace glanced towards her sister's face — she was grinning broadly. 'I think she'll approve, not that you'll listen to her anyway if she doesn't.'

'I don't regret not heeding your advice.'

'That's my little sister, stubborn to the last. You've had a rough year, Grace. It's time for you to do what makes you happy.'

★ ★ ★

Grace wrote to Myrtle to let her know that she'd be arriving in Snargate at the end of the month and that she'd like to move back into Hazel Cottage, if she and John hadn't let it out to someone else in her absence. If that was the case, she and Aggie would stay at the Red Lion until a suitable property came up for rent.

On the last day of January, she said a tearful farewell to Louisa and Jason — and Kitty — before Abel collected her, Aggie and their few belongings, and drove them as far as Hythe where they were forced to stay the night when the grey sky cleared, the temperature plummeted and the pair of bay horses pulling the brougham began to slip on the frozen ground. The next morning, Abel decided that it was reasonable to continue their journey and they crossed the marsh where the mist was pooling between sky and land, like a giant silver sea.

It was the middle of the afternoon when they reached Snargate. As the carriage turned into the lane and approached Hazel Cottage, Grace's heart sank. The gate had been painted, the chimney rebuilt with a cowl on top and the missing roof tiles replaced, which could only mean that her former home had a new tenant.

Abel turned the horses and carriage round, jumped down from the driver's seat and opened the carriage door. 'What do you want to do, Grace?'

'Would you mind waiting while I let my friend at the forge know that I'm here before you drop us off at the inn?'

'Your wish is my command.' Smiling, he held Aggie for her until she'd exited the carriage, tiptoed across the mud and reached firm ground. Grace took the baby back as Myrtle came running out of her house, waving and shrieking with joy, with Abraham and Joseph chasing after her.

'Oh, am I glad to see you! I was wondering where you'd got to. How are you? How's little Aggie? Why did you disappear like that without even a word?'

'Did you receive my letter?' Grace asked.

'Yes, and I had John read it to me several times over.'

'I see that you've already let Hazel Cottage.'

'Oh, we have indeed — to a fine lady and her daughter.' Myrtle's eyes sparkled as she went on, 'That's you, silly.'

Grace beamed. 'You've made me so happy I could jump for joy! No, darling,' she went on, extricating the ribbon of her bonnet from Aggie's sticky fingers.

'We took advantage of the cottage being empty to have a builder in to do some repairs. People have been very kind, offering to do odd jobs to show their appreciation of what you've done for us.'

Grace frowned as Myrtle went on to explain, 'You were the only one brave enough to stand up to George and the Greys — I can't imagine how you must have felt givin' evidence against them. We know all about it — from the news-papers that Mr Prior has delivered to the shop, and the few travellers who pass through this way. It's been a tremendous relief, bein' able to sleep at night without worryin' about who might be lur-kin' about outside with their tubs and guns, and lookin' to steal other people's property.' Without pausing for breath, Myrtle went on, 'Peter's been workin' on the garden in the little spare time he has, tidyin' up and diggin' holes for a couple more fruit trees. I hope you don't mind.'

'I'm . . . I don't know what to say . . . except thank you.' Remembering that Abel was waiting, Grace apologised and settled up with him so he could return to Deal.

Listening to the swish of the brougham's wheels and the clip-clop of the horses' hooves fading into the distance, she turned back to Myrtle who had popped back into her house and re-emerged, waving a letter.

'I almost forgot — this came while you were

away.'

Grace took it and opened it up, quickly scanning the contents.

'Who's it from, then?' Myrtle asked.

'It's from Sarah,' Grace said with delight. 'She's had her mother write to me with her address. Oh, she's well and she's had her baby, a boy — she's named him Joshua. And she's hoping to pay us a visit in the summer, so that she can catch up with the gossip, and tend Digger's grave.'

'John and I took a wreath of holly and ivy to his restin' place at Christmas — we didn't want him to be forgotten,' Myrtle said. 'I must stop talkin' — I expect you'll want to settle in. I'll come over later with tea and cake. And you're welcome to join us for supper afterwards. I'm looking forward to a proper catch-up.'

'My sister-in-law is itchin' to hear all about the demise of the Greys from the 'orse's mouth.' On hearing the sound of a familiar voice, Grace looked behind her to find Peter walking down the path towards them. 'Not that I'm sayin' you're like an 'orse,' he grinned. 'Although I do prefer 'orses to most 'uman bein's. It's good to see you again — there were some dark times when we thought you'd come to 'arm,' he added seriously. 'Still, that's all water under the bridge now.'

'Peter, why don't you show Grace and the littlun what we've done, and get the fire lit?'

'I'd appreciate that,' Grace said when he hesitated, 'but you have work to do at the farm. Please, don't let me stop you.'

'It's no trouble,' Peter said, and he carried her boxes into her home and lit the kindling in the grate. It smoked and smouldered, then burst into flame. He added some sticks, waiting patiently for them to catch before building up the fire with logs from the stack that someone had built for her outside the kitchen door. Through the window, she could see her three hens pecking furiously at the soil where Peter had dug the holes for the trees.

'By the way, Myrtle 'appened to mention that you 'ad a dog go missin', a grey longdog.'

'That's right. Have you seen him?'

'I found 'im wanderin' about four or five weeks ago and took 'im in— 'e's got 'is paws right under the table. 'E's a good dog. I'll be sorry to see 'im go.'

'Then you must keep him,' she smiled. 'His name's Musket.'

'I've been callin' 'im Dog. Are you sure you don't want 'im?'

'It's hard to cope with him and the littlun together. And it would be a shame to move him again when he's just got settled.' It seemed that Musket had chosen his new master well, she thought.

She went to sit down on the bench under the window, letting Aggie down to crawl about on the floor which had been scrubbed clean, while Peter showed her the other improvements: the whitewashed walls; the guard for the fire; the dark oak corner cupboard for storage.

'I think that's everythin'. I'd better be on my way.'

Grace got up to see him out, but as he stepped on to the doorstep, he stopped.

'There was an occasion when you asked me

to call you by your given name,' he said, looking abashed. 'But I insisted on addressin' you by
your married name. I 'ad my reasons. I expect you
can guess, as a partic'larly perspicacious young
woman.'

A flush of warmth spread up her neck and
clothed her cheeks as she smiled and nodded,
understanding exactly what he meant.

'I'd like you to call me Grace,' she said.

He smiled back as he took his cap from his
jacket pocket. 'I'll say good afternoon then, Grace.
I look forward to callin' on you again soon.'

'Goodbye, Peter,' she murmured, watching him
stroll down the path and along the lane, waving
his cap as he went.

She unfastened the chain at the back of her neck
and let the pendant fall into the palm of her hand:
she no longer needed to wear it as a reminder of
where she'd come from and where she was going.
Putting it in her pocket, she went back inside and
scooped Aggie up, swinging her — giggling —
through the air.

She'd been wrong about love. It wasn't dark,
irascible and mysterious. It didn't envy or lie. It
was patient and gentle, and most of all, it was
kind.

We do hope that you have enjoyed reading this large print book.

Did you know that all of our titles are available for purchase?

We publish a wide range of high quality large print books including:
Romances, Mysteries, Classics
General Fiction
Non Fiction and Westerns

Special interest titles available in large print are:
The Little Oxford Dictionary
Music Book, Song Book
Hymn Book, Service Book

Also available from us courtesy of Oxford University Press:
Young Readers' Dictionary
(large print edition)
Young Readers' Thesaurus
(large print edition)

For further information or a free brochure, please contact us at:
Ulverscroft Large Print Books Ltd.,
The Green, Bradgate Road, Anstey,
Leicester, LE7 7FU, England.
Tel: (00 44) 0116 236 4325
Fax: (00 44) 0116 234 0205

Other titles published by Ulverscroft:

A PLACE TO CALL HOME

EVIE GRACE

East Kent, 1876: With doting parents and siblings she adores, sixteen-year-old Rose Cheevers leads a contented life at Willow Place in Canterbury. A bright future ahead of her, she dreams of following in her mother's footsteps and becoming a teacher. Then one traumatic day turns the Cheevers' household upside-down. What was once a safe haven has become a place of peril, and Rose is forced to flee with the younger children. Desperate, she seeks refuge in a remote village with a long lost grandmother who did not know she existed. But safety comes at a price, and the arrival of a young stranger with connections to her past raises uncomfortable questions about what the future holds. Somehow, Rose must find the strength to keep her family together. Above all else, though, she needs a place to call home.

HER MOTHER'S DAUGHTER

EVIE GRACE

Agnes Berry-Clay might have been born into rags but she is growing up with riches. Given away as a baby by her real mother, she was rescued and raised by her darling Papa and distant Mama. Agnes wants for nothing, except perhaps a little freedom. But as time goes on, her life at Windmarsh Court changes. New arrivals and old resentments push Agnes to the peripheries, and finally the consequences of one fateful day shatter her dreams for the future. Heartbroken and surrounded by the threat of scandal, Agnes is faced with a terrible choice: stay and surrender, or flee and fight to keep her freedom.

THE SEASIDE ANGEL

EVIE GRACE

Margate, 1884: When seventeen-year-old Hannah Bentley fled the family home, she never dreamed she'd find her feet working as a nurse on the children's ward at the Royal Sea Bathing Infirmary. She adores her patients and the sea air, and looks forward to a time when she'll have put away enough money so her younger sister can join her. But when her sister suddenly turns up unannounced, she brings more trouble than Hannah bargained for. As Hannah is forced to risk everything to keep her sister out of trouble, she must somehow find the strength to save herself, too . . .